# NAMELESS ACTS OF CRUELTY

A NOVEL OF SUSPENSE

## JULIE CAMERON

SCARLET
NEW YORK

NAMELESS ACTS OF CRUELTY

Scarlet
An Imprint of Penzler Publishers
58 Warren Street
New York, N.Y. 10007

First Scarlet edition

Interior design by Maria Fernandez

Library of Congress Control Number: 2022902939

ISBN: 978-1-61316-304-7
eBook ISBN: 978-1-61316-305-4

10 9 8 7 6 5 4 3 2 1

Printed in the United States of America
Distributed by W. W. Norton & Company

*Tell me, who are you, alone, yourself and nameless?*

—J. R. R. Tolkien

# PROLOGUE

*Mummy and Daddy always said she was a clever little girl and she'd been very clever today. Wolves weren't clever; she knew that. The big, bad wolf might be faster than her across the fields but he wouldn't find her here.*

*At the thought of Mummy, her bottom lip quivered and trembled against her teeth. She thought of Mummy's cuddles; the fluffiness of her jumpers and the lovely smell of her. Her soft, kind hands with their pretty red nails, and her stories at bedtime.*

*Mummy had bought her the new red dress and now it was all dirty—and she'd lost one of her trainers, her favorite ones with the lights in the heels. She hoped Mummy wouldn't be cross. She'd seen her be cross with Jay-Jay sometimes and it was scary, but luckily Mummy was never cross with her.*

*She mustn't cry. If she made a sound he'd hear her with his great big ears—all the better to hear you with. She shuddered at the thought and burrowed deeper into the leaves and ferns that littered the floor of her hiding place. Things were in there with her. She could hear them scuttling. They were running things and creeping things, and she tried not to think about them too much in case they were biting things too.*

*She didn't know what the tumbly-down little house was for, with its letterbox window looking over the lake, but it was somewhere safe to hide. It* was twiggy and rough and it made her think about the big, bad wolf again. She imagined his bristly snout, sniffling and snuffling through the letterbox window. Breath whistling down his wet, red nostrils, huffing and puffing until he blew her house in. Her little house of twigs. A tiny bit of wee-wee seeped into her knickers and she began to cry for real. She wanted Daddy to come and save her, or Jay-Jay.

She felt cross when she thought of Jay-Jay. He was meant to look after her when they came out to play. Mummy had said so, but he'd been mean to her instead. Then he'd met up with the other boys and had left her on her own to get lost and scared. She didn't care now that he'd been mean; she just wanted him to come back.

She suddenly stopped crying and held her breath. She was sure she'd heard rustling outside, and her heart leapt into her throat. Now there was a voice whispering and sniggering. It sounded like a big voice, or a growly voice like Jay-Jay's when he was trying to scare her. She'd never been so frightened. She tried to stay quiet, but a little trill of terror leached its way out between her teeth.

Now it was silent again. She strained her ears, listening, listening, the breath still held in her bursting lungs. Just maybe he hadn't heard her, and slowly she dared to breathe again.

Twigs snapped and crunched, nearer and nearer. A hand reached in through the slit of the window, and the voice was sweet and low.

"Little pig, little pig, are you in there?"

She screamed, shrill and piercing, firing the birds from the trees, but there was no one there to hear her. No one to save her from the big, bad wolf.

# 1

"Crew, seats for landing."

The plane began its descent. The countryside below was a patchwork of fields and hedges, bisected by winding lanes and lazy rivers. Miniature villages of commuter homes with velvet lawns and azure pools unspooled beneath its wings. England's green and pleasant land—an illusion, maybe, but one the people still clung to.

Jeremy leaned his forehead against the coolness of the glass, his eyes tracking the unfolding scene. He'd always liked this part of flying, with the country laid out like a small child's toy, farmyard figures and Matchbox cars, tiny specks slowly making themselves known beneath him; cloud shadows chasing across the fields, smudges of gray on green. It appeared so safe and sanitized, a neat little world where nothing cruel could ever happen. He stole a glance at Sarah, his wife, still engrossed in her book, and despite his best intentions, he saw how the seat belt pulled tight across the softness of her stomach. With a whisper of self-disgust at his evident shallowness, he turned to check on the children instead.

Jack's head was buried in his phone, apparently oblivious to his surroundings, and Jeremy felt the familiar surge of irritation that his son seemed to elicit in him nowadays.

"Jack, your belt," he said, the impatience evident in his voice. "I suppose it'd be too much to think you've fastened it like I asked?"

"Uh?" was the only reply, that plus an unselfconscious yawn, which treated the world to a startling and unwelcome view of the boy's tonsils.

"Jack, you'll wish you'd taken notice of me if—"

He felt the gentle pressure of Sarah's hand on his arm. A note of warning in her voice.

"Don't, Jez, you'll only frighten them. How many times have I told you, you need to learn to pick your battles." She turned to the bundle of sullenness that used to be their darling son. "Belt on, please. There's a good boy."

The seat belt dutifully clicked, and Jeremy fought to ignore the sly little hint of victory in the glance that Jack slid his way.

Sarah's arms were lightly tanned with a sprinkling of golden freckles, and her "holiday nails" shone a vivid pink. She'd lost some weight while they'd been away, and even though Jeremy was ashamed that he'd noticed, he still allowed himself to feel a certain satisfaction. He consoled himself with the knowledge that it was really his mother's fault he thought that way. The very first time he'd brought Sarah home to meet her, she'd smiled across the table with those cool gray eyes, and he'd known what was coming—in one form or another.

"What a pretty dress, Sarah. So flattering. You dress so beautifully for someone your size."

He'd sensed rather than seen Sarah wince. He'd felt the heat of her embarrassment but he hadn't reached out a hand in comfort or even acknowledged that he too had felt the barb. No way. No way would he ever have given his mother that satisfaction, because he'd known. It wasn't really meant for Sarah; it was all for him. The subtext loud and clear—the only one that wanted him, the only one he could get, was a fat girl, a chubby, grateful girl. It wasn't true then and it wasn't true now. Sarah wasn't fat; she was curvaceous and gorgeous. The softness of her skin and the scent of her in the dark did things to him, and they were good things.

Still, the seed had been planted, the damage done, and now he disloyally noticed the soft mound of her belly and the fullness of her breasts and felt a strange ambivalence that shamed him. She was the sweetest, most loving person in the world and he adored every atom of her, but sometimes he wished her thin. Sometimes he found himself vaguely embarrassed—not by her exactly, God no, but embarrassed nonetheless. And then he hated himself for being an arsehole, and for granting his mother her wish. For that was what she'd wanted: to place a little burr under his saddle, to taint the magic of love. Yes, she might hate him but she also knew him too well, she knew which buttons to gently press, and how best to bloodlessly wound him.

He became conscious of his daughter's gaze and turned as she proudly lifted her arms to show her seat belt, safely tightened.

"See Daddy," she said, "mine's all done up."

She fixed him with her round blue eyes, and straightaway he felt it. That flicker of something, that cockroach scuttling across his soul, and he struggled to meet her eyes. The shutter slid down; the sheet of glass that kept him from her, that stopped him ever getting too close. It was another secret shame, that question mark over his love for his daughter. He'd often tried to analyze how she made him feel but he couldn't quite name it. It was a shiver deep inside him, almost like fear or dread.

It was there from the moment she was born. When Sarah first held out her arms to him, eyes bright with tears and said,

"Jeremy, it's a little girl. We've got a daughter."

In that instant he'd flinched away. He'd felt his soul retreating, putting safe distance between them, and he'd felt afraid. Of her, or for her, was the question that still haunted him.

He prayed that she was too young to notice his reserve, and that one day he'd unravel his feelings toward her and they'd all be okay, because to damage her in the ways his mother had damaged him was unthinkable. For the moment, he overcompensated. So much so that, if Jack were asked, he'd say that Lucy was the favorite, his Daddy's Girl, when really it was he who held his father's heart. That lumpen dollop of petulance who could barely bring himself to acknowledge that same father's existence anymore. Sarah reassured him that it was "just a phase," and he marveled at the luxury of it. Such childhood entitlement was never his.

An insistent little voice cut through his thoughts—"Daddy!"—and he smiled at his daughter.

"That's wonderful, darling. You're such a clever girl."

Jack's nostrils emitted something dangerously like a snort, and his father glared at him suspiciously, waiting for him to meet his eye.

"Darling, it's not helping, you keep fussing," Sarah said, the merest hint of irritation in her voice. "Just leave them be, they're fine."

So he turned back to the window and to the neatly ordered world laid out before him.

The holiday had been a good idea, them spending some time together, but it had ended up being far too long. The golden rays had slowly tarnished, and he'd found his joy in his family edging dangerously toward tedium. It wasn't that he didn't love them (he did, with all his heart), but sometimes he needed to be alone—or if not alone, exactly, just able to do what he wanted when he wanted. No pressure. Those last few days he'd longed for space, for his life back. For the routine of the office and the gym, and a drink after work with friends. Time and space to be something other than husband and father, time for some respite from the soft domesticity and the relentless niceness of it all. He'd been like this for as long as he could remember; a man who needed space to keep his head clear. To keep his demons at bay.

The ground was closer now and he could just make out cars and lorries wending their way along neat little roads. Lilliputian animals gently grazed in fields edged by broccoli-floret trees. A golf course drifted beneath him—now that was an idea for tomorrow—sandy bunkers and velvet greens all etched in miniature and swarmed by ant-men.

The plane banked and the world vanished for a moment before surging to meet him once more, suddenly closer. In his line of sight a tiny figure crossed a field at a run, heading for a stand of trees. He glimpsed it for only a second but was inexplicably convinced there were two others running behind, as though in pursuit.

His heart lurched with the plane and the "No!" burst from his lips before terror engulfed him. He strained against the seat belt, his face pressed to the oval of glass, desperate to see the runner's fate. Wildly he clutched at the belt release and lurched to his feet, his head butting hard against the overhead lockers, but the pain barely registered. He tried to cry out a warning but the breath seized in his throat and no sound would come.

Sarah tugged at his arm, her face white with alarm.

"Jeremy! Jeremy, what is it, what's wrong? For God's sake sit down!" She searched his face with her eyes and saw the fear blazing there. "Jez, talk to me, whatever's happened?"

The panic tingled along his fingers, transmitting itself to her and freezing her fingertips.

"Jeremy, please, you've got to sit down!"

Then the stewardess was out of her seat too, bucking against the movement of the plane.

"Sir, you must sit down for your own safety. Please, get back in your seat." Urgency and disapproval in her voice in equal measure as she edged her way along the aisle. "Sir, please!"

Sarah turned to her, voice rising in panic. "He's never like this, there must be something wrong! How much longer is it before we land?"

For a wild moment he feared it was his heart, that he was going to die there in front of his children, thrashing and gasping as his soul fled. He pushed Sarah off and slumped back in the seat, aware of the wild hammering in his chest, his heart a trapped bird, his ribs its cage.

Slowly, he registered Jack's voice against the backdrop of Lucy's frightened trilling. He'd dropped his air of bored indifference and now his voice carried a hint of fear.

"Mum, what's going on? Dad, are you okay?"

Sarah's hand was on his cheek, and he felt its frightened coldness pulling him back to reality. She spoke to him, to the children, softly, soothingly, as though he were a child too, and gradually her words began to make sense.

"Dad's okay . . . You're okay, Jez . . . just hold on, we'll be landing in a moment . . . Breathe, darling, that's right . . . you'll be fine . . . Daddy's fine . . ."

Her face swam into focus, her blue eyes bright with fear. As her hand moved to clutch his, the shame ran through him once more—for scaring her, for scaring his children so.

Slowly his pulse settled and he realized he wasn't about to die; his heart was still working, steadying itself and beating out a reassuring rhythm. Gradually he became aware of the other passengers, of the craned necks and the buzz of excitement at the anticipation of a death on a plane, a thing for the vultures to dine out on, at least for a while.

A hot rush of embarrassment chased away the last remnants of terror. Now he just wanted the damn thing to land so he could get the hell out of there. He'd never done that before, panicking and making a scene. He'd flown more times than he could count and not once had he experienced as much as a flicker of anxiety. In fact he'd never experienced anything like that before, ever. Even as the thought formed, a memory flitted to the surface: him in the night, waking from a nightmare he couldn't recall but which left him trembling in a pool of sweat. Terror dry in his throat and the night a place of nameless dread.

His tongue prised itself from its hiding place at the roof of his mouth. "I'm fine," he croaked, his very tone belying the words. "Honestly, I'm fine."

He squeezed Sarah's hand, trying to suppress the trembling of his own.

"I don't know what that was, I just lost it for a moment, that's all. I'm fine now, really I am, so don't look so worried. I'm okay. Just check the children are all right, God, I must've scared them. I'm sorry darling—I'm so sorry."

The plane touched down on the runway and the reverse thrust kicked in, pulling him forward in his seat. He was jittery, after-shocked, and he desperately tried to label it as no more than a stress reaction, something about returning to the real world. He reassured himself with this explanation, flimsy though it was, and ignored the image of the running figures that seemed seared on his retina. After all, they didn't mean a thing to him.

# 2

Sarah had insisted on driving and now Jeremy was perched beside her. The simple fact of not being thought fit enough to drive made him feel emasculated, enfeebled like some maiden aunt. To make things worse, every few minutes she shot him a concerned look, as though expecting to find that he'd quietly expired on the seat next to her. A limp corpse. Each glance annoyed him further, and he struggled to suppress his rising irritation. He knew it wasn't her fault, but the incident had left him feeling out of sorts and angry. Ever since he could remember he'd always hated making any kind of scene, and even though he understood his anger was self-directed, he couldn't stop himself from projecting it onto her instead.

She looked across again and finally he snapped.

"For God's sake, Sarah, stop keep looking at me. You fussing is doing my head in. I just had a wobble, that's all. It was nothing. Anyone'd think you were my mother or something. Jesus!"

Although on reflection perhaps not *his* mother exactly. Maybe a normal mother, one who gave a shit about her child.

He saw the hurt flash across Sarah's face and wished he'd kept his mouth shut. She rarely reacted. Unlike him, it took a lot to get a rise out of her, and now she kept her eyes fixed on the road and dismissed his selfish outburst with the tiniest flick of her head. An almost imperceptible movement, the twitch of a cat's ear as if to shrug off a fly. He knew his barbs often struck home, but when she spoke her voice was still as calm and kind as ever. It was never her intention, but her equanimity sometimes shamed him further.

"I know you think I'm making a fuss but I'm not going to just ignore it. You were white as a sheet, Jez, and it was almost as though you didn't know where you were. I'm not saying it was, but it might've been a seizure or something, or even your heart. You can't just pretend it didn't happen."

He remembered the tightness in his chest, the struggle for breath, and a trickle of fear ran through him. He was almost at that age, so even though he wanted to, he didn't dare contradict her.

"And I know what you're about to say so don't even bother. I'm the one doing the driving and we're going to the hospital."

She silenced any chance of protest with a wave of her hand.

"I want you to go to A&E, just to get checked out, that's all. I want to be sure it isn't anything we need to worry about, so there's no point in you arguing because we're going whether you like it or not."

Jeremy opened his mouth to retort but then he thought of the children in the back, and how he'd scared them enough for one day. Partly because of them he bit back his words, partly because he knew she was right.

The children were unnaturally quiet; there was none of the messing about and bickering that usually accompanied their car journeys. Jack was happily back on his phone, his earlier filial concern obviously forgotten, but Lucy was clutching the back of her mother's seat, her little face stricken.

Tears welled in her eyes. "Mummeee," she wailed, "I don't want Daddy to have to go to hospital."

*Me too kid*, was what he wanted to say, instead he heard his voice, harsh and unwarranted.

"Stop it, Lucy. I've told you, no one likes a crybaby."

This only served to make her cry more.

The memory rolled in, a ghost from his past. Jeremy's first day at school. All the other mothers wiping tears, soothing, reassuring, his an immovable object, prising his frightened fingers from her skirt. *You're making a dreadful scene, Jeremy. You need to learn, nobody likes a Mummy's Boy, so do you mind not being such a wimp.* And that was before, so what chance did he ever stand afterward?

He shrugged the memory away. He didn't like to think of his mother and her small acts of cruelty, and it irritated him, the way she kept intruding into his thoughts. Anyone looking inside his head might mistakenly think he still cared.

"I'm sorry, darling, Daddy didn't mean to snap. I'm fine, there's no need for you to worry. Mummy's just being careful because she loves me."

He placed his hand on Sarah's knee and gave a reassuring squeeze. He loved his family, so why did he so often fall short of the man he wanted to be?

<hr>

Jeremy dumped the last of the suitcases in the hall and closed the front door with some relief. The hour was late. Sarah went straight upstairs, with the children dragging along behind her. The trip to the hospital had taken far longer than expected, and it was way past their bedtime. They'd been overtired and fractious on the journey back, and it had been all he could do to keep a lid on things.

In the kitchen he opened a beer. Even though he was dead on his feet, he was still too wired to think about bed. It was the hospital that had caused it. Everything about the place had set him on edge. The interminable waiting, the noises filtering through the curtains that enclosed his cubicle, the sound of trolleys, the murmur of voices, the urgent patter of feet on vinyl, the moans, and the fractured cries. And the smell. The smell had been the worst of it. Moist odors of humanity overlaid with the medicinal tang of disinfectant. It had made him think about the passage of time and of his own inexorable progress toward old age. Recently he found his mind straying toward such melancholy thoughts, not often but enough. It was all to do with turning forty. He hadn't realized it before, but it seemed he saw life as a triangle, with forty at its peak, all good on the way up, then the slippery downward slope to infirmity and beyond. To forgetfulness, and frailty, and all those other things that made him flinch but which he supposed were preferable to the final alternative.

The doctor hadn't helped; everything about him had made Jeremy too aware of each and every one of his forty-two years. Midthirties and dark haired, he'd had a square jaw and the kind of casual stubble that looked cool rather than unkempt. If Jeremy ever tried something similar he'd probably look as if he'd crawled out of a dumpster. To make matters worse, he'd been one of those exhaustingly hearty jocks with that easy confidence-cum-arrogance that all doctors seemed to possess. He'd been thorough though. He'd pressed his stethoscope to Jeremy's chest, where his pecs had conveniently wilted into old-man titties before his very eyes. They'd done the works—ECG, CT scan, full medical and social history—before he was allowed to go. As the scanner whirred and spun, he'd wondered what he would do if his head held a stowaway, an evil bundle of cells hiding in the folds and crevices of his brain. Would he be like his father, brave and stoic to the end, or would he become some worse version of himself, yet to be revealed? In the end he didn't find out, as a panic attack had been the verdict. The doctor didn't add, *you great big girl*, but he'd probably thought it.

The memory made him grab a second beer and a bottle of wine from the cooler for Sarah. She'd probably need something to unwind too, after the day they'd had. In the sitting room he closed the curtains and turned on the television. He wasn't sure why but he didn't feel able to concentrate. It might have been just tiredness, but whatever it was it gave him a sense of detachment, as though he were experiencing things at one remove. It was unsettling, and he shook his head in a vain attempt to dispel the feeling.

Sarah chose that moment to join him, eyeing him with some concern as he swiveled his head from side to side. She flopped down next to him on the sofa and pressed her head into the crook of his shoulder, looking up at him with serious eyes.

"Are you sure you're okay?" she asked. "It's just that it's not like you to do something like that, to panic. You looked so . . . I don't know, desperate, I suppose. It frightened me. Have you got any idea what could've brought it on?"

A sudden image of the running figures flitted unbidden before his eyes and an involuntary shudder ran through him, heightening his feeling of unrest.

"No idea," he replied, blinking rapidly as if to dislodge something unpleasant from his eye. "One minute I was looking out the window like I always do and next minute it just kind of happened. I wasn't thinking about anything in particular, and I certainly wasn't feeling tense. I honestly don't know where it came from."

He freed his arm and curled it around her, pulling her closer.

"Look, let's not talk about it anymore. To be honest it's made me feel a bit stupid, and I'd rather just forget all about it."

He bent his head to find her lips, warm and soft and minty. She'd cleaned her teeth while she was upstairs, brushing away the staleness of the plane and the sour taste of anxiety, and Jeremy wished he'd afforded her the same consideration. Somehow he always managed to fall short of expectation. He pulled away and looked steadily into the blue haven of her eyes.

"Sarah, I'm sorry I snapped at you, and at Lucy. I didn't mean to. The whole thing unsettled me, but I shouldn't have taken it out on you two. It wasn't fair."

He was seized by the sudden fear that he might do something to drive her away; that he might manage to mess everything up and lose her too. The thought of losing someone else he loved was more than he could bear.

"You do know that I love you, don't you? Much more than I probably show. You mean everything to me, you and the children."

"Of course I do, and I love you more—even though you don't always deserve it."

She curled herself around to sit on his lap and he felt the firm pressure of her breasts against his chest. Slowly he slid his hands under her T-shirt to release her bra, running his fingers over the softness of her flesh. As her eyes darkened in response he felt his own detachment dispel. He was there in the moment with the woman he loved, his children safely upstairs in bed. Surely all was well with the world.

His eyes opened onto blindness. Velvet-black and fathomless. For a moment he'd no idea where or what he was, just a vortex of terror whirling blindly in the darkness. Gradually sleep receded and his senses returned. The faint outline of the curtains and the familiar scents of the bedroom made themselves known to him, and over the thundering in his head he became aware of Sarah next to him, soundly sleeping, the soothing rhythm of her breathing an anchor pulling him back to earth.

The dream still clung to the edges of his mind like a dark thing. In it, the plane banked and plummeted, the ground rushed toward him, and as it did, the running figure looked up. It turned its face toward the sky and looked straight at him. Emily looked straight at him!

# 3

The day carried a taint of dysphoria. Jeremy had slept fitfully after the nightmare, rising to the surface at every sound, a timid, wee mouse of a man. Here at work, in the cold light of day, he knew it was ridiculous, the terror he'd felt at the time. It was just Emily's face mingling with the present, pulled from the past by his thoughts of his mother. Nevertheless, it'd left him with a hum of . . . not anxiety exactly, more a feeling of being out of step with the world. It was how he felt on the rare occasions when he and Sarah had rowed; a background irritation with everyone, everything. They rarely quarreled, but when they did it was usually his fault. Some minor issue that he latched on to, like a sharp-toothed little terrier with a bone, worrying it to death until even Sarah's patience snapped. Then she revealed a different side; she didn't raise her voice but oh, she was clever, much cleverer than him with his blunt-edged railing against the world. Every one of her words came measured, calculated, designed to wound. Just like his mother, she knew where to poke him so it hurt. It sometimes made him wonder what hidden depths she had. What calculating mind lurked behind her gentle exterior, and what she might be capable of, should he ever truly hurt her.

He turned back to the draft plans and the spreadsheet of cost estimates. There was a meeting planned with the clients tomorrow to run through the numbers, but his heart wasn't in it anymore. Sometimes he longed to walk away from the shopping centers and office blocks and set up on his own. Doing something real, something with soul. Less municipal, more *Grand Designs*. He thought of the view from the plane window. All those little boxes that could be so much more, if form and functionality met art and design.

Out of nowhere the image of the running figure came into his head, and he wondered what had happened to her and whether she'd gotten away. He hadn't consciously thought of her as a girl before but now he was sure, utterly, categorically sure. Logically, he understood that he'd been too far away to properly see, and that he'd only glimpsed her for an instant, but something convinced him, something about the way she'd moved. Like she was a girl in flight, in danger, and now he wondered if he should do something about it. He knew the thought was irrational, but it stuck in his mind and he found himself wondering if anyone had been reported missing, or worse, if a body had been found.

Now he couldn't settle. The background noises of the office grated like nails on a blackboard and his skin began to crawl. He was suddenly agitated and couldn't sit still, so he went to the water cooler, where he stood for a second, trying to gather his scattered thoughts. He felt hot and jittery and so unlike himself that he wondered for a moment if he was having some sort of breakdown. First the panic on the plane, now this.

He downed a cup of water and pushed the hair back from his face. His forehead was damp to the touch and this served to increase his feeling of tension.

Mike appeared at his side, a sly grin smearing his features. "You okay there, mate?" he said. "You look a bit off to me."

He nudged Jeremy hard in the ribs with a bony elbow, slopping the remains of the water onto Jeremy's shirt, a flash of coldness against the heat of his skin.

"Or was it a heavy session last night? Is that it?"

Jeremy looked down at the patch of wetness, then at Mike. There was a crusty remnant of yellow sleep in the corner of one of his eyes, and a tiny tuft of errant bristles on his jaw where he'd missed a patch with his razor. If anyone'd had a heavy session it looked as if it was him. Jeremy could still feel the impact of the elbow to his ribs, and he experienced a disproportionate surge of anger. He'd known boys like Mike at school, pseudobullies who liked causing pain but sneakily and with grins on their faces, as if it was all just a joke. It made them feel big. He could just imagine a spotty, prepubescent Mike grabbing at the front of someone's shirt to inflict the oh-so-hilarious "nipple-cripple." Creepy little sod.

Today he just didn't have any energy for a smart retort.

"I'm fine, Mike, thanks. Just needed to clear my head for a bit, that's all. Think I'm going to take five and get a bit of fresh air."

Suddenly he needed to get out, to get away from Mike and from the almost-overwhelming urge to smash a fist into his face—not that he ever would. That'd happened to him once, at school, and he could still remember the visceral shock such violence had elicited in him.

He took the lift down to the foyer and stepped out into the London street. For a second he felt disoriented, the traffic and the people overwhelming, but the feeling quickly passed and his pulse returned to normal. He decided to go for a coffee and to pick up a newspaper on the way. Usually he got his news online or from the television, but today there was something comforting about the thought of sitting down with a coffee and the paper.

The pavement was bathed in watery sunlight, so Jeremy took a table outside. Even though summer was technically over, there was still warmth in the air. It was probably down to the layer of carbon monoxide that was draping the city but no matter; it was preferable to being cooped up inside with the odious Mike. A group of Japanese tourists went past, viewing the world above surgical masks, and for a moment Jeremy envied their anonymity and the distance the masks afforded them.

He settled at a solitary table and began to flick through the paper, scanning the opening lines of each article as he went, searching for news of a missing girl or of a body found. Needless to say there was nothing, and he experienced a frisson of disappointment. Not that he wanted something to have happened to her, more that he felt sure it had, something no one else seemed to know about. No one other than him.

A sudden thought crossed his mind. Maybe it hadn't made the nationals yet, maybe it was all too soon. Newly invigorated, he finished his coffee and headed back. The costings could wait; this suddenly felt much more urgent.

Back in the office he searched Google for local papers covering the Gatwick area, firstly scanning the latest edition of the *Crawley & Horley Observer*. Nothing. It was the same on Crawley News 24. With growing frustration he went to the BBC News and tapped in "Horley region," but again there was nothing, just drones over the airport and threats of a new runway. Unconsciously he released a sigh and became aware of Mike looking across, craning his neck to see what he had on the screen. With an effort he abandoned his search and returned to AutoCAD and the office designs, where gradually the squares of the site plan, with its trees and walkways, morphed into fields and houses as seen from a plane.

They'd had an early dinner and the kids were tucked up in bed. Sarah had donned pajamas and was now curled up next to him on the sofa, engrossed in *Bake Off*. This week was bread week, and the bun innuendos were coming thick and fast. Usually Jeremy found it vaguely amusing; tonight it grated and he couldn't engage. He felt the same restlessness he'd experienced earlier and found himself fidgeting, unable to settle.

Sarah shot him a pointed look. "Jez, if you don't want to watch it, just go and do something else. I can't enjoy it with you squirming about next to me. Go on, shoo."

He feigned hesitation.

"Are you sure? To be honest, I have got a bit of work to catch up on."

It wasn't honest, not at all. He just felt the need to be on his own.

"This one's *proving* a bit boring," he added, nudging her to let her know it was a joke, albeit a feeble one.

Sarah didn't smile. Usually she indulged his corny sense of humor, but this one failed to rise. Instead a crease of worry sat between her eyes, with all the makings of a permanent fixture.

"Are you sure you're okay, Jez? You've seemed distracted ever since we got back. It's almost like half of you is somewhere else."

"Darling, I'm fine, honestly. I've just come back to a shedload of work, that's all. You know what it's like—you get away for a break, then end up coming back to all the work you would've done if you'd been there. I'll be fine once I've caught up."

Jeremy wasn't entirely sure why he was lying to her. There was nothing that couldn't wait until tomorrow. In any case, Mike had been more than happy to pick up his projects while he was away, probably sidling up to the boss the minute he'd walked out the door, arse-lick that he was.

He just wanted some time to think, to go over what he'd seen from the plane, and he didn't want to say that to Sarah. He didn't want her to think he was going crazy and he knew it'd sound that way. In truth, it was eating at him, intruding into his thoughts like guilt, and he needed to understand why.

He slipped out of the room and went up to the office. It wasn't quite dark yet, but he drew the curtains anyway and turned on the desk lamp. Feeling strangely furtive, he opened Google Maps and zoomed in on Gatwick, closing his eyes in an attempt to visualize the landmarks just before the plane banked. There had been farmland, fields and animals, and a golf course. He remembered the appeal of the bunkers and greens all laid out in miniature.

There were several golf courses near Gatwick, ringing the airport on all sides. The plane would have initially come in from the south coast, but he'd no way of knowing how many times it might have circled, or the direction of its final approach. For want of a better option he started with those more to the south: Ifield, Cottesmore, and Copthorne the nearest, with Haywards Heath and Lindfield lying farther out. He focused in on each one in turn, trying to recall the layout as viewed from the cabin.

Cottesmore looked promising, although he couldn't be sure if it was too far from the airport. There was no way of telling what their air speed would have been either, or the distance from the ground. Ifield looked nearer, and again the aerial view of fairways and sand traps seemed familiar.

The more he scanned the area, the more golf courses there appeared to be. Copthorne and Chartham Park, Effingham, and Mannings Heath; all or any of which could be the one he was looking for. He banged the desk in frustration and laid his forehead against its cool surface. On some level he couldn't fathom why this was so important to him or quite what he was hoping to find, but he felt compelled to look for it anyway.

There was the slightest movement in the air behind him, and he realized Sarah was in the doorway, watching him. He'd been so engrossed that he hadn't heard her come up the stairs, so he had no idea how long she'd been standing there. He had the sudden suspicion that she'd deliberately crept up on him, as though she'd sensed his earlier evasion and was afraid that she'd find him lying in the dark, brooding, or engaged in something vaguely nefarious.

Now, as she went to stand behind him, Jeremy lifted his head from the desk and moved to quickly close the screen. A fraction too late. Sarah saw the aerial view of West Sussex laid out before them, where Gatwick seemed to pulse in the center of the screen, like a beacon.

"Darling, I just wondered if you wanted a coffee or anything, seeing as you're working."

There was something in her voice that Jeremy couldn't read, and she leaned in closer.

"What is it you're actually working on at the moment?"

"Nothing much," he replied. "Just a couple of new projects I've been mulling over."

"Nothing much" was totally at odds with the "shedload" he'd mentioned earlier, and another thread of gossamer added to his web of lies.

"Isn't that Gatwick?" she asked, turning to look at him. Now there was a frank question in her eyes, coupled with a hint of confusion.

"Jez, that's the airport, what are you looking for?" Slowly comprehension dawned. "Is this something to do with what happened on the plane?"

She was too sharp for Jeremy, with her lawyer's mind. Sometimes her flashes of intuition unnerved him. He considered lying—quite why, he didn't know—but instead he decided to answer truthfully.

"Okay, okay." He raised his hands in surrender. "I thought I saw something out of the plane, and for some reason it's troubling me, that's all. I was just trying to see if I could find the area and then I was going to decide what to do. I didn't want to say anything to you just yet, in case . . ."

As he talked she pulled over the other chair and sat down. Concerned now.

"What do you mean, you saw something? What sort of something? And why wouldn't you talk to me about it if it upset you so much that it made you have a panic attack?"

There seemed no choice but for Jeremy to tell her, aware all the while of how stupid it sounded now he was putting it into words.

"Look, it was when the plane banked. The ground was that bit nearer for a moment and I saw a girl, okay? She was running into some woods and she was being chased by three people and now, for some reason, I can't shift the idea that she was in danger. I thought if I could find out where it was I could maybe do something about it. Make sure she's okay or something. I'm not sure what, but I didn't feel I could just ignore it. And before you say anything, I know it all sounds a bit odd, which was why I hadn't said anything to you."

He had no doubts now. It seemed what had started as a suspicion had now morphed into hard fact. Jeremy registered a flicker of surprise at the realization he'd just said there were three people. He knew he hadn't seen three—two, maybe, definitely not three—but now he was convinced there were three. In fact he'd stake his life on there being someone else just out of his field of vision, and the irrationality of that conviction frightened him.

Sarah picked up on something in his face and reached for his hand.

"Jez, to be honest I'm a bit worried about you. If this is what made you panic, it doesn't make any sense. I'm not saying you didn't see something out of the window, but how can you possibly say it was a girl?"

He tried to pull his hand away but she held it tighter.

"Even if it was, how could you know how old she was, or know that she was being chased. She could have been a kid playing or someone out running. Anything. And even if she was being chased, why on earth would you react like that?"

Unconsciously she was using the voice that she used with the children, and that rankled.

"I don't know. It just seemed like she was being chased and that made me feel anxious."

"It really doesn't make any sense. We must've been flying at what, two thousand feet, maybe more? There's no way you could've seen that kind of detail from that far up, or for the few seconds we would've actually been overhead."

"But I did see her. I'm not making it up."

"You'd have maybe seen people from that height but you wouldn't have been able to make out who they were or what they were doing. Darling, it's just not possible."

Her tone was insistent, edged with incredulity.

"And even if you believe you saw something it'd be impossible for you to pinpoint where with Google Earth. And why panic? I really don't understand why you would even be thinking like this."

Her logic irritated even though some part of him knew she was right. It wasn't what he wanted to hear. He wanted her to believe him—to help him find out what happened.

"Oh, so you're an aeronautical expert as well now, are you?" He faced her head-on in a confrontational manner. "Tell you what, if you don't believe me, I suggest you go and see if you can find any more programmes about food. Go on, go and indulge your passion for baked goods."

His voice was mocking and unpleasant, and he was ashamed the moment he said it. Sarah pulled her hand away as though stung.

"Sarah, I'm sorry. I don't know why I said that, I didn't mean it—"

He made himself meet her eye, expecting to see hurt. Instead there was something akin to disappointment, and that upset him more.

"I do," she said. "Maybe it's because sometimes you're a spiteful little prick." And with that she turned and walked away.

He'd wanted to fight with someone all day, so it might just as well be her.

"What's that supposed to mean? Don't come out with a comment like that and then bloody walk away. If you've got something to say to me then come back and say it to my face."

She paused in the doorway but didn't rise to the bait.

"This is weird, Jeremy, and deep down I think you know it. Let me know when you're ready to talk to me like an adult, and I'll be here." And with that she gently closed the door behind her.

# 4

Breakfast was tense. Sarah wouldn't ever let the children see friction between them, but Jeremy could tell she hadn't forgiven him. It was there in the flat exactness of her voice when she spoke to him, and in a certain hardness of expression that turned her irises a steely gray. He knew her well enough to know that inside she was torn: half of her just plain angry with him for the cheap gibe, the other half worried about him and wanting to talk. It made him love her even more, and he felt an ache in his chest when he thought of his spiteful words.

He watched as she prepared fruit and yogurt for herself and the children, making a game of counting out the raspberries for Lucy, putting them on the ends of her fingers.

"Here's a really fat, juicy one," she said, popping the chosen fruit into Lucy's waiting mouth. "There you go, poppet, that one definitely had your name on it."

Sadly, nothing had his name on it this morning. She didn't even make him a coffee—worse, she didn't even get a mug out for him.

Jeremy had often seen her do this; giving the children the cherry off the top, taking the broken cake or the smallest portion for herself. It came with being a mother, that desire to sacrifice for those you love, even in such little ways. For some reason the scene didn't move him as it should; instead of the warm feeling it should've engendered, it brought a stab of something else, something dangerously like jealousy.

His thoughts inevitably turned once again to his own mother. She was never one to give him her cherry—pardon the unpleasant thought that conjured. Any choice morsel was destined for her mouth, never his. He could picture her now, watching him as those carmine lips closed around the last chocolate in the box, relishing his disappointment with something nasty in her eyes.

Someone had once told him—probably Uncle Ian—that carmine came from squashed beetles, a waxy brilliance that cost them their lives. As a child he'd easily imagined his mother pounding their little bodies to a pulp before smearing their crimson secretions across her lips.

A shudder escaped him, a beetle walking across his grave, and he caught Sarah watching him. He flashed her what he hoped was a winning smile but sadly it came last, he'd been aiming for loving, reassuring, normal, but instead it was a rictus bearing of teeth that would do nothing to allay her concern. It was the grin of a wolf in sheep's clothing.

He threw the last of his (self-made) coffee down his throat and headed for the door, stopping to wrap his arms around her as he passed, resting his chin on the top of her head in a gesture of supplication. She stiffened in his embrace; she wasn't quite ready to forgive him yet.

"I'm sorry, Sarah," he whispered into her hair. "I'm such an idiot sometimes, I don't deserve you."

It would take more than a cursory hug and she stayed rigid and silent, so with a sigh, he gave her a quick cuddle and gratefully left the little nucleus of his family.

The office was stuffy and stultifying, and regardless of how hard he tried to concentrate, work was no more engaging than it had been the day before. Even though Jeremy could kind of see things from Sarah's perspective, he still couldn't shake the feeling that she was wrong. He even accepted that what he was thinking might be irrational, but that didn't stop the images from flashing into his brain every time he dropped his guard. It didn't dispel the conviction that somewhere in those woods a girl had come to harm, or lessen the compulsion to find out who she was and what had happened to her.

Emily! The name sliced through his mind like a blade, and sudden beads of sweat rose on his palms. Emily, little Em, and his heart began to beat faster. He mustn't go there. He mustn't think of that missing part of him. Why, after all these years, did it suddenly feel as though she were there in the room with him? As though, if he quickly turned his head, he'd catch the flash of her smile or the play of sunlight on her hair? The air of the office seemed to stir, as though the molecules were shifting and parting to let in the ghost of a dead girl, but none of his colleagues appeared to notice. No one saw the sudden wildness in Jeremy's eyes, or the way his hands trembled.

Grief never dies; he'd learned that at an early age. You just accommodate it. It burrows a little place in your soul and it hides there, waiting. Waiting for the chance comment, the stray memory, the certain scent in the air to conjure it back into life. It was like that now; something had woken it and the pain was as fresh as ever. As if it'd all happened just yesterday.

His thoughts were shattered by the ringing of his phone, its urgent vibrations sending it skittering around the desk in panicked circles. It was Sarah's number, and the breath snatched in his throat. She almost never rang him at work. His mind immediately turned to the children, one of them injured or, God forbid, something worse.

Coming hot on the heels of Emily's ghost, the call felt like a portent, and his nerves pulled taut like wire.

"Hello?" The fear was there in his voice, waiting for the ax to fall.

"Jeremy, it's me. I've just had a call from the hospital in Bristol. It's your mother, she was admitted yesterday evening. They wouldn't tell me much, but from what they did say it doesn't sound good."

The urgency was there in her voice too, her earlier mood with him forgotten.

He hesitated for a heartbeat before answering, trying to make sense of what he felt. There was relief—that it wasn't Sarah or the children—but there was something else. And then it came to him, it was regret. A great wash of regret for what might have been, for what should have been. For the relationship they'd never had, the love they'd never shared, for all the hurts and recriminations, the cruelties that couldn't be undone. All the Christmases and birthdays, the holidays and high days that should've been times of joy. It wasn't just regret for him, it was for her too. That surprised him, that after all she was and all she'd done he could still feel regret for the things that she'd missed. The grandchildren she'd never really known, the daughter-in-law who would've loved her if she'd ever let her near. A great ocean of missed opportunities and time they'd never get back. No second chances.

"Jeremy, are you there? Are you okay?"

"Yes, I'm fine. Sorry it's . . . I don't know, it just took me by surprise that's all. What do you need me to do?"

It was a ridiculous question; it was his mother, not hers, but Sarah had been the one who'd dutifully kept in touch, phoning his mother a couple of times a month, sending her pictures of Jack and Lucy, keeping her part of the family, albeit at a distance. She'd never really understood their relationship, because hers with her parents couldn't have been more different, and in the beginning she'd tried so hard to make things right between them, until she'd realized some families are warped and broken beyond repair. Their pieces buried under a mound of history.

"Jeremy, she's your *mother*. You have to go and see her, you'll never forgive yourself if you don't. Regardless of what you think of her, she hasn't got anyone else. You're her son, her next of kin. Darling, listen to me, you can't run away from this even if you want to."

Jeremy sighed, world-weary and reluctant, but it was all for effect because he knew that once again she was right.

Your pieces buried under a

The drive from London to Bristol was an easy one; basically straight along the M4 motorway, three hours max, and Jeremy felt a twinge of almost-guilt at the length of time it'd been since he'd last made the journey. It was one of those bright September days, crisp and clear, without a cloud in the sky. The trip could almost have been enjoyable, if it wasn't for what was waiting for him at the other end. He'd never been good with hospitals, and the combination of hospital and his mother was never going to be fun. Sarah had offered to come with him and though he'd been sorely tempted, he knew it was something he needed to do on his own. If there was a peace to be made, then he needed to try—if not for his mother, then at least for his own peace of mind.

The car ate up the miles far more greedily than he'd have liked. Once he was past Reading the motorway ran through open coun- tryside where the trees and hedges on either side were starting to show the first tarnish of autumn, a scattering of gold among the greens. Rolling fields stretched away to the horizon, and a distant folly sat atop a rounded hill. Jeremy noted it as he passed, and noted his own folly at the idea there could ever be any reconciliation with his mother. He was suddenly tempted to take the next exit and hide away in a quiet lay-by. Be alone with his thoughts.

His mother. It was strange how often she'd intruded into those thoughts just recently, almost as though on some level he'd known she was nearing the end of her life. Did hate bind them in the same way as love, or were the two of them linked by some kind of morphic resonance born out of trauma and loss? Whatever the reason, he'd felt her presence more keenly over the previous few days.

He stepped into the hush of the side room and there she lay, Mrs. Marian Horton. Filtered light crept through the blinds and dared to touch her face. It was far braver than him. It was the first time he'd seen her in close to three years, and the change was startling. He'd known she had heart failure, but he wasn't expecting her to look quite so ravaged. Her feet protruded from beneath the blankets, their tops smooth domes filigreed with a fine network of blue-gray veins. Her toes were a row of puffy little sausages, with the skin beginning to crack and split as though pricked with a fork. Those were ten little piggies that wouldn't be going to market ever again. Her fluid-filled ankles were the same—elephantine—as were her arms, and her swollen hands were a parody of the slender-ringed fingers he'd known as a boy. Those butter-soft palms and perfect red nails. Now, they lay immobile on the honeycombed surface of the coverlet, putting Jeremy in mind of inflated hospital gloves. A vicious inner voice that shocked him, whispered, "Who's fat now, Mummy?"

Her face was the color of pastry, and her once-fine hair was wispy and lank, stretched across the eggshell of the skull beneath the skin. Each breath she took echoed ragged and bubbly as her lungs struggled against the pulmonary edema marking her journey's end.

While her eyes were closed, Jeremy took a moment to study her face. In his mind's eye he pictured the woman she'd once been, ruby lipped and beautiful, her hair a cascade of spun gold. Always slim and immaculately dressed, the envy at the school gates had been almost palpable. The kind of mother a son could have worshipped—would've worshipped, in fact—if only she'd let him. He was seized by a savage rush of grief and pity. Despite his antipathy, he found his eyes prickling with tears, unsure if they were for her or for himself.

He cleared his throat and her eyes opened.

She was "in and out" now, according to the nurses, but as those gray orbs focused on him, laden with disappointment, Jeremy realized that, for now at least, she was definitely at home.

"Oh, it's you," she said. Her voice was hoarse, with little warmth in it. "I wondered if you'd bother to stir yourself."

Jeremy took a moment to marvel at her resilience. Even now, even in this weakened state, even at the very end, she still found the strength to goad him.

She lifted a bloated hand and impatiently gestured toward a beaker and straw on the side table.

With a Pavlovian response, Jeremy leapt into action, the little boy inside him still apparently panting for her approval. Christ, was he thick or something? He really should've learned by now. He dutifully held the beaker to her parched lips as she took a laborious sip. All the while her eyes never left his, searching his face with an intensity that made him squirm.

She waved the drink away and indicated the chair by her bed.

"Sit with me for a while—unless of course you've something more important to do."

He obediently squeaked into its vinyl-clad seat and tried to ignore the twinge of hurt provoked by her words.

Her eyes closed, and for a moment he wondered if she'd drifted into sleep, but something told him not. He could almost hear the whirring of her brain, the machinations of her thoughts. Oh yes, she was most definitely "in" at the moment.

The doctor had said it was likely a matter of days or weeks, certainly not months, and Jeremy had found himself searching for suitable words and an appropriate facial expression. Both had firmly eluded him.

"Oh dear" was the best he'd managed, coupled with a look dangerously near to bland indifference.

"I understand you're not close," the doctor had said. Oh, what mastery of understatement.

Jeremy looked at her now and wondered exactly what she'd told them. It was bound to be nothing complimentary. Probably some malign painting of a callous, thoughtless son, or perhaps an evil brother bound for hell.

He became aware of the sound of the clock, marking the passing of time. It didn't tick, merely tocked, each strident beat marked by a nervous quiver of its hands. He knew exactly how it felt. He picked at a nail and wished he'd brought a paper or his iPad. Looking for distraction he took out his phone but then remembered the No Mobile Phones sign, and he slipped it back into his pocket with a sigh. Finally he wondered if she'd notice if he snuck away for a bit.

Her eyes snapped open. Apparently she would, and he was struck by the uncomfortable feeling that she could read his mind, that all the time she'd been lying there, she'd been probing his thoughts for weakness. She beckoned him toward her, and he noticed that her eyes had taken on a misty, distant quality.

Maybe this was it then, the deathbed declaration of love, or if not that, at least an explanation, or a plea for forgiveness for how she had treated him. Her voice was weaker than before, so he leaned in closer to catch her words, flinching at the hint of rot carried on her breath. Speech came at a cost, her lungs heaving under the strain, her lips working for a while before the words emerged. When they did, he wished they hadn't.

"I know you," she whispered, "and I've always felt you knew something. Something you wouldn't tell us." Her voice was ripe with accusation. "What is it you wouldn't tell us, Jeremy? Why do you pretend?"

He recoiled as though slapped, more from the unexpected words than from the scent of decay. He tried to back away from her, but she seized his arm in a surprisingly viselike grip, the bones of her hand grinding into his flesh. Even now, even as a grown man he experienced a surge of fear, visceral and bladder loosening. A childhood scar split open. Her eyes had regained their focus and he could see the animosity still burning brightly after all this time. Venomous. She pulled on his arm, raising herself up from the pillow.

"It should've been you," she hissed, "not her. It should be you under the ground."

He felt the breath leave his body as though he'd been sucker-punched. He'd known it all along. Still, to hear her say it was almost too painful to bear. The hurt was like a living thing, and for a moment he thought he'd burst into tears and cry like a baby.

Instead he prised her fingers from his arm, as she once had his, and forced himself to look at her. He almost said it. He almost said *Fuck you*, but even as his lips formed the words something stopped him.

He looked at her, and he sensed her grief like a feral thing. It had destroyed her, losing Em, and somewhere deep inside himself he found a well of, if not forgiveness, then resignation. He'd never been her favorite, nowhere even near, and after Emily she'd had no love left to give. Her grief took it all, leaving in its place bitterness and resentment toward the one who'd survived. He wouldn't be cruel. Instead he leaned forward and placed the lightest of kisses on her forehead, shocking his lips into silence; they'd never done that before.

"Goodbye, Mum."

He turned and walked out the door. He didn't look back or stop walking until he reached his car. Not even to speak to the staff; they had his number for when the time came.

Sometimes Jeremy envied other people, those whose lives seem so—normal. Even Sarah and her parents, John and Barbara. There was nothing but affection between them, an easiness in the way they rubbed along together. Their love was unconditional and honest, and he wondered what it must be like to have that security, that unshakable knowledge that you're loved no matter what. His relationship with his mother couldn't be more different. Dysfunctional, dark, complex, and now to have her finally put it into words. Her resentment that he'd survived and Emily had not. Her suspicions still festering after all this time.

His mind did what it always did when he strayed too close to the past. It skittered away to something else. Instead of going there, he tried to imagine a world without his mother. He relived how it was when his father had died; that Dad-shaped void in the universe that he couldn't quite comprehend, and he tried to preempt how he'd feel when his mother passed. Like the Boy Scout he'd never been, he tried to "Be Prepared'—but it was impossible.

The sun slipped low in the sky, slanting through the windscreen to where he was sitting. It was that which made his eyelids prickle and the tears come; nothing else.

# 5

The house was shrouded in darkness. The windows black, all bar a faint glow of light filtering through the sitting room curtains, like a beacon leading Jeremy home.

Quietly, he unlocked the front door and slipped inside. Every part of him was bone weary, hollowed out, and he prayed that Sarah had forgiven him, for he didn't think he could handle any more tension or thinly veiled unpleasantness. The house was silent, no murmur of television or of music playing. He moved quietly through the hallway to the sitting room, where his wife lay sleeping on the sofa with Lucy curled up in her arms. Lamplight bathed them, exposing their tender vulnerability. He stood in the doorway for a moment and watched them sleep, his wife and his daughter, tight together like two peas in a pod. Lucy was in her pajamas and her fair hair was damp, with wet little tendrils stuck to her forehead. With a tingle of worry he noticed how flushed her face looked.

He slid onto the sofa next to them, quietly so as not to wake them, but still Lucy stirred in her sleep and flexed her legs against the intrusion of his thigh. He marveled at her little feet, at their pink perfection in stark contrast to his mother's ruined trotters. Taking a foot in his hand, he ran a thumb across its velvety softness. Lucy stirred again, and the hint of a smile played at the edge of her lips. As he looked at her Jeremy was pierced by a sudden stab of love for his daughter, and for once it was pure and unalloyed, and it brought with it a welling of relief that he *was* able to feel that way. He stroked the tangle of her dirty-blond hair, so like her mother's, and studied her little features in repose. She was almost five now, the age Emily had been when she died, and he was struck by the unexpected resemblance. Maybe he hadn't allowed himself to see it before, or maybe it wasn't so apparent when she was awake and her face was lit by her own vitality. But now, in sleep, the Horton genes expressed themselves, playing under her features in repose. Jeremy felt that unnerving little flicker of something dark pulling at his heart, and he quickly looked away.

There, in the quiet and the darkness, he allowed Emily to creep into his thoughts—but only a glimpse; that was all he could bear. The long-awaited second child, the beloved daughter, the precious gift, five long years after him. The light that lit his mother's eye and dimmed the rest of them, reducing him and his father to mere insignificances, flickering at the periphery of her vision.

Time and the manner of his sister's passing had perhaps colored his memories of her, but now he sensed a strangeness he'd not considered before. An ethereal, otherworldly quality that had somehow set her apart. The way she'd tilt her head and smile at you was all it took for her to own you, even though you never truly knew what she was thinking. He wondered now, as an adult, if she'd actually been on the spectrum, but it hardly mattered anymore. All that mattered was that they'd worshipped her, each in their own way. He, with a kind of wary awe, as though he'd been entrusted with a princess and it was his job to guard her, to keep her safe. The most miserable failure of his life.

At once, he was that eleven-year-old boy again and the chasm opened up inside him: a great well of grief, confusion, and fear. It was why he never went there. The terror, the silence, the child psychologist's insistent voice echoing down the years.

He stood up and untangled his daughter from Sarah's arms; she needed to be in bed, so he clasped her warm little body to his and headed for the stairs. She was hot to the touch, her forehead like fire, and a flare of panic lit up in his chest. It was his job to keep her safe.

In her room he laid her in the hollow of her bed and gently pulled up the duvet. In the half-light, rabbits balefully glared from its cover and glassy eyes glinted accusingly from the row of cuddly toys perched at her headboard. For a moment his head was a jumble of disjointed sounds and images. A girl running, a tangle of hair flying behind her, feet pounding, a dog barking, a clamor of whoops and shouts. He clamped his hands over his ears, and suddenly he was afraid.

Back in the sitting room, Lucy's absence had woken Sarah, and now she was sitting up on the sofa, bleary-eyed and sleep tousled. As she registered Jeremy's presence she got to her feet, opening her arms to hug him. She'd never been one to hold a grudge, and she could see from the expression in his eyes that right now he needed her.

"Are you okay?" she whispered. "I hope it wasn't too awful."

"It wasn't good," he replied, "not good at all. But I'll tell you about it tomorrow, if that's okay. It's been a long, god-awful day, and right now I can't even think about it, let alone live through it all again."

"Jez, I'm so sorry. It'll be all right, I promise."

He shook his head. "Not for me it won't . . ."

Wordlessly, she folded him into her arms, where he grasped her like a drowning man. The warm scent of her reached his nostrils like a memory of summer meadows. He knew that under her softness lay his rock, and he sometimes feared what he'd become without her.

"You're shaking," she said. "Come on you, let's go to bed."

"No, I just need a bit of time—"

"What you need is to sleep, Jez. It'll all seem that much better in the morning, and we can talk then."

"Please, let's stay here for a while." He pulled her down onto the sofa, to the pool of warmth she had left. "Let's lie here for a bit. I don't want to go up just yet. I need a bit of time to wind down and get my head in a better place."

Truth was, he was afraid to go to bed. Afraid he'd lie awake in the dark, reliving his mother's words. Scared that he'd close his eyes and the nightmares would come to consume him, Em's essence drifting out of the night to haunt him.

Together they lay on the sofa. Slowly the rhythm of Sarah's breathing and the soft warmth of her body dispelled his feeling of dread, and he allowed his limbs to relax as his mind slid ever closer to sleep.

Morning broke, cool and gray and soulless. There was a relentless pattering of rain against the bedroom window, and an ill wind moaned down the chimney and whistled under the eaves of the house. Soon the discordant sounds pulled Jeremy from sleep. For a moment he was confused and disoriented, until he slowly remembered Sarah waking him, deep into the night, and the two of them making their way upstairs to bed. He'd slept, soundly and surprisingly dreamlessly. For a few moments he felt okay, relaxed, more like his normal self, but then his pulse began to rise and anxiety quickened his breath. He reached for the alarm clock. God, it was gone eight thirty, he should be at work already. Throwing back the duvet he leapt out of bed, still wearing yesterday's underpants and shirt. Clad only in this fetching ensemble, he thundered down the stairs to where Sarah and the children were finishing breakfast.

He shattered the scene of domestic harmony, his voice shrill and angry.

"What the fuck, Sarah. Why didn't you wake me? It's half past eight, for God's sake. I should be in work."

"Jez, the children," Sarah said, gently but with a warning frown creasing her brow.

He'd forgotten himself and committed a cardinal sin, swearing in front of the children but he couldn't bring himself to care. It meant nothing to Lucy anyhow, quietly humming over her bowl; her first few days at school hadn't yet laid waste to her innocence. Jack, on the other hand, was looking at his father round-eyed, his expression a mixture of horror and glee.

"Oh, Dad *swore*," he said, just in case anyone had missed it.

Jeremy looked at him smirking and felt his anger ramp up a notch. "Jack, I wasn't even talking to you, so we don't need your input, thank you. Just get on and finish your breakfast or you'll be late for school."

He turned back to Sarah, aware of a low-level hum of rage. He didn't know where it was coming from, but he could feel it bubbling beneath the surface.

"We discussed this last night, Jez, when we came up to bed, don't you remember? We agreed I'd get the kids off to school and then we'd talk. Look, work will understand, you just need to ring them and explain. God, Jez, you mother's *dying*. Surely you're allowed a bit of time off to process that."

Now she'd forgotten herself, and instantly Jack pounced on it.

"*Dying? Who's dying?*" he asked, and something inside Jeremy snapped.

"For God's sake, Jack, don't you ever know when to shut up?"

"Jez!"

"What? He's got an opinion on everything, he just needs to learn when to be quiet."

A look of defiant hurt smeared itself across Jack's features and his eyes glittered with unshed tears.

Now Sarah stood up from the table, her own anger rising with her. "Look, none of this is our fault. If you can't stop shouting and bawling like some madman, just go back upstairs to bed!"

Jeremy had a sudden wild notion of himself sweeping the bowls and glasses from the table, smashing them to the ground in rage, grinding and stamping them into the floor like the madman Sarah clearly thought him. He didn't. Instead he stood there looking at his family with a misplaced, impotent fury building inside him. Not trusting himself to speak, he turned and fled the room, with Sarah's eyes burning at his back, Jack close to tears.

Back in the bedroom he pulled the duvet over his head. He just felt So Bloody Angry. If Sarah wanted him to have a lie-in, then that was what he would do. At least if he was asleep he didn't have to listen to her worrying at him, or think about anything at all. As if on cue, the running girl put in an appearance, forcing herself into his mind. Fuck's sake! He pressed his hands over his eyes to dispel her image, but she was quickly replaced by his mother, a worse and much more insistent presence. Try as he might he couldn't rid himself of the feel of her breath on his face, or the echo of her words, like an earworm, *I've always felt you knew something.* Unbidden, the past surged up to greet him, bursting free of the vault where he'd safely locked it away.

A memory, fresh and immediate. His mother's face, contorted with fear. The hot blast of her breath. Flecks of her spittle peppering his cheeks as she yelled at him, seizing his shoulders and shaking. Shamefully too he recalled the sudden warm surge in his pants.

Then his father's hand on his. The forest of dark hairs on his knuckles. His voice uncharacteristically harsh.

"Stop it, Marian, you're scaring the boy! This isn't his fault."

His father leaning in close to him, his face gentle, coaxing, and there in the present he felt his loss. Grief, sudden and raw and new.

"Take no notice of Mum, she's just scared and upset. Tell me, son, I just want to know where you and the boys were playing and when you last saw your sister. We need you to help us find her."

And he did what was asked of him; he found her—but now the memory was lost to him. He found his sister, or rather he discovered her body, then they found him. Sitting at the water's edge, wet to the skin. Shaking. Silent. Emily, half in the water. So broken, so dead.

Many were the times he'd closed his eyes and summoned her image. Blue eyes open, popping, looking at him with a fixed dead stare. Yellow hair, freed of its braids, fanning out in the water like weed. Her face, white and wrong. His sister but not his sister anymore. But it wasn't a memory; it was a fiction. A fiction he'd constructed to fill a hole, to make a whole. His broken lady of the lake.

# 6

His mother was dead. She'd passed on a wet and windswept October day, quietly, peacefully, while no one was looking—least of all Jeremy, for he'd never gone back. Sarah had visited her just the once, but as for what they'd talked about, he didn't ask and she didn't tell. Nothing, he suspected, or at least nothing he'd ever want to hear.

He wasn't a religious man—the past had damned any chance of that—but he couldn't help wondering: had she sailed into oblivion or, somewhere, somehow, was his mother's soul reunited with the child she'd lost? He wasn't sure what he hoped for her. Maybe nothing.

Her funeral had been a suitably bleak affair. There'd just been Sarah and her parents, and a smattering of neighbors; the kind of wispy elderly folk who turn out for a funeral no matter how tentative the link. Jeremy had watched them through the weeping drizzle, squawking and pecking at the graveside, a murder of avid crows. He'd heard one mutter, "Poor Marian . . ." and was pleased that they did at least know her name. He wondered why he'd even cared—maybe his "compassionate leave" had made him more compassionate—but he had. For a reason he couldn't define, he'd needed to know that she'd had some sort of life outside the little circle of bitterness and loathing that was family. Afterward they'd gone back to her house, the bleak home where he'd grown up, and they'd stood awkwardly over tea and sandwiches while he'd manfully suppressed the urge to scream.

He'd wondered about that too, over recent weeks, when the past had strained against its bolts. If he were to go somewhere deep in the woods and scream, could he let it all come out? If he yelled and cried and pounded his fists into the dirt, could he finally be free of the things locked inside him?

Sarah came up behind him and laid her hands on his shoulders, pulling him back to the present. The children were both at school, so she seized the opportunity to speak to him while they were alone. She'd borne his outbursts of temper with fortitude because she saw how he was suffering, but she couldn't carry on tiptoeing around him.

"Jez, have you thought any more about what I said?"

He didn't answer, so she continued. "We can't carry on like this. It's not fair to any of us. These mood swings, and the anger, Jeremy, it's been going on for weeks now, and I'm fed up with having to tread on eggshells all the time."

Still he ignored her, and a note of frustration crept into her voice.

"I know things have got a bit . . . stressful before, but never anything like this."

He let out the tiniest of snorts at her pussy-footing. He knew he was a difficult bastard to live with sometimes, so she might as well come out and say it. It wasn't much of a snort, just the tiniest release of air, but she heard it nonetheless and her voice hardened.

"Jeremy, you could at least look at me."

The chair swiveled to face her, and Jeremy saw how her eyes flickered over his shoulder to look at the laptop. She couldn't help occasionally checking up on him, and had lost count of the times she'd seen Gatwick airport staring back at her. Today there was just a swirl of blue screen and a misty Window.

"Nothing to see here," he muttered.

"Don't, Jeremy—"

"Don't what? I was working toward an empty head until you disturbed me."

"Look, I'm not going to just stand by and watch you fall to pieces. You've not been right ever since the plane and this obsession with what you think you saw. And now losing your mother as well . . . I'm worried about you."

She knelt in front of his chair and he almost said, *Oh, while you're down there . . .* just to piss her off, but he bit his tongue in time. Truth be told, he didn't understand why he was trying to goad her, or why he felt so angry. He loved her, so he battened down his irritation and made himself look at her.

"I'm okay, Sarah . . ." But even as he spoke, he knew it wasn't true. He felt like a dam about to burst, and he didn't understand why.

"Jez." Her voice was soft. "I've been thinking, and I know you don't like talking about it, but what happened to you . . ."

His "Don't!" fell on deaf ears.

"I know you've never been able to tell me all the details, but I understand enough to know it was bad, and I know it's still with you and that sometimes you dream about it."

"Please, Sarah—"

"I don't know if what's going on with you right now is even linked to what happened back then, but Jez, surely you can see how this obsession with a girl being in danger has a . . . a similarity about it? Look, either way, I think you need some help."

She saw the expression in his eyes. "By that I just mean someone you could maybe talk to about things. Someone who might be able to help you make sense of the . . . issues . . . with your mother, as well."

"Oh, so I've got *mummy issues* now, is that it?"

"Jez, stop, you know that's not what I meant. I need you to see how unhappy this is making you, making both of us, and get some help. Will you at least say you'll think about it?" She delivered her coup de grâce: "If you won't, then I'm not sure how much longer we can go on like this."

With that, she got to her feet and walked away, leaving the veiled threat suspended in the air.

Oh, he understood she was right about him—he did have that much insight at least—but he still couldn't see how talking would help. Emily was dead, they were all dead, and talking wouldn't change the past or exorcise whatever demons might lurk in his private corners. He just needed time to work it out for himself, like he'd always done, ever since he was a boy. He laid his head on the desk—his habitual pose it seemed—and closed his eyes. Everything had been under control until that fucking plane.

He consciously slowed his breathing, trying to still the jittery, strung-out feeling that seemed to be his constant companion, and stared into the darkness of his eyelids, a darkness that began to swirl and pulse with each thump of his guilty heart. Gradually, against that teeming blackness, a picture unspooled. It was vivid and real to him, and slowly, reluctantly, he let his mind slide into it.

A hot day and he's running across sun-baked grass in the fields near his uncle Ian's house; instinctively he knows it's the day Emily died. Someone else is with him. He can hear the pounding of their feet . . .

*They were running; the girl was running. One of her braids had come undone and her hair streamed behind her in a slender skein of gold that shimmered and sparkled in the sunlight. He could sense her fear and it excited him. There was unexpected joy in it; joy because for once it wasn't he who was afraid. He whooped and laughed in exhilaration, thrilled by the sheer devilment. By the growing undercurrent of spite and aggression that he could feel tingling in the air around them. They ran through grass, long and wild. He could feel the brush of it against his calves and smell the sun-scorched scent of it searing his nostrils. He glanced down at his scuffed and grubby knees, at his skinny ankles pounding across the field in carelessly knotted trainers, and he laughed into the baked air. He could hear the others behind him, their breathless laughter as they charged toward the woods. Something, someone, was barking . . .*

Shaken, he pushed the chair from the desk and leapt to his feet, heart hammering. A part of him registered the image as real; another part forced it away, fighting to push back the feeling of menace. Where was Sarah? It seemed he couldn't be left alone with his mind anymore.

She was making Jack's bed, and Jeremy watched her from the doorway as she smoothed down the duvet and bent to pick a stray toy from the floor, her blond hair falling forward to hide her face. He tried to ignore the pounding of his heart as he concentrated instead on the vision of the woman he loved. A tiny voice told him he didn't deserve her, and he knew it spoke the truth. The right words eluded him, so he stood there for a moment, letting the mere sight of her calm him. He took in the curve of her buttocks and the way her hair framed her face in tousled waves. He loved her. He couldn't let anything break them apart.

He'd been hooked from the very first moment she'd walked into his office. It wasn't just physical, although he couldn't deny the sensuality in the juxtaposition of her curves against the severity of her plain gray suit. It'd been more than that. It was the intelligence in her clear blue eyes and the way in which she'd conducted the contract negotiations, calmly managing her bellicose client. He hadn't been able to take his eyes off her, and she'd smiled at him across the table, making hot color sear his face. That evening he'd taken out her business card and rung her, for once setting aside his reticence and almost pathological fear of rejection. He'd hardly been able to believe his luck when she accepted his offer of meeting up for a drink—and the rest, as they say, was history. Later she'd told him it was the blush that'd clinched it. Until he'd colored up like a schoolboy she'd had him down as a bit of a letch.

The memory softened his edges and made him smile.

The intensity of his gaze made Sarah turn to look at him, and the expression on her face in that unguarded moment tore at his heart; it was wariness. He was breaking everything apart and didn't seem able to stop it.

He took a step toward her and tried to speak, but for a moment the words wouldn't come, and he experienced a spike of fear that he'd become that silent boy again.

"I'm sorry," he eventually managed. Words so banal and inadequate. "I don't know what's wrong with me just now but please believe me, I don't mean to be the way I am. I love you so much and it scares me that I'm driving you away."

He took another step and placed a hand on her cheek, pushing her hair back and cupping her face in his palms. She looked up at him, and he was struck by the fact that he had no idea what she was thinking anymore, and that alarmed him. God, if he lost her, his world would cease spinning.

"Please forgive me."

He reached for the steadiness of her, her strength.

"Please, Sarah. I'll try harder, I promise, so don't give up on us just yet."

She let out a long, slow sigh. "I'm not about to give up," she said. "I never said that, but I'm worried about you. I love you and I hate seeing you so unhappy. I just want you to . . . to find your way back to us."

She searched his face, and he tried to smile, instinctively masking the turmoil inside.

"I'm not unhappy as long as I've still got you, that's all that matters. Look, Sarah, if you want me to talk to someone I will. I'll do whatever you want, just don't . . . don't ever stop loving me."

He bent his head to find her lips with his, uttering a silent prayer as hers parted in response.

She placed a palm against his chest, and for a heart-stopping second he wasn't sure if she was pushing him away. Then he felt her fingers unbuttoning his shirt, and the warmth of her hand made his skin tingle. After all the years they'd been together, she still had the power to do that, to make his flesh sing. She bent her head and brushed the lightest of kisses against his chest, her lips smiling at the tremor that ran through him.

He moved to lift her T-shirt.

"Not here, not in Jack's room."

He carried on lifting it over her head. "Why not?"

"It's Jack's *bed*, Jez, it feels wrong."

"Don't be silly, it's not as though he's *in* it, and he's hardly going to come in and catch us."

"That's not the point—"

"Come on, let's be reckless."

She hesitated for a moment, then smiled and leaned her body into his. "All right, but this isn't the answer, Jez. This won't change what I said."

It wasn't the answer but it'd help. All he needed in that moment was to get close to her and to feel something other than a background hum of fear. They'd always been that way together, with the want just simmering under their surface. It was part of what bound them, and right now he needed her to drive the thoughts away and to let him be himself again.

Naked, they stood and faced each other, the air crackling with expectancy. Every time was as if it were his first time, and he hoped it was the same for her, and that he didn't let her down. Sarah pushed him back onto the bed and sat astride him, pinning his arms above his head. Her expression was shadowed by her hair as she slowly dipped her head and ran her tongue from his navel to his nipples, leaving a trail of goosebumps in its wake.

"Do you promise me?" she said. "Promise you'll do what I asked."

"I promise," he told her, and in that moment he'd have promised her anything. "You can even come with me if you don't believe me."

Satisfied, she rolled off him, and then there was nothing but hungry mouths and the rhythm of skin on skin, punctuated by the indignant squawk of unaccustomed bedsprings. All the time Sarah watched him, her eyes dark and unwavering. Once he'd found it disconcerting, now it excited him, and as she cried out into the afternoon, he felt the muscles of his stomach contract, and his mind finally freed itself.

# 7

". . . Although the brain automatically stores experiences as memory, there can be occasions when the mind effectively walls off a memory for its own good."

Carole Jessup, PhD, paused for a moment and her eyes met his.

"If a person, a child in particular, experiences an overwhelming trauma, it can block the memory entirely. It's a process called dissociation, and in this sense it's a protective mechanism. If the cerebral cortex is unable to manage the intensity of the emotional response, a neurobiological survival mechanism kicks in. This cuts off the emotional circuit and blocks the production of adrenaline and cortisol. In doing so it disrupts normal memory formation and recall."

Yadda, yadda, yadda . . . She was solidly midfifties and stern, in a tartan skirt and damson sweater. Neat pearl earring in meaty lobes. A thin white scar ran from her top lip to the edge of her nose, and Jeremy idly wondered how she'd got it. Maybe a deranged client . . . She glanced at the notes in front of her, then back at Jeremy. God, she was intense, but perhaps it came with the territory.

"The family dynamic plays a strong part in how well a child copes with trauma. A child that's raised in a loving and supportive environment is likely to be more resilient and cope better with traumatic events. Whereas an unstable background, where there's, say, fear or mistrust, the child may respond more negatively and may experience dissociation in the way you've described."

Jeremy nodded. He knew all this. He didn't need a psychology lecture. He knew why he couldn't remember much about that day; why he couldn't remember finding her. He knew that the shock of it had broken something in him and stolen away what remained of his childhood.

"You say your relationship with your mother was difficult. Difficult in what way?"

He hated this. Laying everything bare, appearing weak. He didn't need to do it. He was okay. He'd lived with this for thirty years and, after all, he was only there because he'd promised Sarah.

She waited, letting the silence pull the words out of him. She had a mole on her cheek and he deliberately stared at it, conjuring his features into an expression of mild repugnance. Fucking ugly mole. He knew it wasn't her fault, or the mole's for that matter, but he was just so bloody angry. Then he thought of Sarah and of the effect all this anger was having on their marriage, on their children, and he relented.

"I think I irritated her—at best—and if I'm truthful, as a child I was afraid of her. She could be . . ." He hesitated, searching for the right words. There was nothing to quite explain how she'd made him feel. Hated came closest. Loathed and detested would work as well. ". . . unpredictable, vindictive. I don't think she liked little boys very much. Then after my sister . . . after my sister died it was worse. I don't think she ever forgave me."

She leaned forward in her chair. "Forgave you for what?" she asked.

More silence unspooled as she watched him. Unwavering. Waiting.

"For not being the one that died."

The words hung in the air. Now they were finally out there, they hummed with a life of their own. She didn't speak for a moment, taking time to formulate her next words.

"Is that something she said to you, or how she made you feel?"

"Formerly the latter; latterly the former."

He didn't understand his need to be glib but he felt defensive, hostile.

"Look, I'm not here to talk about my mother, or particularly about what happened back then. There was enough of that at the time."

A tremor of anxiety rippled through him at the memory. Those words trapped in his throat. The silence. The choking, paralyzing fear that he'd never be able to speak again.

"All I want to understand is why I'm feeling the way I am right now. Why I feel anxious and angry most of the time. Why I'm dwelling on . . . things and why I feel so out of control. It's been years, decades in fact, and I've been fine. I've dealt with it, so I don't get why this is happening to me now. I really don't need it. I've got a life to lead, my family to think of."

His voice had risen, a wheedling note of neediness creeping in.

She merely nodded and scribbled something in her notes before continuing. "You need to understand, dissociation isn't always total or permanent," she said. "Sometimes a person may see glimpses of a traumatic memory they couldn't previously recall. This can be random, after sufficient time has elapsed, or else it can be triggered. It might be activated by a particular place, a smell. Sometimes the death of a loved one can release emotions that in turn trigger memories . . ."

Jeremy interrupted her with one of his customary snorts. If they were going down that avenue he feared it was a dead end. "Loved one" was hardly an epithet he'd use for his mother.

Before he could say anything, she continued, "In your case I think whatever you saw from the plane may have acted as a trigger."

Suddenly she had his attention.

"Something in what you saw, or believe you saw, has possibly unlocked a memory, and that in turn is responsible for the emotions you're now experiencing."

He went to interrupt her again. He wanted to tell her that he hadn't remembered anything—that the thing, the girl who he'd seen, didn't have anything to do with *him*.

"But I haven't remembered anything. It wasn't like that—"

"It isn't necessarily as straightforward as accurately remembering an event. A trigger may cause the memory to resurface gradually, sometimes taking the form of short flashbacks or intrusive thoughts. It can in itself be a troubling or even traumatic process."

He thought of what he'd experienced in his study. The running girl, the boys in pursuit. It didn't take a genius to see the link between that and what he'd seen from the plane. The realization stirred something in him, excitement or maybe fear.

"I . . ."

Unsure how to explain it, he stopped.

"I haven't remembered anything, but I suppose I have experienced something odd. I've had something like a . . . a waking dream. That's the closest way I can really describe it. It was a boy—me, I think. I was running across a field with some others and we were chasing . . . a girl."

Not Em. It couldn't have been Emily, not with that sense of malice.

"The sensations were real, the excitement of it, the feel of the grass. Even the hot, dry smell of it, if that makes any sense, but it didn't resonate like a memory. It was just a . . . an image."

He watched her expression, all his animosity momentarily gone.

"I'm not explaining this very well. I'm not capturing the immediacy of it. It was as though I was actually there but it still wasn't a memory. More like a totally vivid dream or a film clip."

She nodded. "That's not unusual," she explained. "These recovered memories are often uncontrolled, unintegrated fragments. Just as you describe."

"But if it was a fragment of memory, why did it feel so wrong? There seemed to be malice in it, and that doesn't make any sense. I loved Emily. I love her still, so if it was a memory and the girl was her, why did it feel that way?"

"I'm afraid I can't answer that for you. All I can say is that such memories may retrigger the distress and emotion associated with the trauma as strongly as the original event, and that this is something you may need help to process."

He felt the anger resurfacing. If she couldn't answer that for him, what the fuck was he paying her for?

"If you can't give me any answers, then why the fuck am I paying you? I need answers. I need to know what's happening to me and how to control it. How to make it stop before it ruins my marriage. Everything."

The hostility spat and crackled across the space between them, but she didn't react. She sat calmly, her face a bland mask devoid of expression. No censure, not even irritation. It wrongfooted him, making him feel vaguely foolish, like a rude, petulant child. Maybe that was where Jack got it from.

There was compassion in her face now. "I understand your frustration, really I do, but I'm afraid things are rarely that simple. I think we have work to do in helping you process what's happening to you. You may be able to recover these memories on your own, but you may not be able to cope with the emotions that come with them. In the majority of instances, repressed memories trigger a significant emotional response, and for you this seems to be manifesting predominantly as anxiety and suppressed anger. I wouldn't advise you—or anyone, for that matter—to try and manage this alone. Particularly in your case, as your relationship with your mother and her recent death adds an extra layer of complexity. I think the dysfunctionality of that relationship has influenced how you dealt with the incident at the time and possibly how you have processed things since."

All that registered was her use of the word "we," and he cynically wondered how much of her motivation was driven by the income he represented. Luckily, this time he kept his mouth shut, but something must've flickered across his face because she smiled before speaking.

"I understand your skepticism but would ask that you take some time to consider what I'm saying. There are a range of psychotherapeutic recovery methods that we could explore, all of which have been proven to play a positive role in repressed memory and PTSD. Personally I favor EMDR—that's 'eye movement desensitization and reprocessing'—and sensorimotor psychotherapy."

It must've been working already as Jeremy felt his eye movements involuntarily rolling heavenward, but he let her continue.

"Either, combined with the opportunity to talk things through in a neutral, nonjudgmental environment, can offer real benefits. Please, all I ask is that you take some time to think about it. I would really like the opportunity to see you again."

Something inside him balked at the whole idea. He didn't need *therapy*. He was just a kid who'd gotten scared out of his wits, like any kid would. It was normal, and anyway, it was years ago. He'd come to terms with it. He was fine. If he was going to start remembering things, that was fine too; it was a good thing and he'd deal with it. The last thing he needed was someone else messing with his head. He'd agreed to come here for Sarah, but he hadn't signed up for months of listening to psychobabble. That was a step too far.

"I don't know. It's a big step, and to be honest I'm not sure that it's something I need right now. I'll think about it, okay, and if I want another appointment I'll get in touch."

His tone was dismissive and he stood up to leave. They were done. It was making him feel on edge and he didn't like it. It was making him feel how he'd felt as a boy.

She looked disappointed—probably seeing that Caribbean holiday slipping out of her grasp—and stood up too.

"Please do think about it, I really believe it would help you. And one other thing, regardless of what you decide, please consider keeping a journal of your experiences: any flashbacks or memories and the associated emotions that come with them. If you do decide on some sessions in the future it will be helpful to work through them."

She offered her hand, and Jeremy became aware of how his was adrenaline-iced and drenched in sweat. He self-consciously rubbed it against his thigh before taking her warm palm in his. Somewhere deep in the recesses of his brain, he registered the comfort of her touch.

As a child you hear things, you learn things, and later as an adult you read things, things they didn't tell you as a boy. Slowly you piece together a picture that serves as a memory even though you know it's not.

Still to this day, Jeremy didn't know if he'd seen anything or anyone, or if deep down he knew what had happened to Emily. All he was aware of was that his sister had died. Was it an accidental drowning, an inadvertent, blameless tragedy—or was it something nameless and worse? Had someone held her under the water, cruelly drowning her, washing her little soul away? He wasn't sure why, but he'd always sensed that those woods on that summer's evening were shadowed by evil.

*He looked at the girl; at the ripples licking her face. He felt dead, detached, as though all this was a story belonging to somebody else. Things like this weren't meant to exist, not outside the pages of a book or the flickering images on a television screen. He wanted it not to be real. Some part of him wanted to turn back time and stop it from ever happening, but he knew that he couldn't. She was dead, and all the wishing in the world wouldn't bring her back. He dared to take another look; at her half-closed eyes with their crescents of sightless white, at her tangled clumps of wet hair. His stomach churned at the reality of it, and he feared for a moment that his bowels would loosen, compounding the horror. He felt himself flowing toward the waters at the edge of the lake. It would be so easy to just follow her into the dark, to forget what had happened and the images before his eyes. Instead he hunched there, waiting. Someone else was coming, and maybe soon it would all be over.*

Despite his mother's accusations, it wasn't that he wouldn't tell them; he couldn't tell them. Whatever he may have seen that day became lost to him, along with his voice. Now, talking to the therapist had made it all come rushing back. That feeling of paralysis, of panic closing his throat. At the time he'd wanted to speak but it was a physical impossibility. Nothing, no act of will, could've forced those words from his mouth. His lips had clamped down of their own volition, trapping him inside, and even now the memory of it made the saliva pool and aftershocks of panic buzz along his spine.

She'd tried everything, the police psychologist, even using dolls. To try acting it out, if he couldn't speak it. Fucking dolls, like some abused baby, and him, an eleven-year-old boy. He'd just looked at her dumbly and then thrown them on the floor.

He'd since learned how atypical it'd been, for him to become completely mute—and for so long. It's possible for a child to become mute after a traumatic event, but usually they avoid talking about the trauma itself rather than becoming completely silent. Not him. He spoke to no one. He closed down, while the world played out around him like a movie but one with no speaking part for him. Two long months it was, before the first new words croaked their way through his vocal cords. "I'm sorry," was all he'd said, and he still wasn't sure what for.

His childhood had ended that day in the woods to be replaced by a kind of relentless hell. His mother had fallen to pieces and there were bits of her scattered throughout the house. Dangerous bits that could catch an unwary boy. They'd lain in dark corners, smoking and hissing like lava. Mostly she'd stayed in her room, sedated, but when the drugs wore off he would hear her, screaming, wailing, and he'd press his hands to his ears and hide while she stormed through the house raging at the world. If he'd been afraid of her before, now he was terrified, and she became woven into his nightmares. A part of the horror.

His father and Uncle Ian were shadow men. They talked in hushed voices and dealt with the police. Even his father he avoided. The sadness in his face did something to his stomach. It twisted and wrenched at it and made him feel sick. His dad had given up smoking years ago, but the stress had made him start up again, wrapping him and Uncle Ian in a pall of blue smoke, like a veil of grief. Even now the scent of certain tobacco brought with it an echo of nausea.

He'd wanted to go home. He desperately needed his own house around him, his familiar things, but they couldn't leave. Uncle Ian's house, a place he had loved, became the nine circles of hell.

Every summer, during the long school holidays, they'd stayed at Uncle Ian's. He was Jeremy's mother's brother, and his rambling home, with the countryside beyond, was a childhood heaven. Every year Jeremy would meet up with the others, Ben and Josh, Andrew and Nathan. Even though he didn't see them throughout the year and they went to different schools, they'd always be there waiting for him. It would only take a day or so and they'd be the crew once more.

That summer was the last time he ever stayed there, and he never saw them again.

# 8

It was another foul night. The rain battered the front of the house, and the wind whipped and shrieked under the eaves. Jeremy felt a phantom of anxiety hovering in the wings, but he tried to ignore it like a background noise and focus on helping Sarah with the dishes.

He'd been better lately. Not super-fantastic-great but okay enough to function. To go to work and not attack his colleagues, to not drive away his wife or frighten his children—at least not very much. He'd thought about what the psychotherapist had said and had tried to rationalize things. Whenever he'd felt certain thoughts intruding, he'd rolled with them and tried not to obsess. When he'd felt the anger bubbling, he'd removed myself from the source until it had passed. He wasn't great but he was okay. He was "coping," to use a term that made him want to break things all over again.

He'd had no more memories, or flashbacks, and had convinced himself that once his mother's estate was settled, everything would get back to normal. They were waiting for the Grant of Probate to come through at the moment, until then there wasn't much they could do. Not that he wanted to. Not until Christmas was out of the way.

"Once the kids are in bed, you could go up in the attic and get the decorations down if you like," Sarah said. "Then we can do the tree tonight over a glass of wine. It'll be a surprise for them tomorrow, they'll love that."

He was careful not to sigh. It was best behavior all the way now. The last thing he wanted was for her to suggest another session with Carole Jessup, PhD; once was definitely enough. It'd taken some work convincing Sarah, but she'd reluctantly agreed that they'd "see how it goes." The "it" in question being him.

"Okay, we can if you want to."

It wasn't that he didn't like Christmas. He wasn't some sort of Grinch. He loved it with her and the children; it was just that the first of December was far too soon for him to feel the love. His father never put up their tree until the week before, and that was what he'd have done if he'd had his way. Instead he was facing three weeks of obsessive watering and monitoring of needle drop—after all, it was his job to keep it alive.

This year's lucky winner was waiting in the garage, small but perfectly formed. He'd wanted a bigger one, but apparently that was a "man thing." Dads obsess over size, mums go for aesthetics. There was a parallel there somewhere.

"If you go and start bathing Lucy," Sarah continued, "I'll help Jack finish off his homework. We'll be done quicker that way. Oh, and she'll need clean pajamas. There's some on the top of the laundry basket, you can use those."

Through in the sitting room, Lucy was curled up on the sofa desperately trying to watch TV, but Jeremy could see how her eyelids were drooping.

"Come on, Luce. You've got me tonight." He scooped her up in his arms and headed for the stairs. "Come on sleepyhead, bath time."

". . . and Becca said Father Christmas is going to bring her a Blume doll. Daddy, I wish I'd asked for a Blume doll, do you think Santa will know I want one? Daddy . . ."

He was only half listening to Lucy's chatter, letting it wash over him while he rinsed the shampoo from her hair. His mind kept straying back to his mother's estate and all the things waiting to be sorted. One of which was Uncle Ian's house. He still couldn't quite believe that she hadn't sold it after her brother had died, that she'd kept it as a holiday let for all those years and never once thought to tell him. Maybe she couldn't bring herself to let it go entirely, that last place on earth where Emily was alive. Jeremy knew he'd have to go there himself at some point and he wasn't sure how that made him feel.

"Daddy!"

Lucy let out a sudden wail.

"Ow! Daddy, you're getting the shampoo in my eyes."

"Sorry, darling, I didn't mean to. Let's do it like this instead then. Lean back and put your hair in the water, and I'll just rinse the little bit at the front with the shower. I'll be really careful, promise."

She slid down the bath and tipped her head backward while Jeremy cradled the back of her neck with his hand. He took the shower attachment and gently washed the bubbles from her forehead, taking care to keep the water away from her eyes.

She squeezed her lids tight shut and her hair fanned out in the water, rippling below the surface like golden waterweed; like a memory. An involuntary sound escaped Jeremy's throat, a kind of half-strangled gasp, a noise that made Lucy's eyes snap open. She stared up at him, and the blue of her irises seemed suddenly vivid in the brightness of the overhead lights.

Then the world turned to shit.

Jeremy saw his fingers on her neck and the horror engulfed him. He was going to drown her, he *wanted* to drown her, he was about to push her face under the water and murder his child! With a yell of pure terror he tore his hand away, letting her head slip under. She panicked for a moment, little arms thrashing, then her head broke the surface and she began to cry. Great shocked sobs that echoed in the confined space.

He pushed himself away from the side of the bath, panic making him blind. His shoulder crashed into the cabinet, dislodging an array of bottles that smashed to the floor. The noise was deafening, Lucy screaming and the sound of breaking glass. Bath oil spread in a slick pool across the tiles and he scrabbled through it, pressing himself back against the toilet bowl. Away from her.

Sarah burst into the bathroom, eyes wide with alarm.

"What the hell . . . Jeremy! What's going on now?"

And then he was shouting, "Get her away from me. Get her away . . ."

Lucy's crying took on a hysterical note, and Sarah scooped her out of the bath.

"Darling, darling, it's okay. Shush now, it's okay, Mummy's got you."

She turned to Jeremy, sitting on the floor in a mess of oil and glass.
"Jez . . ."

Words deserted her and he saw something close to fear in her eyes. And something else, a flicker of mistrust.

"Jez, what the hell's going on? What are you doing?"

There was no answer. He couldn't explain. No way could he say that for a moment he feared he would drown her. He only knew he needed her to take Lucy away.

"Please, just take her away. I can't do this."

She opened her mouth as if to speak but instead turned her attention back to the child sobbing in her arms. Aware on some level that something was very wrong, the pitch of Lucy's crying had risen, so Sarah grabbed the nearest towel and swaddled her like a baby. Shushing, soothing, calming her down.

"Shush, darling. You're okay now. Let's leave silly Daddy here and get you sorted out."

She took the crying child away and the relief flooded over him, making him weak. For the third time in as many months Jeremy felt the unfamiliar sting of tears beneath his lids. He turn and leaned over the toilet, retching and heaving until the evening's meal splattered into the pan.

Then he laid his head on his head on his arms and he wept.

⚬⟊⟊⟊⚬

"Jeremy, talk to me. I need to understand what's going on."

Sarah had finally calmed Lucy and got her off to sleep. She'd put Jack to bed and cleared up the mess in the bathroom, and now she was sitting across from Jeremy, who was fighting to stop the ripples of residual panic that were still coursing through him. He'd wanted to drown her.

"You frightened Lucy half to death, and if I'm honest you frightened me too. You looked . . . mad, there's no other way of putting it."

She leaned forward to make him look at her.

"Look, if you're ill I need to know. If I can't trust you to even bathe the children . . ."

He didn't say it, but she couldn't trust him, not ever.

Her voice trailed away and she just stared at him, completely lost. Her expression was stricken, and Jeremy realized just how much he'd scared her, and just how far outside her comfort zone this all was.

"Sarah, I . . ."

What could he say that wouldn't make this worse?

"If you're ill, I'll help you, you know that. I'll support you and we'll get through it together, but I can't if you won't talk to me. If you persist in pretending everything's all right."

It tore at his heart, thinking of his daughter.

"Oh God, Sarah, what did you say to Lucy? What did you tell her?"

"I didn't, not really. I just told her you weren't feeling very well, and then I held her until she fell asleep. Jack asked what all the noise was about and I told him you'd knocked the bathroom cabinet over by mistake and that it'd frightened Lucy. He was okay with that. You know what he's like, away with the fairies a lot of the time."

She briefly smiled at the thought of her son but then her face fell.

"*They'll* be fine, it's *you* I'm worried about. I don't understand what's happening, Jez, and right now I need to."

Jeremy looked at her dear face. He had to try and make this right and to make her understand how scared he was too.

He hadn't told her all the details of his session with Carole Jessup. There were many reasons: he hadn't wanted her to worry about him, he hadn't wanted to appear weak, but mainly because he hadn't ever told her all the facts about that day. She knew that his sister had drowned, and she knew that the details were never fully established, but that was all. Jeremy had never told her how he'd found Emily's body. He'd never spoken about the hole in his mind or about that silent boy. Sarah loved him, so over the years she'd accepted that it was a tragedy he found hard to talk about, and in an unspoken agreement it'd been somewhere they never ventured. Now that had to change.

He'd never told her the truth about his mother either. She understood that there were issues—her word, not his—but never the extent of it. He'd wanted her love, not her pity, and he was afraid that if she'd seen in him that damaged little boy, everything would've changed between them. She'd have felt sorry for him and have wanted to mother him, and that wasn't what he needed from her. It wasn't her job to try and repair the past.

Now he hoped it wasn't too late, that they could find their way through the wall of secrets he'd constructed.

He took her hand in his.

"I haven't been entirely honest with you, about Em," he began, but "honest" wasn't the right word—"open" would've been better. Now he saw fear spark in her eyes, and for a moment he wondered what she thought he was going to say. "Entirely open, I mean. I've told you the bare bones of it—"

Bare bones. That was what Em was now, bare bones. Tiny bones, like a bird's. He pushed the thought away.

"—but not the bits about me. Not what it was like for me and what happened to me afterward."

And now the words tumbled out of him, finally setting themselves free. He watched her face as he told her. He saw the love there and then the pity, and by the time he was finished her eyes were bright with unshed tears.

"So what Carole Jessup thinks is that something has triggered suppressed memories, something to do with what I saw from that plane, and if she's right that could mean that now, after all these years, I might finally remember. I can't begin to tell you how that makes me feel, to think I might finally have all the pieces."

What he didn't dare say, or dare hope—or even dread—is that he might've seen what happened to her. He might know how she died.

"She said I might experience flashbacks, and I think that's what happened with Lucy. Something about her hair in the water made me panic . . ."

"Oh Jeremy . . ." Her voice was barely a whisper.

He could feel his throat closing on the words. He couldn't tell her the rest, how he'd felt the compulsion to push her under the water. He wouldn't think about what that might mean.

"I wouldn't ever have hurt her."

The words brought with them a wave of guilt and he suddenly felt false, hollow. He half expected Sarah to see through him to some darkness deep in his soul. Instead she opened her arms and pulled him to her.

"Darling, why on earth didn't you tell me all this before, why didn't you share it with me? I can't begin to imagine how awful it must've been for you."

"I just couldn't. I didn't want you to feel sorry for me."

Her expression darkened. "As for your mother, to be so hateful to you when you were just a scared little boy, God, that makes me so angry." Her foot did an involuntary little stamp on the floor for emphasis. "I've never really understood your relationship with her until now. I knew she was a bit cold and difficult, but to punish an innocent child for something that wasn't his fault, I can't understand how a mother could do that. No wonder you shut down."

"She managed to make me feel so guilty, as if it was somehow all my fault."

Her voice rose with indignation on his behalf. "But what about your dad, what was he doing while all this was going on? I know I never got to meet him, but if he was such a lovely man, like you say, why didn't he intervene?"

She stopped and looked up at him as though expecting an answer but there was nothing he could say. He'd loved his father, and that love had been returned a thousandfold. The problem was, the man had loved her too, and too often he'd turned a blind eye or taken the line of least resistance. Maybe Jeremy should've hated him for this failing but he couldn't find it in his heart to do so. Unless you knew her, knew what it was like back then, no one could ever understand. His father had been dealing with a grief of his own, and trying to manage his wife's, trying to make sense of it all, and then he was ill and then he was gone, and then it was just her. Slowly, inexorably, her hate had eaten its way into Jeremy's soul, molding the man he'd become.

# 9

The next day Lucy had been wary of her father, and he of her. Sarah warned him against making too big a thing of it, or trying too hard, but he did speak to her about it. She'd fixed him with her round blue eyes while he stumbled through an explanation he hoped she'd accept.

"Daddy's sorry he frightened you," he told her. "I didn't mean to. I let you slip under the water by accident and it scared me. Then I knocked over the cabinet and that scared you even more, and then we were both scared until Mummy came and made it all better. Do you think you can forgive me?"

She'd turned her earnest little face to his. "'Course I can, Daddy. We all get frightened sometimes." And then she'd wound her arms around his neck and hugged him tight.

He'd breathed the soft, clean scent of her hair as she whispered, "I love you, Daddy," and he'd thanked the God he didn't believe in for making it that easy.

"And I love you too," he'd told her, "as much as it's possible to love," and he'd ignored the little voice that hissed inside his head, *Liar. Fraud.*

And that was that—for her at least. Unfortunately Sarah wasn't dealt with so easily. She watched him now. Solicitous, tender, not suspicious—not yet. It saddened him that he'd caused this, that he'd brought this *thing* crawling into their marriage.

Christmas came and Christmas went. Santa remembered Lucy's Blume doll; he felt, in the circumstances, it was the very least he could do. The lights went out, the tree came down, and January skated in. Bleak and cold, and with it came the paperwork for Mrs. Horton's estate.

It was February now, *February that brings the rain, Thaws the frozen lake again.* The old children's rhyme came into Jeremy's head from nowhere, making him start. His mother used to sing that to Emily, and the memory of the warmth in her voice made his skin prickle; for him it was always January's snow. His foot did a reflexive jerk, pressing down on the accelerator and making the car lurch forward.

"Whoops, sorry about that, foot slipped."

He turned and smiled at Sarah and she smiled back, her face devoid of any wariness.

"Are you okay, or do you want me to drive for a bit?" she asked. "If you're tired we can always swap over."

"No, it's fine, I'll shout if I need a break. If I'm remembering it correctly, it's only a few more miles to the village."

He tried to recapture the sense of anticipation that had always accompanied the journey to Uncle Ian's house, but all he could feel was apprehension, and the burn of acid in the pit of his stomach from the hastily eaten sandwich at lunchtime.

Uncle Ian. Jeremy had seen him only the once after Emily died. He must've been about seventeen and home from school for the summer, when he'd overheard his mother on the phone and had gleaned that Ian was in hospital. He'd had a minor heart attack, the first in a rapid series that would eventually kill him, and once Jeremy learned that he was ill, he was seized by the urge to see him again. Time had softened the memory of the days immediately after Emily's death, and he'd begun to remember the good parts, and the way Uncle Ian had always gladly made time for him. That alone was a reason for wanting to see him again: to recapture that rare feeling of being wanted.

Every summer the family would come and stay with Ian for a few weeks, and if Jeremy was lucky, he'd be allowed to stay on when the others went back. Uncle Ian had been a lecturer at the polytechnic, so he was always at home for the holidays, giving Jeremy's mother the opportunity to get her son "out of her hair" for a while. Jeremy would dutifully wave as their car pulled away and then there'd just be him, Uncle Ian—and the crew. Often Ian's friend George would come round for dinner, and in the evening they'd play Monopoly or make models. Those were his Enid Blyton summers, a rare whisper of happiness.

The thought of George tugged at something within him, and he remembered that last afternoon; it came upon him like a chill breeze at the back of the neck.

He'd caught the train down and then a bus to the hospital, as he'd known his mother would never have taken him even if he'd begged. In fact, Jeremy had assumed she'd never set foot in that part of the country again but obviously she had, seeing as she'd kept Ian's house. And kept it secret.

Jeremy had walked into the cardiac unit to see his uncle lying there, with George at his bedside. He'd looked older and thinner, in his pale striped pajamas, with a shadow of blueness to his lips that'd made Jeremy's own heart flip in his chest. Ian's eyes had lit with pleasure—and with love—and it shamed Jeremy even now, the way he'd behaved.

"Jeremy! My boy," he'd cried. "What an unexpected surprise. Come here and let me look at you. Gosh, how tall you've grown!"

He'd held out his arms but it was a fraction too late. Jeremy had already registered George's hand on his, caressing the lightly speckled skin. He'd looked from one to the other and had seen the love-light shining in George's eyes. He didn't know now if it had angered or disgusted him. All he could remember was that he'd been seventeen and stupid. An angry, unloved, unlovable boy, warped by his own misery. He had no empathy. He hadn't learned acceptance. He'd come straight from a school where they taunted the "fairies," and from a mother who showed neither tolerance nor love. He'd been old enough to see but not to understand, so instead of going to him, as he should have, he'd stood a few feet from the end of the bed and stared at him, with two livid spots of embarrassment—and hurt—burning on his cheeks.

"I think I'm fine just here, thank you," he'd said, his voice cold and uncompromising. "I only wanted to check you were all right but I can see you're obviously fine. Both of you," he'd added, letting his lip twist in a sneer of disgust.

He could still picture the hurt on his uncle's face. He'd instantly wanted to take the words back but didn't know how, so he'd pointedly glared at George until he'd dropped his gaze. He could no longer recall what else was said; all he knew was that it'd been excruciating and that he'd made his escape as soon as he could and that he never saw Ian again. Within eighteen months, Ian was dead.

Jeremy wished he could undo it, that he could go back in time and tell him that wasn't who he was. He'd just been a stupid, shallow boy and, if he was honest, a jealous one. He was hurting, and he had hidden that hurt behind a nasty, spiteful anger. He could see that now, but once again he was far too little, too late.

Someone had once told him that he carried a lot of shame. They were right, but shame's okay if you need to keep it like a grain of sand beneath your shell, to remind you of what you really are.

"Daddy, are we there yet?"

Lucy's voice jolted him back to the present, and he realized that they were almost there. He'd driven the last few miles on autopilot, lost in his past. He glanced across at Sarah, but she hadn't noticed he'd been AWOL.

"Almost," he told her. "It won't be long now. You'll be able to see where I spent the summer holidays when I was little. All the places I used to play."

They drove past a farm and turned onto the high street, on past the two pubs and the primary school, until they came to the turning that led to the church. Uncle Ian's had been the last house in Church Road, at the very end where the tarmac gave way to a gravel track that led to another farm, and the fields and woods beyond. On lazy summer days the boys would ride their bikes, past the farm buildings, to follow the footpath across the fields to the dark cover of the trees. For a moment Jeremy was swept with nostalgia—until he remembered what had happened there—then it was replaced by a frisson of dread. He saw that the track and the farmhouse were long gone, and that the road now extended beyond his uncle's house, the route lined with new homes.

He was struck by how small Ian's house seemed. His childhood memories were of long hallways and paneled rooms, winding staircases and secret corners. The house in front of him looked far more modest than those imaginings. Built in the arts and crafts style, it was mock-Lutyens. A thatched roof with twin beamed gables, swooped low over patterned brickwork, and mullioned windows flanked a feature porch and sturdy oak door. Tall chimneys reached ever skyward.

The gardens bore witness to its status as an Airbnb. Gone were the colorful borders and flower beds. All that remained of the former glory was the ancient magnolia, its twisting branches supporting a shady canopy of evergreen, ovate leaves. The grass that lay in its shadow was, like his uncle, long dead.

The key felt cold in his pocket. He was afraid to go in.

Sarah entwined her fingers with his and gave them a comforting squeeze. "You okay?"

He nodded, hyperaware of the noise the children were making, charging round and around the tree. He longed to tell them to stop, that their shrieks were grating on his nerves, but they'd been cooped up in the car for so long that he didn't have the heart.

"It's so pretty, Jez, no wonder your mother couldn't bear to part with it." She looked up at his face. "Are you sure you're okay? We've got all week, so we don't have to go in right now if you'd rather wait 'til tomorrow."

In reality he couldn't be less sure, but he reminded himself that it was only a house. It couldn't hurt him, no matter what memories might lurk inside.

The key slid easily into the lock and the door yawned open. For a moment time stood still, and the wood-paneled walls and checkerboard tiles seem to echo with phantom voices. Footsteps. And then the sensation passed as Jeremy noted, with a mixture of regret and relief, that it was all different. Gone was the dark-wood hall stand, with its jumble of hats and coats; gone was the carved mirror, with its sparkling, age-spotted glass. The old oak staircase still curved upward to the landing with its stained glass window, but the walls were no longer hung with his uncle's paintings. It smelled different too, of emptiness.

He stepped over the threshold and his pulse slowed. There was no smoldering ember of his mother, no shadows of horror or grief. It was just a house.

The family trooped in behind him. Inexplicably, they'd all fallen silent, even the children, which gave their entrance a weight it shouldn't have held. They followed him through to the sitting room, where his memories of his uncle burned so strongly that he half expected to see him, sitting in his wingback chair by the fireplace, marking an essay or reading a book. But the room held no essence of him. The fireplace was still there, and the half-paneled walls, but that was all. The William Morris wallpaper had been painted over in a harsh white that jarred with the dark wood and the leaded windows. The starkness accentuated the weakness of the light filtering through the tiny recessed panes, making the room gray and bleak. Ian's furniture had also been replaced with functional IKEA, which squatted unhappily in its surroundings, a social misfit.

"Oh, it's—" Sarah began.

"—ruined," he finished for her. "I think that's the word you're looking for. This was a beautiful room, and it's been ruined."

He stomped through to the kitchen, where everything else had changed too, and he felt his heart sink further. Once he'd realized the house was still there, he'd desperately wanted it to be the same, a fragment of something good, preserved in amber.

He'd forewarned the woman who looked after the place, so the rooms were aired, and there were clean towels and linens for the beds. Sarah and Jeremy would have Ian's old bedroom, and the children were to share the room where his parents had slept. He'd wondered if he'd be able to sleep there, or whether the memories would be too overwhelming, but there was nothing left to unsettle him.

The door to his old room was firmly closed, and he carefully avoided looking at it as he carried the cases up the stairs.

# 10

Sarah was in the kitchen, opening and closing the cupboards and drawers. The children had gone outside to explore the garden while it was still light, and Jeremy was seized by an overwhelming urge to call them back inside where they'd be safe. He knew it was ridiculous, so instead he wrapped his arms around Sarah's waist and buried his face in her hair.

"What you looking for? There's not going to be anything to eat." He immediately flinched, suddenly afraid she'd misunderstand and think he was being snide. "I mean nothing for us to eat. I thought we could let the kids blow off some steam for a bit and then see if we can get something in one of the pubs."

She leaned back into him. "I'd thought the same thing, but to be honest, now we're here I don't know that I can be bothered. It'll make the children so late to bed and I think they'll just be a pain in the arse if we try to take them out anywhere. Isn't there somewhere where you could pick up a couple of pizzas or something? That'd do for tonight and we can do a proper shop tomorrow." She looked around the spacious kitchen. "What do you reckon we'll get for it then? I think there's going to be a lot of interest, even with the work it needs."

He disentangled his arms and went to the window that looked out onto the garden. "No idea. I would've thought easily eight-fifty, maybe even nine. Could be more, I'm not entirely sure about the prices around here. We'll have to see what the agents say." A sudden grin lit his face. "Anyway, what's up with you? It's not like you to be focusing on the money."

She followed him to the window and looked out at the dusk. "I haven't got a problem with money, Jeremy. I'm just not as obsessed with it as some."

He gave her a playful nudge, desperate to recapture the easiness of being they'd had before. "I'm not obsessed, darling, just a bit less idealistic than you."

She didn't deign to answer, and they stood in companionable silence looking out at the garden. Whoever his mother had been paying, it seemed they only did the minimum, as the lawn was a tangle of tussocks and the flower beds were weed strangled. As they watched, Lucy disappeared into the undergrowth, and his heart did a little leap in his chest. He opened the door and stepped out into the falling dusk, where he could see that beyond the broken back fence lay a stretch of scrubland leading to the distant fields; anyone could be lurking out there.

"I'll walk back into the village and see what I can find. Lucy! Luce! Do you want to come to the shops with me?"

He registered the note of strain in his voice and felt Sarah watching him. He needed to be careful.

Lucy came back into view, skipping up the garden, and his sense of relief was disproportionate. "Come on you, grab your coat. We're going on an adventure to find some dinner."

She bounced off to find it and he turned back to Sarah. "Please don't leave Jack out there on his own. We don't even know if the garden's safe, and that back fence doesn't look any too secure."

"He's fine, Jez, nothing's going to happen, so stop worrying. You go and find us some dinner and I'll keep an eye on him."

He clasped Lucy's hot little hand in his and they stepped out into the February dusk.

The streetlights in the high street flickered and hummed as they passed, each slowly coming to life and sending a trembling cone of golden light onto the pavement beneath. It had the effect of making the surroundings seem darker, with the shop fronts cast in deep shadow. Jeremy felt memories stirring, giving the impression of time looping in on itself to let the past touch the present. It unsettled him.

Lucy skipped along, swinging gently on his arm.

"Daddy," she asked, "where's your uncle now?" Her voice was thoughtful, she'd obviously been pondering this for a while.

"He died a long time ago," he told her. "Way back when I was still at school."

"Were you very sad, Daddy?"

Serious eyes looked up at him, and he wished he'd at least softened it, maybe said that he'd gone to heaven instead. She was too young to talk about death, so he quickly changed the subject.

"What would you like for dinner then? Mummy said to get pizza, but if you want something different, we can see what else they've got. They're bound to have chicken nuggets if you'd prefer those."

She was still young enough for distraction to work and Ian's sad demise was immediately forgotten, replaced by a crispy morsel of breaded chicken.

"Um, I'd like pizza please, and can we see if they've got any crinkly chips? They do crinkly chips at school and I like those, they taste different to the ones Mummy does. They're yummy. The baked beans aren't, they're all brown and yukky."

They reached the pedestrian crossing, and he stopped the budding gastronome at the curb.

"You never know, they might have, we'll have a look. Go on, press the button."

She reached out a hand, and together they stood and waited for the green man to show, Lucy's feet lined up a few safe inches from the road, just like she'd been told.

A lorry thundered past and Jeremy laid a steadying hand on her shoulder, but as he did, a thought came into his head, terrible and unbidden. Her life was in his hands. There was only him keeping her safe, only him stopping him from pushing her into the traffic. His hand looked suddenly hairy and massive, a murderous paw. He was dangerous, and the realization made his scalp crawl. Just the tiniest shove . . . it flashed before his mind's eye. He heard the shriek of brakes, the sickening crunch of steel on flesh and bone, the cry leaving his throat . . .

Even as the thought came, even as it tingled like an irresistible urge, the dread rushed through him. She wasn't safe with him, he shouldn't be alone with her, and he was seized by the need to rush back. He should've left her safely with Sarah.

Desperately, he rejected the thoughts, telling himself it was just anxiety, brought on by being there in the village again. He pulled the child back from the curb, heart hammering.

"Careful, Luce, not too close to the curb. There's lots of big lorries and they come a bit too near."

The red man turned to green and Jeremy turned with him. His pulse slowed and relief washed through him. They were okay, him and Luce. They were fine.

He took hold of her hand again, and they crossed the road together. The release of anxiety had made his legs trembly and weak, but he pressed on. He wouldn't give in and turn back to the house. By the time they reached the supermarket his panic had subsided, and he could almost laugh at how ridiculous it had been to even think he could harm her.

The supermarket was a squat gray cube of startling ugliness but still it was a welcome sight. Even the forlorn string of trolleys, and the scattering of litter that was congregated in angry huddles against its walls, for it meant that Jeremy didn't have to go to the corner shop they'd used as children. After the incident at the crossing he didn't think he could cope with that.

The doors opened with a tired hiss. Seemed "eight 'til late" was almost too much for them, and they sighed wearily as they granted entry. He took a basket and scanned the shelves for the things that they needed, grabbing bagged salad and supplies for breakfast as he passed. He was disproportionately glad to find they had crinkle-cut chips and took a bag from the freezer.

"Are these what you're after, Luce?" he asked, and watched as her little face lit up.

"They're the ones, Daddy. Thank you."

Jeremy fervently wished he could still find happiness in something as simple as a crinkly chip.

There was a stationery section in one of the aisles, and he hesitated for a moment before furtively adding a notebook to the basket. Maybe Carole Jessup was right and he should write these things down. Just in case.

They made their way to the checkout, where a brown-haired woman stood in front of the cigarette shelves, the packs coyly cowering behind gray blinds as though the merest glimpse of them would send the customers hurtling toward the respiratory ward. The assistant had a bland, open face, devoid of curiosity or interest, and there was something tantalizingly familiar about her. Jeremy tried not to think too hard, for he wasn't ready to meet anyone he might know. She began scanning the items when he remembered they needed toilet rolls.

"Wait there for a second, darling," he said, addressing Lucy. "I'm just going to quickly grab some loo rolls."

The woman smiled down at the little girl, and Jeremy watched as her eyes widened in surprise, her features coming alive. She looked startled, and her gaze flitted from Lucy to him, then back again, her eyes scanning his face. As he watched, her expression seemed to close down, and there was a sudden shift in her manner.

When he returned with the toilet rolls, his items were already packed in a paper bag, and when he handed the assistant the toilet rolls to scan, she studiously avoided his eyes, which suited him fine. He wasn't ready to be recognized—and even if he was, he wasn't sure that he'd want it to be by her. Her look wasn't hostile, exactly, more wary, but either way it wasn't entirely friendly. He quickly paid the bill and as they left, he could feel the prickle of her eyes on his neck, troubling the small hairs there.

Darkness had fallen by the time they got back to the house. Sarah had drawn the curtains and turned on the lights. The sitting room window was lit with a welcoming glow, and Jeremy felt a sudden affection for the place. God, he'd had some good times there. Before.

Inside, Sarah and Jack were in the sitting room, one reading a book, the other on his phone. Sarah lifted her head and smiled as they came in.

"Hey, you two were quick. Did you manage to find anything, because Jack's apparently at imminent risk of starvation. Look at him, wasting away over there."

Jack clutched his stomach and looked tragic.

"Yep, we did. We've got pizzas and salad, and some special chips, courtesy of Lucy."

Lucy ran over and jumped onto her lap.

"They're crinkly ones, Mummy. We have them at school and they're much nicer than yours."

Sarah began to tickle her, making her squeal, and Jeremy fought to ignore the way the high-pitched sound jangled on his nerves.

"Is that so? Well thank you for that, cheeky. We'll let you make dinner from now on then, shall we, if my chips are so horrid. I think that's the best idea, don't you, Daddy?"

She tickled her harder and Lucy's shrieks bounced off the paneled walls, louder and louder. He felt a sudden, hard-edged resentment, bordering on jealousy. It was misplaced and wrong, and it made the anxiety come flooding back.

"Stop it, you two. You're being too loud. Come on, Sarah, stop winding her up. Let's get them some dinner sorted, it's getting late."

Jack glanced up from his phone, eyebrows raised. For a second he looked much older than his years as he grinned at his father. It was an unexpected shared moment that thankfully pushed Jeremy's tension aside.

⊙━┿━⊙

Midnight had come and gone, but he couldn't sleep. It was too strange, being there in Ian's room, listening to the old house settling its bones. Sarah could, her exhalations gently stirred the night air, infusing Jeremy's past with her presence. She'd reached for him when they came to bed, but for once he couldn't do it. It'd felt wrong, so he'd gently pushed her away, ignoring her look of surprise.

The moon was up now, and the branches of the magnolia played a shadow dance across the walls. He could feel the pull of his old room, beckoning him along the dark landing. He swung his legs out of bed and quietly padded toward the doorway and slipped out onto the landing, where he walked its length to the door of his boyhood room. It opened at a touch, as though it had been waiting for him all these long years, and he stepped inside.

Moonbeams striped the floor and cast the room in a cool gray light. The old décor had gone but there was still a single bed in the same space, tight against the wall where the ceiling sloped down to form the eaves. The bed was unmade and there was a naked quilt and pillows neatly folded and stacked at its foot. Without conscious thought Jeremy shook out the quilt and threw the pillows to the head of the bed. Then he lay down, pulling the quilt over himself. It felt so familiar, as if he'd never been away. He could almost sense his parents asleep in the next bedroom, Emily safely tucked up across the landing, his friends, safe and snug in their own beds, dreaming of their adventures to come. Nathan and Andrew, Josh and Ben. His eyes gratefully closed and he felt the night carrying him toward sleep.

*He held his breath in the night. His hands gripping the quilt were white-knuckled with tension—would that he could see them in the darkness. The voices were quieter now, just a low mumbling punctuated by ominous silences and tiny whimpers that made his knees clench. He wanted to be asleep, to escape the world and everything in it, but he needed a pee and he dared not get up. If he did, if he drew attention to himself, he knew that the payback would be swift and brutal. He needed to be small and silent, unnoticed and nameless.*

# 11

Sarah was aware of Jeremy's nocturnal wandering, but she didn't comment on his decision to decamp to his boyhood bedroom or ask him to explain it. Instead she brought him tea—once she'd found him—and left him to sleep. It seemed his behavior now had to be truly bizarre to elicit any reaction from her, and she merely shook her head as she quietly closed the door.

He was wide awake now, and he lay in the cramped little bed and stared at the ceiling, a few sparse inches from his face. Lying like that felt oppressive, and mildly claustrophobic; still, he didn't move. His eyes traced the fine cracks in the plaster, and he let his mind drift back to that fateful morning, the last time he'd woken up happy in that room. He believed he'd been planning to meet the others after breakfast, but now he couldn't be sure. He'd thought about those boys only fleetingly during the intervening years, for they belonged to a time he seldom visited—at least not until now. Now, he found himself wondering where they might be and what they'd done with their lives—and whether they ever thought about him.

It was a chance meeting that'd set the wheels of their friendship in motion. Jeremy and his family had been coming there since he was tiny, and it was the first summer where he'd been deemed old enough to be out and about on his own. Emily was still a baby, eternally clamped to his mother's breast, like some love-sucking parasite. He must've been around six years old and his parents' attention had temporarily—at least in his father's case—shifted away from him to focus on the new addition, so he was freer than he'd ever been. The memory wasn't fully formed—he'd been too young for that—but he could just about recall Uncle Ian pottering in the garden while he disconsolately kicked a football round and round the magnolia tree. He'd become slowly aware of a small boy, close to his own age, observing him from the gate. He had a little black dog on a lead and was accompanied by an older boy, with sharp, watchful eyes. The younger boy was stick thin like Jeremy himself, with scuffed and bony knees that protruded from his shorts. A mop of brown hair had topped a tanned face, scattered with a shower of freckles and lit by a pair of light brown eyes. Warily they'd regarded each other, until his dog boldly cocked its leg against Uncle Ian's fence. The boy grinned, revealing missing teeth—just like his—and a friendship had instantly blossomed over Scotty's stream of yellow pee.

Through him—Ben—Jeremy had met the others, Nathan, Josh, and Andrew. Every summer they'd awaited his arrival—and they'd all believed they'd be mates forever.

The memory of Ben and Scotty stirred an unexpected sadness. The boy and the little dog had been inseparable, and he could still remember the summer Scotty died. It was that same summer, maybe two weeks before Emily and now, looking back, it almost felt like an omen. There were already changes on the horizon, with secondary schools looming over them, but for the moment the holidays were still their own. That afternoon they'd arranged to meet Ben by the corner shop, and when he didn't arrive, the boys made their way to the farm to call for him. His family had owned the nearby farm, and Ben lived there with his sister and older brother. He didn't have a mother, and Jeremy could no longer recall whether she'd left or had died. He seemed to think it was the latter, but it was something they hadn't ever talked about or dared to ask. The farm had been in Ben's family for many years, and Ben's aunt lived there too, as unpaid help to his father and a substitute mother to the children. A coolly distant woman, he seemed to recall, with evasive, shifting eyes. Everyone had liked Ben's father though; he was a friendly sort of man, a hair ruffler and a teaser. He always had a welcoming grin on his face when the boys came to call for Ben, and often a ready glass of lemonade or an ice-popsicle on a hot summer's day. He'd been so different from Jeremy's reserved and quiet father that he'd sometimes disloyally wished his own dad could be more like him, more fun.

That afternoon he'd seemed different though. He'd opened the door and his face was a mask. "Ben won't be coming out today, boys, I'm afraid" was all that he'd told them, and they'd immediately sensed that something was wrong. Two more days had passed before Ben reappeared, and when he did, he was alone.

"Where's Scotty-Dog?" someone had asked, and then it was as though a switch had been flicked. He could still picture Ben now, his face contorted with what they'd first thought was rage.

"He's dead, okay!" he yelled. Then his face had blotched and crumpled, and his shoulders heaved. "He's fucking dead, so just leave it."

The others had stood there, shocked by his swearing and helpless in the face of such grief. They'd watched as rivers of tears mingled with snot and the sobs wracked his small frame. Someone, Jeremy couldn't remember who, had reached out a hand but then let it hang there in midair, for they were too young to give comfort, and not yet well versed in sorrow. Of course the following week had changed all that for Jeremy.

Sarah came back into the bedroom, dispelling the memories and bringing him back to the present. She pushed his legs out of the way and sat at the end of the bed, her legs curled under her, feet bare. She had to hunch slightly to accommodate her head under the slope of the ceiling, so he edged over and patted the space he'd created. She lay down next to him with her hands linked behind her head, her T-shirt lifting to expose the smooth skin of her belly. Jeremy curled a lazy arm around her, letting his hand drift across the softness of her flesh. Suddenly he regretted his reluctance the previous night.

"What do you want to do today?" she asked. "We need to do some shopping but then we've got the rest of the morning free. The first estate agent isn't coming until two, so we could make a start on clearing some stuff. It shouldn't take us too long, seeing as no one's been living here." She turned her head to face him. "While you've been hiding away, I've been looking on the internet and I've found a house-clearing company. If we got them booked in, they could come and collect this week, while we're here. Save us a separate trip."

"Sounds like a plan." He yawned and stretched, conscious of the warmth of her body along the length of his. He felt the first stirrings of desire and nuzzled his face in the softness of her neck, letting his finger slide under the waistband of her joggers. "Where are the children?"

He moved to pull her closer but she pushed against him.

"They're downstairs watching television and you're getting up, so you can stop that. You had your chance last night. This isn't a holiday, Jez, there's loads to do and we've only really got this week. Go and have a shower and get dressed, and I'll make us some breakfast." She slid off the bed and stood up. "You can't put this off, Jez. The sooner we get everything dealt with, the sooner you can start putting all this behind you."

He quite admired her optimism.

They were getting the children ready to go to the shops, and Jeremy's throat felt tight with apprehension, despite his efforts to rationalize.

He watched Sarah brushing Lucy's hair, which brought back thoughts of his own mother and Emily, not helpful to his frame of mind. His mother did the same thing as Sarah: pressing a hand to the girl's head, protecting the roots from pulling while she teased out any tangles at the ends. Gentle hands—but never for him. She'd comb his hair roughly, snagging at the knots and pulling until his eyes watered. Now he thought about it, it was always the same. Snatching at his feet to do up his laces. Knotting his ties too chokingly tight, manhandling him into coats in a way that risked shoulder dislocation. It'd never carried enough thought to be deemed deliberate. It was just a careless brutality fed by impatience—most of the time, at least. He wondered, had it been wrong of him to envy Ben his motherless state and to covet his jovial, ruddy-faced father?

*The bathroom mirror glowered back at him, showing him the imprint across his cheek. This had been a good one; four fingers, so clearly defined that there were slices of white skin in between. It marked his skin like a stencil. His summer freckles had turned from the palest hint to specks of livid red, like liver spots aging the handprint beyond its years. Still, it was "only a slap." He leaned into his image where his wet eyes mocked him. His chest squirmed and twisted with a mixture of fear and rage, and he felt the simmering something inside him swell and grow bigger. He cupped his hands under the cold tap and splashed the coolness onto his burning skin. He couldn't go out yet; he needed to wait a while, else the others would know and he couldn't bear the shame of it.*

Jeremy felt shifty but was unsure why, unless it was the thought of facing the pedestrian crossing again and the knowing wink-wink of the little green man. Outside, the sky was gray and flatly threatening and did nothing to lift his mood. Neither did the supermarket. It was no more welcoming than it'd been the previous day, less so if anything, as today there was a reception committee of belligerent teenagers obstructing the entrance with their lumpen bodies and abandoned bikes. Jack looked at them with an expression close to wistfulness and his father herded him into the store. In your dreams, sunshine.

If Jeremy had hoped for someone different behind the counter, he was sorely disappointed as it was the same woman as before, engaged in close conversation with four others of varying ages. One was accompanied by a limp teenager, standing vacuously at her side. He was thin and worryingly pale, bar a livid flare of acne nestling in the hollows beneath his cheekbones. He had the look of one breastfed into his teens, and if he, and the fine specimens lurking outside, were representative of the local youth, then the rude health of the countryside seemed to have passed them by. He gave Jeremy a baleful look from beneath flaky lids, as if sensing his distaste.

The group stopped talking as the family entered and Jeremy was seized by a sudden paranoia, convinced they'd been talking about him. They watched him as he grabbed a trolley, and he felt his features taking on a pugnacious, defensive set. Unlike Sarah, who smiled as she passed, seemingly oblivious to the ripple that ran through the group and to the way they moved together to form a tight huddle. One woman smiled back, almost despite herself, and Jeremy marveled at how Sarah always seemed able to engage with people in a way that he never could. It certainly wasn't naivety, her profession bore witness to that, it was just an easiness with strangers that he lacked. He suffered from a self-consciousness and fear of rejection that only served to repel. An inbuilt self-fulfilling prophecy.

They filled their trolley and made their way back to the checkout where the women were still congregated. After a defiant glance at her friends, one of the group walked toward Jeremy with a smile on her face.

"Don't say hello then," she said, and amber eyes met his.

She was younger than him, slim and very attractive, with light brown curly hair and a peppering of freckles across a tip-tilted nose. Some primordial part of him smiled winsomely back and wagged his tail with an unbecoming eagerness. There was something in her pale brown eyes that ignited a faint memory, but before he could catch it she spoke again,

"It's Laura, Ben's sister. Don't you remember me?"

Her face fell into place, an older version of the tousle-haired child. He recognized her now. She'd been younger than the rest of them but not so much that they would exclude her from their group. Whenever she joined them she was a frenetic bundle of energy, climbing trees and jumping streams, desperate to keep up with the boys. Jeremy hesitated for a moment, unsure whether to extend a hand or to air-kiss, mwah-mwahing at her cheeks in a nod to their previous familiarity. There was a second of awkwardness before she took the decision out of his hands and greeted him with a hug. He was aware of the momentary hardness of her body against his, the pressure of small firm breasts against his chest, and lithe arms enfolding his neck. He quickly supressed an unexpected lure of attraction.

They parted and he became aware of the other women—Sarah included—watching him. One of them had a small child with her, and he could've sworn she pulled the girl closer in a protective gesture. He supressed a wicked urge to bear his teeth at her and growl.

"Sal said she thought it was you," Laura continued, and he glanced at the woman behind the counter; so she *had* recognized him, and now she gave him a look of thinly veiled hostility. "She said how much your little girl looks like—" she hesitated for a moment, then took a deep breath "—like your sister." She continued to stare at him with something akin to amazement. "God, it's been years, Jay, whatever are you doing back here?"

Her use of his childhood name pulled at something deep inside him, an unexpected tug that felt like hurt. "My mother died a few months ago, so we're back at the old house sorting out some things, that's all." He kept his answer brief because he didn't feel the need to give any more detail than he had to. He didn't appreciate the way the women were watching him, and was only too aware of the hum of unease rippling through them.

Laura clasped his hand in hers. "Oh, I'm so sorry to hear that. God, I can remember your mum so clearly, she was always such a glamorous lady. You must miss her terribly."

There was no real answer to that, or at least not one that didn't make him sound like a heartless bastard, so he mumbled his thanks while she continued,

"And Jay, I know it was years ago now but I never got a chance to speak to you at the time, none of us did. I just want you to know, we were all so sorry for what happened back then. Even as kids it hit us hard."

He didn't need this. Not now, not ever, and certainly not with Jack and Lucy in tow; he could almost feel the breeze from Jack's flapping ears. He made another banal rejoinder and backed away to let Sarah pay for the shopping. He needed to return to the sanctuary of the house.

# 12

The sky was clearing as they walked back. The clouds had torn apart to reveal slices of pale blue sky, and a watery sunlight had begun to filter through. Jack and Lucy were restless, jostling and bickering at each other as they walked. There was an odd vibe coming off Sarah as well, he could sense it.

"Have I done something to annoy you?"

"Actually, yes," she said, turning to face him. "In future, when we meet someone you know, would you mind introducing me rather than leaving me standing there like some idiot. It was rude, Jez, and I didn't appreciate it."

"Jesus, Sarah, I didn't do it deliberately, she completely wrong-footed me. I didn't even realize who she was to start with and then it got plain awkward. And when she started mentioning—you know—" he glanced at the children "—I didn't want that conversation in front of them. I just wanted to get away from her, if I'm honest."

"That's fine, I get it. Only it made me feel a bit awkward too, standing there like a spare part. We're probably going to bump into other people who remember you, so I thought I'd mention it, that's all."

"I'm sorry. I won't do it again. I'll be ready for it next time."

She relented slightly and grinned at him. "And since when have you been known as Jay? I must try it if it makes your tongue hang out like that. 'Ooh, Jay, it's been *so* long.'"

He couldn't help but smile at her slightly breathy impersonation of Laura.

"That's better, *Jay*. It's been a while since I've seen you actually smile."

"If you must know, 'Jay' was what the kids here called me back then. I don't remember who started it, but I was always 'Jay' during the holidays." He didn't tell her it was what Em called him too—Jay-Jay. "And for your information my tongue wasn't *hanging out*. She just caught me by surprise, that's all."

Sarah raised an eyebrow and gave him a look that clearly told him he might be a shit sometimes, but he was *her* shit, and she hadn't liked the way he'd reacted to Laura.

"Don't look like that!" God, he hated it when she saw straight through him. "Anyway, she's not my type. I prefer my women more cuddly." He adopted a leering grin and made a playful lunge for her. "She didn't have your marvelous boobies."

She backed away, laughing in mock disgust. "Yuk, Jay, what is *wrong* with you? I think I prefer morose over gross!"

"Sorry, darling, was that too objectifying for you?"

"No Jeremy, I think objec*tionable* is the word you're looking for."

Jeremy felt a surge of relief that they were still able to banter with each other. It allowed him to hope that they'd be okay.

They carried on walking in a comfortable silence, and Jeremy found himself once again mulling over the wariness of the group of women. It still troubled him, the way they'd seemed almost afraid.

"Sarah, did you notice those other women? I don't know if it was my imagination, but they all seemed to be acting a bit strange, almost hostile, like. I'm sure one of them clutched her child as though I was about to bite it, or something."

"I don't know that they were hostile, exactly. A bit standoffish maybe, but then I might've come across like that as well, just standing there like a lemon."

Sarah paused and looked thoughtful for a moment. "It's a small village, and perhaps they don't like being reminded that a bad thing happened here. I don't know, but I certainly wouldn't attach much importance to it. We're only going to be here for the week, so let them gossip and be hostile if they want. I've told you, you worry far too much about other people."

They reached the house and Sarah stopped at the gate. "Jez, how about we drop the food off, and then take these two for a walk? We'll need them to sit quietly while the estate agents are here, but we can't really plonk them in front of the TV all day. You know what they'll be like if they don't at least get out for a bit."

After putting away the shopping, they walked on past the house toward the fields and distant woodland. Jeremy wasn't sure he was entirely ready for a trip to the woods but he couldn't think of any-where else to go, so he battened down the sense of foreboding that was building with each step.

The first of the new homes were already occupied, neat curtains framing the windows, new-laid grass clothing the lawns, but those closer to the fields were empty, with blank-eyed windows that observed the family's progress. The sun was out for real now, and once they'd passed the houses, the scene took on a stark beauty. The fields were plowed, ready for spring planting, and the woods beyond were a backdrop of browns and grays. It was too early for any green on the trees—bar the odd dark yew or pine—but still the image was clear and sharp, a myriad shades defining the detail. The air had a lucent quality that set the distant branches in relief; a filigree reaching into a ground-glass sky of palest blue.

Sarah slipped her hand in his and they let the children run on ahead. Lucy was in front, her bright red anorak a contrast against the sepia of the fields, the hood bobbing behind her like Little Red Riding Hood. She hopped over the ruts and furrows with Jack in hot pursuit. He was laughing and whooping, an echo of his younger self, for once forgetting he was supposed to be *cool* at all times. Jeremy smiled at Sarah and pulled her a little closer. This was okay; he was good.

It'd been wrong of his parents never to come back here as a family—albeit a much-diminished one. It'd made the place take on a sinister significance it didn't deserve; the stuff of nightmares, where really it was a good place where a bad thing had happened. They should've have gone back at least once, if only to dispel the demons, and lay the past to rest. It hadn't been very fair on Uncle Ian either, to deny him the only family he had.

A plane appeared overhead, its vapor trail cutting the blue. The sound of its engines was amplified in the clear air, pulling Jeremy back from his thoughts. He watched Lucy and Jack, aware of the background roar reverberating in his ears. A dog barked somewhere in the distance—and then it was a perfect storm.

It was no longer Lucy; it was Emily.

It wasn't Jack anymore; it was him, Jeremy.

He couldn't draw breath, his throat had closed, and the sense of menace was overwhelming.

He released Sarah's hand and was suddenly lost.

The plane passed over and the roaring subsided, leaving only its echo inside his head. And then the memory came hot and fast. He'd chased her. He chased her into the trees. Into the woods where she died. Hot sun; summer hot. The smell of hay scorching his nostrils. His feet pounding over sun-baked earth, hard and rutted beneath his soles. A dog barking.

And then, somehow, he was on his knees with Sarah's hand on his shoulder, and the sense of evil was like a dark thing, pressing him into the earth. The children's laughter sounded distant, barely audible above the clamor in his ears. He felt the stony ground, the sharp edges pressing into his knees and palms, and somehow he knew he deserved the pain.

Sarah's voice reached him. "Jez, what on earth are you doing? Are you okay?"

She'd assumed that he'd stumbled on the rutted ground and fallen, so there was a note of amused exasperation in her voice as she pulled at his arm. Slowly he rose to his feet. The memory was still there, and instinctively he knew it as real. Dear God, he'd chased her to her death—or worse. He shrugged Sarah off without answering, and began to brush the dirt from his jeans. He began walking but his movements were robotic, distant. He felt disassociated, as though he was stuck somewhere between the past and the present. He watched the two small figures making their way toward the woods and followed in their wake.

"Jez, are you all right?" Sarah's voice had changed, a hint of worry creeping in. "For God's sake, Jez, talk to me. What's going on?"

He struggled to reconnect with the present. "I'm fine," he managed to say. "I just need to think, that's all."

"Jez, let's go back." She tugged at his arm. "You're scaring me. Come on, call the children and we'll go back to the house."

He registered the note of fear in her voice and wrenched himself back into the moment. "No, really, I'm all right. I just remembered being here, with Emily, and it's hard but I need to do this. I need to let myself remember. I'll be okay." He shook his head to dispel the feeling. "We'll go to the edge of the woods and then we'll turn back." He forced himself to smile. "You were right. We need to give the kids a chance to have a run about, blow off a bit of steam. I'm just being foolish, letting all this get to me."

He couldn't go back yet. He needed the memory to consolidate, to take on its true form, awful though it might be.

Sarah wasn't convinced, but they carried on walking, over the stile and across the second field, to the footpath that led deep into the woods. Jack and Lucy wanted to continue on into the trees, but Jeremy stopped them at the first archway of branches, where the air seemed charged with expectancy. The floor was carpeted in a rustle of leaves, and dark waxy holly bushes lurked among the tree trunks like sentinels. Winter sunlight was filtered and became lost in the branches, casting the woods in a gloom that belied the absence of foliage. It gave the trees a sinister, fairy-tale quality; thick dark boles and twisted limbs. There was a stillness that felt alive, as if there was a presence there, watching, waiting. Waiting for him.

Jeremy took a step forward and sensed the air shifting. Busy with a whispering, a chattering, an echo of childish voices. He took another step and the dread overwhelmed him. His fingertips began to itch and tingle and the sweat beaded along his spine. He couldn't go in there. Not today.

"That's far enough, you two." He heard himself speaking, his adult voice strange to his ears. "We'll do the woods another day."

# 13

"Nine hundred and fifty thousand!"

Yesterday's estate agents had both said the same and now Sarah said it again, as though she couldn't quite believe it.

"That, plus whatever we get for your mum's place, is life changing, Jez. Even after we've paid tax."

It would once have been amusing seeing Sarah so excited over money because she'd always had a mildly sanctimonious attitude toward wealth, reminding Jeremy that there were "more important things in life." Normally he'd be the animated one but ironically, now that he was faced with the prospect of more money than he'd ever seen in one go, it didn't excite him. It paled into insignificance in the face of the knowledge that he'd chased his sister into those woods, a fragment of truth that gave him a trill of terror each time he thought of it, and of what might have come after.

He wished Sarah would stop talking so he could process things. He thought about Carole Jessup and wondered whether she'd have some magic trick up her sleeve to speed up his memories, one of her eye-rolling games. He fleetingly considered ringing her but rejected the idea. They hadn't been able to make him remember thirty years ago, when it was all still fresh in his mind, so she was hardly going to be able to do it now, just because he wanted her to. Life didn't work like that.

"Jez, are you even listening to me?"

Apparently not, dear.

"Sorry, darling, I've got a bit of a headache this morning. I might go and lie down for a while, if that's okay with you. I don't know if it's being back here or what, but I've had this band of tension behind my eyes ever since the woods yesterday."

They were surrounded by piles of towels and bed linen, ostensibly—in Jeremy's case, at least—going through them to decide what they might Donate, Keep, Bin. A version of FMK for personal effects.

Sarah sighed—a little unwarranted, he felt. "Okay, I can finish doing this on my own, I suppose. Just look in on the kids before you go up, will you? They're very quiet, so check they're not up to something."

He poked his head around the sitting room door, where Jack was slouched in front of the television watching cartoons. Lucy was sitting on the floor coloring, her blond head bowed over a startling image of bug-eyed monsters and alien landscapes, which gave Jeremy a fatherly twinge of wistfulness for her princess phase. She glanced up as he came in and there was a momentary slippage in time as Emily's eyes met his. It was something about the tilt of Lucy's head or the expression on her face that transformed her; a blink and she'd gone, but it was enough to send his pulse racing. He backed out of the room, leaving them to it. Unlike him, they were fine.

He went into his old bedroom and closed the door. At some point Sarah had put clean sheets on the bed; a pale checked quilt cover and matching pillowcase, a dark blue throw neatly folded at the foot. Her quiet thoughtfulness touched him and made something prickle behind his eyes. He was suddenly afraid of what was happening to him. What if he ended up having a breakdown or, worse, found out something about himself that blew them all apart? All of this because of a chance sighting from the window of a plane, a scene that meant nothing in itself but which had set these wheels in motion. He could picture it still, that tiny figure moving toward a stand of trees, the suggestion of others in pursuit. It all made sense now that he'd glimpsed the memory it had roused from its slumber.

He slipped off his trainers and lay down on the bed, closing his eyes in an attempt to recapture the fragment, letting it play against the darkness of his mind. He could remember the day clearly now. A blue sky, puffed with tatters of high cloud. The field fallow, set to grass, singed to hay by the heat of the summer. He could even conjure the feel of it, and the scent of it, but there was nothing before and nothing after, just a disembodied snapshot drifting in time. He squeezed his lids tight shut and tried to force the memory, straining against the blankness, but his constipated brain held everything in.

With a sigh he opened his eyes and looked at his watch. It was nearly one o'clock. What he really needed was a stiff drink, and he now wished that he hadn't pretended to have a headache.

As he swung his feet off the bed, a realization hit him. Others. Of course there were others; he hadn't been alone. His utter conviction that there had been three people in pursuit suddenly made sense. Someone would've been with him that day, Nathan or Ben, Andrew or Josh. They'd know what they did, and where they went. They would've told it all to the police. His heart raced with excitement; he needed to find Ben.

Sarah had begrudgingly finished sorting through the linens and there were now two black plastic bags and a box waiting in the hall to be dispatched for recycling or charity. To Jeremy they sparkled with opportunity.

"I'll take those now, if you like, and try to find somewhere to dump them. May as well get rid of stuff as we go along." He tried but failed not to sound too eager.

It would give him a chance to go into the village again, and maybe bump into Laura or one of those women from the supermarket. Someone who might tell him where she lived, or at least let her know that he was looking for her. She was his route to Ben.

"I thought you had a headache?" Sarah said. "Funny how it's suddenly gone now all the sorting-out's finished. Thanks for that."

"Don't be like that. I have got a headache, but I'm not going to get rid of it lying up there, am I? I thought a bit of fresh air might help, that's all. Give us a hand to put these in the car, and I'll see if I can find somewhere that'll take them. There's got to be a charity shop in the high street, and recycling bins somewhere around here. Come on, it'll be another job out of the way."

He dumped the box into the back of the car and gave Sarah a perfunctory peck on the cheek. Now that he had a plan he was impatient to be gone.

"I shouldn't be too long, but don't hang on for me if the kids need lunch. I can grab a quick something when I get back."

⚬━━⚬

He drove past the church toward the high street. The day was as gray as newsprint. Naked winter trees and tangled thickets of thorny bush edged the graveyard, as lifeless as its inhabitants. Early daffodils provided the only hint of brightness, showing their sunny faces in the grassy verge on either side of the lychgate. He fleetingly thought of Ian laying within.

Emily wasn't buried there; his parents had taken his sister home. Sadly, the memory of her funeral wasn't lost to him. Instead, the savage brutality of its grief was seared into him. A defiant sun blazing from a watercolor sky, roasting the mourners in their black. A nightmarish day, rendered distant and dreamlike by disbelief. His mother had been sedated close to stupor, her eyes glassy and vacant, devoid of tears; only his father had kept her standing. Him in a suit. Like a hedgehog baked in clay. Guilt like an anvil weighing him down.

He shrugged off the image and pulled into the car park behind the shops. Exactly as he'd thought, there was a row of recycling containers: yellow for plastic, blue for paper, green for glass. He wondered what color the one for unwanted memories would be. Black, probably. He made his deposits before retracing his route back to the road on foot. He wanted to locate a charity shop before he carried a box of junk up and down the high street.

The high street was quiet, just a smattering of solitary shoppers going about their business, and a couple of women standing on the pavement up ahead of him, heads nodding, deep in conversation. They briefly stared in his direction before parting and going their separate ways, one moving briskly, the other lumbering and laborious.

As he walked past the shops he saw a small boy coming toward him, disconsolately kicking a ball along the path. There was something in the slump of his shoulders and his general air of defeat that reminded Jeremy of his childhood self. As he watched, the boy toe-poked the ball and the camber of the uneven pavement sent it rolling toward the road. He started to run after it, but before he could launch himself into the path of the oncoming traffic, Jeremy stopped the ball with his foot and skilfully roll-scooped it back up the curb. He added a few keepy-uppies, just to demonstrate that he was a man of massive talent, then tapped it back to the boy, who looked surprisingly unimpressed.

Jeremy stopped him in his tracks with a paternalistic hand laid firmly on his shoulder. "You should *never* run into the road like that, son. God, if there'd been a car coming . . ."

"Hey!" The sound of a strident female voice spitefully jabbed at his eardrums, and he watched as a stocky woman in her late sixties came barreling toward him, propelled by an excess of righteous indignation. With some surprise he noted that she was one of the pair who was previously chatting, and that now it appeared she was speaking to him.

"Hey you, yes you! What do you think you're doing with that boy? You get your dirty hands off him!"

She was a bruiser of a woman, mean eyes nestling in the meat of her face.

Instinctively Jeremy found himself answering, some previous conditioning making him automatically respond to hostile women. "What do you think I'm *doing*? If you hadn't noticed, he was just about to run out into the road before I stopped him." He was irritated by his knee-jerk justification, so he added. "Not that it's any of your business."

"Well I'm making it my business," she retorted. Turning her ample frame toward the boy, she waved a beefy hand. "You run on home now, Stevie, and make sure to tell your father."

Tell him quite what? Jeremy wondered. How the nice man stopped him from being mown down by traffic? Saved his parents the need to buy black?

The boy adopted a frightened expression—one ideally suited to a narrow escape from abduction and nameless horror—before gathering up his ball and running off down the street. An impotent fury began to unfurl inside Jeremy at the look of outrage and suspicion on the woman's face. One would almost think she'd caught him with his hand down the boy's joggers. He felt the anger starting to build and fought to maintain an air of nonreactivity. Nothing he could say would make the situation better, so she was best ignored, dismissed as someone who'd spent far too long in the shock-horror world of the fevered tabloids.

He didn't even know the woman but it appeared that she thought she knew him. "Yes, I know who you are, and your sort never change," she informed him, with a knowing nod of her bovine head. "We've got the measure of you, so you'd best watch yourself and stay away from the kiddies."

With that she stomped away and carried on up the high street, leaving all the things Jeremy wanted to say wedged in his throat. He found he was thrumming with a delayed rush of adrenaline at the unprovoked attack. He'd been there only three days but already there was an undercurrent of hostility that he didn't understand. Maybe it was nothing more than a village introversion, a parochial suspicion toward outsiders, but somehow it seemed more purposeful and intentionally directed at him.

Having disposed of the box of tat in a suitably grateful charity shop, Jeremy found he wasn't ready to go back to the confines of the house. Instead, he picked up a paper from the nearby newsagent—the least fevered tabloid on offer—and made his way to the Black Swan pub. She was an unprepossessing bird, who balefully glared down from her weathered sign. Bet she could break a man's leg with a single strike.

Inside, the bar was dimly lit and shafts of wintery light made their way through the smudged glass, dancing with dust motes. On a Monday lunchtime it was almost devoid of customers bar a couple of old men at a table near the window, black silhouettes against the glare. They glanced over as Jeremy entered, before disinterestedly returning to their pints. He made his way to the wood-paneled bar, with its row of leather-topped bar stools, where a lone barman was studiously polishing a glass.

He looked up at Jeremy's approach. "Afternoon."

He was sporting a barbell at his eyebrow and a handlebar hipster, above which a tiny yet optimistic "21" was tattooed on his cheek. Jeremy suspected it'd been a long, long while since that'd held any relevance, but he gave a silent nod to his efforts at keeping the dream alive.

He surveyed the beers on offer. "A pint of the Peroni, please, mate, and have you got a menu?" He wasn't intending to stay long but would at least have a look, if only for future reference.

"Here you go." The barman slid a laminated sheet across the bar and proceeded to pull the pint. "We're all out of the beef chili, I'm afraid." He glanced at his watch. "And you better be quick if you're eating, we stop taking orders at two thirty."

As Jeremy perused the menu he realized he was hungry, so he ordered a beef patty in a bun, with a side of chips. Pint in hand, he took a table facing the door, where he spread out his newspaper and surveyed the headlines. His mind began to wander, setting off on its own on a trip to the past, back to his childhood friends, Nathan Kemp, Josh Stephens, Ben McLeish and Andrew . . . try as he might, he couldn't recall Andrew's surname. He idly wondered if any of them still lived around there, and somehow he suspected they did. The place was like a black hole, with a gravitational pull all of its own that held everyone in. Only the lucky few would escape, with the rest ending up but a stone's throw from their childhood homes. He knew he was being patronizing—after all, Bristol to London was hardly crossing the planet—but there was something about the village, a stultifying conformity that must be difficult to break away from.

The barman brought over his food; a cone of slightly undercooked chips and a burger that lacked attitude, lounging on a flaccid bed of salad. Hmm, no brioche bun, chipotle mayo, or pickles appeared to be forthcoming today.

"There you go, sir. If you need anything else, there's ketchup and mayonnaise along the bar."

He pictured it literally smeared across the greasy surface. "No, that's fine, thanks. I'll have another beer though, best make it a half this time, please."

Perhaps he should ask if the barman knew Ben, if he ever went in there for a drink. It was a long shot, but Jeremy had nothing else to go on.

As if on cue, the barman returned with his drink.

"Cheers." He hesitated. "Er, a quick question, if that's okay. You don't happen to know a Ben McLeish, do you? I just wondered if he ever drank in here."

A questioning look crossed the barman's face, not suspicious, not hostile, just waiting for Jeremy to expand.

"He used to live around here and we were friends way back as kids."

He shook his head. "Sorry, mate, I've only lived around here myself for a couple of months. Can't say the name rings any bells, to be honest."

"That's okay, thought I'd ask. Thanks anyway."

Maybe it had been too much to hope for.

The barman went to walk away but then a belated bell did chime and he turned back to Jeremy. "There is a *Mark* McLeish comes in here sometimes though. At least I think that's his name. Don't know if that's any help to you?"

Oh it was, and Jeremy thanked him profusely.

Mark McLeish, Ben's brother, was four or five years older than his sibling, and over the years he'd grown from a sharp-eyed boy into a mean and wary teenager. A lad with a face like a fist, and the memory of him brought with it a hint of threat.

The crew hadn't really had much to do with Mark during those summers; the age gap was too big. By the time everything had ended he was fifteen or sixteen, and he mainly hung out with a group from the local comprehensive: David Kemp, Nathan's brother, and Josh's older sister, Becky. There'd been some others from the village too; they'd roamed the streets and prowled the woods once evening fell, and to Jeremy they'd seemed a frightening mix of hormones and aggression. Suddenly the woman from the supermarket fell into place. Sal, or Sally as was. She'd been one of the group; a quiet girl, a little bit scruffy and downtrodden, with brown hair pulled back in a ponytail, slightly younger than the rest. Just thinking about that group brought a whisper of malevolence. No wonder he'd preferred his evenings at home with Ian and George.

*He pushed his face close to the younger child's, so close that his hot, angry breath tickled their skin. "Stop sniffling, you hear me? Stop crying—crying is only going to make everything worse."*

*He gave them a shake for emphasis, his fingers digging into bony shoulders. "And you don't say a word to anyone about this. Not ever. No matter how much you might think you want to. It won't make it better, only a whole lot worse for you. No one can help you now, so you keep this to yourself, understand?"*

*The child nodded, fighting to suppress the sobs that threatened to shake their small frame apart. They dared to raise frightened eyes to meet the other's but all they saw were two pits of anger—and a dreadful, nameless fear.*

Jeremy pulled into the driveway. He'd been gone for far longer than intended, so he was fully prepared for Sarah to be angry with him. She was. He walked into the kitchen where she was emptying cupboards in that certain deliberate way she had when she was cross, and his heart sank. She turned when he came in and there was something distinctly frosty in her gaze.

"What?"

"What do you mean 'What?' You know exactly what's wrong."

She turned away in apparent disgust, so he went up behind her and wrapped his arms around her waist.

He whispered into her hair. "Darling, I'm sorry I've been so long. Don't be angry with me."

She spun around to face him again, eyes blazing. "Where the hell have you been, Jez? You went hours ago, and left me to do all this on my own—and look after the children."

She gestured toward the work surfaces that were littered with an array of pans and dishes. "This is your family's house, not mine, so why do you think it's okay for you to leave me to do everything? I thought the whole point of this week was that we'd do things together, but no, you think you can . . ." She suddenly stopped and wrinkled her nose suspiciously. "Have you been *drinking*?"

Her voice rose on a note of incredulity and a flush of anger reddened her cheeks.

"You've been to the pub, haven't you." A statement, not a question. "Honestly Jez, I don't believe you sometimes, you've left me here with the kids, to try and clear this place, while you've been in the fucking pub!"

Jeremy understood why she was angry but still it rattled him; it was so out of character, and so unlike her to swear.

"I'm sorry. It wasn't like that. I didn't intend to."

"What do you mean, 'It wasn't like that'? Did someone drag you into the pub and force the beer down you, was that it? Bollocks to it, Jez, I've got a good mind to take the kids home and leave you to do the rest of this on your own."

"You don't understand, I only . . ."

He couldn't begin to make her see how it hadn't been selfishness, how his mind had gone off on a tangent until finding Ben had become the most important thing. He wanted to explain to her how desperate he was but he couldn't do it now, not when it would sound like a lame excuse.

"I'm sorry, Sarah, I honestly didn't mean to be gone so long. I just popped in for a quick one and then I decided to have a bite to eat and time kind of ran away with me. You go and sit down and I'll finish the rest of this."

She slung a Tupperware box into the sink for emphasis, where it bounced reproachfully, and Jeremy watched as the anger drained out of her.

"I'm trying, Jez, really I am. I get that you're not in a good place, but you don't make it easy for me when you do things like this. Sometimes it's like I don't even know you anymore, and it's hard."

"Sarah, that's not fair. I haven't—"

"Jez, let me finish. I've been thinking while you've been out. When we get back I want you to go and see Carole Jessup again. I think this is all getting to you far more than you're letting on, and I want someone to help you with it."

"I don't need to see her again. She didn't really help and anyway, I'm okay."

Sarah ignored his protests and began pacing the kitchen, trying to walk off her agitation.

"I've been going over what you told me, about your sister and everything, and it's too big for anyone to handle on their own. You're not coping. Yesterday in the field you went all remote on us, like you weren't really there, and that scared me."

"But I've already explained. It was just being near the woods that got to me for a minute, I was fine afterward, honestly."

"You're not fine, and I don't know how to help you, or what to suggest, so I think you need someone professional." She saw the skepticism in his face. "I know you don't want to, that it's *not you*, but *I* want you to."

She stopped pacing and placed a hand on his arm. "I just want the person back that I used to laugh with, and dream with, not this obsessed, distant person you're turning into."

He pulled her to him then, and held her, crushing her body tight to his. He didn't ever want to lose her but he couldn't give up on this, not now that he could see a way forward.

"Okay, I think you're making too much of it, but I'll think about it. I love you, and if it's worrying you that much I'll do whatever you want. We'll be okay, Sarah. I promise."

# 14

Sarah snuffled in her sleep, and Jeremy experienced a twinge of irritation at the fact that she was able to switch off and go to sleep like that; she was obviously not *too* worried about him. He was tempted to move to his old room but he didn't dare. He didn't want to upset her even further because, despite how he was feeling right in that moment, he did love her—with every bit of his heart. He sighed into the darkness and decided he'd try and talk to her tomorrow.

They'd finished clearing the kitchen together, but the atmosphere had been strained. She'd made herself distant, her barriers unbreachable, so he couldn't explain to her about the memories teeming under his surface.

He didn't really understand what she was so afraid of or what she thought might happen. Yes, it was frightening, and it was making him anxious, but in part that was the *not* knowing and the fragmented nature of the glimpses he'd seen. To finally understand the past would be liberating. Even if he'd just found Emily drowned by the lake, to finally know the truth of it would set him free. He shook his head in the darkness; what could be worse than not knowing—unless Sarah was afraid it was him who had killed her.

It was a careless, throwaway thought, but it brought with it a wave of fear, rising out of the mattress to engulf him. His throat constricted and he struggled to breathe, the sweat beading on his face. It was reminiscent of the nights when he'd woken from some nameless horror, silently screaming into the darkness—but this time he was awake. There'd been no nightmare, no nighttime terror, but still the panic engulfed him, the same blinding, heart-pounding feeling of impending doom.

He clutched at his throat and reared up in the bed, gasping for air. Spots danced and sparkled before his eyes, and for a moment he thought he'd pass out. Desperately, he reached for Sarah, and his flailing hand found her arm, warm and solid, and real. She stirred in her sleep without waking and just the feel of her, the knowledge that she was there next to him, made the wave break and the panic begin to subside. It slowly seeped away into the night, leaving in its wake a background anxiety. He could hear his heartbeat thumping where his head met the pillow, a steady beating deep in his ears. God, he needed to get a grip if a stupid, meaningless thought was able to bring on a panic attack like that.

He tried to quiet his mind, slowing his breathing, and gradually he tuned in to the rhythms of the night. It had rained in the evening, but now the air was clear and quiet. Away across the fields there was the distant growl of a fallow deer, and nearby he could hear the eerie, high-pitched howl of mating foxes, punctuated by the familiar sound of a faraway owl. Uncle Ian had taught him these sounds, reassuring a city boy that there was nothing out there to do him harm, no matter how threatening their calls. Thinking of Uncle Ian calmed him and he smiled to himself, remembering the first time he'd heard a hunting hedgehog snuffling under his window, and how convinced he'd been that there was a bad man out there, hiding in the garden. Now he wondered if the bad man had been inside all along.

As he finally sank toward sleep another noise invaded his consciousness. He strained to hear but silence blanketed his ears, and just as he began to think he'd imagined it, he heard it again, a sound out of place. It wasn't the call of a creature or the wind rustling the branches, it was a movement close to the house like something—or someone—slowly moving in the darkness. The longer he listened, the more convinced he became that there was somebody out there. An animal would never come this close to humans—unless it was a fox—but the movement was too loud, too heavy for that. There was faintest crunch of footsteps on gravel. There was someone in the garden to the front of the house.

He threw back the quilt and leapt out of bed, moving quickly but quietly. Grabbing a robe from the bathroom door, he slipped down the stairs, muscle memory guiding him over the steps that would creak. He paused on the half landing, listening, unsure if he'd just heard the sound of a car. Silence greeted him but still he continued down the stairs, throwing the front door open onto the garden where the magnolia stood silhouetted against the night sky and a sliver of moonlight slinked through the clouds, illuminating the damp lawn with a faint gray light. All was quiet. There was no sign of anyone, not even an echo of running footsteps, so he made his way down the driveway, past his car and into the road, where he looked up past the church and then back toward the new houses and the fields beyond. He stood there for a while waiting, but no one came creeping from the gardens of the empty houses or slipped through the lychgate from the churchyard. No car came crawling past, lights dimmed, so he turned back toward the house, partly relieved, partly disappointed that there was no one there to challenge. No outlet for some of the tension and anger he was holding inside.

He padded back upstairs to bed, careful to lock the door behind him. He was too wired to sleep. Even though he had no evidence, he couldn't quite shake the idea that there'd been an intruder in the garden. He tossed and turned but couldn't get comfortable. The quilt and sheet were hot and clinging despite the cool of the night. After ten minutes or so, he swung his feet out of bed for the second time, and quietly pulled on his joggers and a sweatshirt. He glanced at Sarah's sleeping form. She stirred at the movement but didn't wake; God, how he envied her the gift of her untroubled mind.

The moonlight suddenly illuminated the smooth curve of her neck and his earlier panic resurfaced. How easy it would be for him to press his fingers to her throat and extinguish the light of her. Was that what he was; was that what he'd done to his sister? He shuddered in the darkness. He needed to put some distance between himself and such thoughts.

As he crept down the stairs, he ran his hand along the smooth wood of the banister. At the bottom his fingers found a hard little nub in the woodwork, and he traced his fingers over the contours of a tiny body and along the length of a tail. Magic Mouse, carved in the fold where the rail met the newel post; however could he have forgotten? A smile played at his lips and he suddenly missed Uncle Ian with a strength of feeling that took his breath away. "He's magic, Jeremy, he was the idea of a wonderful man called Robert Thompson. You just need to rub him and make a wish." He was ambushed by the image of a small boy wishing for his mother to love him, wishing his sister back from the dead. Now a forty-two-year-old man found himself rubbing a carved wooden mouse in the moonlight.

"I wish to know the truth about my sister. I wish to keep my family safe. I wish for this to all turn out right." His voice but a breath in the night.

He threw on a jacket and trainers before stepping outside once more. He walked past the church to the high street, but instead of turning toward the pubs and the shops, headed toward the outskirts of the village, where the road met open countryside. He strode past a forlorn straggle of farm cottages, blank windowed and brooding, their inhabitants safely tucked up inside, past the garage and filling station, where neon lights pooled, green and yellow, in oil-slicked puddles like toxic waste. He didn't know where he was going, he just needed to clear his head. The buildings gradually petered out and the road stretched away into dark countryside. Still he walked, through scrubby farmland edged by low-slung hedges, barely visible in the gloom, past scattered trees, arching their clawlike branches over the road, silhouetted black against the night sky. Finally he came to a stop.

He'd walked off the tension and now he reluctantly retraced his footsteps back through the village. Feeling calmer, he slowed his pace to a dawdle, finally coming to a halt by the church's lychgate. He pushed it open and went inside, where two ancient oak benches lined the walls, sheltered from the elements by the gate's pitched roof. The graveyard didn't bother him. His uncle was there, and other loved ones, quietly resting beneath their stones, with the daffodils fluttering and bobbing over them, white-faced in the moonlight, like friendly ghosts. It was peaceful and he allowed his mind to visit the thought that had so troubled him.

He wasn't given to introspection—that way danger lay—but now he cautiously explored the suggestion that he might've been responsible for Emily's death. The thought held little terror now;

the mere idea of it was ridiculous. He wasn't the nameless fate that befell her. He'd loved his sister, they all had, and he'd wanted nothing more than to look after her and keep her safe. Her image floated before him, Emily, sitting on their mother's lap, those maternal arms wrapped around her—so loving, so tender. His mother, of course! She was the reason for his thoughts, that bitch and her insinuations, her voice, ripe with accusation: *What is it you wouldn't tell us, Jeremy? Why do you pretend?* She was the one who'd put that poison in his mind and made him doubt himself, nothing more. Even now, from beyond the grave, she was still messing with his head.

He left shelter of the lychgate, suddenly eager to be home, hurrying past the neighboring houses hunched in the moonlight. A bedroom light flicked on at one of the windows, and for a moment a shadowy silhouette looked out at the night.

Back in the bedroom he found Sarah awake, illuminated in the glow of her bedside lamp.

"Jeremy, where have you been?" There was no anger in her voice, just weariness. She was well past anger now.

"I thought I heard something moving outside, so I nipped out to check. It's fine though, I couldn't see anything, so it must've just been the wind."

She looked steadily at him. "Don't lie to me, Jeremy. I've been awake for a quarter of an hour and you didn't just nip out anywhere. Your side of the bed was already stone cold when I woke up, so where did you go?"

He rubbed his face with his hands and sighed. "I went for a walk, Sarah, that's all."

In the lamplight her eyes looked too sparkly, too bright, and Jeremy didn't think he could bear it if she cried. He sat down and she took his hand in hers, interlacing her fingers with his.

"Jeremy, I've always loved you, almost from the very start, but there's always been this part of you that's shut off to me. I've kind of accepted it over the years, I've understood there were things in your past you didn't want to share—"

He interrupted her. "It was never that I didn't want—"

"Shush, Jeremy, let me finish. I've been okay with it, but now I realize that I didn't really understand until you told me about Emily and about your mother, I didn't get how much you've been damaged."

He went to pull his hand away. "I'm not *damaged*. I've always tried to be a good person—"

"Jeremy, don't." Her voice broke and a solitary tear splashed onto his hand. "I don't mean you're not a good person, I'm not talking about that. What I'm saying is all these things that you've been through, they've damaged you—probably way more than you realize. None of it's your fault, I'm not saying that either. I'm just scared by what's happening at the moment."

She reclaimed his hand and squeezed it. "You're stirring up memories of things you've suppressed for a reason, and if I'm honest, I'm afraid of what you might find."

Her words brought a resurgence of his earlier fear. "What do you mean? What are you afraid I'm going to find?"

"I don't know, but I don't think you'll be able to deal with it if it's . . . if it's something bad. Can't you see how weird you've been, ever since our holiday? It's like tonight, going off God knows where in the middle of the night. Normal people don't do things like that."

"It wasn't like that, I just went for a walk."

Sarah shook her head. "I don't care. I don't want us to stay here any longer. I want us to go home tomorrow and for you to get some help, like I asked. I know you said earlier that you'd think about it, but I know how stubborn you are. Listen to me, Jeremy, I don't want us to lose you. What if you find out something that . . . I don't want to see you broken . . ."

Her words tailed away and she started to cry for real.

Jeremy pulled her toward him, aware of a slight resistance to his touch. "Shush, Sarah, please don't cry. I didn't mean to scare you, and it's not what you think, honestly. I did hear something outside and I did go out to check, I wasn't lying to you. It was just that when I came back to bed, I couldn't get back to sleep. I was wide awake and you were so fast asleep, I didn't want my tossing and turning to disturb you, so I went for a walk like I said."

He tilted her head to reveal her face, and saw the strangest expression there. It only flickered for a moment but it chilled him.

"Honestly, darling, I hadn't gone wandering off in some fugue state, or anything." He didn't mention the panic attack, nor did he ask her again what it was that she feared he'd find. He'd seen the look in her eyes and he couldn't bear to hear doubts on her tongue as well.

"I don't know if I can believe you anymore, Jez. One minute you seem okay, and then the next minute you're being all weird again. It's worrying me sick and I don't like what it's turning me into. I'm not used to playing the long-suffering wife, worrying and nagging at you like I've been. This isn't us, Jeremy."

He couldn't go home now; he needed a little bit longer.

"I'm fine, really I am, but I promise I'll make an appointment for when we get back. I'll ring Dr. Jessup tomorrow. It's pointless us going home when we're already halfway through clearing. We'll finish off what we're doing and put the house on the market like we'd planned, and then we'll go home."

He gave her what he hoped was a reassuring smile. "Please, Sarah. If you want to help me, then help finish things here. You're right in that I'm letting this place get under my skin, but I'll feel much better once it's all dealt with, I know I will."

Jeremy could sense her wavering and he held his breath.

Finally she gave a little nod of her head. "If you promise me that's all it was, and if you make an appointment like you say, then I suppose it makes sense to finish what we've started. But if you do anything else I don't like, we're going straight home. I mean it."

"Thank you, darling. It'll be okay, you'll see." He gave her a little squeeze. "Come on, let's go to bed. We can always talk again in the morning. God, it must be nearly two and the kids will be up at seven."

He undressed and slipped into bed next to her, looping an arm around her to spoon her close. He was aware of a stiffness still running through her body, as if she was trying not to pull away from him, and he lay there, barely breathing, until dawn broke.

# 15

It was a colder, brighter day, but Sarah's mood hadn't lifted with the weather. Jeremy had phoned Carole Jessup's office and made an appointment for two weeks' time, but it seemed she wasn't entirely mollified. Jeremy sensed, or perhaps imagined, something distant about her, a slight reservation that had never been there before.

Together they'd packed the last boxes of glasses and chinaware, bar the few things they'd need for their stay. Now, Jeremy was standing in the hallway looking up the stairs, his fingers absently fondling the little carved mouse. The intricacy of his ears and the fineness of his tail brought to mind the pole for opening the loft hatch, with its carved handle like an ear of wheat, and he realized they hadn't even thought to check the attic. He made his way up the stairs and surveyed the hatch above with a sense of foreboding.

The pole used to live in the gap between the door frames of the bathroom and the back bedroom but it wasn't there, so he went into the room the children were sharing, where the air still held their scent: that mixture of bath foam and damp hair, and the particular aroma of child. The two single beds were neatly made, Lucy's with her cuddly toys, the friends she couldn't leave behind. Jack's unadorned bar his faithful bear. The sight made him smile. He'd always brought a companion on his visits too, a pair of familiar eyes for company in the nighttime. Lucy's dinosaur, Fuddlewuddle, had slipped onto the floor, so Jeremy picked him up, laying him with his head on her pillow. As he tucked the quilt around the little toy, he felt that familiar tug at his heartstrings, the pull of his troubled love.

The children were in the garden, making the best of the dry weather, and through the window he could see them kicking a ball between the overgrown flower beds, where deadheads weighed down the plants. He looked past where they were playing, to the end of the garden and the land beyond the gap in the fence. From his vantage point he could see that the grass had been cleared and some of the ground was pegged out into plots ready for more homes. Soon this place would be hemmed in by houses, the view of the fields and the woods nothing but a lost memory. It made him feel melancholy so he turned away and spotted the pole he was looking for propped against the wardrobe.

The hook neatly slotted into the catch on the loft door, releasing the hatch and the ladder. Tentatively Jeremy climbed the steps and poked his head into the loft space. He faced a sea of boxes and items of furniture, and all the paintings and prints that had once lined his uncle's stairs. With a growing heartsink he realized it'd take them days to go through it all.

Inside the loft space, the air was still and warm. Slightly musty and wood scented, it felt like old air trapped in time, and Jeremy breathed it in as he surveyed the dust-laden boxes. It appeared that most of Ian's life had been packed away up here and he wondered who'd done it, for he could hardly imagine his mother willingly taking on such a task. Maybe it was George who'd dealt with Ian's effects, those long fingers tenderly taking each memory and stowing it safely away.

At the thought of George, Jeremy was transported back to those long summer evenings after his family had left for home. Dinner on the terrace, or one of Ian's barbeques, his uncle in his striped apron, smiling at them from across the lawn. The spit and crackle of fat on hot charcoal, the air blue-hazed with smoke. He suddenly wondered if George was still alive. They'd seemed so old to him back then, but Ian couldn't have been much over fifty when Emily died, and George was a few years younger. He'd probably be in his late seventies now, so entirely possible. He was someone who would properly remember Jeremy's past and not view it through the lens of a frightened child. Then Jeremy recalled the last time he'd seen him and he rippled with an old shame. Maybe not.

There was a traveling trunk pushed against one of the roof supports, and Jeremy smoothed the years of dust from its surface. Lifting the lid, he stared in confusion at what appeared at first glance to be an animal pelt. He pushed it to one side to reveal a jumble of clothing and hats, a riot of fabrics and faded colors. A cloud of dusty particles assaulted his nostrils as realization dawned. It was the dressing-up box from when they were children, and he marveled at the fact that it was still there after all these years. His fingertips ran across the moth-eaten fur of the stole, and a memory stirred. Him, in a moment of devilment, telling his sister it belonged to the big, bad wolf, that it was his winter coat and that one day he'd come back to claim it; her eyes like shining saucers as she'd devoured his every word. Little Red Riding Hood and the Three Little Pigs became the inhabitants of her nightmares, and in the night she often cried wolf. He determinedly closed the lid—he couldn't face that yet.

Before he could feel any guilt at his childhood teasing, he heard Sarah calling.

"Jeremy, what're you doing? We've got this other box of kitchen stuff to take to charity. Would you rather I went this time?"

"Yes, you go. I'll stay here with the kids." He was obviously not to be trusted out on his own anymore. "Anyway, you don't want to know what I've just found!"

She came to the foot of the stairs. "Why, what's up? What is it?"

"The attic is rammed to the gunnels with a load of junk. It looks like everything of Ian's that would fit has just been shoved up here and forgotten about. It'll take us days to go through it all."

The exasperation was evident in her voice. "We haven't got *days*, Jez. Surely we don't need to look through it. If it's been up there all this time, there can't be anything that's that important. If we just fetch it down the house clearers can take what they want and the rest can go to the tip."

It seemed wrong, almost sacrilegious, to just throw it all away without even checking. This was Ian's life, and there might be photos or things that Jeremy would like to keep.

"Jez?"

"Okay, we'll talk about it when you get back, but I don't mind looking through some of it."

She didn't answer and he sensed her frustration humming in the air. She could do this, transmit her feelings like radio waves. He heard her move away toward the front door and he breathed a sigh of relief. He didn't need any more confrontation.

Lowering the lid on the trunk, he sat back on his heels before randomly opening one of the boxes. It was packed with reference books, all Ian's tomes on natural history. They certainly weren't going to the tip. He stood up to examine the paintings that were stacked against the wall, and as he did, he heard the sound of the front door opening and swinging inward on its hinges with a bang.

"Jeremy, I need you to come down here."

There was some intonation in Sarah's voice that made the hairs on the back of his neck stand to attention. It was a mixture of urgency and fear. He descended the ladder and rushed to join her, taking the stairs two at a time. She'd already gone back outside and was now standing on the driveway just looking at their car. Confused eyes followed hers and then he saw it; black painted letters carelessly sprayed on the side of the vehicle.

"Jesus Christ! What the . . ."

His voice trailed off as his brain caught up with the sight before him: MURDERER. Someone had sprayed the word on the side of their car. For a moment the air stilled and Jeremy was rendered speechless, then a burst of anger carried him down the drive to the car.

"What the fuck!"

The sense of threat—and exposure—heightened his rage and he frantically scrubbed at the letters, but the paint was long dry. He thought of the noises he'd heard in the night and thumped his fists on the bonnet. He'd have caught them if only he'd been quicker. Impotent fury overtook him, and he kicked at the tires of the helpless car, over and over, in frustration and unacknowledged fear.

"I'll fucking kill them when I find out who did this." Oblivious to the irony, he turned to Sarah. "I *told* you I heard someone. Well whoever it was, they're not getting away with this."

She didn't answer and he became aware of how still she was, how quiet, as though frozen with shock.

"Sarah! Where's your phone? We need to call the police!"

Her eyes met his but he couldn't read the expression there.

"Why would someone do this to us, Jez? Why would they write something like that?"

"For God's sake, Sarah, it doesn't mean anything. It's just senseless vandalism."

She just stood there, looking at him and he felt his anger veer toward her. "What? You think it means something? That it's directed at what, us? Or me? Fuck's sake, Sarah, what are you saying?"

He was aware that he was yelling but he couldn't help it. He was angry, and somewhere under that anger, the fear was beginning to register. The coincidence unnerved him, the way it resonated with the thoughts he'd had the previous night.

"I'm not saying anything, only . . ."

"Only what Sarah?" He struggled to control his voice. "Some mindless idiot did this, that's all. It's probably their idea of a sick joke. Well, they might think it's funny now, but they won't when I've caught them."

Even as he spoke, his mind skipped to Sally and the women in the supermarket. They'd looked about the right age to have teenage children; the kind of loutish, knuckle-dragging mouth-breathers who would do something like this. He imagined them gossiping at home, that slack-jawed boy speculating with his mates, and he felt a surge of fury.

Sarah unfroze and took the tiniest step back from him, wariness evident in her eyes.

"All I meant, Jez, was why would anyone do something so malicious? They don't even know us. It doesn't make any sense."

Her lips were saying the right thing but her eyes said something different. There was a shadow of doubt there, and it infuriated Jeremy further. He could feel the pressure building in his head. The lack of sleep, his panic the previous night, and now this—it all conspired and he found himself yelling at her like a madman.

"You think *I* did something, don't you! Go on, say it! I can see it in your eyes. Christ, you've been married to me for all these years and all it takes is for some . . . some fucker to do something like this and then you look at me like *I've* done something wrong! I don't believe you . . ." He was being irrational but this had shaken him to the core. "You think I did this to the car last night, is that it? Or what, that it's aimed at *me*, that I've killed . . . someone?" He wouldn't say *Emily*.

Sarah raised her voice too, but it was more in desperation than anger.

"Jez, will you stop shouting! You're being paranoid. I'm not thinking anything of the sort, so just stop it! Stop yelling like some lunatic—it doesn't help."

Jeremy opened his mouth to retort but the words died on his lips. Jack had appeared round the side of the house with Lucy in tow, their game disturbed by the shouting. The boy's eyes were wide with alarm, and they darted from Sarah to his father then back again. Jeremy watched as he registered the word on the car, he saw how his face paled.

"Dad?" he said, and there was a questioning, upward inflection in his voice.

Jeremy's rage subsided as quickly as it had risen, and he realized he was shaking. He forced himself to make his voice steady.

"It's okay, son. It's nothing for you to worry about. No one's hurt or anything, some stupid person has vandalized the car, that's all. That's what all the noise was about. Take your sister and go back in the garden. We'll be through in a minute."

Confusion clouded his face. "But, Dad, why have they written—?"

Sarah stepped in, calm and collected as ever, her equanimity restored by the need to limit any upset to the children. "It's just someone being stupid, like Dad says. Be a good boy, Jack, and go and keep Lucy occupied while we sort this out. We don't want her being upset by it. She's only little and she won't understand."

As always, her appeal to his elder status won him over. He hesitated for just a moment, another question poised on his lips but then his eyes meet Jeremy's and he thought better of it.

"Come on, Luce, let's go and watch something."

With one last wary glance in his father's direction, he took his sister's hand and led her away. In the silence that followed Jeremy took a few deep breaths before turning to Sarah.

"I didn't mean to shout, I'm sorry. It's just that this kind of caught me on the raw. It just feels so personal, and like you said, it's so malicious. I don't understand any more than you do why someone would want to write that."

One of the neighbors had come outside, alerted by the noise, and now was staring across at them, an elderly man, stoop shouldered, with a lined and weathered face. Jeremy watched as curiosity and concern did battle across his features and felt himself begin to reignite once more. Sarah saw him too and hurriedly gestured toward the house.

"Leave it, Jez, please. Come on back inside and we'll call the police."

# 16

They were waiting for an answer but the words seemed wedged in his throat. The police officer framed the question again.

"So, you say you heard something in the night. Around what time would that've been, sir?"

Jeremy forced himself to look at him and to keep his expression open and neutral, because an unwarranted evasiveness had crept into his manner. It was the word on the car that made him feel uncomfortable, the way it seemed to point to some unknown guilt. He thought he saw the same speculation in the eyes of the officer, as if to say, *Why that word, exactly?*

He was around Jeremy's own age but leaner and fitter. All that chasing down of criminals, Jeremy presumed. Pleasingly, he had noticeably less hair, and Jeremy ran his fingers through his own in an expansive gesture designed to belittle. He knew the police were there to help, but he found their presence vaguely threatening, as though one of them would suddenly whip out the handcuffs and charge him with some crime he didn't know he'd committed. The other officer said little, just jotted down the odd note in his neat little book. He was younger and fresh-faced, with the kind of shiny, scrubbed-looking skin and strawberry-blond hair that was scared of the summer.

"It must've been somewhere around one, I think. I went down to have a look around but I couldn't see anyone. The road was clear and I didn't hear anyone either."

"And did you notice anything amiss with the car then?"

"No. It was dark and I wasn't really sure if I'd heard anything or not. I just glanced around the garden, then looked up and down the road, and then I went back to bed." He didn't mention going for a walk afterward. "I didn't really think to check the car, I was more concerned that someone was looking to break into the house. It'd been empty for a while."

The atmosphere was reminiscent of the time after Emily, when the house had been filled with police, day after day. They hadn't been uniformed officers like these; back then they were detectives, plain clothed and somber, and they'd scared Jeremy half to death. They were watchful and suspicious of foul play, troubled by the fact that Emily was found without her shoes. They'd questioned everyone, his family and the neighbors, even his mates. No one escaped—except maybe a killer.

> *The detective crouched down to bring herself to eye level. He heard the moist little pop of her knee as it bent. All the sounds in the room seemed too loud, from the noise of his breathing to the rustle of his father's clothing as he shifted on the sofa beside him. He averted his gaze, looking instead at the dizzying loops and swirls of the carpet. His glance strayed to his trainers, still stained with brackish water and mud, and his heart did a queasy flip in his chest.*

*"I'm just going to ask you a few wee questions about yesterday. It's nothing for you to be worried about and your dad's going to be here with you all the time."*

*She flicked a reassuring smile at his father, and the boy felt the firm pressure of a paternal hand on his shoulder.*

*"I just want you to tell us in your own words what you can remember about yesterday. Where you and your friends went and what yous all did."*

*He noticed she didn't mention Emily, not then. She didn't even speak her name, and he was glad.*

*The detective's voice was gentle, with a soft Scottish burr. Encouraged, he dared to raise his eyes. She had a kind face. Soft brown hair was cropped close to her head, with a slight curl that made him randomly think of the calves in the fields, of the soft whirls of hair at their foreheads.*

*He felt the words swell in his throat. It would be so easy to set them free, to tell it all to her soft, kind face. He could anticipate the relief of speaking but he knew he could not, he must not. He felt the pressure of his father's fingers, the hard pads of the fingertips against his collarbone, and he clamped his lips tight shut.*

The police officer asked a few more general questions and then got to what he really wanted to know.

"I have to level with you sir, the chances of finding out who did this are extremely low, given what you've told us so far. Close to zero in fact, unless there's anything else you can add, anything more specific?"

When Jeremy didn't respond he added, "Anyone with a grudge against you? Anyone local who you might have had a run-in with?"

Jeremy didn't bother to mention the elderly woman in the high street. She was unlikely to have crept up the drive in the dead of night to vandalize his car—although on reflection she looked quite capable of it, those meaty hands wielding a spray can.

"God no. There's no one like that. We've only been here since the weekend and we don't even know anyone around here." He hesitated and then added, "Well, at least not anyone recently."

The officer's eyes met his. "It's just it seems very targeted and I wondered if you had any idea why they would single you out, and write that in particular? I'm just looking for anything specific that could give us an idea of where to start."

There appeared to be a hint of accusation in the policeman's gaze, and there was no mistaking the way his colleague shifted slightly in his chair, his interest suddenly piqued.

"You said recently sir, so you've been here before?"

"Look, I haven't been back here for over thirty years but this was originally my uncle's house and we . . . me and my parents that is, we used to come here for the summer. There was a family tragedy way back. My—" his throat closed on the words and he coughed to release them "—my sister drowned in the lake in the woods, back when I was a child." He looked him straight in the eye. "The circumstances were kind of unexplained and there was a big investigation at the time. I can only assume somebody remembered it, or heard about it, and this was their idea of a joke. I don't get why that would be the case, but it's all I can think of that's in any way relevant. Otherwise, it's just completely random vandalism." He was aware he was babbling.

The officer's expression softened with something like sympathy—or as if a worry had been resolved.

"You can check if you like," Jeremy added, with a sudden urge to convince them. "It'll all be there in the records."

The younger officer scribbled something down in his notebook and Jeremy pictured them eagerly rushing back to the station to check old case files. Well good luck with that. He'd never consciously covered up what had happened back then, but bringing it out in the open made him feel vulnerable. Unsafe. It made him wonder if their sympathy might be tinged by doubt, wondering if beneath his benign exterior lurked something truly wicked. He felt sweat begin to prickle along his spine and the shiftiness edged back in. His features felt wooden, their expression of innocence unconvincing, but the police didn't seem to notice.

They asked for a few more details, who the family had spoken to since they'd been there, how long they might be staying, and then they took some photos of the car. Before leaving they issued Jeremy with a reference number and the promise to be in touch if anything turned up—neither of which inspired much optimism. He watched them as they walked down the drive to their car and realized he was holding his breath.

Sarah was making coffee in the kitchen, and Jeremy registered a certain tension in her body.

"That's decided it, we're going home. I'd already said I didn't want to stay here any longer, and after this I'm not sure that it's even safe. This has to be a reference to what happened with your sister. Why else would someone write that?" There was a whisper of fear in her voice, and a hint of defiance. "Regardless of what you said to the police, it seems there *is* someone out there with some-thing against you, and the fact they still feel so strongly about it after all these years, and would do something like this is actually quite scary."

When he didn't respond she continued, "It's creepy and it's threat-ening, Jez, and I don't like it. We need to think of the children as well. I take it you saw how scared Jack looked? He's not a baby, he could see what they'd written and how much it upset you, and he's going to start asking questions."

Jeremy looked at the stubborn set of her jaw and experienced a flare of irritation. "For God's sake, Sarah, we talked about it last night and I'm hardly going to go running back home now because of this. You can't seriously think it's a threat."

"It's not running away, Jez, it's just being sensible."

"It's going to be kids, that's all."

"You don't know that. It could've been anyone."

"I don't think so. I reckon it's something to do with those women in the supermarket. I can just imagine that Sal filling them up with all the so-called details, making up what she didn't know. I bet me pitching up here was the first bit of excitement they've had in ages, and they probably started gossiping the minute we'd left. It'd only have taken the dopey-looking kid that was with them to have said something to his mates—"

"But how did they know which house to go to? That doesn't make any sense, Jez."

It seemed nothing he'd said recently made much sense. "'Course it does. Sally knew where my uncle lived, so does Laura. God, I think I even said we were staying at the house, so it didn't take a genius to work it out. Anyway, I can remember Sally, she always seemed a bit rough, so she's probably got exactly the kind of kids that'd do something like this."

He felt his obstinacy biting; the contrariness that made him dig in his heels.

"Look, Sarah, we came here to do a job and I'm not going home until it's finished. We went over all of this last night and nothing's really changed. In any case, we can hardly drive home with the car like that."

He could see from her face that she hadn't considered this, so he pressed home his advantage.

"God, Sarah, we can't exactly go driving across the country with that emblazoned on the side—imagine the neighbors" reaction. Tell you what—I'll contact the insurers and arrange for it to be fixed, and then I'll book us a courtesy car for the rest of the week."

He was talking at her, not giving her any chance to put up more objections because a mounting excitement was taking the place of his anger. This could've been an attempt to drive him out, to make him go home, and that could mean someone was afraid of what he might know. He buzzed with the possibility that the truth could be finally so near, and completely overlooked—or denied—the fact that it could mean somebody knew what he'd *done*.

"And if Jack asks questions, I'll talk to him, okay? Not to Lucy, she's too young, but Jack is old enough to understand."

There was a hard-edged resignation in Sarah's eyes. "You really want to do this, don't you? It doesn't matter what I think—you really want to push this to the limit."

She was right, he really did.

Jeremy took his coffee through to the sitting room to sulk and to see if he could find anything on the internet about removing spray paint from bodywork, anything to make what was written there a bit less obvious.

He called through to Sarah, "Sarah, have you got any non-acetone nail varnish remover?"

"Not with me, why?"

"It says here you can sometimes remove spray paint with it, so I thought I'd give it a go. That way we could at least use the car until the insurers sort something out."

He thought about her concerns for the children and her desire to go home, and how much easier it would be for him to work at finding Ben if they weren't around.

"If I managed to do a good enough job on it, maybe you and the kids could go home? It might actually be easier to arrange the insurers to sort the car out locally."

Sarah appeared in the doorway, a frown pinching the skin between her brows. "What, and you stay here on your own?"

"Why not? You were right, Jack did look really upset earlier, and I don't want that, plus we've pretty much finished. There's nothing much left except the bits we're using, so all that's really left to do is for me to sort through the stuff in the attic."

"But Jez, why don't you just get it all down and leave the house clearance people to deal with it? I've already booked them, and if I moved them forward to tomorrow you could come back with us."

She came and stood next to him, resting her hand on his head. He noticed a slight pause between her stretching out her arm and actually touching him.

"Come on, we could drop the keys off with the agent and then deal with everything by phone and email."

She ruffled his hair with her hand, a deliberate gesture as if to dispel her previous reticence.

"Maybe I overreacted a bit last night, but I still don't like the thought of leaving you here on your own."

"Sarah, I don't want to just dump all Uncle Ian's stuff. It's difficult to explain, but I feel I owe it to him because he's one of my few happy memories. Look, I *want* to do it, but it's pointless you and the children staying as well. I'll be fine. I honestly think it'll do me good."

She perched on the arm of his chair. "I don't understand why it's so important to you. It's hardly like you to be sentimental."

He pulled her down onto his lap. "It just is, okay? Coming back here has made me think about people I've not given a thought to in years. These were people who loved me, good friends, and I've just shut my mind to them all."

Good friends who might hold the key to the past. Suddenly it was massively important that he had that time on his own.

"If I want to get my head straight, I think I've got to start facing up to things. It'll be cathartic. I feel like it'll give me some closure."

He knew she liked that kind of thing, and although it was manipulative it was also true. He did need to devote some time to the past. "Look, we both know I've been a bit of a pig just recently. I've explained why, but that still doesn't excuse it. This'll give me some time on my own to think things through and reset my head."

"I don't know, Jez . . ."

Jeremy was warming to his theme, anything to make her go. "Tell you what, why don't you take the kids and spend a couple of days with your parents instead? They'll love that, and this way you'll be nearer to here. It'll save you driving all the way home and you can come back and pick me up at the weekend. It's Wednesday tomorrow, so that'll give me a couple of days to finish off here and then we're done."

Sarah wavered. The thought of a few days with her parents did have a certain appeal. "But what about the car?"

"Let's see if I can get rid of the worst of it, then we can sort it out properly when we get home. And look, if anything else happens, or if I feel off in any way, I'll ring you and you can come and get me. Promise."

"Okay, if you're sure . . . I suppose it is only a couple of days, and it would be nice to see Mum and Dad." Decided, she stood up. "I'd better give Mum a ring to check it's okay, but it sounds like a plan."

She went to find her phone while relief flooded through him.

A quick jog to the chemist and he'd found what he needed, and now he took a last look at his handiwork. There was still a dull streak along the side of the car, but the hateful word was no longer legible. The driver's window purred down and Sarah looked out at him, doubt and a soupçon of relief flickering behind her eyes. He'd persuaded her to leave that afternoon and didn't want her changing her mind. A couple of hours' drive and they'd be safely at her parents' house; Barbara would have tea ready on the table and both children tucked up in bed by their usual bedtimes. He tried to convince himself that it was their best interests he had at heart.

"Are you sure you're not just trying to get rid of me for some reason?" She searched his face, unsure what she was looking for. "I've never known you so keen to see the back of me."

He leaned in the window and dropped a kiss on Sarah's lips, hoping he'd misread that second's hesitation, as if she wanted to flinch away.

"Don't be daft, 'course I'm not, I love having you around. I just thought it'd be nice for you and the children to have a bit of time with your parents, that's all, and it saves us having to do dinner tonight."

Her eyes scanned his, and he wondered what she was searching for.

"I'll be fine. Remember what I said, I promise."

He stood back from the car, blowing last kisses to the children. "Drive carefully lovely, and you two be good for Grandma and Grandad. Love you loads."

She reversed out of the drive and he waved until the car turned at the end of the road and was lost from sight. He stood there for a moment as dusk softly fell, feeling strangely bereft yet relieved. Determinedly he buried the memory of the doubt in Sarah's eyes.

# 17

Showered and dressed in a clean shirt and jeans, Jeremy surveyed himself in the mirror. He had an even-featured face that didn't quite make it to handsome but came close, maybe lacking that certain engaging sparkle needed to elevate it. Benign, if a little bland, it certainly wasn't a murderer's face. He took a couple of deep breaths and tried to force the word out of his mind. It troubled him on some level far deeper than just the vandalism to his car. His brain had caught up, and now he couldn't help wondering if somebody did it because of what *they* knew rather than what he might know. He shook his head and turned away from the guilty eyes watching from the mirror. He grabbed his wallet and the house keys and set off for the pub, his mission to find Mark McLeish.

The Swan had Happy Hour from six until eight, Monday through Thursday, and it had drawn more customers than he'd encountered the previous lunchtime. The same aging hipster was behind the bar, this time accompanied by a rake-thin woman with lustrous, jet-black hair. He eased his way through a motley throng of mostly male drinkers, and greeted her with a smile.

"What can I get you, love?" she asked, and he settled for a pint of lager before turning to survey the room. The lights were dimmed to a mellow glow that masked the daylight shabbiness and made the drinkers shine, creating the illusion that this genuinely was a rare hour of carefree happiness.

There was no one there who elicited even a flicker of recognition, and no one gave Jeremy so much as a passing glance. The taproom was almost full, mainly with after-workers, groups of men and the occasional woman chewing over the details of their day. There were sufficient numbers of solitary drinkers to render his singular state unremarkable; again mostly men, either with no homes to go to or ones they'd rather avoid for as long as possible, gazing dead-eyed into their drinks. He took his pint and found a free table by the window, well positioned to scan the room and watch the comings and goings. A door at the end of the bar indicated that there was a "saloon" next door—very Wild West—but he sensed Mark McLeish would be a public bar drinker, so stayed settled where he was

He took a mouthful of his drink and felt the ice-cold lager tracking down his throat as he relaxed back into his seat. It was then that he saw him, Mark McLeish. He might have been just sixteen when Jeremy last knew him but he recognized him instantly, even though he was taller, muscular, and fit, with tattooed forearms. There was something in his bearing and in the set of his jaw that peeled back the years, revealing the shadow of the boy he'd once been. He was with a small group of men who looked like builders or farm workers at a guess, and Jeremy sensed that he was the alpha male. It was the lazy confidence in his manner and the way in which he was doing most of the talking while the others listened. He leaned back against the bar and his flat eyes flitted round the room, sliding over Jeremy without interest or recognition. He'd lost the air of wariness he had as a boy; it had since been replaced with the easy assertiveness of a man comfortable in his own skin. Jeremy had hoped he might be recognized—it would've made striking up a conversation that much easier—but Mark's attention returned to his group of friends, so he took another mouthful of his drink and considered his next move. He was aware of a twinge of apprehension, a leftover from childhood.

He picked up his pint and sauntered over to stand near the group, signaling to the barman on the pretext of ordering a packet of peanuts. He wanted to create the impression that whatever happened next was just a chance encounter, he didn't want it to appear as though he was needily seeking Ben. He glanced over at the group and allowed his eyes to settle on Mark.

"Good God! It's Mark, isn't it? Mark McLeish?"

The group fell silent and Jeremy felt a tingle of anticipation.

"Who is it wants to know?"

The words were vaguely aggressive but the face wasn't. Mark McLeish benignly regarded Jeremy, a faint smile on his lips but his eyes belied any warmth in his expression. Not overtly hostile, but there was a hint of menace lurking beneath his gaze, and Jeremy was struck by the uncomfortable certainty that if anyone meant him harm, if anybody upset him in any way, then retribution would be swift and brutal. He understood that Mark didn't need to bully or posture; he knew, and the world around him knew, that he was not a man to be messed with. His pupils dilated, and for a split second Jeremy glimpsed something surprisingly akin to fright but it vanished before he could name it. It was replaced by a look of calm recognition.

"Well fuck me! Jay Horton! Laura said that she'd seen you around but I couldn't quite believe it. Seemed crazy to me that you'd ever set foot back here, but seems I was wrong for once." His eyes took on a mocking quality as he looked Jeremy up and down. "Ooh, haven't you grown."

Someone in the group sniggered, a large, belligerent-looking man with cold, pale eyes, and Jeremy felt a spurt of irritation at Mark's manner. He was trying to make him look small, to make him feel how he'd felt as a child. He'd probably sensed Jeremy's wariness back then, and for some reason he was playing on it now, which didn't make any sense. They'd never had a falling-out or any issue with each other at all. Most of the time Jeremy had remained an insignificance, a child beneath his notice. He decided to ignore the comment and assumed an expression he hoped matched his.

"Yeah, seems you were, and actually it's lucky I've bumped into you. I was hoping I might get a chance to catch up with Ben while I'm here. You wouldn't happen to know where I could find him?"

The sense of threat sharpened for a moment. It was there in the restless shuffling of feet and the heightened attention. One of the group bounced on the balls of his feet and Jeremy recoiled from the blatant aggression in his eyes. It felt personal, and he surreptitiously examined the man's face for any hint that he might once have known him. Mark stretched out a steadying hand and he settled back into the group, although his gaze remain locked on Jeremy.

"Why would you want to do that then?"

"If he's still around I just thought it'd be good to say hello, seeing as I'm here, that's all."

Mark grinned like a wolf. "And why do you think Ben would want to talk to you?"

Cold-eyes sniggered again, revealing a row of small uneven teeth. Jeremy wasn't stupid; he recognized what Mark was doing, deliberately turning everything into a question to put him on the back foot and make him look foolish. He didn't understand the motivation, unless it was to make Mark feel the bigger man. Anger bubbled up inside him, and suddenly he didn't care that the other man was probably fitter, stronger, and backed up by his Neanderthal mates. There was no reason for him to take that attitude, and no reason why he had to accept it.

"I see some things haven't changed around here. You always were a bit of an arsehole."

There was an intake of breath from the circle of men, and Jeremy watched as an answering anger flooded Mark's face. He held himself ready for the onslaught but instead Mark laughed, defusing the moment.

"Whoa, easy Tiger. I was only having a laugh, taking the piss like, but to be honest, I am at bit surprised at you wanting to make contact with him now. After, what, thirty-odd years?" His voice was suddenly accusatory. "He loved you, mate. He couldn't wait for you to pitch up here in the summer, and then you fucked off to that posh school of yours and he never heard another word from you. I might be an arsehole but I'm not a thoughtless bastard." He feigned deep thought. "Or was it that you had good reason for keeping yer head down?"

Jeremy was amazed that a childhood grudge would still rankle enough to be mentioned after all these years, and anyway, it hadn't been like that. Back then there'd been no internet, no mobile phones, no texting or WhatsApp. Ten-, eleven-year-old boys didn't spend their time chatting on the house phone—they weren't allowed, and anyway, he couldn't have chatted even if he'd wanted to. It hadn't been intentional; he'd been scared out of his wits, incapable of even thinking about this place, or the people in it. But he didn't have to justify himself to Mark. He opened his mouth to tell him just that but before he could speak, there was a commotion by the door, and a noisy group of women came into the bar. Jeremy heard a muffled groan come from one of Mark's companions.

Mark turned to the culprit with a grin. "That your missus, Steve? Looks like it's game over for you, mate."

Jeremy looked across at the women and saw that Laura was among them. He experienced an unexpected and totally unentitled twinge of disappointment at the possibility that she might be married to one of the boorish specimens beside him. She began to walk over, and as she reached the group, he realized with some relief that it was Mark she'd come to talk to. Her eyes tracked from Mark to Jeremy, and a small frown wrinkled her brow.

"Hello Mark, Jay."

"Hi, Laura."

She addressed her brother. "See, believe me now?"

"I didn't not believe you. What I couldn't believe was that he'd come back here after everything that happened. I'd just been telling the blokes here about—"

"Leave it, Mark," she said and there was a note of warning in her voice, a subtext Jeremy didn't understand. Her eyes met his. "He's not being a pain, is he?"

He went to answer, but she must've seen something in his expression because she rounded on her brother before he could speak. "What have you been saying, Mark? I don't get why you have to do this, I would've thought you'd have learned to keep your mouth shut by now."

His voice rose in mock indignation. "What? I haven't done anything. Honest to God, we'd hardly spoken two words before you lot came in."

She glared at him and he held up his hands. "Strewth, Laura, give it a rest." He gave Jeremy a conspiratorial look. "What is it with little sisters, eh? Always on my case, she is. You're a lucky man, mate, believe me."

He watched Jeremy recoil and was immediately all contrition. "Shit! Mate, I'm sorry. God, I'm an idiot. Sometimes I just open my big mouth . . ."

His shameface was smeared with apology, his eyes free from guile, but Jeremy couldn't quite accept that it was a slip of the tongue. He wanted to react, to shout and rage, but somehow he suspected that was what Mark wanted, so instead he said nothing. He looked at the blank shock on Laura's face and felt a surge of affection for her. He wouldn't embarrass her and make this worse; he'd rise above it.

Mark turned back to his friends and Jeremy sensed that he'd been dismissed. "Come on lads, let's take it over the road. No point in staying here now the girlies are in."

He heaved himself away from the bar and the others lumbered after him, leaving an awkward silence in their wake.

Jeremy was the first to break it. "God, what was all that about?"

Laura gently rested a hand on his arm and he felt the warmth of her through his sleeve.

"Sorry about that. Take no notice of Mark. He has some anger-management issues sometimes, that's all."

"You're telling me! All I did was ask him about Ben and he seemed about ready to kick off."

"Don't take any notice, he doesn't really mean it. He's a good bloke underneath. He always used to look out for Ben and me, protect us like, but somewhere along the line he's become angrier and kind of antagonistic with everyone. He did a stint in the army, in Afghanistan, and I don't think that helped, and since he's been out he's not really settled. It's sad, really." She jerked her head dismissively toward the door. "Some of the guys he hangs around with don't exactly help matters either. Like that lot. Three of them are local, but the fourth guy came back here with him when they got out of the army and he's a total thug."

Jeremy assumed she was referencing the grinning prick with the too-small teeth. He'd looked like he wanted to hurt something.

She sighed before continuing. "I dunno, Mark's got a wife that won't speak to him anymore, and two lovely kids he hardly sees. Everything seems to have gone wrong for him."

Jeremy felt he should probably say something in response but couldn't summon up any sympathy.

Laura seemed not to notice the omission. "He's got a nice house he's still paying for when he can, but he's not living there. He's out at one of the farms at the moment. Remember Blundell's, out on the main road? Well he's got a place there. He doesn't seem able to get his act together, he's just been doing casual work for the last few years. Drifting, really."

He noticed her friends had already got drinks and appeared to have missed her out. "Hey, do you want a drink or anything?"

"That'd be lovely, I'll have a gin and tonic, thanks." She pointed behind the bar. "A Tanqueray, please."

While they were waiting for her drink Jeremy became aware of her perfume. It was something dark and earthy, so different from the light floral notes of his wife. At the thought of Sarah he felt guilty for even noticing, and he tried to squeeze his nostrils shut against her tantalizing scent.

"There you go."

He passed her the G&T, and amber eyes met his. He was aware of that whisper of attraction, insidious and lethal.

"Thanks, Jay," she said, and that compounded it.

His old name on her tongue made something ripple along his spine. He looked at the bow of her lips and the scattering of freckles across her nose. If he had any sense he should go home, but he wanted to find Ben; that was his excuse and he was sticking to it. A warning flipped deep in his stomach—at least that was what he hoped it was—but he ignored it, and when she suggested they sit down, he willingly followed her to a table. Happy Hour had ended now and some of the earlier drinkers had left; others had hunkered down for the night, their happiness slowly dissipating.

"Don't you want to be with your friends?" he asked.

She shook her head, brown curls bobbing, and he noted how glad he was. "Not really. I can have a drink with them anytime, but it's not often I get the chance to sit down with Jay Horton." She smiled at him. "God, I had a proper little-girl crush on you back then."

Aargh! Don't tell him that. He didn't need to know.

"But you were only what, nine?"

"And? You were the older man." She grinned at him and his stomach flipped again. "You always seemed a bit sad, you know? Underneath, like. Even before your sister there was this little sadness, and it made me want to look after you." A fleeting melancholy shadowed her face. "I suppose I recognized it, looking back."

He was surprised by the depth of insight in one so young and had a sudden memory of her catching hold of his hand. The hot feel of her little palm in his.

He smiled back at her. "You had a lucky escape, I'd have been a big disappointment. Sadness gets tedious after a while—you should ask my wife."

"Oh, so you're married then?" He hoped he imagined the note of regret.

149

"Yes, I'm married to Sarah and we've got two children, Jack and Lucy." He wanted to get that out there just in case. "We're really happy."

He wasn't sure why he felt it necessary to confirm their emotional status and wondered who he was trying to convince. Nervously, he babbled on with more stuff she didn't need to know.

"We're living in London at the moment, but we might consider a change when Mum's estate is all settled. Being back here again has made me wonder if we might be better off in the countryside. More fresh air and space. Healthier for the kids, you know? London's great when you're single or even as a couple, but once you've got family it loses some of the attraction, when you can't go out as much and that . . ."

He bored himself to a halt and there was a vaguely awkward pause. Presumably that conversational gem had withered any remnant of her childhood crush.

"Cool."

There was a moment's silence—probably while she reassessed his attractiveness.

"So what about you? You married? Kids?"

"No and no," she said. He raised his eyebrows in surprise and she colored slightly. "I never really met the right person, I suppose."

It was hard to imagine that there'd never been anyone out there for her, but he noticed how her hand was clenching her glass in a shattering grip and suspected that there was history there somewhere. He wasn't one to probe dangerous personal territory, so he quickly changed the subject.

"What about your dad? Is he still around?"

She nodded and took another sip of her drink. "Yep, the old bastard's still dragging in air, more's the pity."

Something dark clouded her face and venom oozed from her voice. Jeremy had always found her father to be such a nice man, so he struggled to understand the reason for her manner.

"Wow, I always liked your dad. He was such a laugh and so different from mine, I was little bit jealous, to be honest."

She snorted into her glass. "God, be careful what you wish for. It wasn't all fun and ice pops, I can tell you that. It's funny, I always envied *you* your dad. He seemed so kind and gentle compared to ours."

"He was certainly that."

Jeremy pictured his father's face, and with it came a wave of melancholy. He'd been too gentle. Too kind to stand in the face of his wife, the harridan who now made her presence felt.

"I was so sorry to hear about your mum, Jay. I was too little to actually know her that well as a person, but I can remember how gorgeous looking she was. God, that hair! I never really knew my mother because I was only three when she died, but when I was little I always imagined her looking like your mum."

Good luck with that then. "Be careful what you wish for," he echoed. "In her case beauty really was only skin-deep."

He was aware of his own bitterness creeping in, so he pushed the conversation along; he wanted to know more about her, in a way that was perhaps inappropriate for such a happily married man.

"So where's your dad living now? He must've got a packet for selling the farm."

"He did okay. Not as well as he might have, though, because he'd already sold off some of the fields as arable land. Then, when the planners moved in, he realized his mistake and wised up a bit. He was definitely a bit more shrewd with the farmhouse and the remaining land." She shook her head regretfully. "The old fool ended up squandering a lot of it when he was younger, flash cars and stuff, and of course he's always liked the drink and the horses. Lost quite a bit on the gee-gees over the years, but he still had enough for one of those plush retirement apartments where the dairy used to be. He's still there, living like a pig in sh . . . clover."

Jeremy thought he now understood the bitterness and was a little disappointed that it seemed to be about money. Still, he could feel the dangerous pull of a kindred spirit and glanced away from the expression in her eyes. He could feel her glance burning through to his core.

"God, it's so good to see you again Jay. I've thought about you a lot since I saw you the other day, about what happened and that, and I'm glad you're here tonight because we didn't really get a chance to talk before."

They sat in silence for a few minutes. It wasn't awkward, instead it was strangely companionable, as if Jeremy had known her all his life. He felt guilty, even though he'd done nothing wrong—and never, ever would—but the trouble was, being married, loving someone with all your soul, didn't stop you from feeling attraction to someone else. What it hopefully stopped was you acting on it.

He went to the bar for another round of drinks, refusing Laura's offer to pay, and all the while he could sense the curious eyes of her friends. When he returned to their table she greeted him with a smile that made something inside him do a happy little somersault. Down, boy.

"Anyway," he resumed their conversation, steering it to where he wanted to go. He mustn't lose sight of the prize. "How's Ben? I was hoping to say hello if he's still around here. That's what I was trying to tell Mark before he got all chippy with me."

"Yep, he's still around. We all are now that Mark's back as well." She looked thoughtful. "It's funny how you can hate a place, be desperate to get away but somehow end up staying." She sighed. "Maybe we're all cowards deep down. Too scared to leave what we know even as we kick against it. Ben's the same. Even after uni and everything, he still managed to end up back here. I sometimes think this place is like a black hole, always sucking you back in."

Jeremy was surprised by how closely she'd echoed his own thoughts about the place, and was struck once more by that sense of kinship.

"Do you think Ben would want to see me?"

"God, yes. Whyever wouldn't he?"

"It's just Mark implied that I'd really hurt him when we were kids, by not staying in touch . . ." He felt the need to justify himself to her. "It was such a dark time, you've no idea . . ."

His words tailed away and for a moment he had the urge to tell her everything, and that shocked him. It had taken ten years and a crisis before he told Sarah, yet here he was, ready to spill his guts to a stranger.

"Ben was upset, I won't lie to you, but it wasn't with you exactly. It was the whole thing with your sister. I might have only been a kid, but even I could see the way it affected everyone, you couldn't really miss it. Everyone we knew seemed to be touched by it in some way, it was like something dark had settled here and it scared people. God, it was weeks before any of us kids were allowed to play in the woods."

Her gaze turned inward, remembering. "I suppose, looking back as an adult, it was because no one really knew what had happened, whether it was an accident or . . . or something else. It made people wonder, her being a child and everything . . ." She gave her head a little shake, as if to dispel the memory. "Anyway, Ben's always been . . . sensitive, and I think it probably preyed on his mind more than most. I could see how upset he was and he couldn't exactly talk to Dad—or Mark, for that matter. They were too busy . . ."

She suddenly colored and tried to change the subject. "Anyway, let's not dredge up all of that . . ."

Jeremy leaned forward. "Too busy with what?" he asked, troubled by the way she'd clammed up on him. "What were you going to say?"

"Nothing. Just leave it, Jay."

"No, because it's obviously something. What were you about to tell me?"

She sighed and her gaze slid away over his shoulder. "They were too busy speculating. I'd hear them talking sometimes, and Mark seemed to have got it into his head that maybe you had something to do with it, and the minute Dad got wind of it he just egged him on."

*"What?"* His voice rose, shocked, incredulous. "What, that I had something to do with *Emily*?"

An unexpected hurt bloomed in his chest at the notion of Mr. McLeish saying such things about him.

"No, not exactly. You have to remember I was only a child and I might've got it wrong but I think there was like this insinuation, 'If you ask me, it's all a bit odd, the brother finding her like that,' that kind of thing. I'm not really sure who started it, it might even have been Dad who said it first." She saw his face. "God, Jay, don't be upset. If you think about it, there was bound to be speculation, people are just like that. I must admit though, looking back, I'm a bit surprised by Markie, but it's what you'd expect from my father, malicious old bastard."

"Did . . . did Ben think that too?"

"No, of course he didn't. Anyway, he was only a kid. I think he was more scared than anything. It was just Dad and Mark stirring things up."

She was troubled by his expression. "You have to understand, everyone seemed different after what happened. Ben was totally withdrawn, Mark was more aggressive. Nothing like that had ever happened around here, and it sent a ripple through everything. Most people believed it was an accident, but the few that didn't, they wanted someone to blame, and if they blamed you they didn't have to consider that it might be someone local. They didn't have to worry whether their children were safe." She paused and looked worried. "Look, I wish I hadn't said anything. Just forget it, Jay. It doesn't mean anything and it was years ago. God, everyone bar us has forgotten all about it."

He wanted to believe her, but he recalled the expressions on the faces of the women in the shop, the damage to his car, that woman accosting him in the street, and he wasn't so sure.

"I'm not so sure . . ." He related his encounter in the high street, describing the aggression and the woman's accusatory tone. He didn't mention the car though, it was too raw, and it resonated too much with what she'd just told him.

She considered what he'd said. "That sounds like Ann-Marie's mother. Remember Ann-Marie? She used to hang out with Mark and Sally, her mother owned the sweet shop?"

Dimly he could remember a slim hawk-eyed woman, jealously guarding the gobstoppers from her perch behind the counter. Never in a million years would he have equated her with that bovine elder, bellowing her prejudice in the street.

"Well she's certainly not forgotten about it."

"Honestly, Jay, forget it. They're just stupid people. You have to remember how insular this place is and how that breeds small minds." She cocked her head to the side, questioningly. "Why does it matter to you, anyway? Why do you even care what they said?"

The words broke free of their own volition, his voice barely a whisper. It sounded like a confession, as though they might be right. "Because it's all a bit of a blur, that's why. I've never been able to remember anything much about that day, and just recently it's begun to really trouble me. I've started thinking about it again, and being back here has made it all that much worse." He looked at her, imploringly. "That's partly why I want to talk to Ben. I need his memories."

Shock widened her eyes. "Oh Jay, that must be awful for you, not to properly remember something so, so massive. I'm sorry, I didn't realize." She reached out and laid a hand over his. "I'd already told Ben you were back, so I'll let him know you want to see him." Jeremy's skin tingled where it touched hers. "And I really hope you find the answers you're looking for."

Her sympathy touched him, and he was suddenly too aware of her. Her eyes seemed magnified; huge amber irises, sweeping lashes. Her tongue moistened her lips, and he saw the whiteness of her teeth, the smooth pink of her mouth. He ought to go home. He shouldn't stay and drink with her.

He cleared his throat, his words strangely formal. "That'd be wonderful if you could. I may've already said but I'm staying at the house, so he'll know where to find me." He looked over to where her friends were now sitting and glanced at his watch. "I really need to get home and let you get back to your evening."

"You're probably right." She smiled at him and he found himself searching her face for a sign of disappointment. "I'll let him know, Jay. I promise."

They both stood up.

"Thanks Laura, I really appreciate it."

Jeremy held out his arms and went to hug her—just as she'd done to him in the shop—and that's when it happened. She leapt back as though he'd struck her.

"No!"

Her voice was too loud and he sensed the room's attention turning toward them. Her eyes were wide and there was fear there. He recoiled, shocked, and watched as livid color flooded her face. He wasn't angry, not yet, more embarrassed and confused by the ferocity of her reaction. She looked at him like a startled animal and he wondered what on earth she was afraid of. Surely not *him*?

"Really, Laura? You as well?" His voice was weary, suddenly defeated. The bar had gone quiet, focused on them, and at the edge of his vision he saw that one of Laura's friends has stood up.

She reached out a tentative hand. "No, Jay, it's not like that. It wasn't that."

Her dissembling caused the first flare of anger. "No? So what was it then? Please do tell, because I don't quite understand."

Her eyes looked moist. "It's just, it's just that I don't like being touched. Not like that, not when I'm not expecting it."

"But you hugged me the other day in the shop. You didn't seem to have a problem with it then, and you've touched me tonight."

"That's different." Her voice was small. She was close to tears, and Jeremy didn't get what he was meant to have done. "That was on my terms. I just . . . I just don't like to be caught by surprise."

They looked at each other and he wasn't sure that he believed her. She surely couldn't think that he'd hurt her.

"I'm sorry, Jay. It's honestly not anything to do with you, truly it's not. It's only . . . it's difficult. It's not something I can talk about. I wish . . ."

"It's okay." There wasn't much else he could say in the face of her distress. "Really, it's okay, and I'm sorry if I scared you."

They'd lost their previous connection, but she looked so lost that he made himself smile at her. "Look, I've enjoyed meeting up with you this evening, and thank you for offering to talk to Ben for me."

She still looked wary.

"Laura, look, forget it. I'm not upset and you don't need to explain anything. It was my fault for assuming. Come on, go and join your friends, and hopefully we'll see each other around."

She hesitated as if she was about to say something else but then changed her mind. "Goodbye, Jay."

Jeremy fled the bar, aware of the questioning eyes at his back, and pushed his way through the gaggle of smokers crowding the exit. For a moment she'd looked terrified of him, and he suddenly recalled that flicker of something like fear that'd crossed Mark's face as well. His anxiety spiked. He had to speak to Ben. People didn't always like him, but he wasn't usually viewed as a pariah; there was something else going on here.

The weather had blown in while he'd been in the pub. The pavements were wet and a chill wind cut and swirled between the houses, bringing the night with it. It wasn't late but the street was quiet. The elements had driven the locals indoors bar the obligatory huddle of smokers clustered outside the Carpenter's Arms. Jeremy envisioned their interest and felt it prickling his neck as he passed, his latent paranoia coming to the fore.

That same wind carried the aroma of fried chips across the road to find his eager nostrils, heightening his awareness of an empty stomach. He'd intended to eat while he was in the Swan, but somehow the conversation with Laura, and the way it'd ended, had made it impossible for him to stay. The windows of the Carpenter's looked warm and inviting, far preferable to a lonely house devoid of comforts, and for a moment he was tempted by the thought of a hot meal and the convivial company of strangers. Then he remembered that Mark and his cronies had been headed that way when they'd left the Swan, and his appetite waned.

As he walked, he mulled over his conversations with the McLeish siblings, each peculiar in its own way. Laura's hostility toward her father and her reaction to his touch, Mark's barely suppressed aggression, even Laura's veiled inference that Ben was "sensitive." It made him wonder about families and the secrets that lurked behind closed doors.

He then wondered if Mark and his father had voiced their speculations to the police; if the shadow of suspicion had ever slanted his way. It made a shiver play up his spine at the thought of the police viewing his silence as obstruction, as an admission of guilt. He suddenly wondered if they'd planted a seed in his parents' minds to bear the fruit that fed his mother's hatred.

The past closed in, claustrophobic and threatening, and he quickened his pace as if to outrun it. Voices could be heard behind him, a laugh that echoed in the empty street. Somewhere a dog barked. He put his head down and plowed on past the school and the bleak rows of houses, on past the alleyway that cut through to the churchyard, until he reached the turning to the house. His solitary footsteps echoed against the tarmac. As he walked past the church and the graveyard he felt a sensation of being watched, a cool ripple at the base of his skull, and for a moment he wondered if someone had cut through the alley and was waiting in the churchyard to ambush him. Maybe Mark and his thinly veiled animosity. A spurt of raw fear overcame his rational self. It had nothing to do with Mark or his friends; it was something primitive with no basis in reason, and suddenly he was running like a frightened child. Through the blood rush in his head he thought he heard voices, low and malicious, seeping out from the bushes as he blindly ran. The fear center in his brain lit up like a beacon, and for a split second he was a child again, running through the woods, through dark trees and menace, fear making his breath come in anguished sobs.

He reached the house and fumbled his key in the lock. He stumbled into the hallway and leaned against the closed door, heart thundering while his vision cleared. The feeling of panic didn't stay outside; it slipped inside with him and followed him through to the kitchen, where he poured himself some water. As he lifted the trembling glass to his lips he wondered what he was running from: the past or from himself and his secrets.

# 18

He'd dreamed of Sarah, of her hair spreading across the pillow, her eyes dark with desire, but then she'd morphed into Laura, slender limbed and lovely, and the lust and the guilt had shocked him awake. When morning came he'd felt hot and horny, heavy with self-reproach, his mind tortured by the half-remembered dream and the feeling that he'd been unfaithful in his sleep.

Now, a shower and a coffee later, he surveyed the contents of the attic room once more. Furniture and boxes were stacked to the back of the house, where the roof sloped downward and dipped to form the ceiling of his childhood bedroom. With a sinking heart he realized it was going to take far longer than the allotted three days before Sarah came back with the children—particularly if he took time out to rediscover the past.

He pushed the traveling trunk of dressing-up clothes to the side. There was something about the smell when he lifted the lid that formed a hard lump of sadness in his chest. It triggered his limbic system, his emotional brain, awakening a flood of feelings he wasn't ready to face. He opened the box of textbooks instead and thumbed through the volume at the top. Like a window opening onto the past, he saw himself sitting on Uncle Ian's knee while his uncle showed him pictures of birds and animals, of giant fungi like alien beings from another world. Jeremy must've been only four or five, too young to read for himself, but Ian had spoken to him as if he understood every word. The memory was bittersweet, tinged with regret.

Just as he was wondering where on earth to begin, the doorbell rang, cutting through the empty house.

"Hold on, I'm coming!"

He scooted down the ladder and took the stairs two at a time, reaching the door just as the bell rang for a second time.

"Hang on!"

A tall, lean man was standing on the doorstep, wearing jeans and a black Bellstaff jacket. Maybe Jeremy wouldn't have recognized him before, but the likeness to Laura was striking. He grinned, and it was the grin from the very first time that they'd met, except this one had full dentition. It was Ben staring out from a grown man's face, so familiar that Jeremy half expected to see Scotty dog there at his side.

"Hello" was all he said, the grin stretching wider. Then he gestured a hand to his chest. "It's me, Ben," and somehow they were suddenly man-hugging and back-slapping.

"Ben! Bloody hell, I can't believe it's actually you." Jeremy stood back and looked at him. "God, how long has it been?"

"Too long," he replied. Jeremy remembered Mark's words, about how badly he had let him down.

"Come on in. Look, do you want a coffee or anything? I was just about to make myself one." He felt glittery eyed and emotional as Ben followed him into the house. "God, this is weird."

It *was* weird. Ben should've been a stranger to him. For three decades they'd lived their lives apart, and they'd only ever spent five, maybe six, long summers together a lifetime ago. Maybe it was talking to Laura the previous night, or perhaps the intensity of those summers and the sudden, brutal way everything had ended, but whatever the reason, Jeremy felt comfortable in his presence, as if the years had melted away.

Ben perched himself on one of the two remaining kitchen stools while Jeremy filled the kettle.

"I hope you don't mind me just pitching up unannounced like this," he said. "It's only Laura had told me you were back and then, when she said you'd been talking about us meeting up, I thought, why not? I knew if I spent too long thinking about it I maybe wouldn't have come. I might've have ended up feeling too awkward, and I didn't want to do that."

"God no, I'm glad you didn't. I told Laura I wanted to catch up with you and I meant it. It's great to see you—I was just a bit taken aback at you being here so soon, that's all. I only spoke to her last night and I wasn't prepared for her to be quite such a fast worker."

"She told me straightaway, the minute she got in."

He saw Jeremy's questioning look. "Laura 'n' me have got a place together. She'd got fed up with renting and I was on my own, so it seemed like a sensible solution, for the time being at least. If I'm honest, it's nice to have the company, and me and her have always rubbed along okay."

Jeremy observed him as he spoke. Time had been more than kind. A full head of floppy brown hair shaded pale brown eyes, and the same smattering of freckles gave him a touch of boyishness that peeled back his forty-odd years. Even Jeremy could see he was a handsome man.

"So, Laura said you'd lost your mum and that you're back here sorting out the house." Ben glanced round the kitchen. "God, this brings back some memories! I didn't even realize your family still owned this place, let alone that I'd ever be sitting here again. What do you reckon you're going to do with it?"

"I dunno, sell it, most likely. Why, you interested?"

"I wish. I don't think I could stretch to this, unfortunately." He looked at Jeremy and shook his head. "I can hardly believe this, you being back here after all this time. So, what have you been doing with yourself? Laura tells me you're married with a couple of kiddoes?"

She had been busy.

"Yeah, I've been married to Sarah for over ten years now. We've got a boy and a little girl, Jack and Lucy."

"They not here with you then?" Ben asked, glancing around the kitchen as though he might not have noticed them hiding in a corner.

"They were, but now they've gone to Sarah's parents. We came down last weekend to clear the place but when we thought we'd just about finished, I went and found a whole load of my uncle's stuff up in the attic. It was pointless all of us staying, so she's taken the children to her mum and dad's for a few days while I finish off here."

He nodded. "Well if you still need a hand with anything, I don't mind helping out. I'm between projects at the moment so I've got the time, and it'd be good to have the chance to spend some of it together."

"That'd be great." Jeremy placed a mug of coffee in front of him. "So, what about you then? What've you been doing with yourself for the last thirty odd years?"

"Thirty years! Is it really? Jeez, that makes me feel old!" He shook his head as if in disbelief. "Well, I escaped this place, for a while at least. I went off and did engineering at Bath uni and lived there for a few years afterward but eventually ended up coming back." He hesitated for a moment. "It was more to keep an eye on Laura than anything else, make sure she was okay." He saw Jeremy's puzzled expression and added, "It's just she had a bit of a tough time of it a while back."

He didn't elaborate and Jeremy didn't ask. He could remember her reaction when he'd moved to hug her, and wondered if this explained it. Maybe it didn't have anything to do with *him* after all. He suddenly thought of his dream, her naked in his bed, and felt the color creeping up his neck. To hide his confusion he focused on Ben.

"So you never got married or anything then?"

"No. I had a long-term girlfriend for a few years, but we ended up drifting apart and there's been no one since. It was all amicable like, and I still see her sometimes, but it wasn't something we could make a proper go of. We're better off apart." He grinned at Jeremy. "I'm single now, footloose and fancy-free, not like you old married men."

"No kids then, I take it?"

"To be honest it wasn't something either of us was that fussed about and it was just as well given how things worked out." As an afterthought Ben suddenly added, "Oh, I meant to say, I was really sorry to hear about your mum. How's your dad holding up? It must be hard for him."

Of course. He didn't know. Jeremy might feel as if they knew each other, but the reality was that neither knew a thing about the other from age eleven onward.

"Dad's been gone ages. He fell ill only a few years after . . . after Emily, so it ended up just being me and Mum while I was growing up. To be honest, we weren't close latterly and hadn't seen that much of each other, so I'm kind of doing okay despite everything."

An odd expression crossed Ben's face. Something unreadable.

"Still a shock, though," Jeremy added, lest he be considered cold.

"Shit, that's awful, I didn't realize. I'd heard about your uncle but I just assumed . . . if I ever thought really about it, I just imagined everyone still being around, the same as it was back then." He looked pensive. "That's really sad about your dad though. It must've been difficult for you."

It wasn't clear whether he meant the loss of Jeremy's father, or him being left alone with his mother.

"Yeah, it was, and Mum never really got over Emily, so I suppose looking back, they were difficult times all round."

That expression flickered again. "I can imagine. Your mum was always so awfully fond of her." He looked awkward for a moment. "I mean, course she was, she was her daughter and everything, but what I meant was they always seemed especially close."

Jeremy let out a short laugh and hoped Ben couldn't hear the bitterness in it. "You don't need to pussyfoot around it. I always knew she preferred Em. That was part of the problem. Losing Emily left this hole in her, and there was no way I could ever fill it."

It broke them all, but he didn't tell him that. He might have felt a connection, but this was still a stranger.

Ben smiled. "I was always a little bit scared of your mum, to be honest."

Jeremy laughed properly this time. "You and me both."

"God, can you remember what she was like if you were ever late back? I can still picture that look on her face, the one that told you exactly what you had coming."

Jeremy could but he didn't want to; he didn't want to talk about his family, so he shifted the conversation to the McLeishes instead.

"Talking of families, I hear your dad did okay for himself. Laura said he came into the money and that he's got one of those apartments we passed on the way in."

Ben looked down at the table. "Yes. Yes he has. Number six, The Buttery, not that I go there if I can help it."

Jeremy changed the subject. He sensed the same hostility that he'd got from Laura and realized that Ben didn't want to talk about his family any more than he wanted to discuss his. There was a finality to his tone that deterred further questioning.

"Look, if you're serious about giving me a hand with the attic, it'd really help me out. There's more stuff up there than I first thought, and I'm definitely going to need a second pair of hands getting some of the furniture down. And of course it'd be great to have your company as well."

"Dead serious. It'll give us a chance to properly catch up and give me something useful to do at the same time. I hate being between projects. Mark always keeps on at me and then I end up in the pub with him every lunchtime, which I could really do without." He patted his stomach where there wasn't an ounce of fat.

"Come on then. If you don't have anywhere else to be, I can show you what you've let yourself in for."

Together they went up the stairs and into the attic, where they looked at the contents with something close to dismay.

"You weren't joking! Who on earth decided it was a good idea to cram all this up here? It's a wonder it hasn't brought the ceilings down." Ben tentatively tested one of the boards. "Surely your mother didn't do all this?"

"No, I think it must've been George. He probably didn't know what to do with it, and I doubt my mother would've been much help. No matter, however it got up here, it's all got to come down."

"Your uncle and George, I've always wondered, were they like . . . were they like, you know, partners or something? People said stuff afterward, and after he died like, but I don't think anyone knew for sure."

Jeremy felt a ripple of irritation, tinged with protectiveness. It was no one's business bar theirs, and he hated the thought of village gossips speculating. The place was like something out of the dark ages, and it made him think back to what Laura had said, and to wonder where else the finger of suspicion had pointed.

"Yes, I think so, but I didn't realize until I saw them together years later. It's funny, kids nowadays would realize they were gay straightaway and probably think nothing of it, whereas we were so innocent in some ways, it didn't even cross our minds." He grinned at Ben. "Different times, I suppose."

There was no answering grin, instead Ben said, "So you've been back here before then?"

Jeremy detected a note of something akin to hurt in Ben's voice.

"No, not to the house or anything. It was back when Ian had his first heart attack, he was in the Royal and I caught the train down on my own to see him, that's all. God, it was years ago. I must've been seventeen or eighteen because I was still at school, and I only went to the hospital and then straight back home."

He didn't want to think of that visit, instead he focused on Mark's words.

"Look, I'm sorry I didn't try harder to keep in touch after . . . you know, everything with Em. It wasn't that I didn't want to, but everyone in my family was in pretty bad shape. My parents made the decision to never come back here, and that was it as far as I was concerned. I didn't have any choice in the matter, and anyway, I had . . . I had issues of my own to deal with. I couldn't even think about this place without bricking it, if I'm honest." He paused, needing to explain himself. "It's just Mark had a bit of a go at me about it last night and it wasn't like he implied; it wasn't that I'd gone off to some posh school and didn't want to know you lot anymore."

The words sound childish, but Jeremy wanted Ben to understand. He needed him on side if he was to access his memories. There was a prickly moment of awkwardness.

"It's fine, honestly. Mark should stop dredging up the past. It was years ago and we were all just kids, and God knows what you lot were going through. Forget it, water under the bridge."

"Okay, I just wanted you to know, that's all."

They both looked away, uncomfortable in that way only men can be when they detect a whiff of intimacy. To Jeremy it felt almost as though he'd blurted out something inappropriate, and now he couldn't take it back.

Once it felt safe to speak again he suggested a plan of action. "I reckon we need to clear a bit of floor space. If we got some of this furniture down and out of the way it'd give us somewhere to systematically work through the boxes."

Ben took off his jacket and rolled up his sleeves, glancing at his watch.

"I haven't got long and I can't get dirty because I've promised to meet Laura for lunch, but we could make a start. Then if you sort out some rope for tomorrow, we could begin lowering stuff down."

They worked for a while in companionable silence, dragging boxes and shifting furniture. Soon it neared lunchtime and Ben looked at his watch again.

"I'd better get going in a minute, otherwise Laura won't be happy. School holidays are the only chance she gets for a pub lunch in the week and she likes to make the most of it. Her friends are all either in work or stuck at home with kids, so I have to do my brotherly duty and go with her when I can."

"So is she a teacher then or what?"

"Yes, she teaches at the junior school in the village, the year threes. Tell you what, why don't you join us? Laura won't mind, she always had a soft spot for you."

Jeremy had a sudden image of her laying naked in his bed, and it wasn't a soft spot he was worried about. He experienced an unexpected rush of guilty pleasure at the thought of seeing her again—despite the awkwardness of their parting.

"Okay, if you're sure she won't mind me gate-crashing your lunch."

"God no, 'course she won't. She'll enjoy it."

# 19

They went to the Carpenter's Arms, where there was a log fire blazing in the grate, and sofas to sit for a drink before eating. Laura hadn't arrived, so the two men took their drinks and positioned themselves near the fire with its crackling logs and welcoming scent of wood smoke.

"So," Jeremy said, "what about the others? What happened to Nathan and Josh, and Andy?"

Ben took a mouthful of his pint, carefully wiping a line of froth from his lip. "Nathan's still living up in Scotland, I think. He married a Scottish girl and they moved back up there when the children came along. Wanted to be nearer to her family, I suppose. Last I heard he was working on the oil rigs, but I haven't spoken to him for a few years now. As for Andy, he went into the family business. Took over the shop from his father, so no surprises there."

Jeremy frowned, trying to remember the shop he was referring to.

"You know, Durrant's, the hardware shop on the high street?"

Now he remembered. Andy Durrant was the name that had eluded him. Asthmatic Andy, a pale, quiet lad, always slightly on the periphery of the group. He could remember his father too,

Mr. Durrant from the hardware store, who allegedly never took off his brown overall, not even to go to bed.

"He's married as well," Ben continued. "To Josh's little sister, Ellie." His face clouded. "I don't suppose you heard, but poor old Josh isn't with us anymore. Died in a car crash, must be seven or eight years ago now."

Jeremy registered a stab of sadness at the thought of one of their number, gone already. Still, at least it wasn't "natural causes"; when that started happening you knew you were on the home straight.

"Shit, that's awful. Was he married as well?"

"Not as such, not really. He and his wife had split up a few years before. She was still gutted, but it wasn't like they were still together or anything, and there were no kids, thankfully."

Ben looked up and smiled at someone behind Jeremy, dispelling the sense of gloom.

A flushed and breathless Laura threw herself down on the sofa next to Ben. "Sorry I'm late. Thought I'd walk so I could have a couple of drinks but it took me a bit longer than usual. Must be these." She waggled a foot clad in a high-heeled ankle boot. "Not exactly sensible." She smiled across at Jeremy. "Hello again, Jay. You joining us for lunch?"

"Yes, if that's all right with you. Ben invited me along."

She smiled her agreement and looked genuinely pleased to see him, the previous night's awkwardness obviously forgotten. Jeremy took in her appearance, her dark skinny jeans and soft cream sweater. Her hair was loosely wound in a clip, and her eyes were dusted with a shimmer of bronze. He found himself stupidly grinning at her, inordinately pleased to see her again.

"I'll get you a drink," he said, overeager and embarrassing. "Gin and tonic?"

"No, I think I'll have a wine this time, please. A Pinot Grigio if they've got one."

He bounded to the bar, tail wagging as though she'd thrown him a ball. Was he really that shallow, such that the moment Sarah left him on his own, he was lusting and panting after the first pretty female? Apparently yes, and he recalled his hollow promises to be a better man. Unbidden, his mother's voice sounded in his head once more: *Your promises mean nothing Jeremy, they're like pie crusts—made to be broken.* He pictured the mirthless curl of her lip at her joke that wasn't one.

"There you go." He placed the glass in front of Laura, meeting her eyes with a defiant smile, his mother wasn't there anymore, so he didn't need to listen to her ever again.

He'd picked up menus at the bar, and once they'd ordered and gone through to their table, the conversation turned to people Jeremy didn't know and events he'd played no part in. Ben and Laura chatted while he smiled and nodded, and tried his best to appear interested until eventually they realized his exclusion. Two pairs of amber eyes fixed their attention on him, inexplicably making him feel uncomfortable.

"Why London then? What made you decide to settle there?"

"Work mainly, I suppose. It's where the head office is, and if I wanted to get on, that's where I needed to be. It's also where I met Sarah, and we just kind of settled there."

"So what is it you do exactly?"

Laura leaned forward and he felt encouraged to tell her more.

"I'm an architect, mainly commercial stuff, so not what I ideally wanted to do. I'd still love to get into designing homes if I could. You know the kind of thing, those one-off, interesting spaces like you see on the television? That's really my dream."

Laura moistened her lips and nodded as if in absolute understanding, while treacherous, traitorous thoughts marched through Jeremy's head.

"It's important to have a dream Jay, to try to do something you love."

"Ben tells me you went into teaching. I don't know that I could cope with that—a load of screaming kids day in day out is my idea of hell. Don't tell me you actually enjoy it."

"Yes I do, I love it," she said. "The kids are great. Most of them are complete little sweeties, most of the time at least." She smiled but seemed more interested in hearing about him than talking about herself. "So, what about Sarah, does she work as well?"

"She's actually a lawyer, although she's taken a bit of time out while Lucy's still small. I get the sense she's starting to miss the challenge though, so I expect she'll be looking to go back pretty soon. I don't think being at home with the kids all the time really does it for her."

Jeremy saw something shadow Laura's face and she glanced away. He watched as she carefully removed a stray tendril of hair that'd fallen across her face, and tucked it behind an ear, letting her finger trace slowly around the helix. He felt his mouth turn dry as he tried to drag his eyes away from the slender curve of her neck and the delicate whorl of her neat little ear, the velvety plumpness of its tiny pink lobe. He desperately suppressed the urge to reach out a finger too, and gently stroke it, a thought which caused a sudden tightening low in his stomach. She turned back to face him, and he felt hot and distracted as a whisper of his dream floated past. She smiled, and there was a moment of something knowing in her gaze.

"We sometimes wondered what you were doing with yourself, didn't we Ben." She reached out and laid a warm hand on his arm.

"Not often, but occasionally in the summer we'd think about things and wonder what happened to you all. The way you just kind of vanished left a real hole in our summers, especially for me and Ben. We missed you."

"We certainly had some fun back then." Ben grinned at a sudden recollection, oblivious to the undercurrent passing between the two. "Jay, do you remember when we set fire to Josh's tracksuit?"

The memory came back in a rush, dissipating any frisson of desire; Josh, leaping around, trying to free himself from the smoldering arm of his hoodie, while the others rolled about laughing.

"God, yeah! What on earth were we doing?"

"We were trying to make a crossbow, remember? Someone had the bright idea of burning a channel in a piece of wood to make the groove in the stock where the bolt would sit. Didn't work though."

"That's it! We were in Josh's dad's shed. I remember Josh found some petrol from somewhere and drizzled it along the wood, and then tried to set fire to it. It's a wonder the whole place didn't go up."

Ben started laughing. "Remember how his sleeve just melted? It was nylon or something, and it stunk to high heaven."

"Yeah, and remember his mum's face? I honestly though she was going to lose it. I can see him now—his hands were all black where he'd tried to beat it out, and he'd gone and rubbed it all over his face in his panic."

"You weren't much support, were you? If I remember correctly you scuttled off home and left us to it."

Ben wasn't to know how scared Jeremy had been of angry mothers, probably still was.

"Poor old Josh. It's awful to think that he's gone."

"Shit happens," Laura said, and he was struck by the touch of harshness.

"What about when you accidently let Scotty cock his leg on that woman's pushchair, outside the bakers? Her face! I honestly thought I'd wet myself too." Jeremy grinned at the memory.

Ben stopped laughing and a shutter fell across his features. "Don't," was all he said. "Not Scotty."

Raw grief was still there after thirty years, and a hint of something else—anger, perhaps—lurking beneath his surface. He and Laura exchanged a glance that Jeremy couldn't quite read.

"Sorry, mate," he said. "I didn't realize it'd still upset you."

"Yeah, well, it does."

There was an unwelcome moment of awkwardness, which Laura rushed to fill.

"Anyway, Jay, how long are you here for?"

Gratefully, Jeremy turned to her. "It was meant to be just for the week, but having seen what's in the attic, I reckon it's going to need to be a bit longer. Sarah's gone to her parents' and was going to fetch me at the weekend, but I'm thinking it might be better if she takes the children home, and then comes back down sometime next week." He turned to Ben. "Take it you are still up for helping?"

"Yes, sure." Ben smiled, the moment of awkwardness dispelled. "It shouldn't take us more than two or three days, so you might still be okay for the weekend."

Laura reached out her hand once more, this time to Ben, and the sleeve of her jumper rode up as she stretched, revealing the flesh of her lower arm. Jeremy noticed a fine network of old scars crosshatching the skin, and realized with a sense of shock that she was a self-harmer, or had been in the past. She saw him staring, and as she withdrew her hand she pulled down her sleeve in a defensive gesture. Her eyes met his and for a moment she looked guarded and hostile, as if daring him to comment.

She very deliberately returned her attention to Ben.

"So has Jay told you the real reason why he's here?" she asked.

"Yes, course he has." Ben sounded puzzled. "He's clearing his uncle's old house, sorting things out for his mum's will. Why?"

"No, I mean here with us. Why he was so keen to meet up with you?"

Ben looked questioningly at Jeremy and he felt himself begin to squirm. This wasn't how he'd wanted to broach things, and he sensed something intentional in Laura's action, as though she was punishing him for noticing her scars.

"I'm here because I wanted to catch up, that's all, with you, and with the others if I get the chance. It'd be unthinkable to come back here and not look you up, and I only wish I'd done it sooner."

He flashed a look at Laura, who at least had the grace to blush. "What Laura is referring to is that I told her I can't remember anything much about the day Emily died. My mother wouldn't ever talk to me about it, and there's only so much I've been able to pick up from the newspapers. Yes, I'll admit I wanted to ask you about it at some point, but it's not my main reason for wanting to see you, not at all."

It was true. Once he'd begun remembering the good times, he'd wanted to see Ben again for his own sake—to see all of them again, in fact. He'd felt an affection, a nostalgia that was about much more than just finding out what they knew.

He looked straight at Ben. "It's true, mate. I'd have wanted us to meet up regardless of that."

Two bright spots of color began burning Ben's face, a livid redness staining his cheeks.

"You shitting me? What, you can't remember any of it?"

There was a note of disbelief in his voice, and something else, something eager.

"No, not really. I can't remember much at all if I'm truthful. Even after all this time none of it has ever come back."

He didn't want to have to explain, to have to tell them what it was like for him and how it'd been ever since Emily's death, so he was grateful when Ben slowly nodded.

"It's okay, you don't need to explain. It's kind of weird but I get it, I've heard shock can do odd things, and I always wondered how come you . . ." He paused, deciding against whatever he was about to say. "Only thing is, I'm not sure I'm going to be much help to you." His eyes met Jeremy's. "It was years ago, and I didn't have anything useful to add back then, let alone now."

He looked so troubled that Jeremy felt the need to reassure him. "Ben, mate, I'm not expecting you to suddenly solve any great mystery. Just fill in some gaps if you can, that's all. It's weird having this, this blank page." He felt a sudden urge to be honest. "I've recently started having, like . . . like flashbacks, I suppose, and it's been a bit disturbing. I thought if I could remember, or at least put some context around it, it wouldn't bother me so much."

Two pairs of amber eyes regarded him, Ben's wide with concern.

"I don't know if they're memories, or just random ideas my brain's pieced together from things I've been told, so I want to try and get some clarity. If I could only remember . . ."

"Anything I can do to help, I will, but don't you think some things are best left? It was years ago, and nothing's going to change by raking it all back up." There was wariness in Ben's tone.

"I know, but there's always been this hole, and if I could just fill it with *something*, I reckon I'd feel happier about it." "Happier" was perhaps the wrong word.

"Okay . . ." Ben slowly replied. "What is it you want to know then?"

"Not here, not now. There's no rush, we can talk about it another time, when we're back at the house." He suddenly wanted to drop the subject. "Look, does anyone want another drink?"

Ben declined. He had his car parked in the car park. But Laura joined him in another glass of wine while the three chatted about other things. They were easy company, and Jeremy suddenly wished Sarah was there with him. These were people they could both be friends with—as long as he kept his testosterone firmly in check.

When the meal was over, they went out to the car park where Ben's convertible was parked.

"Nice car. Someone must be doing okay."

"It's not bad," Ben said. "It suits me anyway. Look, if you don't mind squeezing in the back, we can drop Laura home, save her walking, and then carry on with the attic. Otherwise I'll only plonk myself in front of the television for the rest of the afternoon."

"I can sit on your lap if you like, save you squashing up in the back. I'm only around the corner."

Jeremy thought of the warm pressure of Laura's buttocks against his groin, and panic sparked.

"No thanks!" A little too hastily maybe. "No, that wouldn't be safe, I'll be fine in the back."

The siblings' house was a renovated end-of-terrace cottage, with a wide swath of landscaped garden at the side. It had the look of a home, with its neat sash windows painted a pale lichen green, to match the smart front door.

"Here we are, this is us here."

Laura leaned across and gave her brother a swift kiss before sliding out of the car. She moved the seat forward for Jeremy to swap, and as he stood, she reached up and kissed him too, the lightest brush of her lips at his cheek, like a butterfly.

"Bye, Jay."

He took her place in the front seat, aware that his face was blazing. She'd taken him by surprise, and he could feel the skin where her mouth had touched, burning like a brand. The blushing was really no more than a reaction to the unexpected gesture, but Ben glanced across at him as he closed the car door, and there was something troubled in his expression. It made Jeremy want to explain himself but he didn't know how. Instead he let his color subside and kept his eyes firmly fixed on the road ahead.

It was almost three thirty when they reached the house, too late to think about working.

"Ben, thanks for the offer, but looking at the time, I honestly don't think we'll get much more done today. How about we can carry on tomorrow, if that's okay with you?"

Ben yawned as the car came to a halt. "Must admit, that lunch is sitting a bit heavy. I've got to see Mark first thing tomorrow but then I'll pop over afterward. How does that sound?"

"Perfect. See you later then, and thanks for the lift."

Jeremy stood on the path and watched as Ben drove away. As he closed the door his mind was already on the half-finished thriller laying splay-backed on his bedside table.

# 20

"It's what we'd planned to do that day," Ben said. "We were going to work on the crossbow in Josh's shed, but then you were told you had to take Emily with you, so we couldn't." His eyes stared back into the past. "Jeez, you were in such a mood, I remember you being so angry with her, worse than you'd ever been."

The two men were taking a break, sitting on two of the boxes in the attic, where the humidity was rapidly becoming unbearable. The space was ripe with the heat from their bodies, and the air carried a tang of sweat. Despite the warmth, something inside Jeremy froze at the thought that he'd been angry with Emily that day. Had he been angry enough to do something truly awful?

"When you say 'angry,' what do you mean? What did I do?"

"You didn't *do* anything. You were just impatient with her, making it clear that she was being a right nuisance." Ben saw Jeremy's expression. "Don't look like that. You weren't doing anything massively wrong. It was just like that sometimes, and I can understand why. I'd have been the same if she'd been my sister. God, I'd have practically hated her."

The frozen part of him crackled like whisky over ice. Hated?

"I didn't hate my sister, I loved Emily. We all did."

"I didn't mean literally hate her, just resent the way everyone was around her." Ben looked thoughtful for a moment. "After all this time I may be seeing it from an adult's perspective, but it seemed that everyone focused on Emily and that you were always the one in the background. Any kid would be resentful, seeing all that attention and love going elsewhere."

They were both silent for a moment, something wistful in their remembering.

*He watched as she smoothed back the girl's hair, her red lips gently brushing the dome of that little forehead with a tenderness that twisted something at his core. He remembered being that small himself and he let himself imagine her pulling him toward her like that, holding him close with love in her eyes. He could almost feel those soft hands and see the gentle smile, all for him. Even though he knew it would never happen he watched and he listened, and he ached for it. Deep in his chest the want still thrummed like a tuning fork, but underneath that want lay something else. It ran through him like a rod of steel, hard and cold, and its name was resentment. Resentment at the world, resentment that others were loved and cherished, and he was not. Resentment fed anger, and anger fed that nameless need, and then all was lost.*

Jeremy recalled that inexplicable flash of bitterness he'd felt in Ian's study, seeing Lucy sitting on Sarah's lap. The tickling and the laughing, and his hard-edged resentment at it all. With an unaccustomed insight he wondered if it hadn't really been aimed at Lucy at all, but instead had been an echo of the past, brought to the fore by being in that house, that room, a place where his mother would've sat, with Emily jiggled on her knee. He'd always remembered his sister with a kind of torn and tragic love, but perhaps he'd pushed aside the bits he didn't want to remember, things that would make him feel even more guilty about the past. Maybe he'd rewritten his role, and shaped his childhood memories to feed his sense of being wronged.

Ben saw the emotions chasing across his face. "Hey, for God's sake, Jay, don't look so bleeding tragic. You're making me wish you hadn't brought this up. Of course she annoyed you sometimes—it wouldn't have been normal for you never to get on each other's nerves. Laura and I, we *hated* each other sometimes, but that doesn't mean I didn't love her, that I wouldn't have done everything in my power to try and protect her."

It was an odd choice of words, as though something bad had happened to Laura. Jeremy almost asked him about her scars, but it seemed too intrusive, and anyway, it was his own past he was interested in.

"I know, I get that. It's just I always think of us as being really close. Me being like her protector."

The look Ben gave him was strange. "Do you really not remember any of this stuff?" he asked. "Nothing at all?"

"'Course I do—some of it, anyway. You're turning it on its head a bit, that's all. It's really just the day itself that's hazy, and the actual finding her. Going back to my parents and . . . and telling them." A shudder ran through him. "I have hardly any recollection of that part at all."

He remembered some things though: the dull thud of his mother's head hitting the door frame, over and over, until his father pulled her away. The red smear that her forehead left on the paintwork. His family adrift in space and time.

Ben's face was tinged with sadness. "Look, mate, I don't know what you're beating yourself up over. From what I remember, you were just normal siblings with a bit too big an age gap. Most of the time you rubbed along okay, but sometimes she got on your nerves."

He hesitated, looking awkward. "I hope you don't mind me saying this, but she was a strange little thing. Most of the time she drifted around like a little lost ghost, just watching."

The thought of his sister as a little lost ghost caused a hurt deep in Jeremy's chest—a turn of the screw, a twist of the knife—for it was what she ended up becoming.

Ben continued, conveniently vindicating Jeremy's sense of victim-hood. "And it didn't help the way your mum totally doted on her and she could do no wrong. I might only have been a kid, but even I could see how your mother was always on your case, like she was waiting for you to step out of line so she could vent her anger. I was seriously wary of her. She always gave me the impression that she was just waiting to explode."

Mostly Ben was only echoing the things Jeremy already knew, but the idea that he'd resented Em sat unhappily. He felt suddenly wretched, and he burned with the longing to unload his secret fear.

"I just wish I knew how I ended up finding her. I hate it that no one really knows how she drowned, and it scares me that I might've been responsible in some way . . ." This wasn't something to be shared, and he quickly shook his head. "Sorry, I don't really know what I'm saying. It's just these flashbacks have given me the sense that I'm on the brink of remembering something awful."

Ben's face had blanched and now he stared at Jeremy, wide-eyed. "Shit, Jay, what are you saying? That you think *you* had something to do with it or, what, that someone else did? Do you think you might've actually seen someone?" His eyes slid away to Jeremy's hands, as if he was picturing those same hands pushing Emily under the water. "And what are these flashbacks you're talking about? Do you like, *see* things?"

His gaze returned to Jeremy's and there was horror lurking there.

"No, not exactly, it's more like dreams, I suppose. I'm not sure if they're even memories or just my mind playing tricks."

Ben forced a laugh. "You need to leave this well alone, Jay. 'Course you had nothing to do with it. God, I don't remember you talking crap like this as a kid, so what went wrong?"

His eyes flitted once more to Jeremy's hands, giving him the urge to hide them from sight. Suddenly he could see water and those same hands at a child's neck, his hand massive on Lucy's back, and panic began to swell. For that single blinding moment he'd wanted to push her into the traffic. Had he stood at that very same crossing with Em and felt the same compulsion? Had he fantasized about throwing *her* under a bus, getting rid of her once and for all? He staggered to his feet and lurched to the hatch, then lowered himself onto the ladder, aware of Ben's worried voice behind him. He needed to get away. He raced down the stairs and through the kitchen, threw wide the back door, and took in gulps of cool air. Slowly his breathing returned to normal, and the overwhelming dread subsided.

Ben appeared at his side, his voice taut with worry. "Jay, mate, what's going on? Are you okay?"

Big exhale. Breathe.

"Phew! Sorry about that. It's a new thing that happens sometimes but I'm fine now. Honestly. Just felt a bit short of air for a moment. It's nothing to worry about."

"Okay, if you say so." Ben didn't sound convinced and paused before continuing. "Jay, I know it's none of my business, but wouldn't it be better to pay someone to finish sorting this out, to just go home and forget all about it? It can't be doing you any good, dredging up the past like this."

He laid a steadying hand on Jeremy's arm. "Starting to talk like you were just now will only stir up all the crap people were saying at the time. Leave it, mate. Go home and get on with your life."

Jeremy didn't answer. He'd spent thirty years forgetting and now it was time to know the truth. It was his whole reason for being there.

"Jay, are you listening to me? I've had a few issues myself, on and off, and believe me, it doesn't do any good to start dwelling on stuff you can't change."

Jeremy managed a weak smile. "I know, and I'm not dwelling through choice. I can't help it. I can't go home until I've done every-thing I can to try and remember. Look, indulge me this once and tell me what you know about the day Em died, and then I'll leave it. I won't mention it again. And don't worry that I'll hear about the rumors that were going around at the time. Laura's already hinted at what people were saying. I know it's crap, you know it's crap. It's fine." He looked at his hand and saw it was no longer a murderous paw. "You always were a good mate, Ben. Thank you."

Ben was talking, Jeremy hanging on every word.

". . . so like I said, we were going to Josh's but your mother insisted you take Emily out with you. She said Em was bored and that you should play with her more. I know that because I'd come to call for you midmorning like we'd arranged, but I got sent away with a flea in my ear."

There was an echo of his mother's censorious tones: "What kind of a horrible brother are you that you never want to play with your little sister? You don't need to spend all your time messing around with those boys. I'm not even asking you to stay in the house, you can go as far as the fields, but you make sure you look after her, and no going into the woods." It had broached no argument, and Jeremy could now recall sullenly trailing out of the house with Emily in tow.

"I thought we met up first thing, straight after breakfast?" he asked Ben.

"No way, it was probably more like eleven. I'd been round to Nathan's first and he was waiting for me outside. We hung about at the end of the lane to see if you were coming out or not, then you pitched up with Emily and we carried on down to the fields."

He took a moment, remembering. "I don't know if Andy was there but he might've been. Josh definitely was; he came looking for us when we didn't turn up at his house like we'd planned."

He grinned at a sudden memory. "You were being a right little sod. You deliberately made us play What's the Time Mr. Wolf with Emily, even though you knew she was petrified of wolves, and you growled and barked like an idiot, trying to scare her. You made us all start off from way back, and it meant Emily got caught almost every time. But to be fair she took it okay, even though you wouldn't let her be the wolf. She was doing that half-scared, half-loving-it kind of thing that kids do, squealing like a piglet." His face shadowed. "Laura was with us for a while and I remember Emily liked that, there being another girl there, on her side like."

He was making Jeremy sound like a mean, vindictive sort of boy.

"We played with her for a bit until we got fed up and then we played football. God, it was all so long ago . . ."

"I know, but just tell me what you can remember."

Ben thought for a moment. "That's right, Andy *was* there. He turned up later, and he was the one who brought the ball. We kicked it about for a while and Emily watched, but then she got bored after Laura left, and started whining, saying she was going to tell your mum that you wouldn't play with her."

He paused and solemnly regarded Jeremy. "This was all years ago, Jay. I told most of it to the police at the time but I've not really thought about it since, so I can't vouch for how accurate this is."

"It's fine. I'm not expecting you to have total recall, only to help me fill in some of the gaps. Then, just maybe, it'll trigger me remembering my side of things."

Jeremy suddenly picked up on the fact that Ben had said *most of it*. "What did you mean 'most of it'? Didn't you tell the police everything?"

"'Course I did. I just didn't mention that you were angry with her." He looked up, expecting understanding. "We were only kids, remember, and you were my mate. I didn't want to get you into trouble or make you look bad. It would've sounded worse than it was."

His gaze slid away and that made Jeremy suspect that it *was* worse. That Ben had needed to lie by omission, to protect him in some way, and *that* made him wonder if there was more than Ben was telling.

"It was a blazing hot day, and at some point we went back to the farm for a drink and a sandwich. I remember the old man moaning about us making a mess. Then afterward we decided to go down to the woods. You weren't keen because apparently your mum had told you not to, but we ended up going anyway."

The look he gave Jeremy was pained and regretful. "That's where it all went wrong. Emily got scared and asked whether there were any wolves in the woods, and you said that there were big ones and that they ate up little girls like her. Understandably she started saying she didn't want to go, and then you told her *you* were the big bad wolf and that you were coming to get her."

Jeremy was aware that his pulse had quickened. "So I deliberately frightened her. God, that makes me feel awful."

"I don't think for one minute she believed you, but she started running anyway, and then we all chased her. We ended up chasing her into the woods."

Jeremy pictured Jack and Lucy running across bleached winter fields, Little Red Riding Hood a contrast against the sepia earth, and now he understood the context. He'd deliberately chased a frightened child into the woods where she'd died. The question that remained was how she had died, and the things that Ben was saying made him fearful of finding out.

"Go on, then what happened?" He needed to know, no matter how bad.

"We thought it was funny to start with," Ben continued, looking ashamed. "We chased her as far as the woods but then you got worried and told us to stop. You shouted for her to come back, that we were only messing about, but she kept on running. I think she was properly scared by then and had started to believe she really was being chased by wolves." He shook his head at the memory. "She carried on into the woods and you kept calling out to her to stop, but she ran into a tangle of bushes and then we couldn't keep up. Because she was so much smaller than us she could get through gaps where we struggled, so it slowed us down and eventually we lost her."

His heart was beating a rapid tattoo; his limbs tingled with adrenaline. Jeremy wasn't sure he could bear any more, but Ben's words bored relentlessly into his head.

"At first you were cross with her for running off but then you panicked, Jay. You weren't usually that mean to her, I just think you were particularly pissed off that day because we'd wanted to finish off the crossbow."

"You're telling me she died because I wanted to finish a bloody crossbow?"

"When you couldn't find her you got really upset because you knew you were going to be properly in the shit. I remember we looked for her for ages, you, me, and Nathan. Andy and Josh had to go home—Andy's parents were going out and Josh was still doing penance for the tracksuit incident—so it was just the three of us." He concentrated, dredging up the past. "We saw Mark in the woods but he hadn't seen or heard anything, so in the end you went home to get some help, or at least that's what you said."

There was a question mark implied over Jeremy's intentions, but he let it go. He was more interested in the fact that Mark had been there, and that afterward he'd felt the need to spread rumor and suspicion.

"What was Mark doing? Why was he there?"

For the first time Ben revealed a different side, a glimpse of anger that darkened his features.

"He wasn't *doing* anything. If you're trying to suggest he had something to do with what happened, then you're way out of order. He was there with his mate David, and with Sally and another girl, I think. They were messing about down by the swing."

Jeremy raised his hands in a gesture of submission. "I wasn't trying to imply anything." Not strictly true. "I was just trying to get a full picture of what we did and who we saw, that's all."

Ben's anger dissipated as quickly as it had flared. "It's okay. I didn't really think you were. It's just so many people seem to have a problem with Markie, and he's a good bloke, really. He'd do anything for you, anything at all, but people only see the snarkiness."

That was certainly all Jeremy had seen, but again he declined to comment. "So what happened after I went home?"

"Nathan and I carried on looking for her for a bit, but in the end we gave up as well and we both went home."

"What, together?"

"Yeah, pretty much I think. There was nothing more we could do, and if you were coming back with your parents we were pretty sure they'd find her soon enough. Once she heard your mum's voice she was bound to come out of hiding."

*The woods smelled verdant and alive, and the sunlight that had managed to find its way through the high canopy of leaves was tinted with chlorophyll. It bathed the spaces between the trees in a green and watery light that rippled and changed. Tiny insects danced and sparkled in the shafts of light, swimming in the air and making the boy feel as though he were wading through a secret underwater world.*

*It had all started as a bit of fun, teasing her with tales of the big bad wolf, preying on her fear of the time-honored tale. He privately remembered how good it had felt, how he'd reveled in her fear. But then everything had changed, she'd panicked and had gone running off into the woods, ignoring their calls to stop. She'd left the path for the tangled thicket of brambles where they'd tried to follow but had lost her in a jungle of undergrowth. Jay had shouted and shouted until his throat was hoarse, his voice edged with panic. But the forest had swallowed the words, and though they'd strained and listened for an answering call, all it'd offered them back was the sound of silence.*

Ben's hands were trembling, and he looked almost as upset as Jeremy felt. "Look, Jay, I feel truly awful about what happened back then, and going over it like this makes me realize I was a part of it as well. If we hadn't chased her like that, none of it would've happened, and that makes me feel dreadful. To think you . . . we frightened her so much that she ran all the way to the lake and ended up . . . falling in . . . it's horrible."

There in his voice was his unquestionable belief that she'd simply fallen in and drowned.

"Don't be daft, Ben. No way was any of it your fault. If anyone's to blame it's me. I was her brother and old enough to know that what I was doing was spiteful and wrong. Look, I'm grateful to you for doing this, and I'm really sorry if I've made you feel bad about it."

They were finished for the day. Neither had the heart to go back into the attic to blow yet more dust off the past. The traveling trunk loomed somewhere above Jeremy's head, the gray fur stole curled in its depths, and it was almost as though he could hear it murmuring to him, a menacing hum reverberating through the house: *Who's afraid of the big bad wolf?*

⚬

After Ben left, Jeremy decided to go for a walk, to get out of the house and clear his head. He set off in the direction of the woodland, following the same route he'd taken with Sarah and the children just a few short days before. There was no sun today; instead the sky hung flat and heavy, pressing into the rutted ground. Jeremy's limbs felt weighted, but he forced himself to walk briskly across the barren fields toward the trees. He needed to face those woods and exorcise whatever demons lurked in the silent undergrowth. There were no planes overhead today, no barking dogs to hurtle him into the past, but still the darkness of the trees held a sense of malevolence. The trunks at the woods' edge stood in serried rows, watching his approach, and a shiver rippled through him as he pressed on, following the footpath they'd used as boys. The branches arched overhead and the trees seemed to lean in ever closer the deeper he went. Silence folded around him, the hush of winter woodland. Jeremy continued to walk, even as his muscles resisted, ignoring the sense of expectancy that seemed to vibrate in the air. He realized his breathing had shallowed, and he made a conscious effort to loosen his limbs and breathe more deeply.

He arrived at the clearing where the boys had once hung a rope swing, long since rotted and gone. The place was melancholy and partially overgrown with brambles and spreading holly. It seemed the local children no longer played there; why run through real trees when such pleasures could be replaced by the virtual worlds contained inside Xbox and PlayStation?

Jeremy left the clearing and carried on toward the lake, his heartbeat growing louder the nearer he got, its pounding drowning out the sound of his footsteps and muffling the rustle of leaves under his feet. Weak-limbed, he reached the bank and looked out over the lake where the water lay dark and flat, barely a ripple creasing its surface. There was no burst of recollection; his memories remained as undisturbed as the lake itself. Even the spot where he'd found Emily's body remained obscured. It all looked the same: an uneven oval of earth, ringed by dark trees whose branches dipped in places to touch the water, their twigs festooned with fronds of waterweed and dammed with clumps of leaves. Jeremy stared down into the depths but saw no secrets there, just a brackish wetness, brown and humus laden. Impenetrable like the past.

*She made barely a sound. Just a frightened gulp and a tiny
splash, and then the water closed over her face, her hair pooling
in a golden tangle. Gradually her thrashing movements slowed,
and a trickle of tiny bubbles popped to the surface amidst the
weeds. She was gone, taking the dark secret of her death into the
water with her. The breeze still ruffled the uppermost branches,
the birds still sang their songs, and there, by the lake in the
woods, the silent trees looked on.*

Time looped and swelled until Jeremy sensed a residual prickling
in the skin between his shoulder blades, a sense of being watched.
A heron soundlessly swooped from the trees like a ghost and glided
across the water, its mirror image rising to greet it like a watery dop-
pelgänger as its wingtips brushed the surface. The spell was broken.
With a start Jeremy realized he'd been holding his breath and he
pulled in a lungful of air as spots danced before his eyes. His vision
cleared and he could see there was nothing there, no answers. It was
just a place, at once both familiar and strange to him.

Suddenly he felt old and tired, and decided to turn back, retracing
his footsteps toward the welcome light and air of the fields. For a
moment he could hear the voice of a young boy calling, but it was
just a trick of the wind in the trees that had set his heart racing. As he
broke from the cover of the woods he spotted a lone figure walking
the rutted track some distance ahead. It was Mark, moving quickly,
head down, and Jeremy slowed his pace. He had no desire to catch up
with him and risk subjecting himself to more goading. Mark's presence there was an enigma; he seemed hardly the type for a solitary
walk in the countryside, more one to sweat off the previous night's
beer pumping iron in some steroidal show of macho dominance.
Jeremy vaguely wondered what he was doing there.

# 21

The pair of them stood on the doorstep. Ben was the first to break the increasingly awkward silence.

"I thought I'd bring Markie along to give us a hand, if that's okay? Those last bits of furniture are pretty heavy and I thought it'd be easier with three of us. You all right with that?"

As if Jeremy could say no. "Yeah. Yeah, sure." Words glinting with frost.

He stood back to let them come in while adrenaline raced his pulse. *Rat-a-tat-tat*, little fists beating at his pericardium; it seemed his heart wanted nothing more than to punch Mark squarely between the eyes. Jeremy didn't want him there in his house, or at least the house that was his for the moment. It wasn't so much his mocking, sneering manner in the pub, it was more the knowledge that he'd tried to smear his name, and that he'd been there that day in the woods. What might *you* be hiding, eh, *Markie?*

As Mark pushed past, Jeremy could smell the scent of stale beer and cheap aftershave on his skin. It served as a trigger, and he felt a wild surge of anger pushing to the fore. He wanted to hurt him. He wanted to feel the gristle of his nose popping under his knuckles. It shocked him to the core, but the knowledge that Mark and his father had spread rumors, had implied that Jeremy had a hand in his own sister's death, made the rage burn in his throat.

Mark turned to him as though sensing his hostility, contrition written across his features. "Look, Jay, I wanted to have a word with you anyway. I'm sorry about the other night, okay? I'd had a few sherbets and gotten a bit lairy. You were right, I was being an arsehole, and it was totally out of order."

Jeremy mistrusted his blokeish apology; unlike Ben's obvious sincerity, it didn't ring true. In fact it was hard to believe that the two men were even brothers, for they couldn't be more different. Everything marked them apart. From the way they were dressed to the difference in size and bearing. Jeremy looked at the heavy boots and the oversize jacket that Mark was wearing, with its bulging pockets that amplified his already impressive bulk. Unlike Ben, everything about him had a whisper of intimidation and masculine threat, as if he even pissed testosterone.

"It's okay," he squeaked. "We've all been there." In reality they hadn't, only knobs like Mark.

He wanted to ask why Mark had felt the need to slander his name; what was it he had been trying to deflect or to hide? He didn't, not because he was intrinsically a coward but because he was unsure how, once started, it would ever end. Instead he took a few deep breaths and tamped his antipathy down to a background hum. One snide comment, one wrong move, and he knew it'd burst free, but for the moment he'd be the better man. He didn't offer coffee though, his good intentions didn't stretch *that* far.

Up in the attic, the three worked in near silence. They lowered down the parts of the dining room table, followed by the chairs and a heavy oak ottoman. Finally, Jeremy scooted back up the ladder to where there were just the last couple of small boxes and the traveling trunk remaining. Mark moved to lift the trunk's lid but Jeremy stopped him with a warning shout.

"No! No not that one! Just give me a hand to get it down and I'll go through it later."

It was suddenly important that no one other than him touched the trunk, heart-in-the-mouth important. There were memories in there of his family, of Emily, and of Uncle Ian. Jeremy wanted the opportunity to look through it on his own, when he could deal with whatever emotions it conjured into being. He didn't want to do it there, not even in front of Ben, and certainly not under his brother's mocking gaze.

Mark lifted his hands in the same gesture he'd made to Laura in the pub. "Whoa! Okay mate, fine. We'll just give you a hand to get these last bits down and then we'll get off."

Once the boxes were on the landing and the trunk safety stowed away in one of the bedrooms, Jeremy took one last look around the empty space. He could hear the brothers engaged in murmured conversation on the landing beneath him, and a spark of suspicion made him wonder what they were saying. There was something in Mark's tone that sounded like disagreement. Jeremy lowered himself through the hatch door for the last time, his foot flailing to find the upper rung.

He began his final descent and that was when it happened. The bottom section of the ladder split where it was hinged, and the lower rungs folded under and away from his reach, leaving him suspended, clutching the ladder while his feet peddled in midair. He heard someone say "Shit!" and hands made a grab for him but it was too late. His grip failed and he fell, bouncing painfully against the newel post at the top of the stairs. The air was knocked from his lungs, and before he had time to react, he was falling, pitching and rolling down the steep staircase toward the hard polished tiles of the hallway below. Frantically he threw out an arm to clutch at the banister posts as he hurtled past, all too aware of the likely outcome if his skull hit that floor. His hand found a lucky hold and he lurched to a halt, almost ripping his arm from its socket. The pain made him yell out in shock and hurt, and the first thing he registered, through a haze of red, was a tiny carved mouse passively regarding him. Smug little bastard. Slowly he became aware of the clatter of feet on the stairs above and Mark's face swam into view, his brother close behind him.

"Fuck's sake! Jay, are you okay? God man, you scared the life out of us. What the hell happened?"

He couldn't answer, too close to vomiting from the force of the pain.

"Someone didn't click the safety latch properly, that's what happened," Ben said, a note of accusation in his tone. "Jesus, Jay, you need to be more careful. You could easily have been killed. In fact any one of us could've fallen and might not have been so lucky."

If laying there with broken ribs and an arm hanging off could be considered "lucky" then in a way he was right, but it didn't feel like that to Jeremy. It was funny how they'd both manged to get down safely, odd how it'd all been fine until Mark was there.

"I'm sure it was properly secured," he eventually croaked. "Are you sure one of you didn't knock it on the way down?"

The brothers exchanged a glance.

"I'm pretty certain I didn't," Ben said, helping him to stand, "unless it got caught on one of the bits of furniture." He looked at Jeremy's face. "Shit, Jay, you're white as a sheet. Don't you think you need to get checked out?"

Jeremy flexed his shoulder and a bolt of pain ran down his arm and across his chest.

"It feels as if I've done something pretty terminal to my shoulder and I think I might've heard a rib go. I'm going to need a lift to the hospital though."

Gingerly the brothers helped him to Ben's now stupid and impractical car—funny how the glamour paled—and lowered him into the passenger seat. He was convinced he was about to be sick but right at that second he didn't care. Sod Ben's upholstery. He was more focussed on the ripple of very real unease trickling along what was left of his spine, for he could swear that the ladder had been fully secured.

It was late when Jeremy and Ben returned from the hospital. The house felt cold and spartan, and Jeremy experienced a heart sink at the prospect of the lonely evening stretching ahead of him. His shoulder ached and his ribs ached, despite the anti-inflammatories pumped into him at the hospital. There was nothing broken, nothing that time, rest, and pain relief wouldn't mend, but it still hurt like hell.

Ben picked up on his mood, his obvious lack of enthusiasm. "Look, Jay, why don't you come over to ours this evening? Neither of us have got anything planned so we could maybe get in a takeaway and a few beers. What do you say?"

"I dunno, I probably won't be much company, it's okay, I reckon I'll be fine here."

"No you won't. Come on, I want you where I can keep an eye on you."

Jeremy was touched by his thoughtfulness but he hardly needed a babysitter.

Ben's face suddenly brightened. "I know, I could give Andy a ring if you like, see if he's up for joining us. It'd be a shame for you not to meet up with him at least once while you're here."

Jeremy thought of the empty house and felt himself weakening. Maybe Ben was right, and it would be good to see old Andy again.

⸺

Ben and Laura's home was warm and inviting. The front door opened onto a narrow hallway, with deep blue wainscot and stripped wood doors, its walls covered with a variety of prints in quirky, mismatched frames. The sitting room to the front of the house was painted in a sumptuous shade of aubergine, which gave the walls a velvety appearance, almost as though they'd be soft to the touch. Two elegantly slumped and faded sofas faced each other in front of a fireplace, where a wood burner nestled, flanked by two stacks of chopped wood. The oak mantle above was lined with candles, some in brass candlesticks, others free-standing, ivory columns in various stages of decline. The wax from previous generations had been allowed to run, covering the surface of the wood with intricate folds and runnels, spilling over the edges to form lacy waterfalls and stalactites, the brittle ghosts of candles past. There were glossy-leaved plants, liberty-print floor cushions, a batik rug, and throws in vibrant emeralds and golds. The whole was an eclectic mix that came together into something warm and wonderful.

Ben had rung ahead, and now Laura came out of the kitchen to greet them, a smile lighting up her face. Jeremy felt an answering

200

NAMELESS ACTS OF CRUELTY

grin creasing his own and he was suddenly glad to be there, and not alone with his thoughts as unwelcome company.

The evening had an easy, companionable vibe. Andy joined the three of them later, arriving with a takeaway and a twelve-pack of lager. In the intervening years it seemed he'd evolved into his father, albeit a younger, happier version. The likeness was there in the tilt of his head and in the way his lean face carried the same creases and folds, as though those paternal features had become superimposed over his own. Time had stolen away most of his hair, and now a few optimistic strands were carefully arranged over his scalp in a way that made Jeremy feel mildly embarrassed for him.

Andy's eyes were frank and friendly, and he seemed unreservedly happy to see his boyhood friend. He enthusiastically pumped Jeremy's hand, causing the nerves in his bruised and injured muscles to shriek with pain. Suppressing a shriek of his own, Jeremy gamely returned the greeting.

"Andy, it's great to see you."

"Jay," he said. "Good God, man, I can hardly believe it. After all these years." He looked Jeremy up and down. "I'd have recognized you anywhere though. You've hardly changed a bit—unlike some." He grinned and made a self-deprecating gesture toward himself. "So, what have you been doing with yourself these past however many years?"

A momentary shadow crossed his face, and Jeremy knew he was remembering Emily. He didn't want to go down that road, so he quickly regaled him with details of Sarah and the children, of work and the circumstances that had brought him back there, before asking Andy about himself.

"Nothing too exciting, I'm afraid. I took over the family business when Dad retired, and I've been running it ever since." A note of pride crept into his voice. "We're doing okay. Actually, we've expanded a bit, opened a second store across at Pewsey, and I may be looking at a third next year. We'll see." His face softened. "I married Ellie and she's got to be the best thing that's ever happened to me. Remember Ellie, Josh's little sister? Well we've got two boys now, Aaron and Joshua, and if I do say so myself, life's pretty good."

Something must've shown on Jeremy's face, or Andy imagined that it had, because he was suddenly defensive, as though he'd been somehow judged and found parochial.

"Being happy is what matters. We're not all going to change the world or find the cure for cancer. Some of us are content with what we have, and there's nothing wrong in that."

Jeremy smiled at him. "I hear you," he said. "I totally get that."

Truth was, he didn't. He'd always felt the need to strive, to try and be something better, something more, but maybe that was because he believed himself lacking to start with. For a second he envied Andy his contentment.

Laura had lit the wood burner and the candles, and the warmth and mellow glow added to the ambience of the room. Jeremy stretched back on a floor cushion, easing the stiffness in his shoulder, and he smiled at them, dear friends all. An unexplained sense of guilt popped up in the wings, but he ignored it. It wasn't as if he was doing anything wrong, he was just relaxing with some old friends, and God knew he deserved it.

Ben dished up the takeaway, and the aromas of cardamom and cumin mingled with the tallow scent of the candles. The four sat in a congenial silence eating rich spicy Balti and sweet Peshwari naan, crisp onion bhajis and golden pilau. Jeremy leaned back, replete, the food and the beers mellowing him out. It was the first time in months where he'd felt so relaxed, almost as if he'd escaped from himself for a few precious moments.

Laura took the plates through to the kitchen and returned with a bottle of whisky and one of After Shock, and something else, a nasty and viscous-looking tequila.

"Come on you lot, it's time to move on to the serious stuff now you've lined your stomachs."

She sloshed out huge measures of whisky and pressed a tumbler into Jeremy's hand, meeting his look with something dangerously close to a challenge. There was something else there too, something avaricious that made him feel at once excited and uneasy. The spirit slipped down like fire, easing out the kinks in *his* spirit and numbing the pain gnawing at his ribs. Laura topped up his glass without asking and flopped down on the floor next to him.

"It's a shame we haven't got Nathan and Josh here," she said. "Then it'd be just like old times, all of us together again."

She was including herself as a member of the crew in her personal rewrite of the truth. In reality, she'd been so much younger and a girl, so she had only ever been allowed to join the others as an occasional and a generous concession. Jeremy remembered how dejected she'd looked on the days when they'd excluded her, and how that dejection had been shot through with a fierce little anger.

The drink flowed and soon Jeremy's eyes were having trouble maintaining their focus, and his diction had become slower and overly precise. Somehow Laura's head had found its way into his lap and he was having to resist the urge to twiddle his fingers through her tangle of curls, while ignoring the warm pressure of her cheek against his groin. He was still sober enough to scent danger, so he used a need for the loo as an opportunity to extricate himself.

The downstairs bathroom was a revelation, a small space, entirely papered in near-black wallpaper covered in a riot of full-blown roses. Voluptuous crimson and pink blooms, thorny stems, and deep green leaves tangled and coiled in a fecund mass across the walls and ceiling. The lighting was low and a blistered, gilt-edged mirror lit Jeremy's face with a golden glow. He noted how he looked mildly dissolute and was glad to escape the unsettling image.

On his return he reclaimed his cushion, careful to position himself in such a way as to deter Laura from resuming her previous pose, tantalizing though it had been. The After Shock had been opened in his absence, and now the scent of cinnamon mingled in the fragranced air. Ben handed him a shot glass and Jeremy noticed how his eyes had taken on a glittering, unfocused quality.

The After Shock burned in a good way, and soon Jeremy was swimming in a hazy affability. They were getting slightly maudlin and nostalgic, and now Ben began repeating the story of Josh and his flaming tracksuit. Somehow it seemed far funnier than before, until Jeremy spoiled the mood.

"It's weird to think he's not here anymore. It creeps me out if I really stop to think about it. I didn't imagine for one minute that any of you guys would be . . . gone."

"I know. It still gets to me pretty badly sometimes, particularly when Ellie's mum gets the family photos out. You kind of can't get your head around it."

"Yeah, well, you and him were always best mates. Probably more so then the rest of us."

Andy nodded. "He was a good friend and I miss him."

An unwelcome air of melancholy settled over the group.

"Remember those godawful jokes he used to find so funny when we were kids?" Ben asked, desperate to lift the mood. "What is it with kids that they'll laugh at anything?"

And then they were back there, competing to see who could remember the worst.

"What do you call a man with a bag of leaves on his head?" Jeremy asked.

"Russell!" the others yelled in unison.

"Have you heard the one about the constipated mathematician?" Ben snorted. "That was one of Josh's favorites."

"He worked it out with a pencil!" And then they were laughing as though it was the funniest fucking thing a grown adult had ever heard.

Andy solemnly announced, "That one always resonated with me as well. My mum was bloody obsessed with checking we were regular." He kept a straight face but Ben and Jeremy started sniggering again.

"There's a name for that," Ben offered.

"Yeah, scatology," Jeremy added, tears rolling down his face. "That what your mum's into?"

"Perhaps that's why his dad keeps his overall on."

"Come on children, don't be dirty," Laura said in a tone of mock disapproval, and then they were off again, Andy looking confused but the rest of them in fits of hysterics, regressing to the smutty schoolkids they'd once been. Somehow more After Shock had appeared in Jeremy's glass, and he was coughing and spluttering as the room began to tilt.

"Anyone up for a smoke?" Ben asked, and then a rolling tin appeared from nowhere.

He expertly ground the buds, folding the roach and rolling a neat, fat joint. A twist and a light from one of the myriad candles, and they were away. The deft way in which Ben handled the gear gave Jeremy the impression that this was a regular feature. After a moment of surprise, he pulled in a lungful of the earthy smoke before passing the joint to Laura. She was already loose-limbed and slightly vacant, and was once more pressing her body into his, her aversion to being touched apparently dispelled by the alcohol. She hesitated for a moment, casting a concerned eye at Ben, then relented and took the joint in her slender fingers.

The high was a warm beneficence that took Jeremy back to his university days, huddled in some skanky student room letting worries about exams and the future float away in a haze of musky smoke. He leaned back against the sofa, and the floor cushion swallowed him up like a fat marshmallow. He should definitely do this more often.

# 22

More disjointed boyhood reminiscences were being shared, floating in and out of Jeremy's consciousness, when there was a loud knock at the door. Ben got up to answer it and returned with Mark in tow—hmm, that certainly harshed his mellow. Mark's presence brought with it a whisper of malice, making Jeremy's mood shift to one of wary hypervigilance. The candles sent up warning threads of dark and sulphurous smoke, and he suddenly felt his skin begin to itch.

Mark benignly surveyed the room before throwing himself down on one of the sofas.

"Looks like I'm a bit late for the party." He glanced up at Ben. "Get us a drink then, bro, where's your manners?"

He plucked the joint from Laura's limp fingers and took a long, slow drag. He nodded wisely, as if giving the mix his approval, then leaned back into the cushions. "So, what's occurring?"

"Just chewing the fat about the bad old days," Andy said, his words ending on a stifled hiccup. "Remembering some of the stuff we got up to, some of the crap we thought was so hilarious at the time . . . just stuff like that. Nothing major."

They desperately tried to recapture the earlier mood, but something had shifted with the newcomer's arrival. Mark joined in but there was an undercurrent now, which only served to feed Jeremy's feeling of unease.

"Here's one you'll like," Mark eventually said, his cold eyes fixed on Jeremy. "Ever heard the one about the two gay ghosts?"

No one answered and he continued to stare. "Come on, Jay. What with your uncle and everything, you should know this one."

Still no one answered and Ben shifted uncomfortably. He reached for the joint but his brother moved it out of reach.

"No, Ben, come on, you've had enough."

Mark exchanged a glance with Laura, one marked by a look of concern. His features momentarily softened and there was something almost paternalistic in his voice. But then his focus swung back to Jeremy and the jeering, antagonistic expression returned.

"They put the willies up each other!" Mark shouted, guffawing with a forced and false laughter.

Suddenly Jeremy longed to go home; he wanted to get away from Mark. He wasn't sure whether Mark was trying to be amusing, or was having a dig at him, or a bit of both, but either way he didn't appreciate it.

"Come on Mr. Memory, you forgotten your sense of humor as well?" Mark asked. Jeremy experienced a stab of outrage at the fact that either Ben or Laura had obviously been talking about him.

Now he wanted to get away from all of them. The high was turning bad and he scratched at his arms, which were crawling with a nervy paranoia. The aubergine walls felt too close and seemed to swell and recede as though breathing. He was sure they were, and that was nasty! He stumbled out of the room, seeking refuge in the downstairs bathroom, where he hoped to find space and a moment of calm to still the anxiety. He was aware that what he was feeling wasn't real, but that didn't make it any better. He sat on the lid to the toilet and put his head in his hands, trying to push back the sense of threat. It didn't work. He could feel the roses squirming out of the paper, their stems twisting and writhing, encasing him in a wall of thorns like in some febrile fairy tale.

Time seemed to ripple and fold. Whatever Jeremy had smoked, it was stronger stuff than the weedy weed he'd puffed on at uni. He was suddenly consumed by a ravenous hunger and was just contemplating eating the soap when a tentative knock sounded at the door.

Laura's voice. Small. Worried.

"Are you okay in there, Jay? You've been gone ages."

He nodded, his head like a giant puffball, wobbling on a willowy stalk.

"Jay, you in there?"

Of course she couldn't see him. He gripped the sink, pulling himself to his feet, and opened the door onto the narrow hallway. "I'm hungry."

Laura smiled, grabbing him by the hand. "I'll sort you out in a minute. Right now I need to know you're okay. Lightweight," she added with a sly grin.

Her face swam in and out of focus, and Jeremy found himself mesmerized by the freckles peppering her nose.

"Thank you for rescuing me," he said. "I could've been trapped in there for days." He gave a theatrical shudder. "Those roses were close, you know, they almost had me."

She shook her head. "Come on you, let's go and join the others. And take no notice of Mark. He doesn't mean anything by it, he just tries too hard to always be top dog. Alpha male and all that macho crap." She smiled but her lips were hiding something else. "Try to see it for what it is: his defense mechanism. And anyway he'll be going in a minute, he's only popped in on his way home from the pub."

She was still holding Jeremy's hand, and the sensation carried a snug little echo of childhood. He could feel the sense of threat slowly receding and he allowed her to lead him back to the sitting room, where Andy had become the butt of Mark's "humor."

"For fuck's sake, just shave it off, mate. It makes you look like that fat guy off TV, back in the nineties."

The mood had lifted again. Everyone was laughing, even poor comb-over Andy.

"Oh yeah!" Ben chipped in. "Baldy Man. Remember him, Andy? The bloke with the ginger comb-over?"

"Fuck off, you two," Andy retorted, good-natured to a fault. "Ellie loves me just the way I am."

"God knows why, she's well out of your league, mate." Mark turned to Jeremy, his face now open and friendly. "You ever seen his missus, Jay? She's bloody gorgeous."

Jeremy shook his head.

"Well, you should. Lovely girl, isn't she, Andy? Face like a wrench." He saw Jeremy's look of confusion. "What? She has. Every time I look at her my nuts tighten."

Jeremy was seized by a chemically induced mood shift and had to suppress a disrespectful urge to laugh while Andy fumbled around for his phone before handing it across. Jeremy had nowhere else to be, so he dutifully looked at the photo of the woman on the screen. Ellie was dark haired and elfin, pretty enough to be called beautiful, and as he stared at her face, his befuddled brain was convinced that she'd winked at him. There was a shadow of Josh in her twinkly brown eyes, and Jeremy was swept with a wash of melancholy.

Mark leaned across and looked at her picture, grinning lasciviously.

"Any chance you could send me a copy of that, Andy? I could do with something new for the wank bank."

Andy didn't respond, but something fierce slid beneath his features, a glimmer of something protective and deadly. It was only there for a second, quickly replaced by a look of expectation as he waited for Jeremy's reaction.

"She's stunning, Andy," and he meant it.

"And these are my boys."

Andy swelled with pride as he showed a picture of two dark-haired boys, with maybe two years between them. Both had their mother's coloring and even features, combined with their father's kind eyes. In a mawkish rush Jeremy thought of Sarah, and Jack and Lucy, and sentimental, drunk-stoned tears shone in his eyes.

"I'll show you mine," he said, ignoring Mark's childish snigger, and proceeded to writhe about for a while, trying to locate his phone in the back pocket of his jeans, a phone which seemed to be mysteriously swapping sides.

"Here's my Sarah." He looked at her face, at the intelligence in her eyes and the soft swirls of her blond hair. "And these're the children. This is Jack—" he passed the phone round the group "—and this is little Lucy."

Ben had blanched and beads of sweat stood out, glistening against the pale skin of his forehead. The phone trembled in his hand, and his eyes widened as if in recognition. It appeared the skunk had kicked in with a vengeance, and he suddenly looked jittery and unwell.

He's stared at the picture of Lucy. "But," he said, "but she's, it's Emily . . ." He looked at Jeremy, and there was something like panic on his face. "It's Emily!"

"I know," Jeremy replied. "Uncanny, isn't it? She's little Em all over again."

"I noticed the minute I saw her in the shop that time," Laura added. "But it's so much more obvious in this photo. She's Emily to a T. God, if you didn't know better it could *be* her."

She passed the phone back to Jeremy and the room went quiet, as they each remembered the one bit of shared past that they'd rather forget. Even Mark had fallen silent. He cast a worried glance at his brother, who was still staring at the phone, as if bemused by the image there. Jeremy's stomach chose that moment to give a monumental rumble as his munchies kicked back in.

"Food," he whispered to Laura. "You promised me food."

"I did, and that I can fix. Come on," and she reached for his hand once more.

So focused was he on his craving for food, Jeremy didn't notice the way Mark's and Ben's eyes were fixed on the pair as they left the room.

Laura led them through to the kitchen, and he was vaguely aware of stripped wood units, mismatched and quirky, dark tiles, copper pans, swaths of dried hops festooned around the door frame.

"Fire hazard," he inanely said, pointing at them.

Laura shook her head. "God, you're in a bad way. Come on you, you need to eat something."

She hacked off a chunk from a dark, nutty loaf and slathered it with butter and golden honey. Jeremy's salivary glands went into overdrive at the thought of all that sweetness, and he devoured it like a starving man. Instantly he felt better, clearer, and more like himself.

He smiled at her. "Thank you again for looking after me."

She was standing close, too close. He could see every line and fleck in her golden irises, and the brush of her lashes against her cheek. The scent of cinnamon on her breath was mingled with the earthy tang of weed, and he could feel the moist warmth of it as she breathed onto his skin. She stepped into him and then her lips were on his, the taste of her tongue and the sweetness of honey filling his mouth with sin. Her arms wound around his neck and his own encircled her slender frame, limbs moving with a mind of their own to enfold her and pull her closer. She felt so different from Sarah. So slight. So lean that he could feel the bones of her vibrating beneath her skin. Her mouth moved against his, her hips pressed into his groin, and a hand strayed toward the place where his flesh quivered and stirred. Then it hit him like a thunderbolt. The wrongness of it. The betrayal and the hurt. The love he had for Sarah filled him like a physical pain and momentarily he was sober, coldly and frighteningly back in the room. Panicking, he disengaged her mouth from his and stepped away from her, running his palms down her arms to catch her hands in his. The scars on her skin were a barcode beneath his fingertips, and they spelled out her fragility, and the message that he was a slimy, duplicitous bastard.

"Laura, I'm sorry, I can't do this."

She pulled her hands away and her eyes met his.

"It's not that I don't want to, I do. You're beautiful and if circumstances were only different . . ."

He realized that even that wasn't true. Yes, he was attracted to her but it was more to the idea of her, to the thought of something illicit and forbidden. Now the reality was literally in his hands he didn't want her. He never had and he was ashamed. More than anything he wanted his wife. He didn't want to be there, half off his head with a group of almost strangers. He wanted his family around him, to be wrapped in their love, but he had to be kind. After all, he'd given off the signals that had led to this, he'd thought he wanted it, so he owed it to Laura to at least be gentle in his rejection.

"I'm so sorry. If I wasn't married it'd be different but I can't—"

She cut him off and her eyes hardened. For a moment she looked more like Mark than Ben.

"It's okay, I get it. You love your wife and that's fine." Her voice was brisk.

"Laura, I—"

"Look, don't flatter yourself. God, I'm not in *love* with you or anything. I'm not *heartbroken*. I just thought, you know, we're both here and we're adults, so why not. It might've been fun, that's all. No big deal. Just a one-night stand that's not going to happen, so get over yourself."

She crossed her arms and just looked at him. There was contempt in her gaze, rather than disappointment, and for a second Jeremy thought that he glimpsed something else. A murderous fury.

The intention had been for him to stay there for the night, snugly tucked up in their guest room, but now the idea was intolerable, impossible to contemplate.

"Look, I'm sorry, I think I'd better go. This isn't a good idea."

She didn't deign to answer so he turned to leave the kitchen, only to come face-to-face with Ben in the hallway. He still looked pale, with a glittering, uncontrolled look in his eyes.

He grabbed at Jeremy's arm. "Did I hear you say you were leaving? I thought you said you were staying over, what with your shoulder and everything. You can't go yet, the evening's only just getting started, and anyway, I really need to talk to you."

The anesthetizing effect of the alcohol had wiped all thought of his injuries from Jeremy's mind and now he gamely flexed his arm. Bad move.

"It's fine, honestly, and I'll be far better off sleeping in my own bed. I've had a great time tonight, but I reckon I've had about enough now." He was in control of sufficient faculties to manage a sheepish grin. "To be honest, I'm not used to this amount of fun anymore, so I'm only going to end up making a fool of myself if I don't quit while I'm ahead." He'd already been there, done that, but Ben didn't need to know.

"But how are you going to get home? Nobody . . . none of us can drive you." A fact that was obvious from the slurring in Ben's voice and the disjointed quality to his speech.

"It's fine, I'll walk. The fresh air will do me good. It'll clear my head, and God knows it needs it."

Jeremy was looking straight at him but had the unnerving sensation that he was viewing him from the end of a very long tunnel. For a moment he stood mesmerized, watching it pulse and swirl toward him, until he realized Ben was still speaking.

"But it's miles, four or five at least. You can't walk that at this time of night."

"I'll be fine, honest, Ben. Leave it."

He needed to get out. He grabbed his jacket from the coat pegs in the hall and poked his head around the sitting room door.

"I'm going to make a move, I think." He addressed himself primarily to Andy, although he could feel Mark's watchful eyes. "I'm going to have to dash but maybe we could try and catch up properly before I go back. Ben's got my number if you want it." He was conscious of his precipitous departure but he had to escape. "See you both later"—but not if he could help it where Mark was concerned.

Before he could close the door, Andy called out to him. "Hang on, I'm on your way, so I'll walk with you if you like. I'd better be going as well; otherwise I won't hear the end of it. We've got a lot on tomorrow and I promised Ellie I wouldn't be too late." He lurched out of the room. "Just give me a sec, I'll need a pee before I can go anywhere."

He trundled off down the hall, leaving Jeremy with Ben, who seemed even more restless and agitated than before. His eyes had a wild look, and he shifted from foot to foot, his movements jerky and nervous. Jeremy was seized by the sinking feeling that he'd seen, or at least heard, the exchange in the kitchen.

"So, what are you going to do?" he demanded, compounding Jeremy's suspicions.

"About what?" Best to feign innocence.

"About her, for fuck's sake, what else . . ."

Ben looked manic, and even in his current state Jeremy was worried about him. There were beads of sweat standing out on his forehead, breaking into feverish trickles running down his temples. He took a couple of deep, shuddering breaths, and for a moment Jeremy was afraid he was about to splatter the evening's meal all over the hallway floor.

". . . Sister . . ." he managed to mumble, so there was no point in denying it.

"Nothing, Ben, I'm not doing anything. You weren't meant to see any of that, and it's not what you're thinking anyway. Let's just forget about it. There's no harm done."

Ben's voice rose, a slight hysteria in its pitch. God, someone needed to tell him to leave off the smokes. "What do you mean, I wasn't meant to see? What, you were going to try and keep it from me? And how do you expect me to forget about it? Fuck, it's massive."

He jigged from foot to foot, agitated, unable to stay still.

"God knows what she's going to do, what she's even capable of. I knew something bad was going to happen the minute I heard you were here. It's your fault for ever coming back, so it's up to you to make this right."

"Look, she's fine. We're all fine. Just talk to her when you've sobered up, you'll see."

Ben's eyes flitted wildly up and down the hall. "Talk to her? No way, *I* can't fucking talk to her!"

The man looked terrified. Jeremy sagely shook his head: bad high.

"Look, Ben, it may not be my place, but I really think you need to call it a night. Get rid of Mark and get yourself off to bed, get some sleep, for God's sake, and talk to Laura tomorrow."

Thankfully, Andy reappeared and he hastily opened the front door.

"Here's Andy, so thanks for a great night, Ben, and let me know what I owe for the takeaway."

He didn't answer, and the two men left him staring vacantly into the street.

# 23

The fresh air hit Jeremy like a bowling ball, and the street tilted and rolled. The night was overcast, no moon to illuminate the pavements, the air February-cold. He was glad of his thick jacket but abandoned the effort of trying to insert his octopus hands into the gloves that he'd found in the pocket. He was all fish fingers, or . . . were octopi mollusks? Andy was in a far better place, and he happily chattered away as the pair began walking. Most of his words barely registered because all of Jeremy's effort was focussed on remaining upright and determinedly placing one foot in front of the other. The concentration helped him to ignore the more irrational ideas that were playing at the back of his mind. Eventually Andy's words began to penetrate, so he abandoned the challenge, and turned to face him.

". . . I just wanted you to know that in case we don't get to see each other again, that's all."

"Sorry?" The word dragged out in Jeremy's ears like a vinyl playing at the wrong speed. He was a seventy-eight on forty-five.

"This is me, here," Andy said, gesturing to a tree-lined side road of tidy suburban homes. "I was just saying, I didn't want to bring it up back there, but I was sorry for what happened with your sister, and I never listened to any of the crap some people were saying at the time."

Andy's features were barely discernible in the gloom. Jeremy gleaned an impression of his long face, both literally and figuratively, and watched as his mournful voice misted the night air.

"It was an awful thing to happen, and I just wanted you to know I thought about you a lot back then."

Suddenly near to tears, Jeremy placed a hand on his arm. "You're a good bloke, Andy," he slurred. "But from what I've been hearing recently, I was a nasty little bastard to her most of the time and I as good as killed her."

Andy's voice was ripe with indignation. "Well, I don't know who told you that, but you were a pretty good kid from what I remember, and always kind to Em. Okay, you might've been a bit pissed off with her that day but you weren't usually that way, and how the hell was anyone to know that things would end how they did?"

They stood in silence for a moment or two until Jeremy released a half sob, a despicable, drunken sniffle.

"You sure you're okay from here?" Andy asked, his concern and doubt both evident in his voice.

Jeremy nodded, not trusting himself to speak.

"You know where you're going?"

He reeled off a string of directions that drifted away into the night, then patted Jeremy once on the shoulder and turned into his road, appearing and disappearing as he moved between the cones of light from the streetlamps. Jeremy stood there, staring blankly, long after he'd vanished from sight.

The fresh air made everything worse, enlivening the weed and the alcohol that was flooding Jeremy's veins. He walked but he didn't seem to be gaining any ground; his legs gave the impression of movement but he appeared to be standing still. He tried walking with his eyes closed to see if that helped to cover the distance more quickly, but each time he opened them he seemed to be on the same endless stretch of road. He experienced a mild panic, a sense that he could be pounding the street for all eternity, and he closed his eyes once more, deciding instead to count his steps as he went.

He was up to 432 when he heard it, a car approaching from behind. It slowed to a crawl, and Jeremy had the uneasy sensation of its lights fixed on his back like raptor eyes. It was the change in the cadence of the engine that alerted him, the shift from a lazy purr to a frenzied roar, accompanied by a squeal of tyres as the accelerator hit the floor. Even in his present condition some hardwired, primordial part of him registered danger, and he watched the angle of the headlights' beam shift as the vehicle mounted the curb. Light now streamed from directly behind him, casting his shadow in a long, dark splatter, like a body on the pavement ahead of him. Just in time, he managed to throw himself to the side as the car screamed past, so close that the wing mirror caught at his jacket as it went. It moved too quickly for him to see the make, and it was too dark for him to see the license plate, but he was vaguely aware of harsh laughter before the car regained the tarmac and hurtled away into the night. His balance faltered and he fell, and suddenly somebody was on him. Floundering and flailing, he thrashed and struggled, but they seemed to be at him from all directions, clawing and jabbing at his skin.

It was moments before he realized that he'd fallen into a hedge, and he staggered back to his feet, adrenaline teeming through his veins, adding to the already-heady mix of chemicals. The shock made him dizzy and his stomach constricted, expelling a stream of alcohol and curry onto the pavement. He was shaking and angry. Drunken idiots, he could've been killed. The thought reignited a spark of his earlier paranoia and made him wonder if that had been the intention all along. He thought of the whiff of hostility from the locals and that very personal damage to his car. Suddenly a warning was there in the very air, the night whispering to him, *Go home, you're not welcome here.*

It was irrational but the thought persisted, prickling his scalp. He wasn't safe. He needed to walk with his eyes peeled now in case they came back. The expression stirred a sudden fear that his eyelids might actually peel away and fly off into the night, like little pink flamingos, and he had to remind himself it was just the drugs making him think that way. He needed to focus, to stay alert in case the car returned.

Andy had said something about cutting through the estate, so he turned off onto the estate road, his thinking being that the car wouldn't find him there, but he was soon lost among the shadowy hulks of unfamiliar buildings. Eventually he found himself at the rear of a small shopping precinct, where the back entrances to the shops crouched like cave mouths in the darkness, and dumpsters overflowed with flattened cardboard and billowing plastic sacks that swelled and rustled in the stiffening breeze. They seemed alive and made him feel queasy. Somewhere deep in his core he was sober enough to know that his decision to move off the main road hadn't been wise. Nothing about the night had been wise. Now he rounded the bend where the shops gave way to houses, and under a solitary still-functioning streetlight lurked a cluster of hooded youths, all shadowy faces and sharp, glinting eyes. Feral creatures of the night. His skin tingled as he sensed their latent thuggery.

"Oi-oi!" one of them shouted but he kept his head down. Lurching and stumbling slightly, he exposed his vulnerability, his crunked condition.

"Got a light, mate?" another called, and there was sniggering and more catcalls as he staggered past. He thought of the car and had the urge to run but knew it was beyond him, so quickened his pace as much as he was able. Unwise. The broken curb caused him to miss his footing and fall into the road, where he landed hard on one knee with a sickening crunch. Instinctively he threw out his hands to save himself and the pain seared through his shoulder, making him gag hot alcohol into his throat. Defeat washed over him and he was struck by an urge to just lie there, maybe get run over by a delivery truck the following morning if the car didn't get to him first—that would be after he'd been robbed of his wallet and watch, of course. Lucky him. He closed his eyes in anticipation of the kicking to come but nothing happened, just more shouts and jeering.

"Had a few shants there, mate?" Hard-edged laughter.

"Wanker!"

Eventually he picked himself up. The knee of his jeans was damp where he'd landed, and something smelled bad. He was in the shit, in more ways than one, and self-pity swamped him as he limped on.

After trudging past interminable rows of blank-faced houses, he came out on a road that looked familiar, and hope sprang eternal. Finally he spotted the spire of the church rising above the rooftops, and it had all the power of a conversion. He was born again; if he could see the church he could find his way home.

A break in the cloud allowed watery moonlight to illuminate the lychgate and the church beyond, and as Jeremy passed he was seized by a sudden drunken compulsion to find his uncle's grave; to apologize for how he'd behaved toward him all those years ago.

The previous dangers forgotten, he pushed open the gate and walked through into the graveyard, where he lurched and staggered among the nearest graves like one of the undead. The moon winked in and out as the clouds chased one another in the breeze, strobing the gravestones like a scene from a horror movie. He was vaguely aware of kicking over a vase of flowers, of crunching through green granite chips in drunken disregard for the souls slumbering beneath. It was futile and shameful. There was insufficient light to read the inscriptions, not that he'd be able to make any sense of them in his current state, so he floundered back to the lychgate to flop in the corner of an oak bench. It was sheltered from the wind, and as he sat, he was swept with an overwhelming tiredness, such that the last few meters to Ian's door were more than he could face. With his jacket pulled tight around him and his hands thrust deep in the pockets, he allowed oblivion to claim him.

The unforgiving cold woke him. A weak February dawn cast a shaft of gray light across the flagstones, which was enough to make his eyeballs throb. For a moment he was disorientated, then the evening came floating back to him in disjointed, toe-curling fragments. He'd slumped sideways during the night, and now the ground righted itself as he tentatively returned to a sitting position, his shoulder yelling in protest. A dull throbbing reverberated through his temples and he bit back the urge to vomit, although during the night he'd been less restrained, as a shameful splatter of puke stained the flagstones near his feet. His mouth tasted of sweet cinnamon and stale sick, and his teeth had grown fur while he slept.

He remembered blundering between the graves in a futile search for Ian's resting place, and he felt ashamed. Trembling and sweating with the effort, he stepped out into the cool morning air of the churchyard, where the bushes were slung with spiderwebs that glistened with dewdrops in the soft morning light. The world was scented with yew, but he was still far too wasted to appreciate its fragrant beauty. A wraith of low mist swirled between the stones, rendering the scene ethereal and peaceful, and through it Jeremy could see toppled vases and spilled flowers marking the previous night's passage. More shame engulfed him as he gathered up the scattered blooms, righting vases and replacing the flowers with shaking fingers.

"Sorry, Elsie Morris," beloved wife and mother; "Apologies, Harry Grant," never far from our thoughts.

Once he'd salved his sorry conscience he straightened up and leaned back, hands on hips, hearing his spine pop. There were hundreds of souls laid to rest there, and the idea that he could ever have chanced upon Ian's grave seemed even more foolish in the cold light of day. Still, he couldn't shed the hope that he might find it, so he followed a grassy track that led through the tombs to the brick-and-flint church with its towering spire stretching heavenward. He studied the stones as he passed, trying to remember what year Ian had died; he'd been nineteen at the time so it must've been around 1997. The graves appeared to be roughly in date order, so he sauntered backward from the 2000s, through the '99s and '98s. Then by sheer chance he saw it, standing out from the crowd in its neatness. Freshly trimmed grass, smooth as a bowling green, a granite vase brimming with alstroemeria, past their prime but still a flash of brightness amidst the misty greens. Ian Cahill, beloved brother, teacher, friend.

Emotion forged a ball of iron in his throat. There was something unbearably poignant about finding the grave, something that conjured his uncle's image far more vividly than his home. Jeremy read the wording on his headstone for a second time. No mention of "beloved uncle" then. That absence, that failure to acknowledge all that he'd been to him, made tears spring to his eyes, and he knelt in the damp turf alongside the grave. Leaning forward, he laid his pounding head on the cool grass, where grief, desolation, and the indulgent self-pity of his hangover made him weep, and that was how he was found . . .

He didn't hear the approach, so deep was his wallowing. The first awareness of another presence came by means of a genteel cough. Jeremy looked up, his sorrow instantly giving way to embarrassment, and came face-to-face with a familiar stranger, holding a bunch of purple anemones. An elderly man, tall and elegant, with a sweep of white hair and pale, Paul Newman eyes. He was sporting a cashmere Crombie and an expression that was half puzzlement, half wariness, with a generous hint of suspicion thrown in.

"Can I help you?" he asked. Cut-glass diction. Imperious.

The two regarded each other in awkward silence. The man's appearance was in stark contrast to Jeremy's own, and he became painfully aware of his sick-stained and disheveled state. Their recognition dawned in unison; it was partly his voice and partly his striking eyes, which Jeremy now watched widening in astonishment.

"Good Lord, Jeremy Horton!" he said. "Is it really you?"

Jeremy relished the small pleasure of hearing his given name. He wasn't Jay, he was Jeremy. He didn't want to be Jay ever again.

He nodded, his voice failing him.

"Good Lord," he repeated. "What on earth are you doing here, lad?"

"I wanted to see him," Jeremy croaked. "I needed to explain."

The man registered his appearance and his expression changed.

"Are you all right?" he asked. "You don't look at all well."

"I'm fine," when he so obviously was not. "I met up with some old friends last night, that's all." As if that was sufficient to justify his condition and his early-morning presence in the churchyard.

"But what are you doing *here*? I mean here, in the village?"

Of course, George wouldn't know.

"My mother died back before Christmas, so I'm here sorting out the house. Trying to get everything in order for the probate."

"I'm very sorry to hear that, Jeremy," George said, but the briskness of his tone somehow belied the sentiment. Even as a child Jeremy had picked up on a certain coolness between his uncle's partner and his mother. His voice lifted in sudden interest. "I assume you're talking about Ian's house. So she ended up keeping it then? Good Lord, I had no idea. I assumed she'd got rid of the old place years ago." His eyes met Jeremy's, taking his unexpected reappearance completely in his stride. "It must be rather difficult for you, Jeremy, being back here after all this time, I'm sure. How are you holding up?"

"I'm . . ."

He wanted to say he was coping, that he was all grown-up now and doing okay, but the words failed him. There was sympathy in George's gaze, and Jeremy recognized the look from his childhood. It resonated with a small, lost part of him and made him feel strangely forlorn.

"It's been hard," he finally said. "It's kind of bringing a lot of things to the fore—and I won't lie, it's not been anywhere near as easy as I thought it'd be." He surprised himself by his honesty toward this stranger he'd once known. Maybe it was the chemicals talking.

"Surely you're not here doing it all on your own? I hope you've at least got some help?"

"Sarah . . . my wife was here with me and she's been brilliant, but she's had to take the children home. They're back to school on

Monday, so she's had to leave me to finish off on my own." He registered how plaintive his voice sounded.

Once again George's eyes flitted to Jeremy's clothing. There was no judgment as he took in the stained knees of his jeans, the dregs of curry drying on the collar of his jacket. He steadily regarded him before arriving at a decision.

"If you're happy to wait while I do this, I think I'd quite like to take a stroll back to the house with you, if that's okay. It'd be good to hear what you've been up to over the last . . . however long it's been." He smiled but this time it didn't quite reach his eyes. "Ian was so very fond of you, and he'd have wanted to hear what you ended up doing with your life." He suddenly looked shocked. "Good Lord, has it really been decades!"

"It has, and yes, I'd like that."

He truly would. George had been part of those wonderful, long-ago summers and always so kind. The night had completely destroyed any resilience Jeremy once had, and now his eyes began prickling once more at the memory. George tactfully looked away, busying himself with the task before him, chattering as he replaced the alstroemeria with the fresh flowers, and plucked any stray leaves from the grass around Ian's headstone. Jeremy watched him as he worked, the unfaltering quality of his movements that gave an illusion of youth. He was still the same. Older but unmistakable.

"I tend to do this every Saturday morning now. It keeps the place neat for him, shows that he's not forgotten and that someone still cares."

Clear blue-gray eyes met Jeremy's, and for a moment he wondered if he imagined the hint of challenge in their gaze.

"Rain or shine. It gets me out of the house for a bit of exercise and a spot of fresh air." He finished and straightened up. "Let me just pop this little lot in the bin and then we'll get going." He gave a small knowing smile. "In fact you look like you could do with a good breakfast and a spot of company."

"I met up with Ben and Andy last night, and it all got a bit out of hand. It's not what I normally do, honest." Sheepish now.

George patted an unstained arm. "No need to explain to me, lad. I can remember the kind of scrapes you lot got into as boys, so I can just imagine what it was like, meeting up again after all this time."

The two men began the journey back to the house. Rather than slowing his steps to accommodate the older man, Jeremy found himself struggling to keep up. George's pace was assured, his frame erect, an echo of the successful solicitor he'd once been. It was only when they arrived at the house that he displayed any vulnerability, standing at the gate for a moment, as if afraid to go in. Jeremy realized that the place held far more memories for George than it did for him, so he waited in silence while the man composed himself.

# 24

Once they were inside the house, George gave a shake of his head and took a single, shuddering breath, and then was all business. If being back there upset him, he didn't allow it to show.

"You go and have a shower and clean yourself up," he said. "I'll get some coffee on, if I can still find my way around the place. Can't say this new kitchen is much of an improvement, preferred the old oak myself."

Jeremy left George busying himself finding the remaining mugs and the kettle, and once in the shower he let the steaming water flow over his body, trying to wash away the guilt of the night and ease the pain. It couldn't rinse away how he felt inside though. He had the urge to call Sarah and confess but knew that was selfish; it would just be him assuaging his guilt while wounding her. Instead he had to console himself with the knowledge that he'd come to his senses in time and that nothing had really happened. He maybe couldn't undo what he'd thought and felt, but at least he hadn't acted on it. He let his mind trawl back through what he could recall of the evening and realized there was something else that felt out of kilter, something other than the incident with Laura. It made him feel prickly and uncomfortable. He wasn't sure if it was just the residual effects of the joint or a hangover depression, but he had a creeping feeling of unease and a sense of having missed something significant.

He pulled on a fresh T-shirt and tracksuit bottoms, and joined George in the kitchen, where the comforting smell of toast filled the air. George placed a plate of freshly scrambled eggs in front of him along with a steaming mug of coffee. He'd always been that way, one of life's instinctive nurturers.

"There you go," he said with a smile. "I took the liberty of rustling you up some breakfast while you were upstairs. Trust me, you'll feel better once you've got some food inside you."

"There was really no need to go to all that bother, but thank you."

He sat down opposite while Jeremy ate, his slender fingers wrapped around his mug.

"So," he said. "You're clearing this place then. That must be a task and a half." The look he gave Jeremy was sharply focused, belying the casual tone of his voice.

"It's not been too bad. The fact that no one's been living here meant there wasn't much clutter and personal stuff—or at least that's what we expected." Jeremy sighed. "We thought we'd finished a couple of days ago until I went up in the attic and saw what we'd missed. Loads of Ian's things that must've been up there ever since he died."

"Good Lord, is all that still up there?"

Jeremy registered George's surprise, and something else, a sudden keen interest.

"Your mother left it to me to deal with Ian's personal effects—she wasn't much interested in his things. I didn't have the heart to get rid of it all, and I couldn't keep everything, so I listed anything of value and put what I could in the attic." His features assumed a look of sadness. "Other than some furniture it was mainly his pictures and books, and a few bits and pieces he'd gathered throughout his life."

"I know, I've looked through some of it."

"I'd always intended to speak to her, to arrange coming back at some point when I felt more able to deal with it, but time passed and then I just let it go. I assumed she'd eventually sold the place and that it had all taken care of itself."

"Seems she didn't, and I knew nothing about it until I saw her will."

George sighed. "It would've been so much easier if Ian had made a will because it would've given me authority to deal with everything how he would've wanted." He shook his head at the memory. "I used to keep on at him to get his affairs in order after the first heart attack, but he wouldn't listen. For an intelligent man he could be remarkably resistant to good sense if it was something he didn't want to think about."

There was nothing Jeremy could say so he sat quietly and ate his eggs.

"So," George continued, "the stuff in the attic, are you really going through it all bit by bit?"

"Yep, I've been going through every box. I kind of feel I owe it to him."

He nodded. "Well you've certainly got your work cut out." Then, after a pause, "So have you found anything interesting yet?"

It was hard to read his expression, there was that keenness again, and a certain evasiveness quality, which made Jeremy suspect that there were things of Ian's that George would like but found it too awkward to ask.

"Look, George, you probably know better than me what's up there, so if there's anything of his you think you might like, you only have to ask. I certainly shan't be keeping all of it."

"Thank you, I'd like that. I couldn't really think straight at the time but now I might quite like one of his pictures or maybe his books. He did so love those books."

Slowly Jeremy felt his head clearing, his body coming back to life, and eventually he heard the question he'd been expecting.

"So what exactly *were* you doing in the churchyard earlier? You looked like you'd been there all night."

"I had. Not intentionally though," he added. "It was one of those things that seemed like a good idea at the time but then just kind of unraveled." He forced himself to meet George's eyes. "It was the drink I suppose, but I felt the need to see Uncle Ian's grave." His eyes flickered away. "To say I was sorry."

Now he felt an urgent need to explain. "Look, the way I behaved back then, when I came to see him in the hospital that time, it was unforgivable. I behaved like a complete arse and I'm sorry."

George didn't say anything, but it was obvious from his face that he remembered the incident too.

"I think I was jealous more than anything else, but that doesn't excuse it. It was stupid and hurtful, and the fact that it was the last time I ever saw him makes it worse. I've thought about it on and off, and it's one of those things I wish I could undo but—" he faltered "—it's just that I loved him when I was a boy, he was good to me, and it was awful to treat him that way."

George reached across and placed his hand on Jeremy's arm. "He forgave you," he said. "He knew that you didn't really mean it; he was far more astute than you're giving him credit for. You were the son he never had, and it would've taken far more than that to make him stop caring for you. If anything he blamed your mother—she wasn't likely to foster much kindness in anyone." His face suddenly clouded, and he looked at Jeremy with an expression akin to disappointment.

"You should've realized that from his letter. Now that *did* hurt him, the fact that you never replied or took him up on his offer."

"What letter? I never received any letter." Jeremy felt his pulse quicken. "What offer?"

"It was a few months after he came out of hospital. He sent you a card for your eighteenth birthday, along with a letter inviting you down. He never heard anything back, so he assumed you were still angry with him, but he always hoped you'd eventually come around."

Jeremy felt a lurch; a thumping at his temples that was more than just the hangover. "I didn't receive anything. No card, nothing." He could see that George believed him but still he repeated it. "Honestly, I didn't receive it. I never got a thing."

A hateful suspicion was forming. He hoped it'd been lost in the post but part of him knew otherwise. His mother had deliberately kept it from him. She would've opened it and seen what it was and been angry that he'd gone to see Ian without her knowledge. That would've been enough for her to punish him. Something twisted in Jeremy's chest at her cruelty, that she would wound her own brother just to hurt her son. The thought that Ian had died believing that Jeremy had ignored his letter, that he was that spiteful and small, was unbearably sad.

"It didn't ever reach me. I'm so sorry."

The familiar anger toward his mother bubbled to the surface. It took his breath away once more, the knowledge of how much she must have hated him. He hadn't thought about her that much since he'd been back, but now the memory of her made his chest tighten.

"Shush now," George said, sensing his distress. "Don't take on so. It doesn't matter anymore, it's all in the past now."

"But I hate the thought of him dying not knowing that I cared."

"He did know, deep down, and he loved you too."

There was something about the way the old house settled around them that encouraged confidences, the kind of things that normally remain unsaid. When George next spoke his voice was suddenly old and tired.

"Some days even now, I miss him so." A sad smile touched his lips. "You know, it's nice to be able to actually talk to somebody about him. There's been no one for years, you see, no one I could really talk to, and even after a lifetime together, it's sometimes felt as if he didn't really exist. So much time has passed there's almost no one who remembers him."

His voice was quiet, the words spoken in tacit acknowledgement of all that they'd been to each other.

"I'm sorry," Jeremy said, "truly I am. I remember the two of you, and you always seemed so happy together. It must be unbearably hard to lose the person you . . . you love."

He needed to acknowledge them too, to make George realize he wasn't really that prejudiced and bitter boy, that he never had been.

George nodded in silent acceptance of what remained unspoken. "I'm grateful for what we had, and there was no one before him and there's been no one after." He suddenly grinned at Jeremy and the years fell away from him. "So you can imagine my initial consternation at finding a young man weeping over his grave."

Jeremy could feel a weight lifting, just being there with him and having the chance to right at least one wrong. He started to understand just how odd his life had been, to almost have no past life. No parents, no elderly relatives, no one behind him to care about him or to know who he'd once been. Just him in the present with Sarah and the children, his history a locked door at his back. He'd missed the comfort of family without ever realizing it.

The pair chatted for a while. Once again Jeremy related the potted version of his life so far, until eventually the conversation came back around to his uncle.

"I can't help but be sorry that I ended up hurting him, even if it wasn't entirely my fault. I sometimes feel as if everything I touch ends up going wrong."

"Why on earth would you think that?"

"Oh, I don't know. I was supposed to look after Emily and look how that worked out, and right now I seem to be managing to make a mess of my marriage as well. Even my relationship with my little girl feels tainted."

He wasn't sure why he was telling George all this. It was out of character, brought about by either the sympathy he exuded or the fact that George was someone who had once cared about him—was a link to his uncle and to happier times.

George hesitated before he answered, "Jeremy, you can't blame yourself for what happened with your sister, or let it overshadow your life. No one could've ever foreseen what was going to happen to her. You were a good brother, you always looked out for her, no matter what." He looked thoughtful for a moment. "To be honest, it would've been more understandable if you'd resented her, given how your mother was with the two of you."

"I don't think my mother ever liked me very much."

"You were probably too young to realize this, but it was some-thing that caused a big rift between her and Ian. He didn't have a lot of time for the way she treated you, to say the least. You were a good lad and he could never understand why she couldn't see that." He smiled at a sudden memory. "I honestly think he'd have adopted you if he'd had the chance. I've told you, you were like the son he never had and you brought him a lot of joy, so stop feeling guilty. He lived for those summers when we had you to stay."

Silence settled around them as they each relived their memories of those halcyon days, and Jeremy wondered who he would have become, how much better a person he might've been, had he grown up in Ian and George's loving care.

George suddenly looked at his watch. "Good Lord, is that the time? I'd better be getting back for Gracie."

"Gracie?"

"My dog. She's getting on now—like me, I suppose—and her hips aren't what they used to be. I usually bring her with me on my morning walk, but the cold and the damp is starting to be a bit much for her, so I left her curled up in the warm this morning."

"Whereabouts are you living now? Still the same place?"

"Yes, still the same old house. I can't imagine living anywhere else after all this time. Too many memories to leave behind, I suppose."

Jeremy pictured the elegant town house, with its tall windows and high-ceilinged rooms. A house somehow like the man himself, and he liked the thought of him still living there. A permanence, a sense of things unchanged. As George left, Jeremy asked him for his phone number because this time he had to stay in touch; he couldn't let his past slip through his fingers again.

# 25

After George had left, Jeremy retreated to his bed, pulled the duvet over his head, and sank into a deep and dreamless sleep. Now, as the winter sun lowered its head toward the horizon, he was woken by an insistent knocking at the front door, a staccato hammering that shattered the silence of the house.

Ben was on the doorstep looking gray and drawn, and he jumped nervily when Jeremy answered the door.

"Hi," he said, avoiding Jeremy's eye. "I tried ringing a few times but I couldn't get any answer, and I just wanted to check you'd managed to get home okay last night. You were in a bit of a state when you left ours . . ."

There was a slight furtiveness in his manner, which Jeremy hoped was guilt over having blabbed to Mark about his memory loss, and he experienced a fresh spurt of anger at the recollection of the elder brother's snide comment. He hadn't said that the information was in confidence, but still.

"No, I mean yeah. Yeah, I'm fine." He pushed limp hair from his forehead. "Sorry, I was dead to the world and my phone was downstairs, so I didn't hear it ringing." As his lips moved they recalled the touch of Laura's mouth on his, and he crackled with a sudden awkwardness. "You didn't need to go to all the trouble of driving over to check on me, but thanks anyway."

Ben didn't move, and Jeremy struggled to read the vibe coming off him. There was still something out of kilter, a remnant of his weirdness the previous evening.

"Look, you may as well come in for a minute seeing as you're here."

He felt the need to try and explain to Ben that what he'd witnessed between him and Laura wasn't what it seemed. He stepped back from the door, gesturing for Ben to follow, and noted his hesitation before entering.

In the kitchen, Jeremy filled the kettle, all the while uncomfortably aware of Ben's eyes on his back. The feeling caused a remnant of last night's paranoia to coldly ripple across his skin.

"Jeez." He forced himself to grin. "I don't know about you but I'm still trying to gather my wits after last night. Thanks again for inviting me, it was a great laugh and good to catch up with old Andy. Certainly better than being here on my own."

It wasn't in the end, but no one wanted to appear an ungrateful bastard. He placed a coffee in front of Ben without asking. His old friend looked as though he needed it; he appeared hungover and ill, and something else undefinable that Jeremy couldn't quite name. He noticed how edgy Ben was, tapping his feet and crossing and uncrossing his legs. There was an odd, inward-looking quality about him, as if half of his brain was engaged elsewhere. Jeremy decided to seize the initiative. Ben's manner was unsettling him and making him wish he'd just come out and say whatever it was that was bothering him.

"Ben, about last night, I don't know what you saw but I don't want you getting the wrong end of the stick. I feel really awkward about it and I never meant for it to happen—well nothing did happen, really—but still, I want you to know there's nothing going on between me and Laura. It was just a stupid spur of . . ."

He realized he was babbling, so he stopped and forced his eyes to meet Ben's.

Ben's look was questioning, and there was another hesitation before he answered. "Well I'm glad to hear it." He picked at a fingernail, and the momentary silence was weighted with significance. "You do realize she likes you, don't you?" he eventually added. "And don't take this the wrong way but it wouldn't be right if you—"

Jeremy leapt to interrupt him. "God, no, you've got it all wrong, Ben. There's nothing like that on my part, not at all. Honestly, you've got absolutely nothing to worry about, I'd never do anything like that to Sarah . . . nor to Laura. God no."

"That's okay then," Ben said, and took a sip of his coffee. Jeremy still couldn't read his expression and suspected that he'd now offended him by protesting a little too vehemently. After all, she *was* his sister and she was hardly repulsive.

"Not that Laura isn't lovely. I'd be mad not to have noticed, but I'm honestly not interested in her that way, not when I've got Sarah and the kids."

He recalled the thinness of her arms, the ridges of scar tissue whispering under his fingertips, and felt compelled to ask.

"Ben, I know it's probably not my place to say anything, and you can tell me it's none of my business if you like, but is Laura all right? I couldn't help but notice all those scars on her arms."

Ben hesitated, and at first Jeremy thought he wasn't going to answer but then he twitched his head, blinking rapidly as if to dislodge an unpleasant thought.

"She wouldn't like me talking about it, but maybe it's best you know. I wouldn't want you doing something thoughtless and hurting her."

Jeremy tried to protest again but Ben wouldn't let him butt in. "You mustn't repeat any of this, mind, not to anyone ever, but she's been through some pretty dark stuff."

He didn't elaborate and now Jeremy's interest was piqued.

"From what I remember, she was always such a happy little thing, more so than some of the rest of us, it's sad if something happened to change that."

Ben slowly nodded. "Yeah, once she was out of that house it was like she was able to push it to the back of her mind and forget about it, but I think that was just her way of coping. It's why no one realized what was going on, at least no one outside."

Were they talking about something that had happened when she was a *child*? Jeremy felt his heart start to pound, as if maybe *he'd* done something to her but couldn't remember.

Ben released a long sigh. "She couldn't keep it bottled up all the time though, nobody could. I remember how she'd have these outbursts, proper out-of-control rages where people just thought she was being a pain, attention seeking or something, but they didn't know what was going on." His eyes slinked toward Jeremy's. "She had to move schools over it at one point, because of some incident where a girl got hurt."

"Laura hurt someone? What, badly?" Jeremy couldn't hide the shock in his voice.

Ben's gaze retreated and he tried to backtrack. "No, course not, I shouldn't even have said anything. I was still a kid too, so I never got to know the full details of it, but I don't think it was anything that serious." He tried to smile but it didn't ring true. "Probably more a case of the other girl's parents making a fuss, but Laura ended up having to move schools anyway." He shook his head at the memory. "She was bloody good at hiding things, but I suppose it all had to come out somehow."

He was confusing Jeremy. Laura had been a happy child. He could remember a little live wire with curly hair and a wide grin. Into everything, her hand in his. He couldn't reconcile that little girl with the idea of her hurting another child.

"What are you talking about, Ben? She always seemed fine to me."

"The cutting came later," Ben said, almost as if Jeremy hadn't spoken. "It was only the start of it though. She completely unraveled in the end, which is partly why I ended up coming back. Then it all came tumbling out." He gave a tight little smile. "Not that I hadn't already worked it out years ago. Neither of us have anything much to do with the old man now if we can help it. Except for Markie—he still sees him sometimes, but then that's him all over, too soft for his own good."

Soft? *Markie?* Jeremy let that one pass as realization blindsided him.

"What? Your *father* . . . ?" He couldn't articulate something so awful.

"I don't know why I'm even telling you this. God, she'd totally hate me if she knew, but she always was a bit smitten by you, and I want you to be careful around her. Sometimes she's not entirely . . . she's a bit vulnerable, and to answer your question, yeah."

Ben's face was suddenly hard and cold. "Let's just say that some nights, when he'd had one or two more fucking drinks than he should've, Dad found himself missing our mother a bit too much for comfort." He spat out the words, his voice drenched in bitterness, and his hands began to shake.

Jeremy felt sick, for her, and for his own lascivious thoughts. "Fuck's sake, that's . . . God, Ben, I don't know what to say. That's awful, horrific. Didn't anyone, like do anything? Go to the police or something?"

"She didn't want to. She didn't want anyone to know, so you must never let on that I've told you any of this, and you mustn't ever repeat it. Her way of dealing with it is to try and pretend none of it ever happened. She'd be mortified if she thought people knew."

Jeremy could identify with that: push all the crap back in the box and try to ignore it. Guess it never quite worked though.

Ben continued, "The only reason I'm telling you is because I've seen how she is around you—and the way you look at her, despite what you're telling me now—and I don't like it." There was accusation in his tone. "She'll be fine once you've gone home but at the moment I'm worried for her."

It was Jeremy's turn to shake his head. "Ben, I've already told you, nothing's going to happen, you really don't have to worry. And look, you didn't need to tell me all of this but now you have, I won't say a word. Promise. Not to her, not to anyone."

"Okay, okay, I believe you," he says. "I just want you to understand how things stand, that's all. What she can be like . . . "

He was still edgy and distracted even though he'd got that off his chest, and when Jeremy made a few futile stabs at conversation, he didn't seem able to engage. He was still remote, and there was something searching in the gaze he let stray around the kitchen.

"So, you still intending to go home this weekend? I bet you'll be glad to get back as soon as you can and put this place behind you."

Jeremy was struck by the impression Ben was trying to get rid of him, as though he now viewed him as some kind of sexual predator.

242

For someone who'd been so keen for the two of them to spend some time together, he'd certainly changed his tune and it rankled.

"No, I've put Sarah off for the moment. I reckon I need at least a couple more days to finish off here, so I've suggested she take the kids home and get them back to school on Monday. We'll sort something out midweek."

He remembered his conversation with Sarah, the surprise in her voice when he'd said that he wanted a few more days. It wasn't about her, he'd told her that, it was more about his need for the closure he hadn't managed to find yet—and which he was beginning to doubt even existed.

"We're not really meant to take the children out of school, but she's going to pick them up at lunchtime on Wednesday, and then drive down here in the afternoon."

"So they're all coming then, the . . . both the children as well? Surely it'd it be easier for you to get the train back rather than dragging them all this way?"

Jeremy was vaguely irritated by Ben's sudden interest in his family arrangements. If he wanted them to come they would—it was hardly Ben's decision.

"We'll see," he replied. "It'll depend on whether she's managed to get the damage to the car sorted out."

He hadn't mentioned the vandalism to his car but Ben didn't ask. Instead he remained distracted, only half listening.

Despite how odd Ben was being right now, Jeremy still felt the pull of their previous friendship, so found himself making an impromptu suggestion. "Look, Ben, it might actually be nice for you to meet Sarah, she'd like that. She's always said how she doesn't get to hear anything about my childhood or to meet any of my old friends. She knows the reason but she still finds it kind of weird. Maybe we could all spend a bit of time together if you've not got anything on. What do you reckon?"

Ben looked momentarily startled. "Yeah. Yes, I think I'd like that."

His expression slowly changed to one of eagerness, as if it was perhaps a good idea after all. "Tell you what, could you show me those photos of the kids again? I was well out of it last night and didn't get to have a proper look."

Such interest from a man with no children of his own was a bit unusual, but Jeremy dutifully grabbed his phone and flicked through his photos until he found the ones of Jack and Lucy. Ben gave Jack's picture a cursory glance, but he studied Lucy's little face intently, poring over every detail. Jeremy knew what was coming and it unnerved him, the way everyone was making such a big thing out of her resemblance to Emily. He didn't find it that striking but everyone else seemed to think so. Even the woman in the shop had looked as if she'd seen a ghost.

As if on cue Ben looked up at him. "Has she always looked like this?" he asked. "Like . . . like her?"

"As a baby? I don't know. I was too young to remember what Emily looked like when she was small, and anyway, all babies looked pretty much the same to me. I can't really remember Em's face that well, if I'm honest, it's more just an idea of what she looked like unless I see an actual photo."

He took the phone from Ben's hand and looked at the picture of his daughter. She was staring straight into the camera and had a beaming smile splitting her face. To him she just looked like Lucy, and he experienced that familiar whisper of conflicted love.

"I only recently picked up on the fact that she looked like Emily at all. Up until a couple of months back I hadn't really noticed, so I think it must've got more marked as she's got older."

"So, she's changed then?" Ben asked, his voice sharp with interest. "Is she like her?"

"What, like Emily personality-wise? No, not at all. Like we said before, I remember Em being a quiet little thing, whereas Lucy's the polar opposite. She's a right little chatterbox. It's hard to get her to be quiet sometimes."

Ben went quiet too, and Jeremy picked up on that strange air of introspection, as if he was mulling a problem over in his mind. He thought of the way Mark had stopped him smoking and wondered if the weed didn't agree with him, because he was decidedly odd at the moment: first sharing all that stuff about Laura when he didn't need to, and now quizzing Jeremy about Lucy.

"You don't believe in reincarnation then?"

His words gave Jeremy a jolt and he scanned Ben's face to see if it was a joke. "Fuck no! What rubbish are you talking? You need to lay off the cannabis, mate, if it's going to make you talk crap like this."

Ben gave an odd little grin but underneath he looked troubled. "You're right. It's just some nonsense me and Laura were talking about last night after everyone'd gone. She's into all that kind of thing, ghosts and karma and that, and it all got a bit heavy. It's proper spooky, the resemblance, that's all."

Jeremy closed the photos and put his phone on the side. It made him uneasy to keep comparing Lucy with his dead sister, and he wished they'd stop it. He didn't like all the fuss about the apparent likeness—and as for reincarnation, no way. He wasn't normally spooked, but being back there seemed to have upset his equilibrium.

"Whatever. I can't see it myself, but if you say so."

Ben picked up on the undercurrent of irritation and was suddenly keen to leave. "Anyway, suppose I best be getting back. I only popped over to check you were okay." He stood up and started to make his way to the door. "Look, I reckon we're pretty much done here, but if there's anything else you need a hand with, just give us a shout tomorrow, otherwise we'll catch up in the week. You can let me know when you want me over." He briefly paused on the doorstep. "See you later then, Jay, oh, and thanks again for the coffee."

Jeremy watched him hurrying away before pushing the door closed on a sad gray world. What he'd just learned had shaken him. It seemed that everything Ben told him ended up turning something from his childhood onto its head. Those good times before Emily had already been tainted by the thought that he was a spiteful, jealous brother and now by the idea that their days had been overshadowed by cruelty and abuse. He thought about Laura's aversion to people touching her without her permission, and now he understood it—and Ben's reaction the previous night. It all made sense in the context of what he'd just been told. He pictured Mr. McLeish, his smiles and his bonhomie, and shuddered at the way he'd coveted him over his own dear dad.

This village was full of dark secrets and hidden cruelties: Laura hurting a girl at school and so full of pain that she cut her own flesh, her father a sexual predator of the most abhorrent kind. A cold finger ran up Jeremy's spine at the thought of his own little sister alone in those woods, but he shrugged it away. He mustn't let this place get under his skin. Even if the police had been unaware of Mr. McLeish's predilections they would surely have looked at him, particularly with the farmhouse being closest to the woods. Jeremy had to believe that for his own sanity.

⚬─┼─⚬

Jeremy lifted the lid, and the past came wafting out on a breath of mustiness. He had nothing else to do with the remainder of the day, so he might as well tackle the dressing-up trunk; after all, his mood could hardly sink much lower. The moth-eaten fur lay on the top and he didn't want to touch it. It elicited a sense of revulsion now. The memory of tormenting Emily with it had taken on a sinister significance; it was no longer just a spot of childhood teasing, instead it now had an undercurrent of spite, a whisper of something darker. It compounded the suggestion that he was perhaps not the boy he remembered. Not him at all. The self-image of a quiet, contained boy, touched with sadness, had been replaced by someone sharper, a mean boy, slyly malicious and gnawed by jealousy. Jeremy liked him even less than the one who'd gone before.

Beneath the stole lay capes and masks, a pirate flag and cowboy hat, a crude wooden sword, and a grubby bundle wrapped in a plastic bag. Jeremy unearthed gold-buckled belts and fringed chaps, and he wondered where it all had originally come from. With no children of his own, Uncle Ian must have gathered it together just for those summers with Emily and him. He took out a child's dress, a fairy costume, complete with pale blue tulle and wire coat hanger wings. Anxiety slid out with it, for he could picture Em wearing it, her chubby little legs and snowy white ankle socks poking from beneath its folds, the lacy wings lopsidedly flopping at her back. Briskly he shook out a refuse bag; there was no place for mawkish sentimentality, this all had to go. He stuffed the fox fur into the bag and gathered up the costumes and the small bundle, which appeared to have a hard lump wrapped up inside it. Gingerly, he pulled apart the Sellotape that was binding the plastic. The bag was yellowing and brittle with age, and it tore open under his fingertips to reveal a piece of tightly wrapped fabric. The cloth loosened and an object rolled out onto the floorboards, where it slowly trundled to a stop. A second of confusion followed before Jeremy's heart stopped with it.

It was a child's trainer and the sight of it caused Jeremy's skin to tingle and tighten, and his scalp contract, each follicle crawling with a sudden horror. It was a small girl's trainer, mold stained and grimy. Instinctively his hand reached for it, but his brain wouldn't let him touch it. Instead he stared at it laying there, a tiny trainer that he knew was once pink. That knowledge was there inside him, in the same way that he knew Emily's trainers had been missing, that her feet were bare when she was found. The canvas might be water ringed and faded, the lights in its sole long dimmed, but he knew what it was. He looked at it in a kind of awed horror, then leapt to his feet and began pacing the room, back and forth, back and forth, as if the motion alone might make it disappear.

Its significance rolled over him like a chill. Deep down he'd secretly hoped that there was no mystery to unravel, that Em *had* just tragically slipped and drowned, but this changed everything, and the knowledge turned his insides to liquid.

At first his thoughts flew to Uncle Ian—after all, it was his house, his attic, his things. He regarded the trunk full of treasures and for the first time considered it in a less benevolent light. It was perhaps a strange collection for a single, childless man, and he pondered whether there'd been a darker purpose behind his uncle's smile, something sinister lurking beneath his indulgent gaze as he'd watched the children play. Even as the idea flashed through his mind Jeremy rejected it. He *remembered* his uncle and felt remorse for even entertaining such a thought. In any case, Ian had been there with his parents for the whole of that day, and Jeremy could recall the hours the adults had spent behind closed doors, the drone of their voices, as the police explored every avenue. No, not Ian.

Frantically he paced, fighting to still the panic; avoiding the sight, letting his eyes slide unseeing over the object on the floor.

He considered George, who'd been so keen to come back to the house. He pictured his long fingered hands curled around his mug, and remembered his questioning. Had there been any unease, any whisper of fear beneath his urbane exterior once he'd known that Jeremy was going through the things in the attic? He couldn't tell.

Jeremy cast his mind back into the past, searching for anything out of kilter, anything malign, but all he had were golden days and balmy evenings, straight from the pages of a children's storybook. If there'd ever been anything there to remember, it was lost, obfuscated by the mists of time and by his longing for something in his past to be perfect.

Slowly, cautiously, he picked up the trainer, turning it over and over in his hands, the feel of the canvas rough against his palm. The Velcro fastening was brittle with age, and a brown tidemark stained the fabric where lake water had once soaked it. He carried it down to the kitchen, along with the cloth and the plastic it was wrapped in. He'd wanted to finally know the truth, but this scared him, and he remembered his own sudden insistence that he alone look inside the trunk. For some reason it felt like a secret, but he knew he couldn't ignore it, he had to go to the police regardless of the consequences.

Suddenly he longed to go home. He wanted to be away from that place, to put the past back in its box and never have to think of it again.

# 26

The trainer was so laden with significance that it weighed like lead in Jeremy's hands. Ben had asked him if he believed in reincarnation and, even though he'd laughed at the idea, it seemed the past was returning to haunt him. Last night the trainer had featured in his dreams and had been the first thing he'd thought of when he awoke, even insinuating itself into his morning run. Normally running cleared his mind, the rhythm of the pavement a mantra pushing thought away, but not today. The simple act of putting on his running shoes had brought the image of it crashing into his head, and the sound of his soles pounding the tarmac became the echo of it hitting the floor.

Now, as his gaze rested on it, he gradually became aware that he'd done this before, that he'd seen the trainer like this, not on Emily's foot but orphaned, stained, and dirty. He allowed the memory to creep up on him, time shifting like sand until the shoe no longer lay in adult hands. Instead it was held by a boy's skinny fingers, a trainer, waterlogged and wet, with lights still merrily blinking in its heel. The memory was pin-sharp, alarmingly vivid. The hands were tanned, summer hands, small hands trembling in fright. He could see the dirt under the fingernails, the grass stains in the creases of the knuckles, and he could feel the emotions that came with it: heart-stopping, gut-churning dread and fear. It was real. *He* remembered feeling that way, and in a sudden panic he hurled the trainer across the room and leapt from the stool, leaving it to crash unheeded to the floor behind him. No, not that! His mother's accusation came roaring into his head, and he felt his control slipping.

He looked at the crumpled plastic bag and the cloth that the trainer came wrapped in. No! He shook his head in denial; he hadn't seen these things before. Tentatively he smoothed out the piece of gray fabric, laying it flat on the kitchen counter, where he saw it was a plain cotton T-shirt, dull and unremarkable. With a reluctant hand he gathered up the neck, looking for the label, and with a sense of dreadful presentiment, read: M&S Boy, AGED 10–12. His fingertips prickled and he stepped away until his back was flattened against the wall, the beads of his spine pressed into the plaster, and he slid to the floor. Pulling his knees to his chest, he wrapped his arms around them, and there he crouched, staring at the trainer as if expecting it to spring into life at any moment and kick him to death.

*He wanted to scream, to vent the horror he felt inside, but he stayed silent and still, waiting for a solution to come to him. He risked another glance at the trainer accusingly perched on the edge of the bath, and a spurt of adrenaline made him feel shaky and weak. He should never have let it into the house, but now he had and he didn't know what to do with it. Even the thought of it made him want to regress and cry like a baby. Like the baby she'd been—but no, he mustn't think of that, he mustn't think of her and how her face had looked with the water rippling over it, the fronds of weed caught on the lashes of her sightless eyes. For the time being he must hide it because he didn't dare burn it or bury it, at least not yet, for if he was caught, the very act of disposal would scream his guilt, and none of this was really his fault at all.*

*Once he was sure there was no one outside he flushed and washed his hands, although he wasn't sure why he was even bothering; his hands would be soiled by this forevermore. He reached into the dirty linen basket and pulled out a T-shirt, a plain old one he hoped no one would miss. Back in his room, he wrapped up the trainer so he didn't have to look at it, opened the wardrobe, and pushed the bundle far to the back. It would do for now; tomorrow he'd have to think of somewhere better until he could get rid of it for good. He closed the closet door and turned away, his soul shrinking inside him. It was time for him to grow the fuck up.*

Jeremy examined the burgeoning fear that he'd drowned his sister, that his mother had been right and it was him all along. He tried out the idea, picturing it alongside the image he'd constructed of Emily in the water, her hair a golden fan beneath her head. It elicited nothing, no flicker of memory, no unlocking of the past. Surely, regardless of the vagaries of the mind, that knowledge would be *somewhere* deep inside him. He looked at the T-shirt and the bag, searching both items for any whisper of familiarity, but there was nothing except that lingering unease, and a shameful desire to keep this a secret—just in case.

There was a bottle of red wine on the side, and now he opened it. All the glasses had packed up and left—much like he wished he'd done now—so he rinsed out a mug instead. The queasy "never again" of two nights ago evaporated as he took the first mouthful, waiting for it to hit the spot where he could breathe more easily and push past the panic that threatened to overwhelm him. He needed to think.

The flashbacks brooked no argument, the sense of spite in his flight across the fields, the terror in his memory of that bath time with Lucy. He thought of his daughter and of that strange ambivalence in his feelings toward her, and he understood at last. It was a subconscious echo of his feelings for Emily, a hidden guilt at what he'd done that came bubbling to the surface, summoned by Lucy's likeness to his sister. He remembered his urge to push her into the traffic, and horror engulfed him once more. It was there in the prickling of the hairs on his arms, and in the way his breath snagged in his throat. He mustn't let Sarah bring her there; he was a danger. Everything, his silence all those years ago, the memory loss that'd haunted him ever since, all of it was no more than his hateful, solipsistic little self, lying to save his sorry arse. His mother's last words came back to him: "Why do you pretend, Jeremy?" Why indeed.

He drank some more wine on a hollow stomach, mind racing. He could dispose of the trainer, burn it along with the things it was wrapped in, as though it had never existed. The idea came on a furtive rush of self-preservation. It would be easy to pretend he'd never seen it, to shut down his mind and go on as before, but there were two things that stopped him: if by some chance it wasn't him, then that meant his sister's killer was still out there; and if it was him, however could he live with that knowledge and deny the consequences it deserved?

⊙━━⊙

Sometime and more wine later, he rang Sarah; he was falling apart and he needed her.

"Sarah," he began, "Sarah, I have to talk to you."

"Jez . . ." She was breathless and he realized she was running. "Can't it wait until I'm home? I'm just out for a run, I'll ring you when I get back."

"Yeah, I suppose, I just . . . I don't know . . . "

He heard the muffled noise of the traffic recede. She must have stopped. Probably sheltering in a shop doorway to better hear him.

"What is it, is there something wrong?"

Suddenly he felt panicked, terrified of losing her, losing his family. Going to jail. It wasn't what he'd meant to say; he'd only wanted to hear her voice to remind him of who he really was, but somehow other words came tumbling out.

"Sarah, I need to know. Would you still love me if you found out I'd done something terrible, would you stay with me?"

"Jez, what on earth are you talking about?" There was a touch of irritation in her tone.

"I just need to know that you wouldn't leave me."

"What's going on, Jeremy?" Her irritation was giving way to anxiety, evident in the slight rise of her voice. "What have you done?"

The hint of suspicion in her last words brought back the memory of Laura's kiss. Everything had gone wrong, and now he was going to lose her.

"Nothing, I don't *know* that I've done anything. But if I had, would it change things?"

"Change what? What are you talking about?"

"It's just that I've . . . I've found something."

"Found what?" A hesitation, then, "Jeremy talk to me, what's happened?"

This time it was unmistakable, the doubt in her voice.

"Sarah, I've found something that could mean it's been me all along. I'm afraid I did something awful to her but I can't remember doing it."

"To who? Jez, you're not making any sense. What are you talking about?"

"What if I did it? What if it was me who drowned her?"

"What, *Emily*? Jez, don't be so ridiculous, of course you didn't. Why on earth would you even think such a thing?"

He could sense her doubt, stronger now. He knew that she loved him, but she wasn't stupid, she'd seen things on the news, the same as he had. The women who'd lived with killers, apparently oblivious while those same husbands raped and murdered, then came home to their children and kissed their loving wives good night. Those wives who were always the last ones to know . . . He could almost hear her thoughts: *was Jeremy a danger, to her, to the children?*

"I don't know that I did, but—"

"But then why are you saying it? Jeremy, what's going on?"

"Nothing, I just need to talk to you—"

"You're scaring me now. I'm going to come and—"

God, he didn't want them coming there, not until he knew what he was dealing with. Until he knew what type of monster he was.

"No, I'm fine, I'll sort it out. I just wanted to talk to you, but it doesn't matter. I'm fine, forget it."

"Forget it? Look, you need to come home. I told you this wasn't a good idea you staying there on your own, I'll come down first thing tomorrow—"

"No! No Sarah, I just need a little bit longer. I'm so close to finding out."

"Finding out what?"

"What happened to her. I'm closer than I've ever been. I just need a couple more days."

She sighed with that familiar note of resigned frustration. "When are you going to give this up, Jeremy?"

"When I finally know the truth," he told her. "Please, don't come just yet. I'm okay. I just need to work out what to do."

"Jez, why don't you want me there? I don't understand."

"Please, Sarah, just stay away! I shouldn't have rung you, I'm sorry."

Jeremy rang off and buried his head in his hands. He'd just messed everything up, made it all worse. In sudden anger he glowered at the bottle of wine before picking it up and hurling it at the wall, where it shattered into myriad shards of dark green glass, a shower of emeralds. A bloom of pink trickled to the floor, but none of it made him feel any better.

⚬━━⚬

Jeremy was dragged from a deep and surprisingly dreamless sleep. A little wine-induced death. Unsure what had woken him, he listened into the darkness, ears straining to pick up any sounds still vibrating in the night air. There was nothing bar the settling of the old house, and he was just drifting back to the place that he'd left when he heard it again, the tinkle of broken glass. Adrenaline pinged through his system and he was instantly alert, listening. Instinctively he reached for his phone before remembering it wasn't there. He'd left it downstairs charging, and the knowledge gave him an extra little jolt. Another faint noise came from the floor below, and he tried to orientate it in the unfamiliar layout of the house, maybe the dining room, where the French doors opened onto the terrace and lawns beyond. He swung his feet out of bed and silently slid to the doorway, thankful that the cold night had forced him to sleep in T-shirt and joggers, and not half naked as he normally would. Beyond the bedroom the landing was in darkness and he stood at the head of the stairs, looking down into the hallway below. No moonlight filtered in through the panes of the front door, but he could still make out the black and white checkerboard of the floor and the dark shapes of the boxes and furniture from the attic, chess pieces yet to move.

He grabbed the pole for opening the loft hatch, feeling the comforting ridges of the corn ear beneath his fingertips. It was hardly a weapon, but he balked at the thought of venturing down unarmed. Slowly, he made his way down the stairs, keeping close to the wall to lessen the stress on the treads and minimize any chance of creaking. He held his breath, edging one foot and then the other onto each step, a tremulous, geriatric descent.

Having reached the bottom undetected, he considered his options. He could've maybe stayed safely hidden in the bedroom but didn't relish the idea of being found in bed like a tortoise on its back, the duvet no protection for his soft and vulnerable underparts. Still, he'd no wish to confront anyone or play the hero. His phone was the sole priority; he had to find it before the intruder found him.

He safely negotiated his way along the hall and gently padded toward the kitchen. He knew exactly where the phone was; he just needed to get to it and call the police. His heart was beating so loudly he was sure the trespasser must hear it. Muted voices slowly drifted through from the dining room, confirming the presence of more than one person, which increased his sense of urgency and hardened his resolve to just grab the phone, head out through the back door, and call from the garden.

At the end of the hallway he slid open the kitchen door, a gap just wide enough for him to slip through. He felt his way along the work surface in the darkness until his hand found his phone, and relief let him breathe again. But as he unplugged it, it burst into life, emitting a shrill beep and illuminating the screen to cast the kitchen in a blue-white glow. Jeremy shoved it in his pocket and made a dash for the door, aware of a commotion in the hallway behind him, and unaware of the glass that still littered the floor. A shard sliced into the ball of his foot, and he cried out in pain before he could stop himself.

"Quick, he's in the kitchen!" a voice said, and then they were on him.

He was vaguely aware of three darkly clad figures before they slammed him hard against the door, knocking the breath from his lungs and his makeshift weapon from his hand. Something was pulled over his head, a rough cloth that smelled earthy and damp, and which muffled the cry that burst from his lips at the shock of what was happening. He flailed his arms, the pain searing through his injured shoulder, and blindly tried to make contact with his assailants as they dragged him back into the hall. There was an arm around his throat, cutting off the air and stifling any attempt to call out. He tried to struggle free from the grip that held him, but his efforts were rewarded with nothing more than a swift blow to the solar plexus—hard, brutal contact, which made him want to double up in pain. For a moment he was unable to breathe, and he heaved for air, fearing that he'd vomit into the sack that was covering his face. Fright rendered his legs weak, and a mewling whimper wormed its way out between his lips.

Other lips were pressed to his ear. "Is that the noise she made, you bastard?"

Another voice, the one that seemed to be in command. "Not here, the neighbors are too close, someone will hear." There was an almost gleeful excitement in his tone.

Jeremy realized in a sickening rush that they weren't there to burgle the house; they'd come for him. Fear made his bowels rumble.

There was the sound of the front door being opened and then the cold of the night hit him, slicing through his thin T-shirt. The gravel was sharp, and pain seared through his injured sole while a hand still pressed the rough fabric against his lips. A car door opened and then he was being bundled inside, into a small square space with ridged metal flooring beneath his knees, and air heavy with the tang of machine oil and dust.

At least one of his abductors joined him in the back of the van, pushing his arm up his spine and grinding his face into the floor. It was unnerving, how he seemed to know exactly what he was doing, something almost military in the way he handled himself. With a renewed strength born of panic, Jeremy twisted sideways, trying to throw off his captor. He couldn't let them take him away. The man was bigger than him; he could feel the muscled heft of him pressing into his back. In response to Jeremy's struggling he merely grabbed a handful of sack and hair and lifted his head, slamming it back into the steel.

"Stop fucking struggling, you nonce. You're not going anywhere."

Nonce? What was he talking about, who did they think he was? Stars sprinkled his field of vision, and a dazzling pain shot across his forehead like a lightning strike. This couldn't be happening. He didn't live in a world where things like this happened. He was an architect, for fuck's sake.

Fear made it impossible to think, but he made the effort to listen, to work out how many there were and what their intentions might be. Nothing good, obviously, and for a wild, irrational moment he wondered if they meant to kill him. Their ringleader seemed infinitely ready for it, and Jeremy queasily recalled the glee in the man's voice. To stem the panic he tried to focus on the other voices, to see if there was anything there he could recognize or could use later. But his hearing was obscured by the rough fabric and by the reverberation thrumming up from the floor of the van.

The vehicle moved steadily through the village, with no rush, nothing to draw any attention. Jeremy tried to note the twists and turns they took, but it was beyond his terrorized brain to absorb. At some point he asked what they wanted with him, but all it gained him was his face pushed harder into the ridged floor. A knee in the back.

Eventually the vehicle turned off the road and onto an uneven surface, jolting and bouncing through potholes until it came to a halt. The front doors opened and closed, disgorging the other two abductors, before the back of the van was pulled open and Jeremy was unceremoniously dragged out onto cold, wet ground. Then the pain began. He was pulled to his feet and slammed against the side of the van, where something hard and unseen made contact with his gut and his already bruised ribs. With a shudder he pictured his liver, his spleen, those tender parts of him swollen with blood, and he tried to protect himself but hands held him fast while the blows rained down. Some were half-hearted slaps, but one man put body and soul into it, encouraging the others to do the same. He felt the searing crunch of gristle and his nose spouted blood, which trickled in a hot, salty rush down into his gasping mouth and over his chin. He gagged. He felt his lip splitting against his teeth, and all the time, all he was aware of was the hate; these strangers hated him and he didn't know why.

"Go near his boy again and we'll kill you, you murdering bastard. We know what you did. Yeah, you might've been just a kid yerself, but that makes no fucking difference."

What boy? What was he talking about? Even through the gritty cloth that was smothering his head, Jeremy could smell beer, hot and stale with something sharper beneath, whisky or brandy cutting through it. Dutch courage to do cowards' work.

He tried to fight back, but he wasn't a fighter. He designed buildings; he didn't hurt people. His muscles trembling, he flailed at them, clawing at arms, swinging blind punches into the darkness, every movement making his shoulder scream with pain. Through the burgeoning shock words came to him, disjointed fragments:

"You've been fucking warned . . . we don't want you here . . . "

"A little girl, you sick fuck . . . "

"We've got the kids to think about . . . "

Random insults:

"Nonce . . ." That word again.

"Murdering piece of shit . . . why don't you go back where you came from . . . "

Finally his legs buckled and he slammed into the dirt, where he tried to crawl away, stones and wetness beneath his palms and knees.

Someone else muttered, "Come on, leave it, he's not worth it." There was reluctance in the voice, fear even, at the thought that they'd gone too far. Then they were scrabbling back into the van, and after a shower of grit and a squealing turn, Jeremy found himself alone in the quiet and the darkness.

He lay still, a chill wind scraping over him, too shocked, too hurt to move. He was acutely aware that he seemed to be weeping, not crying, more an involuntary seeping of tears in response to the sheer violence of it. It'd happened so fast, so brutally, that part of his mind was still back at the house, still safely tucked up in bed.

Somehow he managed to get a grip on the cloth and pull it from his head. It was a hessian sack of the sort used to hold grain or feed, and even in the semidarkness he could see that it was marked with blood, dark and sticky under his fingertips. Gingerly he put a hand to where his face used to be. His nose was surely broken, and his tongue found a split in his lip, salty and stinging and tasting of iron. He staggered to his feet, the world tilting and spinning, and carefully felt his ribs and stomach. Everything was tender yet slightly numb, and he suspected the worst of the pain was waiting for the adrenaline to recede. A wave of dizziness felled him once more, and his legs buckled. He sank to his knees, and vomit splattered the ground in front of him.

Like Jeremy, dawn was close to breaking, and a gray light sliced the lower reaches of the sky. As his head slowly cleared he took in his surroundings: Hills of metal rose on either side, pile upon pile of broken vehicles, car parts, and crushed steel. Fossils covered in rust-stained paint. A track led back to a high-wire fence and a double gate, which was now hanging open onto the road. He was in a breaker's yard with no idea where or how to get back. The shock had kicked in properly now, and his teeth violently chattered despite his attempts to still them.

The priority was to get help, so he surveyed the yard, where a Portakabin hunched in the gloom. Slowly and painfully he made his way to it, limping and stumbling over the uneven ground, panting with the effort. All was in darkness at that early hour but he tried the door anyway, hoping for shelter and a telephone. It was firmly locked, and a sign warned of guard dogs patrolling the area. This news brought a fresh spurt of fear at the thought of slathering jaws poised to finish what the assailants had started, but there were no dogs that he could see, and no sign of any CCTV either, which might have borne witness to the attack. A hard presence at the side of his joggers reminded Jeremy of the existence of his phone and he reached for the pocket, praying that it was still working. Relief flooded his lungs in ragged, juddering breaths.

With near useless fingers he began to dial, nine, nine . . . then he paused. It was what he should do, but something stopped him. He thought of the things they'd said to him, the certainty in their voices. A murdering bastard they'd called him, and he belatedly realized they were talking about Emily. Now he understood the warning hissed into his ear; they were referring to the boy in the high street. God knows what that woman had said but they thought he was a danger to their *children*. A cold, rational voice spoke to him, one he didn't recognize, and it spelled out the possible implications for him if he involved the police before he'd thought things through. If everything was dragged up again and he was accused, he didn't have the means to defend himself against such allegations, against a crime he didn't remember committing. He thought of the trainer sitting there in his uncle's house, how he'd touched it, smeared it with his DNA, and how he'd as good as told Sarah that he'd found it.

The immediate threat had pushed the thought from his mind but now he revisited the possibility of his guilt. It carried a note of resignation about it, as if deep down he'd known it all along, his capacity to disappoint finally fulfilled. With faltering fingers he deleted the numbers he'd pressed. Right now he had to get somewhere safe, where he could tend his wounds and consider his options. He wanted to ring Sarah but couldn't face her. He wanted everything planned out in his mind, what to say to her and how much he intended to tell her, before he saw her again.

He could feel his old life splintering under his fingertips. Perhaps he should go on the run.

# 27

It was a stately old Mercedes, and if Jeremy still had any sense of humor he'd have smiled at the seemliness of it. He watched as it slowly glided around the potholes, carefully traversing each hump and hollow. This might have been a mistake, but it'd felt like his only option, and it was too late to worry about it now. He admired the man's unflappability in the face of a dawn phone call from an incoherent almost-stranger, the way he'd gathered himself and agreed to help. As the car neared, Jeremy ran through his earlier rationalizing: Yes, George could be the one who'd hidden the trainer, but it wasn't likely. Even without the events of the past day there was no logic to it. Why would he keep it, why would he wrap it in a boy's T-shirt, and—most unlikely of all—why would he choose to hide it in the home of the man he loved? It made no sense—not to mention why he would ever have harmed Emily in the first place. No, Jeremy himself was the much more likely suspect—the spiteful, jealous sibling—so now he had to trust the old man and use his memories to fill in the gaps, and his legal knowledge to advise.

George pulled up alongside and Jeremy was struck by the urge to stumble away and hide among the skeletal vehicles. Strange how quickly he seemed to be developing a criminal sense of self-preservation. He didn't though. He stayed where he was, slumped against a van that, now it was properly lit, revealed itself to be an old ice cream van, adorned with streamers and inanely grinning cows. It was an incongruous picture, a bruised and bloodied man against its jaunty backdrop. It was pink and white, at least where the paint hadn't succumbed to rust, a Tonibell van, in fact; the slogan "Make mine a 99" called from faded speech bubbles. In the time he'd been leaning there Jeremy had developed an irrational hatred for it, and now he wanted to beat his fists into it—see, he could be brave when things couldn't fight back.

He felt unsound, strangely disassociated, and he wondered if the blows to his head had done some permanent damage.

George stepped out of the car and approached with wariness in his eyes. Not totally unflappable then.

"Dear God, whatever's happened, who did this to you?" He peered at Jeremy's face in thinly disguised horror. "Look at the state of your face! You need to get that looked at."

"No!" Jeremy replied, more harshly than he'd intended. "Just get me home. I'll be fine."

"Don't be ridiculous. You need to see a doctor."

"No George, please. I just need to get home." George moved to take his arm but he pulled away. "No hospitals, I can't go to hospital." He didn't know their protocol in situations like this, but he was afraid they'd automatically inform the police.

George looked confused. "But Jeremy, something could be broken . . ." He noted the way Jeremy's other arm was wrapped around his midriff as if to stop his innards from flopping out and dangling in the dirt. "Or, you could have internal bleeding, or Lord knows what other damage. This is foolishness." He made eye contact. "I take it you've called the police, like I said?"

It'd been his first instruction on the phone, but now Jeremy shook his head. "No, not yet."

"But why on earth not? You needed to report this immediately. Where's your phone?"

"No, you don't understand. I can't, not yet. Please just take me home and I'll explain everything. I'm fine, honestly. It looks worse than it is. Once I'm cleaned up I'll be fine."

George looked like he wanted to argue the point but eventually just shook his head.

"Well I disagree, I think you're being foolish but there we are, we can discuss that later. Come on, let's get you in the car."

He took Jeremy's arm once more and led him to the passenger door of his Mercedes. Every bone, every muscle shrieked at each step. Jeremy was wary of leaning on him too much, but George was surprisingly strong for his age, with no whisper of frailty about his movements. He opened the door to reveal the buttery cream leather of the car's interior.

"George, I can't . . . your car . . . "

Jeremy gestured at the blood on his hands and down the front of his T-shirt, at the grime and wetness soiling his pants, but George seemed unperturbed.

"Don't worry about the car. Just get in before you fall down."

With George's help he eased himself into the warmth, grateful for the hot blasts of air coming out of the heater. There was a classical track playing, soothing and rhythmical, and Jeremy leaned his head back into the headrest and closed his eyes. He was aware of pain on each inhalation, a persistent throbbing from his nose and lip, and a dull headache blooming in intensity somewhere behind his eyeballs. He was broken. He clenched his jaw and squeezed his eyes tight shut, fighting for control. He could sense an unraveling starting deep inside him, and his teeth resumed their restless chatter—unlike George, who remained silent. He sensed Jeremy's distress, so he didn't talk for the entire journey, merely turned the volume of the music down a notch and let the gentle purr of the car carry them home.

The car pulled into a driveway and came to a stop, but when Jeremy finally opened his eyes it was to the sight of George's elegant town house.

He turned to him in surprise. "Why . . . "

"If you think I was going to take you back to that empty house on your own, in this state, then you're mistaken. Besides, I'm sure there'll be nothing there to patch you up with, and if you're insistent about not going straight to casualty, we'll need to at least clean you up and try to assess the extent of your injuries."

Jeremy made no objection as George helped him out of the car, up the front steps, and into his home, where he took him through into the tranquility of his sitting room. There was a cream Regency chimney piece flanked by bookshelves on one side and an ottoman on the other. A cane bergère chair sat in front of the fireplace, with an open book draped on its arm, and two Chesterfields faced each other across a Bidjar rug and an inlaid table. Jeremy knew all of this from Sarah's obsession with *House & Home*, and now it provided a welcome focus for his mind, anything to distract from the pain and harsh reality of his situation. In fact it was the kind of look his mother had once strived for but never quite achieved.

"Sit down there," George ordered.

He'd quite taken over Jeremy's care, who at that moment was happy to relinquish control of everything—of his wounds, his life, his future—into George's capable hands. He was grateful for the way George had unquestioningly decided to help when he knew almost nothing about him. In the decades since they'd last seen each other, Jeremy could've become anyone, but George had taken him at face value as though he were still a harmless boy. The thought made him shudder, maybe not so harmless after all.

George bustled out and returned with a navy-striped dressing gown and an elderly dog in tow. She was speckled white around the muzzle and moved stiffly, in hopefully unwitting mimicry of Jeremy's tortuous gait. She stopped when she entered and sniffed the air suspiciously, her rheumy eyes scanning the room for the intruder. When she saw Jeremy she bristled and a low rumble came from her throat.

"Gracie!" George said. "Don't be so rude, growling at our guest." He turned to Jeremy. "I don't know what's gotten into her. She never does that."

Jeremy thought he knew; she was a good judge of character and could scent evil.

"Maybe it's my face," he offered, gifting the dog with an unlikely level of intelligence and observational skill. Still, better that than to suggest she could sense his murderous soul.

"Come on, let's get you out of those clothes," George said. Seeing as the dog wasn't wearing any, Jeremy assumed George was addressing him.

He was beyond any humorous rejoinder, so he meekly dropped his joggers and struggled out of his T-shirt, crying out at the effort of lifting it over his head. The sudden sound made Gracie growl a second time, and a ruff of hair raised itself at the back of her neck. Maybe she could smell blood. George whisked the offending garments away, leaving man and dog warily regarding each other. Jeremy didn't think he could handle a further assault, although Gracie's advanced age made it likely that, this time at least, he'd emerge the victor.

Arm-to-tooth combat proved unnecessary, as George quickly returned with a towel and a bowl of warm water, cotton wool balls, antiseptic, and dressings. These he placed on the inlaid table and asked Jeremy to lie back on the sofa.

Jeremy made some feeble objection. "No, not here, I'll ruin your things."

"Oh for goodness' sake! I don't remember you being this stubborn as a child. If you won't go to hospital then at least let me do what I can."

George laid the towel across Jeremy's chest and got to work, sponging the dried blood from his face. Jeremy winced as George touched the cartilage in his nose, and he huffed and tutted as further injuries revealed themselves.

"You're going to have a proper shiner tomorrow," George said. "Two, if I'm not mistaken. I'm pretty sure that nose is broken. I'll get you some ice for it in a minute."

He leaned in to examine the split lip, and Jeremy caught the resinous scent of Dunhill cologne. It was weird, the way in which his brain was homing in on irrelevant details, skittering around the bigger issues of who had attacked him and why. Now there was suddenly childhood in his nostrils.

"Why are you doing this for me, George, why are you helping me? You barely even know me anymore."

George paused his ministrations and looked thoughtful. "Thinking about it, I suppose it's for him. He always was so awfully fond of you." He turned his attention back to the offending lip, suddenly flustered. "That needs a butterfly, otherwise it's probably going to scar. I really think you should reconsider the hospital, Jeremy."

Jeremy didn't care. He'd probably get much worse in prison. He cringed even as he thought it. God, he disgusted himself with his relentless capacity to be the victim.

"Leave it, George. It's fine."

When George had finished picking the grit from Jeremy's injured foot he smoothed the hair back from his forehead and looked into his eyes.

"Have you really no idea who did this to you, lad?" he asked, shaking his head. "I can't for the life of me understand why you haven't contacted the police. I've a good mind to ring them myself."

"No," Jeremy caught at his hand. "Please, not yet. I need some time to think."

George didn't answer, distracted by the marks blossoming on Jeremy's torso. Instead he began to gently probe the patches of redness on ribs and abdomen, his long fingers expertly prodding and pressing. "Does that hurt?"

"Ow!"

"I'll take that as a yes. What about here?"

There was an assuredness about his actions that made Jeremy believe he'd done this before.

"Army Medical Corp," he said, in answer to the unasked question. "Only support but still . . ." He sighed. "I was just about old enough to catch the tail end of national service and I couldn't see myself doing very well at the killing side of things."

He finished his prodding and straightened up. "I expect you've got a cracked rib or two but there's no sign of anything more serious, at least not that I can see." He peered intently. "I take it you can still breathe okay—no coughing up blood or anything?"

"God no, I just ache like hell. I feel as though I've been run over by a truck."

On balance that would probably have been less painful, what with the fall from the loft and now this.

"I'd be much happier if you'd agree to go to the emergency department, but if you won't be persuaded, you're welcome to stay here for the next twenty-four hours or so. You've been hit in the head, Jeremy, and here I can at least keep an eye on you."

He opened his mouth to protest but closed it again at the thought of going back to the house, of being alone there in his vulnerable state. "Thank you."

Cautiously, Jeremy pushed himself up to a sitting position and tied the robe, before burying his head in his hands. George bustled off to get some ice wrapped in a tea towel, before taking a seat on the sofa opposite.

"Now Jeremy, do you think you're ready to tell me what's really going on?"

Jeremy looked back at him, at the genuine concern creasing his old face, and had no idea where to begin.

"Jeremy," George prompted. "How about you start by telling me how you ended up at the breaker's yard in the first place?"

It was as good a beginning as any, so Jeremy took the ice pack from his mangled features and told him about the intruders, and his nighttime abduction. George listened impassively, the lawyer in him coming to the fore, as the nightmare unfolded. When he got to the part about the beating and the things that they'd said to him, Jeremy stopped. His mind shied away from it.

"And you're sure you have no idea who they were? Nothing familiar in their voices, no clue in anything they said to you as to why they were doing it?"

"No, it all happened so fast, so unexpected. One minute I was asleep in bed and then . . . I was too shocked to take much in . . . "

He began to shake at the memory, his knees jiggling with a life of their own. He couldn't repeat the things they'd said to him and watch suspicion blooming on George's face too. Instead he focused on the other question spinning round in his brain—what might happen to him if he were guilty.

"George, I need to ask you something . . ." He hesitated and felt his throat start to close. For a second he didn't think he could speak, and he coughed nervously, hyperaware of George's eyes upon him. Then the words came.

"If, if for instance, someone was . . . someone who's now an adult was charged with something they did . . . with a crime they committed when they were a child, what would happen to them?"

George didn't question the question; he just gave it due consideration, as though Jeremy were a client. "What sort of crime would we be talking about here?" he asked.

Jeremy's voice stuck again but he pushed past it. "I'm not sure . . ." He could hardly bring himself to speak its name. "Killing someone. Murder, I suppose, or manslaughter, maybe if it was an accident . . ."

George's eyed momentarily widened and Jeremy wondered what he was thinking, his earlier unflappability now seriously flapped.

"I'm talking about something that might've happened years ago though, back when . . . they were a child."

George cleared his throat, his eyes fixed on Jeremy's. "Well firstly, it doesn't matter how long ago."

Jeremy already knew this, but still his pulse quickened.

"Because unlike most other countries, there's no statute of limitations in the UK, and in any case it wouldn't apply to murder or manslaughter."

Jeremy nodded his understanding, not trusting himself to speak.

"But then we get onto the sticky issue of the age of the child in question." He waited, expecting Jeremy to fill that gap and when he didn't, he continued, "In England and Wales the minimum age of criminal responsibility is ten. It was set way back and is lower than any other European country, but there we are. Any child of ten or over is considered to have capacity to understand the implications of their actions and, ergo, be responsible for them. Below ten, the presumption is that the child is morally and intellectually incapable of committing a crime by reason of age."

He warmed to the legal theme. "It used to be a bit of a gray area between ten and fourteen, as *Doli incapax* could be applied to children up to the age of fourteen, but it was abolished at the end of the nineties." He looked thoughtful for a moment. "You're probably too young to remember, but there was a dreadful case back in the early nineties, which tended to focus the mind somewhat on the whole issue of age and responsibility. Venables and Thompson? The James Bulger case?"

Dread coursed through Jeremy's veins. He might have been only fifteen or so but he could remember it well, the horror of it. Was that what he was, a monster no different from those two boys? He fought to calm himself. He didn't know that it was true. It might be the secret fear he'd carried through his life, the thing that inhabited his dark places, but he didn't know it to be true.

George continued, oblivious to Jeremy's distress. "Usually between ten and seventeen, cases are dealt with in youth court, but in the matter of serious crime, children of that age can face adult crown court." Finally, he noticed. "Good Lord, Jeremy, you've gone white as a sheet."

Jeremy wondered if he saw it then, the first whisper of suspicion, but George gave little away.

"I suppose, in the situation you're proposing here, the individual concerned would be charged and tried as an adult, but their age at the time of the index offense would be taken into account when sentencing—on the assumption they're guilty, of course."

That was it then; off with his head.

"Jeremy, may I ask where this is all leading?"

He might ask, but Jeremy had no intention of telling him. "Nowhere, really. I was just speculating, that's all. Some of the things I've heard in the few days I've been back here have made me wonder."

"Wonder what, exactly?"

"Nothing specific, just that there seem to have been a lot of rumors flying around back when Emily drowned, and it's made me wonder whether someone was trying to deflect suspicion, and now this . . . Maybe somebody doesn't like me asking questions, poking around in the past."

"Is that what you've been doing then, asking questions?"

"Well, yes, but only some general stuff, about me mainly. My memories of that day have always been a bit hazy, so I asked Ben a couple of things, that's all. No big deal." He managed a painful grin. "I think I'm letting my imagination run away with me, if I'm honest."

George seemed satisfied with this, at least on the surface, and Jeremy allowed himself to relax. He was suddenly unbelievably tired and released a long and shuddering yawn.

George got to his feet. "I think you need to rest for a while—we can talk some more later. I'll get you something for the pain, and then you best try and sleep if you can."

He came back with a glass of water and two lurid pink tablets nestling in his palm. "Here you go, these'll help. I was given them by the doctor when I pulled my back. Marvelous things, they'll do the trick."

Trustingly Jeremy swallowed them down, aware of the intentness of the older man's gaze. He leaned back against the cushions and closed his eyes.

"Thank you for doing this, George. I don't know what I'd have done without your help."

He felt the warmth of a hand patting his.

"The least I could do, lad," George said. "Now you try and get some rest."

His footsteps receded and Jeremy heard the soft click of the latch before the shock of his experience and the warmth of the room overwhelmed him, and he crashed into sleep.

When he woke he felt floaty and warm, courtesy of George's marvelous pink pills. The door was still closed, the house silent. Tentatively he sat up, testing his muscles and bracing himself against the pain that surely must come, but mainly he felt stiff. Every muscle had contracted in on itself, and he cautiously stretched to release his limbs. He edged his way up from the sofa and moved toward the door, each step making his side ache and his breath snag in his throat. Opening the door, he moved through into the hall, where the tiles of the floor were cold against his bare feet. George could be heard moving about in the room at the end of the corridor, and Jeremy entered to find himself in a bright and spacious kitchen. George was standing by the window looking out at the garden, and he turned at the sound of Jeremy approaching.

"Ah, you're awake. How are you feeling now?"

"Achy, stiff, but nowhere near as bad as I thought I would." He stretched his back. "My ribs are the worst and my stomach feels bruised, but otherwise it's mainly the stiffness."

"I told you those tablets were good," George said. "You've been out for the best part of four hours. Your clothes are in the tumble dryer. I took the liberty of rinsing them through while you were asleep and they should be almost dry now."

Startled, Jeremy glanced at the clock. George was right, it was almost midday.

"Sit yourself down and I'll make you a coffee and something to eat if you feel up to it." George gestured toward a scrubbed pine kitchen table ringed by six matching chairs.

"Please," Jeremy said. "Just a piece of toast will be fine. No need to go to a load of trouble."

He gratefully sat down at the table, wobbly legged and suffused with a pleasant, spacey mellowness. God knew what those pills were, but he certainly appreciated their effects. Through a warm haze he watched as George cut slices from a crusty white loaf, the blade of the bread knife a flash of silver in the watery sunlight filtering in from the window.

"So," George said, "what was all that talk about earlier? About the legalities around child crime?"

He glanced round and his pale eyes bored into Jeremy, penetrating the haze of affability induced by the drugs.

"Oh I don't know, I was just speculating I suppose, wondering about the implications if . . . if one of the kids back then had something to do with what happened to Emily. I was really just trying to come up with reasons why someone would want to beat me up."

"It seems rather extreme lengths to go to, to me," George observed. "Breaking into the house and effectively abducting you. Good Lord, Jeremy, it's more like something you'd see in a film rather than encounter in real life. Surely if they wanted you to stop asking questions, then they were going about it in entirely the wrong way. It doesn't make any sense—and I still don't understand why you won't inform the police."

Something about the warmth of the room and the aftereffects of the medication made Jeremy lower his guard and gave him the urge to confide.

"I think they'd got the wrong end of the stick. They seemed to think I'm guilty of something." He gave a little half laugh to convey the ridiculousness of such a thing.

George's eyes locked on to his, and Jeremy was aware of Gracie slinking around the leg of the table to sit by his side. "Why ever would they be thinking something like that?"

"You tell me. It seems I featured in a lot of the rumor and speculation that was flying around at the time."

George nodded as if in understanding, and Jeremy was moved to say more. "You know, I've always had this feeling that, deep down, I knew more than I could remember, that there was more to Emily's death than just an accidental drowning, and now I've found something . . . "

George turned away from the work surface where he was cutting the bread, a quick, fluid movement that belied his age. The knife was still clutched in his hand, and there was something unsettling in his expression. Something avid, overly eager and probing. The dog picked up on the shift in the atmosphere, and her throat emitted another low growl as George stabbed at the air, using the knife to punctuate his next question.

"Found what?" he demanded. "What have you found?"

Jeremy was suddenly wary of saying too much. Of incriminating himself or of showing his hand. He'd been so ready to assume George's innocence because of his relationship with Ian and because of his own childhood memories of those idyllic summers, but now he paused. He'd been a child. What did he really know of this man or his predilections? All he had were rose-tinted recollections of those summers that were a haven of happiness in a fairly wretched childhood. Romanticised, unreliable recollections. He looked at George now and got a sense of threat.

He found himself backtracking, his mind working quickly. "Not found something, found *out* something that makes me suspicious. Apparently Ben's brother was particularly keen to incriminate me, and it makes me wonder if he had something to hide." He wasn't lying; it was true. He had wondered why Mark was so ready to cast suspicion his way.

George looked doubtful. "You said you'd found something," he insisted.

"No, it was a slip of the tongue. You misunderstood me."

Jeremy looked at the way George was holding the knife, the blade pointed toward him. There was something vaguely threatening in the gesture, and he suddenly mistrusted him. George followed his gaze and quickly lowered it, a faint smile edging its way to his lips.

"Good Lord, whatever must you think of me, pointing at you with the knife like that. How rude, please forgive me."

There was an awkward silence while he made some toast and a mug of coffee. Jeremy could sense how much he wanted to continue his questioning, and he tried to put it down to the man's profession, an ingrained tendency to interrogate and establish the facts, but it didn't help. He was uneasy now and wanted to go home. He didn't know whom he could trust anymore, not George, not himself, and he needed time to think things through.

When he'd finished the toast he broached the subject of leaving. "George, I've been thinking, there's no need for you to go to all the bother of putting me up here for the night, making up a guest room and everything. Now I've had a sleep and a bite to eat, I feel reasonably okay bar a few aches and pains. Sarah was meant to be coming down later today anyway, so I'll be fine." Only a half lie—she was *meant* to be.

"Don't be silly. You're more than welcome to stay here, and it's not good you being in that house on your own. At least stay a while longer—you haven't finished telling me what happened."

Jeremy hoped it was just loneliness feeding his insistence. He'd sensed it before back at the churchyard—George's need for company, for someone to talk to—but he wouldn't be swayed.

"I don't want to seem ungrateful, but I think I'd be better off getting back. I'll ring for a taxi once my clothes are dry, I've imposed upon you more than enough for one day."

George didn't answer, just nodded his acquiescence. Jeremy wasn't sure if he was disappointed or angry. He reached into the pocket of his joggers for his phone, but of course he was still wearing George's dressing gown.

"Have you seen my phone? I last had it to ring you, so it must've been in the pocket of my trousers."

George shook his head, and guileless eyes met Jeremy's.

"No," he replied. "I checked both pockets before I put them in the wash and there was nothing in either of them. Best check the sofa in case it slipped out."

Together they returned to the sitting room, where George scrupulously felt between the cushions but there was no phone. Jeremy cast his mind back to when he'd made the call. He couldn't consciously remember doing it, but he was sure he would've automatically put the phone back in his pocket.

"Are you sure it's not there?"

"Nope, nothing," George replied, pulling out the seat cushions to demonstrate. "But don't worry, it'll turn up, I'm sure. It's bound to be somewhere." Straightening up, he smiled but Jeremy felt a deep rumble of mistrust. "Look, I can see you're dead on your feet. Trauma gets you like that sometimes. It's the body's way of telling you it needs to shut everything down and focus on recovering and healing. I know you're in a hurry to get back, but the house isn't going anywhere. You'd be better served by getting your head back down and giving yourself a bit of time to recover."

He was right about the tiredness. Jeremy was suddenly bone-crushingly weary, as if the trip to the kitchen and back had used up his all reserves. His body craved oblivion. George took his elbow, and despite his unease Jeremy didn't resist. His energy was sapped, and he honestly wondered if he'd even be able to make his own way home.

"Come on, the guest room is all made up, so you're honestly not being any bother." George glanced at the clock. "You'll be all right to take another couple of painkillers, and then you must get yourself off to bed. In the meantime I'll have a look in the car for your phone, that's probably where it fell out, and then you can sort out that taxi when you wake up. Believe me, everything will seem better after you've had some decent rest."

Jeremy let George lead him up the stairs, trying to ignore the feeling he had of being trapped—hopefully by good intentions.

George was right about the guest room too. The bed was made up just as he'd said, and Jeremy gratefully slid between cool cotton sheets. They had the vaguely clammy feel of bedding that had lain unused for a while, but he was past caring. Being beaten up was an entirely new experience for him, and if this was what it felt like, then it wasn't one he was in any hurry to repeat. He'd been on the receiving end of a few well-deserved thumps at school, but never anything like this. He tried to go back over the events of the night, but his brain wouldn't function. By the time George reappeared with water and the pills, his eyelids had grown heavy. He swallowed down more tablets and watched while George fussed with the curtains, ensuring they were closed against the intrusion of light, and then there was nothing at all.

# 28

The phone burst into life with a series of excitable beeps, and a stream of messages, voice mails, and missed calls flooded the screen, all of them from Sarah. Jeremy pictured her obsessively checking her phone in case she'd missed his call, while her mind imagined the worst.

She picked up on the second ring. "Jez?" There wasn't quite the relief he'd expected, instead there was a strangled quality to her voice, as if she was suppressing an urge to scream down the phone at him.

"Sarah, it's me. Darling I'm so sorry . . . "

"Jez, where the hell are you? I've been trying to get hold of you all night" Through gritted teeth. "I've been worried sick. Where are you? Why aren't you at the house?"

Angry tears burbled beneath the harshness of her tone, threatening to rise to the surface at the sound of his voice.

"It's okay, I'm fine and I didn't mean to worry you. I lost my phone and it was flat by the time I'd found it, so I didn't know you'd been ringing me until now . . . "

"But where have you been all night, why aren't you here?"

"I'm at . . . Look, it's complicated. I'll . . . "

How did she know he wasn't at the house?

"Sarah, where are you?"

"We're here at the house, all of us. I've had to drag the children here as well. After you rang and were so weird on the phone, I got worried and I drove down. We got here late yesterday, and I've been up all night trying to get hold of you, imagining all sorts of things . . . "

"Oh God, I'm so sorry. I'll come home and I'll explain everything."

"And where did these things in the kitchen come from, this old T-shirt and trainer, and why is there broken glass all over the floor? And . . . and *blood*, Jez, why is there blood? What's been going on?"

"Sarah, that's . . . that's nothing, just . . . just some stuff I found in the attic, and the blood's from where I dropped a wine bottle and cut my foot, that's all." He suddenly pictured her tidying up and throwing everything away. "Look, don't touch any of it, okay? I'll be there as soon as I can and I'll explain everything, but there's nothing for you to worry about, honestly." Not yet.

He was standing in George's study, with the errant phone clamped to his ear. Confounding all his earlier suspicions, George had found it in the car and set it charging while he slept—through the remainder of the day and most of the night. It wasn't until three in the morning that a burst of pain had finally woken him, alone in a strange bed, hot and disoriented and needing a pee. Even then he'd manged to go back to sleep, not surfacing again until eleven in the morning, hurting in all the places he'd expected, and desperately, ravenously hungry.

His previous paranoia and mistrust seemed misplaced in the cold light of day, particularly when George had presented him not only with his phone but with a massive plate of bacon and eggs, and a rack of buttered toast.

Now George was standing in the doorway holding a mug of fresh coffee and watching him. He waited until the call was finished before handing Jeremy the steaming mug.

"There you go. Drink that before it gets cold. It'll help you to feel a bit more human." He cocked his head to the side and examined Jeremy's face. "How are you feeling now?"

Jeremy took the offered coffee but felt too agitated to answer. He could sense his life crumbling around him, washed away in a flood of questions for which he had no answers. George didn't move, instead he just stood there, head still slightly on one side, staring intently at Jeremy's face, like a seagull spying an ice cream. One of Jeremy's eyes was swollen shut, the skin livid purple and stretched tight like a damson. His nose hadn't fared much better; it had a squashed, misshapen quality and, as he'd found to his earlier horror, a worryingly mushiness to the touch. He'd prided himself on being a bit of a looker in an understated kind of way, and for a shallow moment he'd wondered whether his prison mug shot would still be a thing of beauty. On balance, he might be better off if it wasn't.

George stood there, fixing him with those startling eyes. He might be old but he was far from stupid, and he could sense that Jeremy was keeping something from him. Something significant that he needed to know.

"What?" Jeremy asked. "What is it?" The burgeoning stress made his words curt and accusatory, and he felt the previous day's mistrust resurfacing under the older man's laser-like scrutiny.

George moved into the room and proceeded to straighten the pens on his desk with exacting fingers, lining them up on its burnished surface. He didn't glance up from the task as he spoke, but Jeremy could feel every atom of his attention focussed on him.

"I wasn't eavesdropping, but I couldn't help overhearing you say that you'd found something in the attic?"

The words ended on an upward inflection, an unspoken question, and a cool finger of doubt touched the base of Jeremy's skull. What was it with the man, this interest in the stuff from the attic?

"Yes, but it wasn't anything that important."

Even to his own ears the answer sounded disingenuous, and Jeremy found himself pinned like a moth by that unwavering gaze.

"Really, Jeremy? You mentioned the same thing yesterday, and regardless of what you said afterward, you seemed rather upset by it at the time. I'd be grateful if you could tell me what's really going on."

"No I wasn't upset, not really, and like I said, it was nothing important."

Questioning, everyone questioning him.

"Forgive me, Jeremy, but it didn't sound that way, not when you were asking me all those questions. You seemed really quite bothered by it. Maybe I'm just being overly curious, but I would quite like to know what you found."

His words were casual, but his face had an intentness that said something different.

"But why? Why does it even matter to you?"

"It doesn't, not as such. It's just that I don't remember there being anything unusual about any of the stuff I put up there. But the way you're talking makes me think I may have missed something important, and that troubles me."

Jeremy offered nothing, so he continued, "So do you mind telling me what it was?"

He did mind, actually. This was his family, his past, and he wanted to tell him so, but something in George's expression stopped him.

"Look, George, I'm not trying to hide anything but I still don't get why you're so interested. It doesn't really have anything to do with you."

It came out more aggressively than intended, and for the first time George's equanimity slipped, a hint of steel entering his voice. "Everything isn't just about you, Jeremy. From the way you were talking yesterday, I'm assuming that whatever you found, you think it has something to do with your sister's death, and what you need to realize is there were others of us who were affected by what happened back then. Badly affected, as it happens." A flicker of anger played beneath his features. "I'm not suggesting for one moment that it was anywhere near what your family was going through, but still—"

"Yes, but—"

"No, Jeremy," he interrupted. "You weren't the only one who attracted the rumors. There were some who tried to imply things about Ian because . . . because of us. Probably about me as well. Ignorant, bigoted people who couldn't separate men like Ian and me from the type of men who would harm children."

"But that's ridiculous. I had no idea . . ." Jeremy ignored the uncomfortable knowledge that he too had cast suspicion their way, if only in his mind.

"No, and I didn't expect you to. But you need to understand, there was no closure for any of us, and even though it doesn't matter to Ian anymore, it matters to me. For his sake if nothing else."

Jeremy went to speak but George silenced him with a wave of his hand.

"Look, if you've found something that sheds some light on what happened back then, I'd like to know about it. All those things you were asking me, I'm not stupid, Jeremy, I think I understand what that was all about."

With a sense of inevitability, Jeremy capitulated. Whoever had hidden it, it didn't really matter anymore; it was all going to come out anyway. He looked at George's face and its expression of anticipation, and fleetingly wondered what he'd do once he knew.

"Look, I found one of Emily's trainers, okay? One of the ones she was wearing that day." The words came out on a long sigh of resignation. "It was all stained, and it was stuffed in that trunk of dressing-up clothes that we played with as kids. I don't know how it got there or what it even means, but it was definitely hers, and before all this happened—" he gestured at his face "—I was trying to decide what I should do about it."

George had blanched, his pupils dilating in shock, and as Jeremy watched that shock was replaced by a look of deep puzzlement.

"But that's impossible!"

"Maybe so, but there it was, wrapped up in an old T-shirt. I couldn't believe it either, to start with."

"So was anyone there with you when you found it?" He sounded dubious, as if he didn't entirely believe it.

"No, I was on my own, but I've—"

"I don't understand—it can't have been there."

"Well it was, whether you believe me or not. The whole thing was wrapped in a plastic bag and sealed up with tape." Jeremy saw him shaking his head. "Look, why would I make up something like this?"

"You don't understand. I went through that trunk. I refolded all those costumes and packed them away. I can remember doing it. It was one of the bad days, there was just too much sadness, and I couldn't cope with it anymore, I couldn't bear to just carry on throwing his things away." He stabbed an insistent finger at Jeremy. "I tell you, there was nothing wrapped up in plastic, no trainer or anything like that. I would've seen it if there had been."

"But George it was there. I found it myself, in amongst—"

And then knowledge crept up on him, along with a delayed, incredulous anger that took a while to sink its teeth. He hadn't been the only person to go into that attic.

"Are you sure it wasn't there? Would you swear to that in court?"

"There was nothing like that, nothing at all."

Jeremy thought of Mark spreading rumors, Mark who'd been so unwarrantedly hostile and aggressive. He thought of his unexpected arrival at the house, ostensibly to help, and a violent rage engulfed him, one that obliterated any relief that just maybe it hadn't been him or any of his family after all.

"He put it there. My God, *he* did it."

"Who? Jeremy, who are you talking about?" George grabbed his arm, squeezing the flesh 'til it hurt. "Please, tell me what you're talking about."

"Not now, George, right now I have to go home." Jeremy turned to him. "I need you to drive me!"

"Jeremy, who do you think put it there? Who are you talking about?"

"George, please! Just take me home. You'll find out soon enough if I'm right, soon this whole damn village will know."

George wanted to question him, to make him sit down and tell him what he knew, but instead he busied himself with fetching his keys.

"And do you have anything for my feet? Anything will do, and maybe if I could borrow a jacket or something?"

Jeremy slipped his bare feet into the proffered pair of shoes and pulled on a fleece, pacing the hallway in his eagerness to leave. His fury was mingling with a feverish excitement; this was it, finally he'd know.

The day was surprisingly clear and bright. Drifts of thin cloud trailed across a pale blue sky, like wisps of smoke, and birds made commas against the blue. The air smelled fresh, as though winter had surrendered to spring while Jeremy slept, giving the impression that he'd been at George's for far longer than just one night. The sense of time warp lingered as they reached the house, and it elicited in Jeremy the same feeling he'd had when he'd first arrived: of a long absence and a slippage in time. Everything felt dislocated, turned on its head, as if the world wasn't quite the same place as it had been when he left it. His car was parked in the driveway, and he noticed the streak along its side with a fresh stab of injustice, heightened by the new possibility of innocence.

George dropped him at the curbside. He'd been quiet on the journey there, sensing some momentousness in Jeremy's discovery.

"Thank you, George, for everything. For helping me when you didn't have to. I won't forget it and I'll . . . I'll let you know what happens, I promise."

"Do you need me to do anything? I . . . I could come with you if you like."

Jeremy understood George's reluctance to let the moment pass. The anticipation of vindication, of shaming those who'd slyly whispered, must hold an irresistible allure—if not for his own sake, then for the memory of the man he'd loved.

"No, honestly, George, it'll be fine."

"Okay, if you're absolutely sure." Still that unwillingness to relinquish his own small role. "But you will be careful, won't you? You won't do anything stupid."

Jeremy shook his head, not trusting himself to answer; he could be about to do the most stupid thing in his life so far.

Sarah opened the door to Jeremy's pounding, her mouth already opening too—in admonition. The words died on her lips, to be replaced by a sharp intake of breath, and for a moment she stood motionless, before slowly raising a hand to the round O of her mouth. He'd forgotten how he looked; the sudden realization, and the adrenaline that came with it, had driven all other thoughts from his head and had dulled the pain. But now Jeremy saw the full horror of his appearance reflected in Sarah's face.

A stunned whisper: "Dear God, Jeremy, what's happened to you?"

He rushed to reassure her. "Don't panic, Sarah, it's worse than it looks, honestly. I'm okay. It's really just bruises, there's nothing serious. I've been checked out, I'm fine."

"But what on earth happened? Who did this to you?"

The stricken look on her face tugged at something deep inside him, and he moved to take her in his arms—he needed the feel of her. But she pulled away, staying him with a hand against his chest. Jeremy let out an involuntary gasp, faltering and stumbling against her.

"You're not okay at all, you're hurt. Dear God, look at you, your face is a mess. Come inside before you fall over."

She took hold of his arm and helped him into the house, at the same time questioning him about what happened and where he'd been. Anxiety made the words pour out of her and all the while Jeremy was considering how much he should tell her; if he said too much she'd want to call the police, but he had to confront Mark first. He wanted to hear him say it.

"Sarah, listen, I know it's hard, but I need you to trust me. I will tell you everything, but first there's someone I've got to speak to. I had to see you first, to let you know that I'm okay, but right now I need to go out. I'll explain when I get back."

"No, Jez, you're not going anywhere in this state, and not until you tell me what this is all about. Where you've been and who did this to you—and who that was in the car just now."

"That was George, he was Ian's . . . my uncle's partner, and he helped me. He's been brilliant, patching me up and checking I was okay." He took her hands in his. "Look, I won't be long, and when I get back I'll tell you everything, I promise. I have to do this, Sarah, then it'll be over, I'm just asking you for this one last thing."

She snatched her hands away, and he saw how pale she was, the dark circles under her eyes and the hard edge to her gaze.

"No, Jez. If you walk out of that door without talking to me first, I won't be here when you get back. I won't have you shut me out like . . . like I'm a child." She stepped away from him, eyes blazing. "I've taken our children out of school and driven halfway across the country because I'm worried about you, and then when I get here I find—" she waved her hands in his general direction "—this! So you either tell me what the hell's going on, or that's it. I've had enough."

The tremble in her voice and the tightness of her mouth warned him not to call her bluff. She glared at him, determined.

Jeremy hesitated while his future fluttered in the wind. He instinctively knew that if he walked away this time they'd probably be over. He'd waited thirty years to find out the truth; surely another hour wouldn't matter if it meant saving his marriage.

"Okay, okay," he said, surrendering. "I'll tell you everything, but you've got to promise me you'll still let me do this. Regardless of what I tell you, you've got to let me see this through."

Sarah took his bruised hand in hers, and led him through to the kitchen. It was empty, and with a sudden burst of anxiety, Jeremy remembered the children.

"The children, Sarah, where are the children?"

"They're fine. It's a nice day and they're out in the garden, so let's not disturb them. Anyway, I need to talk to them both before I let them see you like this." She looked at his face once more, flinching slightly as she did. "Are you sure you're all right, that you don't need to go to hospital or anything?"

He shook his head. "Maybe I'll get checked out properly later on, but I'm fine for now. Sit down, Sarah . . . "

And then he talked.

He'd never really got the concept of catharsis before but he could feel it now, the relief of letting go as the words tumbled out of him. He told her everything, filling in the gaps in the story he'd shared before, bringing her up-to-date with all that had happened in the few days since she'd left him—right up to his discovery in the attic and his suspicions about Mark. He didn't mention Laura's kiss, that would add nothing but hurt, and he didn't speak of the ambivalence in his feelings for Lucy or the dark thoughts that he'd had. The shadow that would cast over his family might never lift, and he instinctively knew it was the one thing that Sarah would struggle to forgive.

At first she said nothing, processing what he'd told her and deciding how much she believed him.

"So for all these years, you've had this . . . this thing going on in your head? This fear, or guilt, that you had something to do with your sister's death?" She sounded incredulous and almost disappointed, as if she'd found out he'd been living a secret life.

"God no, not all the time. Most of the time I've not even thought about it, not unless there's been something that reminded me, but ever since the holiday and the . . . those flashbacks starting, yeah, it's been pretty much constantly in the background."

"Oh Jez . . . "

He remembered his mother and her relentless suspicion. "Mum dying and the things she said to me didn't help either, and neither has the way everyone's been since I've come back here."

He shuddered at the memory of the night terrors he'd experienced ever since he was a child. "I suppose if I'm honest, it's always been there somewhere. Not that it was me necessarily, but that there was *something* there. It wasn't like I'd notice it on a day to day basis or anything but recently I've not been able to stop thinking about it."

Sarah shook her head. "I sometimes can't even try to imagine what it must be like to be you, with all this past behind you, all these questions."

She paused for a second, as though reaching a decision, then laid a hand his arm. "Look, every single thing you've ever told me about your sister tells me how much you loved her, so I don't understand why you'd think for one minute that you had something to do with her death." She took a deep breath. "You were just a little boy yourself, Jeremy, and I think you lose sight of that."

Being a child was no defense; George had reminded him of that. Even his assailants had reminded him.

"Don't you see? It's been the not knowing. I started to wonder *why* I can't remember, and whether it's because I did something so awful. And then when I found the trainer I began to think, what if my mother was right all along and that I *was* pretending, that I'd deliberately suppressed the memory of what I'd done." He saw her expression and sheepishly added, "I've read stuff over the years about memory loss, and that can happen."

"I know, but why would you think it applied to you? You loved Emily."

"Yes but I was jealous of her, so I thought I might've . . . "

292

"For God's sake, Jeremy, loads of siblings are jealous, but they don't *kill* each other."

"I know, but—"

He stopped. Speaking it aloud had somehow rendered his fears foolish.

"Okay, you're right but now it seems there's somebody else out there who maybe *did* kill her and has gotten away with it for all this time. I need Mark to give me some answers."

"So what do you intend to do?" she asked, and he was surprised by how matter-of-fact she sounded. He'd expected something else, some resistance or disbelief. "Shouldn't we just take all of this to the police"—she indicated the trainer and the T-shirt—"and let them decide what needs to happen next? It's not down to you to talk to him. They'll have to reopen the case and investigate everything properly." A tremor ran through her. "Jez, are you absolutely sure that it's even hers?"

The question was rhetorical, the conviction already there in her voice. Jeremy was overwhelmed with love for her, and for her apparent faith in him.

"So what are we going to do?" she asked again. "You're not going to do anything stupid. I won't let you."

Not her as well.

"I just need to be sure, that's all. I want to understand what happened, which is why I have to talk to him."

"Oh God, that reminds me, someone came here looking for you earlier. A tall guy with floppy dark hair. He didn't give me his name. It wasn't him, was it? It wasn't Mark?"

"No, that sounds like Ben. What did he want?"

"He didn't say. He just asked for you and I told him you were out. To be honest, there was something a bit off about him—he seemed edgy, and he hovered about on the step for longer than necessary. He kept staring at Lucy too, in this funny, intense way that made me really uncomfortable."

Jeremy remembered how strangely Ben had acted when he saw Lucy's photo and the odd things he'd asked afterward. His anger reignited at the thought of him perhaps knowing all along what had happened to Emily but sowing the idea that her own brother had hated her enough to harm her. All to protect Mark.

"He'll be feeling more than uncomfortable when I find him. He's going to tell me where Mark lives."

"No! I still think we should go to the police because if you're right and this Mark had something to do with Emily's death, then God knows what else he's capable of." She forced him to look at her. "Jez, listen to me, he might be dangerous. You've already been beaten up."

"I have to confront him Sarah, I have to be sure before we go involving the police, just in case George was lying, or . . ." That flicker of personal doubt again. "And anyway, I'm pretty sure Mark wasn't one of the men who attacked me. I think I'd have recognized his voice." Even through the heat and the pain, through the cloth covering his head? "At least I don't think it was him."

"Oh come on, Jez. You've just said you thought one of them was military and you told me Mark's ex-army. Even if he wasn't there himself he could've put them up to it." Her voice was terse, exasperated. "What about the father of that boy you spoke to? Who do you think has been fueling the fire over that? It's all too much of a coincidence to be anyone else."

"I don't understand. I thought Mark's animosity was because he believed *me* to be the one who killed Emily, but if it's not that, then why? I'm hardly any threat to him, God, I've not given him so much as a thought in thirty years." He looked at Sarah in puzzlement. "And why would he risk bringing that . . . *thing* into Ian's house? What was he trying to achieve by doing that?"

"Jez, maybe you are a threat without realizing it. What if you really did see something?" She clutched at his arm with urgent fingers. "Did you ever tell any of them about the memory loss and how you were afraid you might've been responsible? Did you give them any reason to think they could convince you that it was you instead?"

They all knew. He'd told Laura and Ben, and one of them had told Mark. Maybe they all knew what happened and had conspired together to convince him of his guilt. The ultimate act of deflection.

"I may've mentioned it, yeah, but I didn't ever dream they'd try to use it against me."

"Look, Jez, if you're insistent on speaking to them, then I want you to be careful. You can't be sure that this Ben isn't involved, you can't trust any of them, so promise me you'll be careful."

"I will. And you don't need to worry about Mark, he's not going to be stupid enough to try anything in broad daylight. I'll make sure of that."

The words were braver than their owner, and Sarah anxiously awaited while Jeremy changed his clothes.

"If you're not back in an hour, Jez, I'm calling the police, regardless of what you say."

# 29

It niggled at him. It floated at the edge of his consciousness, a little flotsam almost bobbing within reach until the very effort of trying to grab at it made it drift further away. The feeling was strong; that sense that someone had told him something significant, if he could only remember what it was. Reaching the house, Jeremy pulled up behind Laura's car and made his way to the front door, his anger tinged with apprehension in case he'd got it all wrong.

It was Laura who answered the door, and Jeremy was struck by her changed appearance. Today her hair was lank and flattened to one side of her head, as if she'd just gotten out of bed, and her eyelids looked pink and swollen, the skin beneath chafed and sore as though she'd been crying. Whatever; he was too angry to find much sympathy for her. Her expression was haunted and she looked past him, craning her neck as if expecting someone else to be following behind.

"Where is he?" To hell with a greeting. "Where's Ben?"

"So, he's not with you?" Her shoulders slumped in defeat.

"No. Where is he? I need to speak to him."

"He isn't here. I haven't seen him since Sunday, and I'm worried about him." The anguished look deepened. "Mark says he probably just needs some space, but I'm terrified that he's made himself ill again. Have you seen him at all, has he been over to the house or anything?"

Jeremy was surprised at her mention of Ben being ill but was too wrapped up in his own mission to ask what she meant. He looked at the wretched expression on her face and it took some of the edge off his anger, so rather than immediately demanding Mark's address, he found himself taking her by the elbow and steering her back inside the house. In the stark afternoon light the sitting room lacked the charm of the evening; now the surface of the coffee table was ringed and stained, peppered with ash, and the sofa was littered with a snowdrift of used tissues. A blanket lay crumpled on the floor, along with a skanky pair of balled-up socks and two empty glasses, sticky with residue. The air in the room struggled under the weight of stale smoke, and the glossy leaved plants gasped and wilted in their pots.

Laura looked at him properly for the first time and flinched at the sight of him.

"Oh Jay, your face! I told him to stop it . . . that it'd only end up with someone getting hurt." It was hard to catch her mumbled words, as she averted her face from his. "I don't know what's got into him recently . . . I'm sorry."

The breath caught in Jeremy's throat. "Told who?" he demanded, as if he didn't know, and his anger sparked back into life. He had to resist the urge to grab her by the shoulders and shake her until she told him. "Told who? Are you talking about Mark?"

She nodded glumly.

"So it *was* him did this?" he said, gesturing at his mangled features. "I thought as much, even though he didn't have the guts to let me see his face. Where the fuck is he, Laura?" He knew she'd mentioned one of the farms, but he couldn't recall which one. "I need you to tell me where he lives."

"What? No, no, you don't understand. Mark wouldn't have done it, that's not what I meant. I meant if he kept on saying those things about you, something like this was bound to happen."

He didn't need to ask her what things. "I want his address, Laura. I need to speak to him."

"No!" She shook her head, her curls springing into life. "No, I'm not telling you. Listen, he didn't do this to you. He may have said some things about you, but it wouldn't have been him that did this. No way."

She began to cry with a jagged rawness, the sobs only broken by her need to draw breath. "Jay, I need to find Ben, have you really not seen him?"

"Look, forget about Ben, I haven't seen him for a couple of days, okay? I need you to give me Mark's address—"

"Jay, you don't understand, Ben's not well. He's got . . . he's had these . . . like breakdowns in the past, where he just loses it and there's been something . . . something off about him recently, and I'm scared it's happening again. I need to know where he is and that he's okay." She glared at him accusingly as if it was all his fault. "Everything's gone weird since you came back."

"Laura, Ben's your problem, I don't care. But I'm not going anywhere until you tell me where to find Mark—"

"No, you need to leave him alone—"

It suddenly came back to him—she'd said he had a place at Blundell's farm. "Forget it, I don't need you, I can find him myself."

He turned to leave but she grabbed at his arm with bony insistent fingers. "Please, Jay, don't hurt him."

"*Me* hurt *him*? Look at what they've done to me already. I think I'm more the one who should be worrying about getting hurt, don't you?

"Jay, he didn't do this, that's not who he is. I don't get what he's got against you, but—"

Her blind defense of Mark infuriated Jeremy, and he blurted out words without thinking. "Seems he's got plenty against me. How about he's afraid that I'll find out what *really* happened to Emily? That maybe I'll find out what he did?"

Shock stopped her crying and she shook her head vehemently. "What? No! How dare you say things like that about him. I don't know what's wrong with all of you, making these dreadful accusations against each other." Her voice rose. "I don't understand why you're dragging everything up, why you can't just leave it alone. Mark didn't hurt Emily, and you're mad if you really believe that. He wouldn't hurt anyone, let alone a child. He might not like you very much but he's a good person. He looks after us, he *protects* us, he always has."

*Protects*. It was the word she'd used before.

"Protects who, Laura? Why would anyone need protecting?" He locked eyes with her. "Speak to me Laura. Why would anyone need protecting?"

Her eyes slinked away, and two spots of color rose on her cheeks. "He keeps an eye on Ben, makes sure he's okay, that's all, and he looks out for me . . . "

Her words made him think of what Ben had told him, and his mind unlocked. That was it, the thing that he'd been clutching for. Maybe he *did* have this all wrong—perhaps it was *her* that they'd all been protecting. He looked at her anew, and noticed the guilty way her eyes flickered back to his. Her disheveled appearance took on a new significance and now, as he stared into those amber irises, he thought he could see a deadness there that made him shiver.

"If it wasn't him, then is it *you* they're protecting?" He felt his control slipping. "Did . . . did you drown my sister?" He admonished himself for the noticeable quiver in his voice.

Her face reacted as though he'd slapped it, wide-eyed with astonishment and hurt, while a rising redness mottled her skin. For a moment she looked ugly.

"No! Surely you can't think that? I was just a child when she died, I had nothing to do with any of it, course I didn't—and neither did Mark. None of us did." She pulled in a gulp of air. "This is madness, Jay, these things you're saying, and I think you should leave now."

The idea, once formed, gained traction, a train of thought that dragged him along behind it. It could explain the state she was in, and why she seemed so frantic.

"I think you know what happened, and I need you to tell me the truth." Without thinking he reached out and grabbed hold of her arm, shaking her. "Laura, you've got to tell me."

"I don't know what you're talking about, I haven't done anything, I was just a kid myself, for God's sake, not much older than Emily." She was panicked, and angry now. "Don't touch me! Let go of my arm and get out! You're scaring me!"

"Yeah, right, like you were just a kid when you hurt that other little girl? How scared do you reckon she was?"

The effect was immediate. Jeremy watched as her expression froze. She tried to pull away and her freckles, so much like Ben's, stood out in stark relief against the sudden whiteness of her skin. Her mouth gulped like an air-drowned fish, and Jeremy's anger spiraled away from him. He was yelling at her now.

"Yes, Ben told me everything. He told me what happened to you and how you used to fly into rages." He tightened his grip on her arm, turning it to expose the crosshatching of scars. "You evil little bitch, is that how it was, did you hurt other children until you learned to do this instead?"

Her other arm moved so quickly that he didn't realize until her hand made contact with his face. The pain was indescribable; his nose screamed out in protest against this latest offense. Shocked, he released her, and they glared at each other as if neither could quite believe the lines they'd just crossed. She recovered first, her face blazing with fury.

"You're crazy. I didn't touch your sister. You've no right to talk to me like that, about things you know fuck all about."

He reached out to grab her but she stepped away until she was pressed against the fireplace, her hand reaching behind her, fingers blindly searching for a candlestick. Clutching the heavy brass she stood and faced him down.

Jeremy stared at her hand, white-knuckled around the candlestick, and then at her face. He tried to read her expression. There was something unfathomable in her eyes that gave him pause, and he found himself edging away from her, just in time as she swung the candlestick in a lethal arc. He felt the breath of it against his cheek as it whizzed past his head. He raised his hands, palms outward, partly in defense, partly in supplication. He needed to defuse this before someone did something irrevocable.

"Laura, I'm sorry. I should never have touched you. I don't know what I was thinking."

"I want you to leave now. I swear I didn't hurt your sister and neither did Mark." Her eyes met his, cold and determined. "I mean it, Jay, get the fuck out of here!"

He had no choice other than to leave, but it didn't matter anymore. He didn't need her, not now that he remembered where Mark lived. Whatever any of them had or hadn't done, for her or for Mark, it would soon be all over.

He turned when he reached the door. "I'm going to find out the truth and God knows, I hope you're right, Laura, because you're going to be the ones telling it all to the police."

Her parting words were spoken to an empty room, but they reached him as he opened the front door, piercing him like a dart.

"If anyone hurt your sister, Jay, it was most probably you."

Jeremy drove out of the village on the road that led past Blundell's farm. He was so far inside his own head that he almost pulled out in front of an oncoming car before its angry horn blasted him back to reality. He was trying to work out what exactly he felt, but he couldn't name it. He'd anticipated a raw and furious grief, but it was all too distant, too long ago for him to feel that kind of immediacy. Mainly what he was getting was a sense of vindication and a burning curiosity. If it was Laura, then it was likely the result of the things that she'd been through, but Mark? He'd hardly had any contact with Emily, he'd barely even noticed her, so why? It didn't make any sense.

He reached the farm and pulled into the yard, where a square, redbrick farmhouse directly faced the entrance. It was flanked on either side by a long dark barn and a range of outbuildings, outside of which two men were hosing mud from the undercarriage of a tractor. Jeremy tried to compose his features into something marginally less menacing before asking for directions, but he needn't have bothered. One looked up at his approach, eyebrows raised momentarily at the sight of his face but nothing more.

"Hi, I wonder if you could help me. I'm looking for Mark McLeish? His sister said I might find him here."

He mentioned Laura to give the inquiry some legitimacy, in case they were the mistrustful type.

"Round the back," the man said, vaguely gesturing toward the barn on the opposite side. "There's a couple of statics—his is the one with the green trim." He turned back to his task, any interest he'd had apparently exhausted.

A track at the side of the barn led to a patch of rough ground, with a wide expanse of open fields stretching into the distance beyond. Jeremy walked past a pile of broken wood and stopped to pick up a length, weighing it in his hands for a weapon, although he wasn't quite sure what he'd do with it. Perhaps he should've asked Laura, given how readily she'd wielded that candlestick. He reached an area of uneven gravel parking, which housed the two static caravans, one of which was sporting the promised green trim. He took a fruitless moment to examine the three cars that were parked there, in case any were reminiscent of the one that'd tried to run him down. With mounting apprehension, he walked toward Mark's caravan, conscious of the crunch of the gravel underfoot, loud in the blanketing hush of the countryside.

Laura had rung ahead. The door was suddenly flung open, and Mark was standing there, barefooted, arms folded. A malevolently grinning skull leered out from his upper arm, nicely setting the tone. Jeremy took another moment to register the unwelcome bulk of him and the size of the biceps on display, and not for the first time he questioned the wisdom of what he was doing. From their higher vantage point, Mark and the skull watched him approach, both seemingly alert to any sudden movement. Jeremy sensed wariness, and it was somehow reminiscent of that flicker of fear he'd glimpsed in Mark that very first time they'd met.

There was no point in prevaricating. "I know what you did," Jeremy said, and his voice was surprising steady given the circumstances.

"What do you want?" Mark tried for the old aggression but his heart wasn't in it; he knew exactly why Jeremy was there. There was an inevitability about it, a relief even, for he'd carried the burden for far too long.

"Why did you do it?"

That was suddenly the most important thing for Jeremy, to understand why.

"To make you leave," Mark replied. "To make you fuck off and let things be."

"That's not what—"

He interrupted. "Look, you'd better come in." He glanced toward the farmyard as if to check whether anyone was within earshot. "And you'd better get rid of that unless you're intending to use it—or are you afraid?" he added with a nod to his old contempt, but it rang false. His veneer of aggression seemed to have cracked, exposing something raw beneath, and now there was an air of resignation about him that wasn't what Jeremy expected. It pushed aside any hesitation he might've had at the thought of being in a confined space with him, of being alone on his territory.

"You need to know, I've notified the police," he said. A cautionary mention just in case, but Mark merely nodded.

"Thought you would've, somehow."

Jeremy discarded the piece of wood, and his feet took the three steps up to the doorway almost of their own volition; finally, he'd know. Mark stepped back as he reached him and then he was inside, head thrumming with something close to excitement.

Like Mark's attitude, the interior of the caravan was contrary to expectation. If Jeremy had imagined anything it would've been surfaces littered with beer cans and dirty clothes, air fetid with the stench of sweat and farts, and rancid bedsheets. Instead it was clean and neat inside, with a fresh breeze jauntily wafting the checkered curtain at the open window. A sparsely ordered living space, clear of clutter except for the shotgun dismantled on the pull-down table. His heart lurched at the sight of it, until he saw the rag and the can of gun oil. It was a farm, so the presence of a shotgun was hardly unexpected. In any case, it was in pieces, so unless Mark intended to beat him to death with the stock, it was unlikely to do him much harm. Mark noticed him looking and his expression flickered with something faintly mocking, a whisper of a more familiar man.

"Laura told me you'd be coming," he said. "So it seems it's all over."

Mark looked at Jeremy's face with something akin to regret and once again there was that sense of a different man from the one Jeremy had encountered before. It was disconcerting.

"That wasn't meant to happen, you know. They were just meant to warn you off, maybe rough you up a little if you wouldn't listen to sense. You weren't supposed to get hurt." Before Jeremy could respond he continued. "You just wouldn't leave it, would you? You wouldn't take the hint that you're not welcome here, and fuck off back home. No, you had to carry on poking around and questioning Ben." He shook his head. "You couldn't just leave well alone."

"So all of it was you—the damage to my car, the attack, everything, all . . . all that was you." He couldn't bring himself to ask about Emily. Not yet.

"Not the car—I can't take credit for that. It was one of the kids, but I daresay it was me put the idea in the little bugger's head."

He was so matter-of-fact, so calm in the face of all he'd done.

"But you tried to fucking kill me. What happened to me not getting hurt when you were trying to run me down and when you tampered with the loft ladder? I take it that was you too, so where was all this concern then?"

He shook his head again. "The rest of you might've been off your tits, but I was pretty much sober that night. I'd never have hit you; I was just scaring you a little, that's all. And as for the loft ladder, I had nothing to do with that, that was purely an accident. Ben must've knocked it on his way down. Just an accident."

He was too emphatic, saying it almost as if to convince himself. "It wouldn't have been deliberate. He must've accidentally caught the catch with his jacket."

Jeremy pictured the big padded jacket Mark had been wearing that day, and the package concealed inside it.

"It's over, don't you realize? It's all in the hands of the police now, the trainer, everything. They're with Sarah, she's telling them everything, and you'll be going to jail for what you did." He still didn't understand Mark's reasoning for hiding the trainer. "Why *did* you hide the trainer? I can't see what you thought it'd achieve—other than this. Did you not think I'd guess that someone had planted it there?"

"They told me you couldn't remember anything, that you were afraid you were somehow responsible for your sister's death, and that's when I thought of it. I knew it would still be where I'd hidden it, so it was just a case of a trip to the woods and then working out how to get it into the house." Mark smiled, as if at his own cleverness. "You were meant to think that you'd hidden it there but couldn't remember, or if not you, then at least suspect that your dear old uncle had a hand in it. I thought you'd destroy it once you found it." He looked suddenly sly. "To make sure you didn't get caught."

He stopped. A thought had just occurred to him. "How did you know I'd put it there? I was pretty sure the trunk hadn't been touched. I even asked Ben."

"I just knew, okay? And once I knew, it didn't take a genius to realize it was you. It had to be you or Ben, and you were the obvious choice." He wouldn't think about Ben being part of it too—that betrayal felt too much like a wound.

The hint of a smile played at Mark's lips.

"I'm glad you find it funny. I'm glad killing my sister amused you."

The emotion he'd been waiting for flooded through him, and he took a step toward Mark, propelled by the urge to really hurt him. But he was halted by the look of confusion on Mark's face.

Mark raised his hands in a gesture of submission or denial. "No, no you've got it all wrong, that wasn't me! I thought you'd worked it out, but you've still got it wrong. I came along afterward—she was already dead by the time I got there."

"Afterward?" Jeremy was aware of a feeling of sadness cutting through his anger, and the realization that he'd been hoping that it wasn't Laura, that it hadn't been that broken child. "So do you mean that all this time you've been protecting—"

"I was just a kid myself," Mark continued, "and at the time it seemed like the only thing I could do, to help him hide it, to try and make it go away."

Now it was Jeremy's turn for confusion.

"'Him'? I don't understand . . . "

"Yes, *him*, not me. He didn't mean for her to die, so regardless of what he'd done I couldn't let him get caught. It was wrong, I saw that afterward, and it didn't solve anything either. It made it worse for him in the end"—a look of regret crossed his face—"but when something's gone that far you have no choice. We were in it together and my father would've . . . "

His father? Understanding forced the air from Jeremy's lungs and for the first time he was near to tears. She was his sister, his little sister.

"So it was him, him all along?" He was shouting now, uncaring of who might hear. "And you protected him after everything he was? After what he did to Laura, you still fucking protected him?"

"No, you don't understand . . . "

Mark's denials were drowned by the sudden frantic shrieking of Jeremy's phone, its urgent vibrations drumming against his hip. He snatched it from his pocket and rushed outside; he needed to be away from Mark and from the things he was telling him. That bastard, that animal had touched little Em.

"Sarah . . . "

At first he couldn't understand her. Her words came in a rush, disjointed, distorted by panic.

"Sarah, Sarah, slow down! What is it, what's happened?"

It wasn't like her to panic and the first cold fingers of horror crawled across his scalp.

"She's gone . . . "

"Who? What's happened?"

His first thought was her mother, that Sarah had received a phone call from her father to tell her she'd died.

"I thought she was outside with Jack but she wasn't, he thought she'd come back indoors with me but I can't find her . . . "

Slowly he pieced together what Sarah was telling him. Lucy had been playing in the garden and now she was gone.

"Jez, the hole in the back fence . . . I've checked in the field but she's gone . . . Jez, I can't find her. She wouldn't wander off . . . "

He was shouting into the phone. "He must've taken her, McLeish has got her. Sarah, phone the police and tell them McLeish!"

Then he was running to the car, aware of Mark shouting behind him,

"No, not Dad . . ."

He was out of the caravan, trying to stop him.

"Who's McLeish? Jeremy, who is he, who's got her?"

"Sarah, listen to me, I'll find her but you have to ring the police. Tell them McLeish . . ." He wracked his brains for the place Ben had mentioned. "The Buttery, he lives in the Buttery, tell them."

He pounded down the track toward the yard and the place where his car was parked. Mark was still yelling after him, trying to keep pace, but his bare feet slowed him down. Sarah was crying in his ear, as every parent's worst nightmare unfolded around them, the sound of her tears drowning out Mark's words.

"Sarah, I promise you, I'll find her."

Ignoring the shouts from the farmworkers, Jeremy ran across the yard. Then he was inside the car, fingers fumbling at the keys. His legs on the pedals were weak with fear. Mark reached the door as the engine fired into life and he grabbed at the handle, wrestling with the door as the car pulled away. For a moment his face was pressed against the glass, shouting, and even through his panic Jeremy registered the expression in Mark's eyes. It was desperation.

# 30

And then he was running, oblivious to the pain, his heart bursting in his chest, across well-tended lawns toward the smart new apartment blocks that stood on the site of the old dairy. Reaching the entrance to the first low-level building, he scanned the numbers on the entry system, looking for apartment number six. He tried the doors, rattling the handles and pounding the glass with his bruised fists, but they were firmly secured, so he randomly pressed numbers one through four, praying for someone to answer. The intercom crackled into life at apartment four, and a tremulous voice wobbled from the speaker.

"Hello? Hello, who is it?"

Jeremy searched for a reason for her to let him in.

"Delivery," he finally said. "Delivery for McLeish."

Somewhere inside she tutted, oblivious to the tension in his voice. "Can't you people read? McLeish is upstairs, number *six*. I'm four."

Despite the irritation in her tone he heard the door unlock as the intercom clicked off, and then he was inside. Like sweets from a baby—and the unbidden thought made him want to cry.

In the lobby a harsh reality brought him stumbling to a halt. There, dejectedly slumped at the foot of the stairs, was Fuddlewuddle, and the bright beads of his eyes implored Jeremy to find her. If there had ever been any ambivalence in his love, any doubt in his mind, it had fled in the time it had taken him to drive there. He'd kill for this child. He'd die for her, a thousand times over if he had to. All the foolish thoughts, all the ghosts of the past he'd let overshadow her, they all meant nothing now. She was the one that mattered, only her.

Before he'd consciously made the decision, his legs started moving again, painfully carrying him up the carpeted stairs, two urgent steps at a time. Every muscle was tensed, every one of his senses fine-tuned. He felt the hairs on the back of his neck pulling the skin into goose bumps.

He reached a landing with a muted light that felt forbidding, unreal, and he was now so close that the terror slowed his limbs. What if he was wrong and she wasn't there? What if he was too late? His guts churned in anticipation of a nameless cruelty to come. He wilfully slowed his breathing and pushed through double doors into the corridor beyond, where four identical apartment doors blankly stood sentinel. The urge to pound his fists on each in turn was almost overwhelming, to scream her name, to shatter the opulent peace of the building. Instead he edged down the passageway, moving quietly so as not to raise any alarm. When he reached number six, he found the door to be off the latch, and this shrieked to him a warning of something very wrong. His bowels gave a threatening flip as he purposefully pushed wide the door, which opened onto a small internal hallway, with a cloakroom off to the side. Despite the plushness of the carpet and the opulence of the wallpaper, there was an unmissable hint of dust and urine, of stale clothes and old age.

Another smell slowly reached him, slyly invading his nostrils like an afterthought: it was the metallic, iron-rich scent of blood, overlaid with a stench of rot. Faint but unmistakeable, the sickly sweet aroma of death. A fractured moan escaped his lips, a whimper of pure terror, before logic kicked in. A coolly analytical part of his mind saved him. It couldn't be her; it was too soon for decay. He'd only taken her today.

Jeremy followed the smell through into a living room, richly furnished but littered with empty beer cans and bottles, and over-flowing saucers serving as makeshift ashtrays. The air was hot and ripe, heavy with the smell of unwashed bodies and putrefaction. Instinctively he gagged, the bile rising in his throat as he scanned the room. There was an electric fire recessed in a faux fireplace, and this was belching heat into the already fetid atmosphere. A smell of scorching wool emanated from the trousers of the old man who was slumped in a wingback chair, and Jeremy didn't need to feel for a pulse to know that he was very dead. The man's face told him that: There was a blackened mass of congealed blood and gore where his eye should be. An eye that had fooled the world. An eye that'd looked at his child and seen not a perfect being worthy of love, but a creature at his disposal. Jeremy tried to look away from the hellish sight, to not see the dried mess of brain matter staining the chair behind his head, to not hear the buzz of eager flies, but he was momentarily transfixed. He gazed at Mr. McLeish, at the waxiness of his flesh, at the bluish tint of his skin, marbled by livid veins, and he tried to see the jovial ruddy-faced man he'd thought he knew and liked. That man wasn't there. There was nothing but the bullet hole, no vestige of the person who had once lived around it. The smell was overwhelming, and he pressed his hand to his mouth, breaking the nightmare spell.

Then he heard it. The softest of movements from the room beyond. A stifled whimper, a hurried "shush." A surge of adrenaline almost undid him, and then time slowed. The seconds it took him to cross that room felt like a lifetime. The things around him assumed a frightening clarity: the pattern of the wallpaper, the swirls on the carpet, the green and yellow budgie, rigid in its cage. There was no opportunity for surprise, no chance of stealth, so he walked directly into the bedroom, where the scene before him knocked the breath from his body.

The curtains were drawn, and in the half-light he could see his daughter there on the bed, hog-tied and helpless, a cloth stuffed in her mouth. Her eyes were wide and unseeing with terror, her face smeared with tears and snot—but she was alive. The temperature in the room was unbearable—another electric fire spewed heat like a furnace—and her hair lay in matted, sweaty clumps against her forehead. A memory flickered behind his lids—Emily—and he was seized by the urge to weep. He held out his hand, as though to a frightened creature, and took a step toward the bed.

"Don't!"

The voice was firm but calm, and he turned to see Ben standing in the shadows.

"Ben . . ."

"Don't touch her. She's not of this world."

He stepped into the light from the doorway and he looked the same as always: friendly, benign, a half smile playing at his lips. His appearance belied the utter madness of his words.

Jeremy's eyes flew to the rifle, its barrel trained on Lucy. Trained on his little girl. It looked like Ben's father's old .22, and Jeremy knew the damage that could do. The abomination in the other room was testimony to that.

The fear caught in his throat and made his voice break. "Ben, you can't do this. It isn't the answer. You need to let Lucy go."

He tried to keep his voice calm and level. He tried to match Ben's, as though they were just two mates chewing the fat about old times, as though this was the most normal thing in the world.

"She isn't Lucy anymore," Ben replied, and Jeremy's heart shrank.

There was a knife on the bedside table, a long, bladed kitchen knife with a sharp, pointed end. Jeremy allowed his eyes to stray toward it, wondering if he could reach it in time. But Ben read his mind, his eyes tracking the same path. Casually, he moved closer to the bed, momentarily dropping the rifle to his side as he picked up the knife and slipped it into the pocket of his jacket. Jeremy weighed up his chances in the split second while the gun was lowered, but he'd be too slow and Ben was too close to Lucy to risk it.

"Ben, please . . ." There was pleading in his voice, desperation that made him whine, and an echo of the past filled the room. "Please Ben, she's just a little girl, you don't want to hurt her. Please, let her go."

Ben impassively regarded the child on the bed.

"I can't hurt her, not anymore. Everything that's going to happen already has."

He tilted his head to one side and looked at Jeremy. His calmness was unnerving, an icicle melting down the spine.

"It's your fault, you know. You were warned, you had the chance to go home, but you didn't take it. It couldn't have been made clearer that you weren't welcome here, but you wouldn't go. You could've made it all go away, but instead you had to bring her back."

Ben nodded his head as if in agreement with something unheard. "Yes, it's all your fault. You had the chance to deal with it, but oh no, you chose not to. I asked you, I begged you to do something about it that very first time you showed me her picture, but you took no notice. Told me to just forget it and that there was no harm done."

"Ben, what are you talking about? I—"

Ben's benignity faltered, and a note of accusation crept into his voice. "Don't try to deny it! You'd summoned her up by coming back here, so it was down to you to make her go away. I don't know why you couldn't see that and stop all this from happening."

"Summoned her up?"

The question died on Jeremy's lips as he realized. Ben thought she was Emily, little Em. That time at his house, he'd been talking about *Lucy*, not Laura, about *Jeremy's* sister, not his. He was talking about the photo he'd seen on the phone, never the kiss in the kitchen that he hadn't even seen.

"She's an evocation. Didn't you know?"

For a moment Ben's psychosis glittered in his eyes, a window onto insanity. His fragile hold on reality had snapped, leaving him lost in a world of his own imagining. It was what Laura had said but nobody was listening. Jeremy instinctively knew not to challenge him, not to antagonize him and make things worse, so he held out his hands, palms up, supplicant, submissive.

"I don't know what you want from me, but I'm here to talk. Whatever you want, we can work this out without anyone . . ." his voice failed ". . . anyone getting hurt."

It was as if he hadn't spoken.

"If I turn my head quickly I can see the water over her. She hides it well, but I know it's still there."

Ben began snapping his head from side to side, a fleeting glance at Lucy and then away again. Over and over he did it, and Jeremy watched him with a deepening, visceral horror at the extent of his madness.

"Come on mate, do it," he said. "Then you'll see it too."

Jeremy didn't move and suddenly Ben screamed at him. "Fucking do it, I said. I want you to see what I see."

It was the first time he'd lost control. Obediently Jeremy swiveled his head from side to side, the motion making him dizzy. Each time he saw Lucy's petrified eyes and each time the urge to kill Ben grew stronger. He was the nameless creature of nightmares. Never his father, him.

"I didn't mean for it to happen." Ben addressed the terrified child on the bed. "I tried to save you, I pulled you out of the water afterward and I tried to bring you back. You know that, so why are you doing this to me?"

A trill of fear seeped through the rag clogging Lucy's mouth.

"Don't argue with me! You know that's the truth."

He turned back to Jeremy. "Don't listen to her, she's trying to trick us. They're sly like that." He jabbed the rifle toward him. "Look at her, see what she is, see the creature she's become."

Lucy's eyes locked on her father's, beseechingly, and he wondered how he could ever have doubted his love for her.

Ben saw the tears welling and suddenly his voice was melting, soft with compassion. "Don't, Jay. Come on, don't get all upset. Can't you see it's for the best? She needs to go back where she came from. I know you loved her and all that, but this isn't the answer. I can't let her stay here and tell people what I did. It's time for her to go back into the water."

For the first time Jeremy became aware of the sound of a tap running in the bathroom adjoining the bedroom. The sound of a bath filling, a bath overflowing, water flooding onto the floor, and he realized Ben wasn't going to shoot Lucy—he intended to drown her. The terror he'd felt that night when he'd bathed her came surging back, the image of her face under the water, and with it came the irrational feeling that he'd made this happen, that he'd somehow glimpsed the future. His need for guilt, his self-obsessed wish for it to be all his fault, came rushing to the fore. But hot on the heels of that thought came another. This time he could change it. This time he could stop the bad thing from happening.

Without hesitation Jeremy dropped his shoulder and charged at Ben. The scream he'd been holding in his throat burst free, shattering the baking air, and he saw Ben startle, his pupils dilating in surprise. Time slowed and Jeremy watched as he raised the rifle, and in that moment he knew he'd failed. For the second time he'd failed to keep her safe.

The noise was deafening at close range, far louder than Jeremy had expected, an adrenaline rush and a physical sensation bursting his eardrums. His eyes closed and he waited for the pain but it didn't come. Instead a figure charged past him, pushing him aside. Slowly he lifted his head and opened his eyes, and there was Ben, his hands clutched to his neck, his own eyes wide with shock and fear. A deep, viscous crimson pumped from between his fingers and the side of his jaw was peppered with black and red. Beneath his hand Jeremy could see a mess of livid flesh, enmeshed with the tattered fabric of his collar. All this he saw in the split second before Ben's brother reached him. Mark threw his shotgun to the side and gathered Ben into his arms, stopping him from crashing to the floor. Understanding bloomed beneath the ringing in Jeremy's head, and he rushed to the bed, pulling Lucy to him and pressing her face to his chest, hiding her eyes from the scene before them.

"Lucy, Lucy! I'm here. Daddy's got you, you're safe now."

He lifted her off the bed, still crushed to him, and carried her out of the room, past the old man's body slumped in the living room and out into the safety of the hallway. Only now did he pull the rag from her mouth and fumble to untie her. Lucy's mouth opened and closed but no sound came, and for a hideous moment Jeremy feared that she couldn't speak, that history had repeated itself and rendered her mute. Then he understood. The blast of the shotgun so near to his head had deafened him. His head was tolling like a bell and his ears felt plugged with cotton wool.

"Daddy's here, it's over. Lucy, darling, you're safe."

He was bellowing at her, rocking her, and his own tears were flowing freely.

"You're safe, he can't hurt you now."

Over the ringing in his ears he could hear the faint sound of the police sirens' frenzied wails. He felt the vibration of feet pounding up the stairs and he closed his eyes and held his daughter.

It was gone—all his reticence in loving her, all his fear of her and for her, was gone. It no longer mattered that he couldn't remember, that he might never remember, what he saw that day. All that counted was that this time he done it, he'd saved the thing that he loved.

# EPILOGUE

*The woods smelled verdant and alive, and the sunlight that had managed to find its way through the high canopy of leaves was tinted with chlorophyll. It bathed the undergrowth, and the spaces between the trees, in a green and watery light that rippled and changed as the canopy shifted in the breeze. Tiny insects danced and sparkled in the shafts of light, swimming the air like arboreal plankton. The saplings and low-hanging vines, the holly bushes and the mossy floor, muffled all sound and made the boy feel as though he was wading through an underwater world.*

*It had all started as a bit of fun, teasing the little girl with tales of the big bad wolf; preying on her fear of the time-honored tale, but it had gotten out of hand and soon they were chasing her across the fields, reveling in her fright. He remembered how it had felt. The liberating joy of, just for once, being the one doing the scaring and not the one who was afraid. But then she'd panicked and had gone running off into the woods, ignoring their calls to stop. She'd left the path for the tangled thicket of brambles, crashing her way through the underbrush, fear making her flee. They'd followed her, calling her name, but had lost her in the shin-tangle of bushes. Jay had shouted and shouted, his voice edged with panic, but the forest had swallowed the words. Though they strained and listened for an answering call, all it offered them back was the sound of silence.*

*They'd seen Mark and David in the clearing, where the boys' rope-swing listlessly dangled from the branches. They were sitting on a moss-covered trunk, laughing and jostling with a couple of the girls while their bikes lay abandoned, pedals and wheels shamelessly akimbo. The girls were muss haired, all flushed and giggly, and the air was heavy with cigarette smoke and the whisper of pheromones. The undercurrent of things sexual and unspoken made the boy feel awkward and he tried to sidle past unseen, but Mark spotted the group and called out to them, "Hey, bro. Where're you and your little mates off to in such a hurry?"*

*Jay told him they were looking for Emily, that they'd scared her into the woods.*

*"Okay, we'll keep a look out for her," Mark said, his arm carelessly looped around Sally's shoulder, but the boy knew that they wouldn't. He knew by the way the secret had closed around them the moment the children moved on. He knew by Sally's giggled "Stop it!" that their minds were on other mysterious things.*

*Finally, white faced and afraid, Jay had gone home to tell his parents, leaving Nathan and Ben alone. Soon Nathan had lost interest too—like he always did—and now it was just Ben among the trees. He wasn't ready to go home, he was never ready for that, so instead he went deeper and deeper into the woods. The trees seemed to lean in, closing their trunks in stripes of light and shade, but Ben wasn't afraid. The others rarely came in this far, but he did. He'd often followed this hidden track all the way to the lake, with Scotty at his side.*

*The thought of his little dog made his guts twist, and something dark and bloodied swam behind his eyes. He felt his heart begin to race, suffused with a feeling too complex to be called anger, too wrenching to be called grief. One day he'd do to his father what that bastard had done to his dog. Some* nights his dreams were filled with Scotty's whimpers as the barrel pressed his little eye, and he awoke to the sound of his father's rifle, and smelled the pungent nitro on the air. Some nights the image of those final twitches rose up out of the darkness to sear themselves onto his retina once more. He thought he now knew how hate felt, and it was a secret he'd never shared with his friends. His hands were thrust deep into the pockets of his shorts, but he felt his fingers twitch in anticipation. He could almost feel the steel of the trigger.

As he neared the lake he heard muted voices, and he hung back for a while. He wasn't sure he wanted to bump into his brother again, not while the memory of Scotty was still fresh in his mind. He hadn't forgiven Mark yet; he'd done nothing to help. Instead he'd just stood there with a face as shocked and scared as Ben's own, while their father tormented him.

Silence enfolded him once more and cautiously he resumed his route. As he neared the lake he saw two figures through the trees. His brother and Sally, leaning against an oak, not far from the tumbledown birdwatching hide. He stood and watched as his brother slid his hand under Sally's T-shirt, tentative fingers fumbling for the curve of her breast. He looked on as their mouths met. He saw the flicker of tongues and the wet glisten of saliva, and he tasted bile rising bitter in his throat. He didn't want to watch but his eyes were pulled toward them, riveted by what he saw, and it was with some relief that he watched Sally suddenly push his brother away, laughing as she pressed her hands against his chest. Finally the couple turned from the lake and were lost once again in the trees. The scene left Ben with a tingling tightness in his shorts—the same thing he felt some mornings now—and even as he liked the feeling he also hated it, for it made him think of his father and the dreadful things he did to Laura when he thought no one was watching or listening.

Once he was sure the pair had gone, he made his way toward the lake. He had no idea where he was going or why; he only knew he wasn't going *home. He passed the remains of the hide, now not much more than a tangle of twigs, and as he did, he caught a sound from within, a small outrush of breath. He stopped and waited until he heard it again, the tremulous sound of frightened breathing. His pulse leapt. Just maybe it was Emily. He could be the hero, the one they all talked about, the one who brought her safely home. He let himself imagine Jay's mother pulling him toward her in a grateful hug, holding him close in the way she did with Emily.*

*The skin of his eleven-year-old heart contracted with sudden loss for the mother he barely remembered, and he stood for a moment trying to conjure her gentle smile. For a while she'd lived on in the guise of an angel, one that he'd glimpsed in the dark corners of his room. He'd talked to her sometimes but soon learned that, though she might listen, and even speak to him inside his head, she did nothing to save them from their father.*

*Ben shook his head and hardened his heart. He wasn't a baby anymore—his father reminded him of that often enough—so he shouldn't still long for a mother's love. He shouldn't feel that dark twist of envy he sometimes felt toward his friends.*

*He trod gently, slowly moving toward the hide. He didn't want to have to chase her again. A twig snapped beneath his foot and he caught the sound of a muffled sob. A wet little hiccup that made him think of himself in the night, with the quilt pulled over his head, and he felt a ripple of anger and shame. She had no reason to be scared; she was an odd little thing, but everyone loved Emily. "A little angel," he'd heard her called. If anyone had a right to be afraid it was him, not her.*

*The thought made him spiteful, and he reached his hand through the letterbox window. "Little pig, little pig, are you in there?" he slyly called.*

*The child's scream caught him by surprise. It was loud and shrill, accompanied by the sudden updraft of birds taking flight from the trees. The boy rocked back on his heels, momentarily losing his balance as a startled flash* of red flew out from the hide and toward the lake. Ben scrambled back to his feet.

"Emily, wait! Emily it's me, Ben!"

Blind panic carried the girl to the lake's edge, where the moss and the tangle of rushes and waterweed masked the point where earth became liquid. She stopped dead in her tracks, trapped between the expanse of water and the boy at her back. She spun to face him, her terror blazing in her eyes. Ben glanced from her face to her feet and cautiously extended a hand.

"Emily, it's me, Ben. Just stay where you are, don't move until I get there."

He looked back at her face, where the fear slid and flickered, her eyes darting from side to side like a cornered animal.

Ben felt something stir in response to her fear, something unfurling and slithering deep within. He was suddenly like the lake: calm and clear on the surface but underneath a dark tangle of emotions, like the weeds. In a blinding moment of clarity, he understood his father. He understood how it made him feel when he held his cigarette close to Ben's face, or left his handprint on his skin. When he did the things to Laura that left her sobbing in the night, and when he pulled that final trigger to end poor Scotty's life. It was power, and now Ben felt it too. He was too young, too lacking in insight to name it, but it was there in the flare of Emily's nostrils and in the stark terror in her eyes. He had power over her. He could gather her up and take her safely home, or he could make her take one final step into the deep, dark water.

Emily let out a whimper. A weak, mewling sound that fed Ben's sense of power. He felt spite, like a dark thing, enfolding his heart. Unlike him, she was loved and cherished, but if he chose to, he could take all that away from her. Why did she deserve love but not him? If he was lost, he bet no one would come looking, no one would scour the woods to bring him safely home. He took a step toward her and watched as her foot, the one that was *missing its trainer, took a step backward, in time with his. Slowly the mud swallowed her heel, the dank water darkening her sock to brown as her foot sank from sight. Her eyes widened in surprise and her arms flew out from her sides as she fought for balance, but Ben didn't move. He could if he chose to; he could just step forward and grab her arm. Instead he stayed rooted to the spot. He watched as she slowly tipped backward, her fingertips frantically scrabbling at the air. He saw her pass the point of no return and watched as her knees folded under her and her body fell into the lake. She made barely a sound, which surprised him. Just a frightened gulp and a tiny splash, and then the water closed over her face, her hair pooling in a golden tangle. The boy stood frozen, looking on as her arms splashed and flailed in panic, her body arching and thrashing against the water. He watched as the movement slowed and a trickle of tiny bubbles popped to the surface amid the weeds.*

*As Emily's body stilled, Ben's sprang to life. He raced to the lake's edge and fell to his knees, his hands raking the mess of muddy water. He grasped a foot and pulled but his hand came away with a trainer, mud-soaked and ruined, the lights in its heel an incongruous twinkle of green and red. Panic consumed him as he delved into the water again and again until, at last, his hand found a slender ankle. This time his grip didn't fail him, and he pulled the child free from the water and onto the bank.*

*Ben looked at her face, at the ripples still licking her skin, and terror beat a tattoo behind his ribs. So loud he could hear it echoing among the trees. A death knell. He hadn't meant this to happen; he'd never, ever, intended to harm her. He looked at her half-closed eyes, with the peeping slices of sightless white, and he feared she was dead.*

*Still he tried to pull her upright, shaking her shoulders as if sheer force alone might stir her back to life. A trickle of foul water dribbled from her parted lips as her head lolled and wobbled, and Ben knew that all the wishing in the world couldn't bring her back. He let her slump back into* the mud, her hair in matted clumps about her head, and sobbed as though his heart would break. His guts churned and his bowels clenched and loosened, and for a fearful moment he thought he would mess himself there in the woods. He wasn't angry anymore; he was terrified, and ashamed. He was evil, even worse than his father, and for a wild moment he considered throwing himself into the lake and letting the waters claim him too. Instead he stayed there, sobbing over the girl's broken body with the muddied little trainer clasped to his chest.

The breeze still ruffled the uppermost branches, the birds still sang their songs, and there, by the lake in the woods, the silent trees looked on. The forest was ancient and the rhythms of life and death passed unheeded in its leafy stillness.

❦

Sally stormed into the clearing by the lake, heedless of the brambles that snatched at her clothes. Her eyes were swollen with unshed tears, and two bright spots of color seared her cheeks. She could hear Mark behind her.

"Wait up, Sal! I didn't mean it like that, honest!"

She didn't stop because she knew that he did. She'd seen the way his eyes followed Rebecca in class, and the way they lingered on her school blouse where it strained across the swell of her breasts. She should never have been so stupid as to let him kiss her—and more. Now she supposed he'd laugh about it with his mates, all at her expense. In her agitation and her need to get way, she didn't notice the boy by the water, or hear his muffled keening over the pounding in her ears. She ran on, back to the path that led to the main track out of the woods.

Mark watched the disappearing figure and slowed his pace to a walk. He wasn't going to chase after her. For God's sake! He'd only asked if Becky Stephens was going to the party on Saturday; he didn't mean anything by it, so there was no need for her to get all weirded out over it. Even as the thought formed, he knew it wasn't true. Becky was the girl who filled his daydreams and fuelled his nighttime fantasies, Sally was just the more willing.

He came to a halt and rested his hands on his knees to catch his breath, and as he did he became aware of a sound as familiar to him as his own voice. A sound out of place in the still of the forest, a sound that sometimes haunted his sleep. He turned and looked toward the lake, in the direction of the smothered sobs, and there by the water's edge he saw a small figure hunched over something laying on the bank. He could see a flash of red, and his mind leapt to the image of an animal slowly dying in the woods. He remembered the shrill cry he'd heard a while back, of some poor creature meeting its fate, and a fond smile lit his face, momentarily softening the sharpness of his features; his little brother could be such a softie sometimes.

"Hey Ben, what's up, mate? What've you gone and found this time?"

As he neared, the words died in his throat and his brain struggled to make sense of the scene before him. A child lay unmoving by the lake, while his brother sobbed over it. Fear prickled along his spine.

"Ben?" His voice sounded strange in the hush of the woods, bouncing and echoing off the trees. "Ben . . . "

Ben turned a dirty, tear-stained face toward his brother. Between the hiccups and sobs, Mark heard his words but they held no meaning.

"She's dead and I did it . . . Markie, I drowned her . . . "

The older boy looked at the girl on the ground, at the blue-white pallor of her skin, and his soul shrank. Some instinctive part of him sensed the absence of life and his voice, when it came, was shrill and harsh.

"Fuck's sake, Ben, is that Emily? What's wrong with her, what's happened?" Panic set the blood pounding as he looked at his brother's stricken face. "Answer me, Ben! What are you taking about, you drowned her? Shit, bro, don't even say things like that!"

Ben said nothing, just stared mutely at his brother.

"Ben, speak to me! What the fuck's happened?"

"It was me, I made it happen, Markie, I pushed her into the lake." Fear and shock made the boy's teeth chatter, and tremors wracked his body. "I made it happen. I killed her!"

Disbelief rendered Mark stupid, and his brain raced ahead of him, trying to understand what he was hearing. He saw the terror in his brother's eyes, and love, fear, and anger rolled themselves into one. He paced back and forth, his agitation making stillness unthinkable.

"Shit, shit . . ." He needed to think.

He was overwhelmed by the urge to just run away, but much as he wanted to pretend he hadn't seen this, he knew that he couldn't leave his brother. He had to try and do something to make this right. Finally his pacing came to a halt, and he turned to his brother.

"Ben, what the hell have you done?"

Even as the words left his lips Mark knew that no matter what Ben said, he couldn't have deliberately done this thing, and he wouldn't let him be blamed for it. His brother didn't have it in him to shoot a bird, let alone kill a child.

He forced himself to look at the girl. Just maybe she wasn't dead after all. His limbs felt paralyzed, but he willed them to move. Kneeling down in the mud, he stretched out a hand toward her. Everything in him recoiled, but he made his trembling fingertips brush the lifeless flesh of her face. He prodded her cheek, watching her eyes as he did, but there was no flicker of her lids, no change to the rinds of white that made his skin crawl.

"Come on, Emily, wake up!"

Grasping her shoulders, he shook her. "Come on Emily—please!"

The movement caused her head to slip back into the water, submerging her face once more. No bubbles seeped from her nose or escaped her parted lips; instead, her face stayed blank as a mask, and Mark knew there was nothing he could do. He'd seen death often enough on the farm and he knew *its signs. Still, he dragged her from the water and pressed his hands to her chest, rolling her onto her side like he'd seen on TV, but it was hopeless.*

*He was sixteen years old and he hadn't cried in years, but now he felt the tears forcing their way from beneath his lids. Visions of police cars and men in uniform swam before his eyes; his brother being hauled away to juvenile court and prison. He couldn't let that happen. The poor little sod had enough to put up with, and he'd never survive something like that.*

*Mark looked around at the silent forest. No one else was there, and he was pretty sure Sally hadn't seen anything; she was too mad at him to notice anyone else. The only thing he could think of was for them to just walk away and keep their mouths shut, pretend this had never happened. No one need ever know they'd been there. He let the girl flop onto her back, leaving her half submerged at the lake's edge, and all the time Ben sobbed and wailed until Mark thought his head would burst.*

*"Stop crying and listen to me, Ben. This is nothing to do with us and we don't say anything to anyone. We're going to walk away now and we're never going to talk about it again, not ever. Understand? Emil—" He balked at speaking the girl's name "She fell in the lake and she drowned, okay? It doesn't matter what you think you did, that's what happened. She just slipped and drowned, and that's the truth, okay?"*

*Still Ben sobbed and the older boy pushed his face close. He had to make him stop; otherwise his father or their aunt would realize that something was wrong.*

*"Stop sniffling, Ben, you hear me? You have to stop crying—crying is only going to make everything worse. You've got to act like nothing's happened."*

*Fear made him harsh, and he shook the boy for emphasis, his fingers digging into bony shoulders. His breath hot and angry against Ben's skin.*

*"Listen to me. You don't say a word to anyone about this, not ever. No matter how much you might think you want to. It won't make it any better;*

it'll only make everything a whole lot worse for you—and for me as well now. What do you think the old man'll do to us if he finds out about this? He'll fucking kill us for real, so you keep this to yourself, understand? If you don't, there'll be nothing I can do to help you."

Ben nodded, fighting to suppress the sobs that threatened to shake him apart.

As his weeping subsided Mark hauled Ben to his feet, frantically brushing the worst of the mud and wet leaves from his legs and clothing. It was lucky their farm was the first house after the woods because it gave them a chance to get home without anyone seeing the state he was in.

The younger boy's eyes had taken on a glazed quality, and Mark could sense him shutting down.

"Hey, come on, Ben. You've got to stick with me. Once I've got us home it'll all be okay. You've just got to do exactly what I say, always."

There was no response and Mark tugged at his arm. "Come on mate, you've got to get moving, we've got to get away from here."

He saw that the boy was still clutching the mud-soaked trainer and moved to take it from him, but Ben held it tighter, clasping it until his knuckles were white. Mark saw that his brother was in shock and he wasn't going to risk upsetting him further. He could deal with the trainer later.

Slowly he coaxed Ben away from the lake and gently led him toward the cover of the trees. They didn't look back. If Mark tried really hard, he could almost imagine there was nothing behind them, no nameless horror bobbing at the water's edge.

They pushed through the brambles and onto an overgrown deer track, where the woods seemed to fold around them. A faint breeze rustled the leaves, and to Mark's ears it carried a whisper of accusation. His pulse jumped and raced at the thought of the woods ahead of them teeming with people searching for the missing girl, but he kept calmly going forward, leading his brother safely home.

*Eventually the pair emerged onto the main track. Mark cautiously parted the underbrush and listened for the sound of voices. The afternoon had moved on and the sun had dipped lower in the sky. Sunlight no longer reached the forest floor; now it played in the treetops, bathing the uppermost branches with gold. The effect was to deepen the shadows in the lower reaches of the woods, reducing the holly bushes to dark shapes floating among the trees. Mark hurried along the path, pulling his brother behind him, pausing only at the point where the woods broke into scrub and the scrub became meadow. It wasn't possible to see the route all the way to the farm. Once they were out in the open there was nowhere to hide, but they had no choice; it was the only way home.*

*The boys set out across the fields, crossing the first without incident. Mark began to breathe more easily. If they could just get home without being seen it would all be okay. He could talk to Ben, calm him down and make him see that this thing, awful though it was, wasn't his fault. Then they could put it behind them and never, ever, speak of it again.*

*The fields were washed in late-afternoon sunshine and the air was heavy with the warm scent of hay. The birds had begun their evensong and the day had a pastoral calmness that made it easy to believe that nothing cruel had ever happened.*

*Mark was first to see the small figure running toward them, and he was seized by the urge to turn and run too, but they were far from the cover of the woods. As the figure approached, Mark saw that it was Jay heedlessly charging across the grass, his face a bleached disc beneath a shock of brown hair. He skidded to a halt in front of them, his eyes red-rimmed and afraid.*

*"Have you found her? Have you seen Em anywhere?" Jay was on the point of tears and seemed much younger than his eleven years. "Ben, please tell me you've seen her . . ." Then he registered Ben's grubby face and his wet and mud-stained clothes. "Ben, mate, what's happened? Why are you all . . ."*

*The question died on his lips and a look of confusion crossed his face. "Ben, is that . . . is that Emily's?"*

*Mark turned to his brother and saw that he was still clutching the muddied trainer to his chest. He hardened his features and thrust himself between the two boys, forcing Jay to back away.*

*"Fuck off, Jay. I dunno why you're questioning him but he found it, okay? You're the one who should've been out there looking for your sister, not him. But you cleared off home, so don't start having a go at him 'cos you feel guilty. Maybe if you hadn't left him, you'd have found her by now."*

*Mark fought to keep his voice steady. Now that Jay had seen the trainer everything was ruined. It meant he couldn't burn it like he'd intended—at least not yet, it would look too suspicious. They'd have to hide it somewhere, and if they were asked about it, say that they'd found it in the woods but been too afraid to say. Fear spiked his chest when he thought of the lake water soaking it through; how could they ever explain that away? He could feel himself beginning to panic, his breath coming hot and fast. Shielding his brother, he moved closer to Jay, his face confrontational and aggressive.*

*Jay saw the warning in Mark's eyes and he hesitated. He was afraid of the older boy, but he knew his parents wouldn't be far behind, and he had to find his sister before they did. This was all his stupid fault, and he had to set things right.*

*He took a deep breath. "Ben, please . . ." he said, reaching out his hand. "I just want to know where you found it." He didn't understand the glazed look on his friend's face. "Ben, please. Talk to me. I have to find her . . ." There was pleading in his voice, a desperation that made him whine.*

*Mark lunged forward, his fright making him vicious. He pushed the other boy hard in the chest. A flat hand that felt more like a fist.*

"I told you, leave him the fuck alone! Don't you get it? He doesn't know anything about your stupid sister, so stay away from him," and with that he pushed past, dragging his brother behind him.

The fear center in Jay's brain lit up like a beacon, and some primitive part of him began to sense that a very bad thing had happened. He turned to face the woods and began to run, faster and faster, toward the dark opening between the trees. On he ran, as fast as his legs would carry him, rushing toward the thing that would leave him changed forever.